"You're not any sort of a man as I can see," snarled Johansen.

Fuming, Fergus leveraged himself upright with the cane. "Look, Eric, that's quite enough! I *was* a mate on a buoy tender, but that was before I began this crusade to rid the oceans of the filth who are quite prepared to destroy it. Now, if they won't negotiate, and they won't listen to the pleas of environmentalists who *know* that their overfishing is crucifying the planet, then I will make it my business to stop them."

"Even if it means killing them." The chief's voice was somber.

"This is *war*, Chief, and in war there are casualties. I detest this act, and I will surely hang for it, but it is the first shot to save the oceans. And I do not mind giving my life for its revival."

The chief mate just stared, seemingly unconvinced. "Now, I really don't give a rat's ass," continued Fergus, "if I'm remembered in the same light as Jack the Ripper or Ted Bundy. But people will remember me, and realize that I fought for the planet against those who would destroy it."

Jonathan sniffed as he finished the speech in which his accent had transformed from that of an English grammar-school teacher to a Coast Guard second-mate and back again. But Johansen was not buying it.

"Well, *Planet Man*," Johansen countered in a low, threatening tone, "I suggest you go back into your phone booth and change out of your costume or this ship's as good as dead in the water. Because, let's face it, if I don't play ball, the ship don't go, 'cause none of your dweebs could float a toy boat. Especially without the codes. Now, stop this ship! Now!"

Ice Break

by
Kim Kinrade

Commonwealth
Publications

A Commonwealth Publications Paperback
ICE BREAK

This edition published 1996
by Commonwealth Publications
9764 - 45th Avenue,
Edmonton, AB, CANADA T6E 5C5
All rights reserved
Copyright © 1995 by Kim Kinrade

ISBN: 1-55197-164-X

This work is a novel and any similarity to actual persons or events is purely coincidental.

Designed by: Federico Caceres

Printed in Canada

For Heather, Sam and Tony

"Westward to the Davis Strait
Was there t'was said to lie,
A sea route to the Orient
For which so many died,
Seeking gold and glory
Leaving weathered, broken bones,
And a long, forgotten,
Lonely cairn of stones."

The Northwest Passage
- Stan Rogers
1981 Fogarty's Cove Music, Inc.

FOREWORD

The following story is strictly a work of fiction and *not* intended to be an accurate portrayal of the Canadian military, the Canadian Coast Guard and the Royal Canadian Mounted Police; nor the governments of Canada and the province of Nova Scotia. I wanted to capture some of the spirit and dedication that is demonstrated daily off both Canadian coasts and the Arctic archipelago by men and women of the Canadian Armed Forces and Canadian Coast Guard; as well as the skills employed while providing surveillance and maintaining rescue services over a vast area in some of the world's worst weather conditions.

I would like to thank the following people, whose information and dedication made this work possible: Paul Wrench, Roger Gosse and Guy Paproski were invaluable guides through the maze of military technology and protocol; the Halifax Public Library, Dartmouth Regional Library and King's College Library, a wealth of information on almost every topic that I needed to research; officers and crew of the Canadian Coast Guard, Dartmouth Base, for their input; Jane Buss and the gang at the Writers' Federation of Nova Scotia who fielded my endless editorial questions with decorum; and last, but not least, Joan and Eileen at Author Author Literary Agency.

Kim Kinrade. August 15th, 1995

Author's Note: After the completion of this manuscript the Canadian Coast Guard was transferred from Transport Canada ministry to Oceans and Fisheries Canada, thus the cabinet minister in charge of Transport Canada is no longer responsible for icebreaking as portrayed in the following story.

PROLOGUE

1.

October 19, 1993
Murmansk, Russia

Bracing themselves against another gust of freezing wind off the Arctic Ocean, the three figures stared in awe at the shadowy, monstrous shape which lorded over the dimly lit dock facility. In the next instant, the frigid blast subsided leaving minute ice crystals billowing around them, brownish colored under filthy, bare light bulbs which swayed back and forth on their long, tightroped tethers.

"If this is to be the last one, I'm glad, at least, that it is worthy of our heritage." Clouds of vapor poured into the dark, frosty night as the old man dragged out the last syllable. He grinned with admiration, the cold spout of the small vodka bottle rising to his lips once again to deliver more of the biting liquid.

Huge fur mittens extended past the elbows of his woolen greatcoat, exaggerating the sweeping motion as the flask raised and lowered again. They were like flippers and, along with his short, stocky build and heavily wrinkled face, gave him the look of a walrus without tusks. A satisfied belch followed.

"Are you sure you don't want any?" The old man's large eyebrows raised inquisitively, two wire brushes polishing the rim of his cozy fur hat. The visitors shook their heads. "Well then, comrade...uh, sorry, I guess that venerable name has been stricken by the *New Order*."

Instinctively, he felt his spine tingle. If it were difficult for him to accept the demise of the party, it was even harder to dispel the fear of saying too much; even though the new KGB no longer had the inclination, nor the manpower, to persecute citizens for speech offenses anymore.

As he relaxed again, the old *zampolit*—political officer—sighed, feeling the ironic taste of nostalgia. He almost longed for the days when people were fearful of the State and could be arrested without pretense. At least back then everyone knew they would be cared for when old age finally caught up with them, and never had to worry about digging around in the garbage for food, or living in cardboard boxes. That is, those who weren't first imprisoned or sent to *gulags*—prison camps—for speech offenses.

"Excuse my vices, please. And thank you for the gift," he went on, glancing back at the cases of vodka stacked up in the snow. "It allows an old patriot to warm himself on such a night." This brought a smile from one of the visitors, the man built like Hercules. His much younger accomplice, however, just stared in awe at the gargantuan ship, which seemed to twitch as the wind played with the dim strings of light bulbs—the only illumination in the large shipyard since the power shortages.

"Shall we go?" he asked, his black-leather trench coat groaning as he adjusted his hands in the fur-lined pockets.

The ancient sailor, Igor Anatoli Larenko, nodded, clumsily depositing the bottle into a large pocket in his greatcoat. It had been many weeks since his "young compatriot" had contacted him. How many weeks he could not recall, as the vodka, which eased the pain of his arthritis, had also eroded his capacity to remember many details. But he was very proud that one of his "students" had come back to help him, even if it was for a favor. At least one person remembered him from all those he had boosted up to better lives.

Before Gorbachev, a man of his stature, honored as a *Hero of the Great Patriotic War* and good party member, did not have to indulge in such clandestine operations. He made a comfortable living as director of the Murmansk Shipyard, including a large apartment and a car, as well as a driver, who took him to and from work and chauffeured his family around. And they never had to queue up for food or, for that matter, anything. Everything was the best: meat, fresh fruit, caviar; and lots of wine and vodka.

Larenko enjoyed other perks as well, like the privilege of being poached every morning in the best health club in Murmansk. Yes, despite having to live in a city which begged for the sun half the year, life had been grand under Leonid Brezhnev, his old friend and the man who had overseen his good fortune.

Now, although he was allowed to hold the director's position at the yard and keep his apartment, his standard of living was lower than a laborer's had been under the Soviet system. The once-thriving Murmansk Shipyard, which used to bustle around the clock to meet the demands of the Soviet navy, had descended to a mere shadow of its former capacity. The Russian government, it seemed, could not provide enough fuel to keep even the present ships of the Northern Fleet at sea. And the other half of the Great Fleet was rotting away in the Black Sea, a political pawn caught between two formerly allied regions, Russia and the Ukraine. Stalin must be spinning in his grave, he mused.

It took the trio more than ten minutes to walk the three hundred yards through the deep snow to the rear access of the large shipbuilding compound. Larenko had to stop and rest many times. As they approached the gate, a watch officer strode out of an adjoining blockhouse standing to the side. Taking out a key, the man, a captain, flipped open a metal box attached to the thick, metal gate post. Then, as if barely interested in the proceedings, he tapped in his code on the keypad inside the box and then turned and plowed briskly through the knee-high drifts, scanning the area briefly before he disappeared back into the concrete shelter.

Larenko then followed the officer's actions and punched in his own set of numbers. There was a metallic clanking sound and then a heavy, steel gate swung open with a tortured groan.

The inner fencing of the compound consisted of a heavy wire fence strung with three rows of deadly razor-wire. The coils of wire bristled with thousands of small knife points which shivered and hissed like a snake as the howling wind tried to dislodge it.

Between the two barricades there was a thirty-foot space where, up until Boris Yeltsin took power, armed guards with dogs diligently patrolled in the never-ending hunt for "capitalist saboteurs." Now there was no one. Who would want to break in and attack a bunch of Canadian ship workers?

The outer chain-link fence was no longer electrified, another casualty of the energy shortage, but its barbed-wire sections were still formidable barriers to human intruders. Beyond that set of defenses were acres of snow-dusted, diagonally-juxtaposed, concrete dragon's-teeth. Like the maw of an enormous creature, the white obstacles, set in curving rows, glistened in the moonlight, jutting outward to face a land foe that threatened from another era.

Larenko chuckled as he stared at the shipyard's contribution to the Cold War. *Now* the compound was guarded against the thievery of organized gangs who would strip what was left of the facility, including this last project that was being built here, if the place were left unguarded. But so far, those thugs had neither the wherewithal nor the inside information to try.

As the outer gate popped open, an engine sputtered to life, followed by another, and then two more. Soon the dark shapes of medium-sized trucks could be made out as they lumbered toward the warehousing area near the dock, following the heavily snow-covered road that wound through the compound. The last truck stopped in front of them, and Larenko's two associates lifted up the canvas flap and climbed into the back. Once aboard they pulled the old man up after them.

The truck came to a stop by an open door on the seaward end of one of the dozens of nondescript warehouses in the shipyard. Dark figures emerged from the trucks and began off-loading the contents of the vehicles into the large shed. After twenty minutes, the trucks turned around and left as mysteriously as they came, taking Larenko's two guests with them. As he waved good-bye with one of his mittened hands, the old man reached for the vodka container with the other hand. He chuckled as the warmth of the liquor seeped through his chest. Fifty-thousand dollars in American currency would keep a seventy-three-year-old sailor in vodka and steaks for a long time.

"Ah," Larenko remarked as the hum of the engines died away, "it was good that some people remembered an old man."

Bouncing in the cab of the Mercedes truck, the two departing men bathed in the delicious flow from the heat vent. As the tall, husky one in the leather coat rubbed his hands under the duct, he moaned in pleasure. "I'm getting soft, Alesandr. Since I left the *real* service, not so many years ago, I'm not used to such frigid temperatures anymore."

The younger partner chuckled as he piloted the truck along the snaking path through the new snowdrifts which had collected on the narrow road during the evening. He kept his eyes glued to the red taillights in front, which acted as beacons in the blinding swirls of snow that the seaborne winds were creating.

"Do you think that the old man might say something," the driver asked. "I mean, he does drink a lot and his tongue might wag too much to the wrong person."

The big man, young-looking for his forty-odd years, shook his head. Unlike his young associate, he did not have Slav features. In fact, he looked more Germanic with his blue eyes and blonde hair, most of which he had tucked up under his dark toque.

"No, Alesandr, he won't talk. Right about now he should be snoozing in his office. Then, tomorrow morning, when the duty officer comes in to wake the old man up he will find that Admiral Igor Anatoli Larenko, a glorious hero of the once-great

Soviet Union, has passed away peacefully in his sleep."

Startled, Alesandr took his eyes off the road and looked over for an instant. "Do you mean you poisoned him? Won't some doctor figure it out?"

The passenger's smile, ghoulish under the dash lights, sent a shiver up Alesandr's back. This was one man, thought the youngster, that no sane person crossed. "No, not at his age. He will be just another old veteran who died from the effects of too much vodka."

The passenger's mouth was stretching wide into a yawn during the last sentence and it took a keen ear on the part of the driver to decipher his last words. His face remained in that position, contorted and motionless, for almost a minute before returning to normal.

Then, suddenly breathing deeply, he deadpanned, "The sad part is, Larenko won't get the large state funeral that all his old friends received, the ones that are entombed in the Kremlin wall. Modern Russia hasn't a budget for that sort of thing anymore."

When his face relaxed, the passenger almost appeared childlike, the look of a youngster who was truly sorry for breaking a friend's toy. "But I will make sure he gets a funeral befitting a war hero. My friends will take care of it for me.

"After all, he was my mentor."

2.

January 3, 1994
Bosnia-Herzegovena

"Get down from the tank! Get down, now!"

The words in halting English were loud and nasal, sounding somewhat like the impish dialogue from an old Pink Panther movie. In fact, thought Dorey, the speaker could have even been a lighter-haired version of Inspector Clouseau.

But the Canadian wisely kept his brevity leashed, for this speaker was heavily armed and was probably not alone. Because in Bosnia-Herzegovina, especially on lonely, snow-covered roads like this one in the mountainous center of the former Yugoslavia, humor came in short bursts, like the firing of automatic weapons.

The man was dressed in Soviet-style winter fatigues, a camouflage pattern giving his torso the appearance of a white tiger from the famous Las Vegas show, Seigfried and Roy. However, the similarity ended there. For when he moved, his legs appeared skinny and bowed under the flapping of the baggy fatigues held tightly at the calves by large, black, rubber boots.

Strutting like a tom turkey, the armed man moved to within ten feet of the blue-bereted soldier who stared down at him in a composed manner from the upper hatch of the white United Nations APC—armored personnel carrier. In the hatch below and to the left of the APC commander was the driver, Corporal Eddie Anderson, who appeared only as a nervous head moving back and forth between the armed man and his officer up in the hatch.

Anderson's hopes of a rational discussion between the two men dimmed when the man brought up the barrel of his assault rifle, held by its pistol grip in his right hand, and pointed it up in the vicinity of the vehicle commander's head. Then, keeping his eyes pinned to his two captives, he began waving theatrically with his left arm.

From his perch above, Captain Tom Dorey shot another glance down at his helmeted driver. "Eddie," he whispered, speaking out of the side of his mouth, "slowly ease inside and then, on my signal, pop the door and get everyone out." Without a moment's notice, Anderson disappeared like a gopher down a prairie hole.

This motion startled the ambusher. "Where is he?" he bleated. "Get him out, now!"

The blue-bereted officer acted as if he hadn't heard the man. "We are Canadians, with the United Nations," he announced slowly and calmly, stressing the obvious and hoping that its pronounced, verbal confirmation would somehow prevent the escalation of tensions. "We are on an errand of mercy—"

But the proclamation seemed to fall on deaf ears. "I don't care! You are not welcome. Get down, now!" the gunman barked, gaining confidence with each bellow.

Then the peacekeeper soon found out the reason for the aggressor's continued arrogance and silently cursed himself for not just running the guy over and heading back down the mountain. Because, bathed in the last, weak rays of the winter afternoon, snow-encrusted figures began appearing from behind the snowy trees on the surrounding cliffs. Over half-a-dozen in number, they carefully negotiated the ditches running alongside the road, their mixture of civilian and military apparel in stark contrast to their leader. To the APC commander, they looked like street people he had seen in Chicago; except that the faces of these men looked far more desperate than anything he had ever witnessed staring out from behind an old shopping cart.

Dorey glanced at the .50 caliber machine gun beside him and instantly put any thoughts of firing it out of his head. It was loaded, but UN regulations, which seemed to change daily, forbade peacekeepers to use aggression unless fired upon.

Besides, the vehicle manufacturers, obviously not military engineers, had mounted it to the side of the hatch, not in front where it would do the most good. *Like a limp dick*, he snorted in disgust.

Upon reaching the level surface of the road, one of the motley soldiers kneeled in the ankle-deep snow and pointed an unwieldy-looking APG—armor-piercing grenade—launcher at the vehicle. Then, as each ambusher joined the growing entourage on the road, more automatic weapons raised to threaten the white vehicle and its occupants.

There were seven "bad guys". They had to be Serbs, the peacekeeper guessed at first glance, because the TDF—Muslim forces—checkpoint was twenty miles back and this was too far into Bosnia for the Croatians, even the most persistent ones. But whatever they were, they were dangerous. That toy aimed at them, thought the worried commander, could rip the belly out of the APC and roast him and the other three Canadian peacekeepers in a diesel brazier.

Enough of this shit! Dorey grunted. Panning his eyes back and forth over the ambushers he carefully stood up in the hatch and swung his legs over to climb down, the C-7 assault rifle,—a Canadian version of the automatic-firing, 5.56mm American M-16—swinging from his shoulder. Startled, the camouflaged Serb backed off a few feet as the imposing figure of Tom Dorey jumped off the vehicle and landed on the snowy road with an audible crunch. At the same time, there was a motor sound and the rear hatch of the APC began to open slowly, like a large, white beetle about to give birth.

The tactic should have worked. However, instead of forcing a discussion like Dorey had hoped, the white-clad leader coolly signaled with his right arm and two of his men scrambled toward the opening door. So, when the four United Nations soldiers stepped onto the snowy road, they found themselves in the gun sights of their captors.

Like their commander, the men in dull-green combat fatigues wore light-blue, Kevlar flak jackets which made them look larger and, with their grim, expressionless faces, more than a bit intimidating to the militiamen. These were professional soldiers, a foe the nervous men before them had never faced before. In the next few seconds the two bewildered Serbs searched each others' eyes for signs of courage.

The UN soldiers shifted their attention toward Dorey. His resigned look was all too plain. In unison they all lowered the muzzles of their weapons.

That was all the attackers needed to bolster their resolve and the importance of their mission began to outweigh their former uncertainties. One of the braver ones stepped forward and shoved a Canadian with his weapon. Although there was contempt in his eyes, the UN soldier just stepped back.

"You are like chickens!" the Serb chuckled, repeating the remark in his own language and producing whoops of laughter from the rest.

However, one bark from their impatient leader ended the distraction. The group immediately stopped their badgering and sprung into action. Four rifleman trained their weapons on the peacekeepers and two more joined the jokester and his companion, carefully searching through the APC for more soldiers. When they were satisfied that no one remained inside, the man in white turned back to Dorey. "Drop your weapons and leave, now!"

The Canadian, the muzzle of his rifle rubbing

against his polished, black boots, never answered. Instead, he held the Serb's stare and started to walk toward him, slowly and methodically, the frozen surface crunching and squeaking underfoot.

As he had predicted, the nervous Serb militiamen turned away from his soldiers, jamming their bolts back and clicking safety catches as a warning against his unwelcome advance. The threatening moves seemed to go unnoticed by Dorey. Because, instead of backing off, the UN commander continued, slowly closing the fifteen-foot gap that separated him from his aggressor.

When the Canadian officer got to within ten feet, the Serbian saw the tall man's badges: captain's bars and maple leaves, denoting the peacekeepers' nationality. But it was the man's light-brown eyes that held his attention. Though soft in color, they had a hard edge to them, and the impenetrable sheen of one who has seen many battles.

When he was two feet away, the Canadian stopped. The other peacekeepers held their breath and tensed for action, each one mentally picking out his target. But no signal came from Dorey. He just stood in front of his foe as if his metallic stare was enough to blow him off the snowy road.

In the next instant, the eyes softened into merry, mahogany orbs. Carefully he raised his right hand and motioned toward to a pocket in his flak jacket.

"May I?"

The Serb nodded, unsure of what he was up to. But his experience had taught him that peacekeepers were negotiators, not tricksters.

In a slow, deliberate movement, Dorey pulled out a package of Export "A". Flipping open the top with one motion he reached out with the cigarettes to the Serb who nodded and accepted one. The Canadian then took one for himself and his light-colored eyebrows raised as he pointed to another pocket. Again his captor moved his head up and down and Dorey pulled out an old Zippo. Snapping it open to expose a wavering blue flame, and cupping it with his hands to ward off the breeze, he reached out with it. Cautiously, the Serb pushed his face toward the flame, his eyes watching for any movement from the Canadian. The end glowing orange, he drew back puffing, watching carefully as Dorey lit his own. Soon the air around them was stained with a bluish haze.

"Thank you, Captain," said the Serb. "Now please, there is little time." There was a moderate change in the smaller man's tone but his purpose remained unshakable. "I want you to take your men down the road."

The Canadian's cinnamon eyes scanned the mottled forms that were the tense, Serbian militiamen, memorizing any specifics for later debriefing. A few years ago, he surmised, a few of these men and teenaged boys had probably been shopkeepers and farm workers, even teachers. But some were most likely thugs, criminals who hid behind a "cause" to pad their pockets and exact their misplaced vengeance on those who could not defend themselves.

And the Serbs did not have a monopoly on this type of low-life. He had seen them dressed as Croats, Muslims and Greek and Turk Cypriots, not to mention those in another time who had once masqueraded as South Vietnamese and American army officers. Wherever there was conflict, they waited in the wings like jackals.

Dorey's attention returned to the Serb commander, who looked more Slavic than anyone else in his darker-skinned party. This one, Dorey reflected, had most likely been a career officer in the regular Yugoslavian army before the war, maybe even part Slovenian, judging by his blue eyes and sandy-blonde hair. Another thing he saw about the man was that he had only a slight growth of beard in comparison to the heavy, dark whiskers of the others. A day tripper?

"Uh, Captain?" he guessed.

"Major. Major Dragutin Ilic," the Serb answered, proudly.

The major, the Canadian noticed, did not offer any other information. That was strange. Usually the three warring parties were brimming with exuberance and self-importance, loving to brag of their exploits to anyone who would listen.

"Sorry, Major, I'm Captain Tom Dorey." Still clutching his weapon in his left hand he extended his right to the Serb, his eyes squinting as the smoke wafted into his eyes. The man took it and gave it a firm but brief shake.

"As you probably know, we are on a patrol, leading the way for a food convoy that has been cleared by both *your* government and the Serbian militia authority in this locale...so this intrusion is not necessary."

Despite the below-freezing weather, Dorey noticed small sweat droplets on the major's face and the nostrils of his hawk-like nose quivering over his bushy mustache.

"Yes, that may well be. But on this road, Captain, *I* make the rules, and *I* say that you and your men must go.

"We do not make war on Canadians, or other United Nations' soldiers. But, please, you are in the way and you must leave!" Ilic's voice was still curt but a sense of immediacy was replacing the arrogance.

Captain Dorey, his eyes now narrowly focused on the major's blue irises, shook his head in a slow and determined fashion. "Sorry, Major. I get my orders from the United Nations, who have their assurances from *your* President Radavic that this convoy has complete authorization. Now, as a commander, what would you do in my position?"

Ilic tried again, his voice softening.

"Captain! I understand that you have your orders, but this is a war of *liberation!*" Ilic's eyes bulged as he mouthed the last word. "All we need is for you to leave, nothing more. Just leave the tank and walk away. Is that too much to trade for the lives of your men?"

Lives? You tell me about lives, you dismal prick? Dorey fumed beneath his breath, his anger barely showing in his burnt-sienna eyes. After so many previous encounters with these people, Tom had the drill memorized. Threat, intimidation, maybe a slap or two; that's usually all. But here, now, to threaten to kill peacekeepers in cold blood? Maybe a reckless militia group, but not this man, especially not if he was a former career officer.

A very familiar set of teeth began gnawing at his insides, an old friend that had followed him around since his days in Vietnam. It had saved his life then, and a few times since, so he rarely ignored it. And today was no exception; he knew that this was no ordinary encounter.

Actually, no confrontation with the Serbs had ever been routine, especially since a small cache of arms, no doubt destined for the Muslims, was discovered on a food convoy a few weeks back. As a result, he realized that Serbian trust in humanitarian aid shipments for Muslim civilians was at an all-time low, which also meant greater concerns by many UN officers on whether or not the UN flag actually guaranteed their safety. Today, that apprehension was brought to fruition.

"Major," the Canadian reassured Ilic, "it's just carrying food. We personally went through every inch of every truck to make sure. Look, if you and your men are hungry, I'll stop the convoy myself and give you as much as you can carry. No problem, I—"

Dorey stopped in mid-sentence as the sound of engines reverberated through the snowy mountains, like a harbinger of doom. *High noon?*

Ilic's lips tensed and he began fidgeting with his cigarette. His men gazed down the steep, white mountain pass, trying to catch a glimpse of the invisible convoy that was now snaking up the lower switchbacks. It would arrive in less than ten minutes, he calculated, flashing a fearful look at Dorey.

Then, his eyes widening and smoke puffing from his nostrils, Ilic bellowed a command. Two of his men picked out a member of Dorey's party, Corporal Anderson, and shoved him to the middle of the road. Before Captain Dorey could protest, one of the Serbs drove the metal-ended stock of the AK-47 assault rifle into Anderson's back. The Canadian grunted in pain. Stunned, but saved a serious injury by the flak jacket, his knees shook as he fought to remain standing on his rubbery legs.

The gun went up again for another hit, stopping in mid-air as the assailant waited for another word from Ilic. Dorey, his teeth grating with anger, spun around to Ilic and barked, "Major! Order them to stop!"

Startled by the icy rebuke, Ilic backed up a step, prompting three of his men to rush forward and grab Dorey around the neck and arms. He started to struggle but immediately froze when he felt the icy steel of two AK-47 muzzles jam into the back of his head. His blue beret had slipped of his head and lay in a snowy rut on the road.

Ilic snapped his fingers at the attentive militiamen and they reluctantly loosened their hold on the Canadian. Dorey wrenched his arms away from his captors, his icy stare a reminder to them of his dangerousness.

"I am sorry, Captain, but before any more of my men lose control, *please go!*"

As if ignoring Ilic, Dorey casually bent over and picked up his snow-encrusted beret. Studying it for a moment, he brushed off the white powder and placed it on his head, subconsciously adjusting it to regulation pitch and height above his eyebrows. "Sorry, Major," he sighed as if brushing off a United Nations bureaucrat, "not until the food is safely in Gorazde."

Uttering what Dorey recognized as a curse, the major pointed to Anderson and the rifle stock came down again, this time jamming into the corporal's upper leg. With a stifled cry, the peacekeeper slipped and fell sideways into the snow, clutching his thigh.

Dorey, his mind racing for ideas, fought to keep his temper. *No more stupid outbursts, Tom boy. These are not the ordinary Serbians who yelled threats; these bastards meant business. Now, come on! Use your head. Think man or we'll all die!*

Watching his corporal writhing in the snow, he unslung his rifle and said, in a resigned voice, "Alright, Major, you win. We'll go." Then he laid the weapon on the road.

The Canadians, including the injured Anderson, looked up at him in disbelief. It wasn't possible. Dorey quit?

"Enough of this bullshit, guys. We've done our

job. Now let's get out of here and get whisky to warm ourselves." Grumbling, the men nodded and dropped their automatic rifles on the snowpacked road.

A slight smile came over Ilic. His chest felt larger and he further enlarged it by breathing deeply. Barking a command in Serbian, the others lowered their rifles and flipped on their safety catches.

Switching roles to that of the benevolence of the victor, the major looked up at the sheepish face of Dorey. "Captain, you are a brave man but you cannot stand in the path of our *destiny*. No one can I'm afraid so—"

The move was so swift that nobody realized what was going on until they saw the Serb major's back pressed tightly against Dorey's chest, facing his men, and a large, black knife pushed up into his skinny neck. Obviously in some pain from the arm that was unnaturally extended up to his neck, Ilic's frightened eyes searched his men for some sort of answer to his dilemma. But there was nothing they could do. The Canadian had the Serb's head yanked back so that the white neck faced the militiamen with the throbbing jugular vein of their commander evident beside the lethal blade. Ilic's boat-style cap slipped off his head and rested on his shoulder.

"Major, tell them to drop their weapons and do it now, or I'll start cutting you a happy face below your chin!" As the terrified Ilic swallowed, the razor-sharp edge of the US Marine KABAR knife rode the movement of his Adam's apple. Feeling the cold, pristine sharpness, he nodded and called out weakly to his men. Disbelief showing on their bearded faces, one by one the militiamen dropped their weapons.

Dorey never relaxed his hold. "Alright, guys, gather them up. Jamesy, cover them!" Sergeant Terry James smiled and brushed the snow off one of the liberated Kalashnikov rifles. He then got up on top of the APC to get a clear view of his captives and, for effect, aimed at the head of the one who had struck Anderson.

Dorey lowered the knife and spun Ilic around, his face lording over the features of the Serb, his voice as cold as the knife. "Major, I'm *supposed* to charge you with gross violation of UN ordinances, but I'd still rather slit your lying, fucking throat as pay-back for all the dead and starving children I see everyday, and the ones that you bastards shoot like rats as they run the gauntlet of snipers for water!"

Ilic fought for control of himself. Breathing deeply, he felt the adrenaline fade and then began calmly to appraise his situation. His initial thought was to curse his stupidity for letting the Canadian trick him into surrendering, but then he scanned for options. He knew for a fact that this man would not hurt him. Because this man was a commander under the blue flag and was on *his* land, Ilic knew nothing could happen to him that would not be met with stiff reprisals by his own forces and also diminish the credibility of the United Nations. UN commanders knew the rules, and they always played by them—*always*.

"Captain," he said, his voice regaining some of its former control, "the convoy is almost here, so you can stop with your meaningless rhetoric. You know you don't have the authority to detain us and neither does the UN. And if you turn us in we will be released within hours and you will be severely reprimanded!" With that he defiantly spat on the ground at Dorey's feet.

The Canadian officer grabbed Ilic by the camouflaged collars of his jacket. "Major, you better hope, for your own sake, that the convoy gets here before I forget my mandate and rip that fucking mustache off your face!" In disgust, Dorey pushed the skinny major away and James motioned with the rifle for the Serb to join his comrades.

A groggy Corporal Anderson, assisted by Lieutenant Brad Flemming, was just now getting to his feet. Dorey helped him brush off the caked snow.

"The convoy's almost here, Eddie. We'll make sure to get you a hot rum for your imitation of a punching bag!" The corporal smiled painfully, steam wafting up from his face like he'd just run a marathon.

"Captain," he croaked, "I'll be alright. I just may be pissin' a bit of blood tonight. Nothin' big time, sir."

Dorey nodded. "Sorry, Eddie, but it's a long way to the LZ—landing zone. I'll get a Red Cross guy to take you and the APC back, we'll hitch a ride on the communications truck."

Just then, the first UN vehicle, a white, Cougar personnel carrier, rounded the corner like a large rodent and stopped behind Dorey's APC. It was followed in turn by the large transport trucks, which made up most of the convoy. Jumping down off its upper hatch, a confused, blue-helmeted, UN official landed on the road. Another man in green fatigues and the boat-styled cap of the Serbian forces climbed down off the Cougar and stood behind him. Then, upon seeing Major Ilic and the others under arrest, the second man plowed through the snow toward the major and began a tirade in Serbian.

"What the hell's going on, Tom?" asked Brigadier-General Jay Carruthers as he doffed his Kevlar helmet, his eyes taking stock of the assorted militiamen with their hands still on their heads. Before Dorey could begin, Carruthers spun around and barked at James, who still had a rifle pointed at the ambushers.

"Sergeant, it's over! Lower that goddamn weapon and get down here!" By now, other UN soldiers were gathering around, picking the weapons out of the snow and handing out cigarettes to the Serbs. James saluted the officer and tossed the Kalashnikov into the snow. Then he disappeared over the far side of the APC.

"Dammit, Dorey, what the fuck's going on?" The irritable tone told the captain that his superior was in dire need of sleep. Usually Carruthers was quite animated, even jovial at times.

"Ambush, General," replied Dorey, flipping his Zippo and sucking in the smoke from another Export "A". "Only these pissants meant business."

"Yeah, but who ambushed whom?" Sighing, Jay Carruthers scratched his bushy, gray-flecked hair. At six-foot-six-inches, 225 pounds, he had a lofty view of the confusion milling about him as UN soldiers checked the identifications of the Serbs. It was then Carruthers noticed that the Serbian official was standing beside them. The man's thin mustache made his face look fatter than it actually was, giving him the look of Wimpey, Popeye's hamburger-chewing friend.

"General Carruthers, I must protest this incident very strongly. These men were on a routine patrol when they were ordered to stop by this *gangster*!" He pointed a chubby finger at Dorey. "Then, he threatened Major Ilic, here, with a big knife and almost let one of his men kill them all!"

Captain Dorey, his six-foot frame filled out with

broad chest and shoulders, was regarded as a for-
midable-looking figure to the Serb ambushers.
However, he paled in comparison to Brigadier-
General Carruthers who, at half-a-foot higher, was
just as broad.

At just a couple of months shy of forty-six years
old, Carruther's keen, gray-blue eyes had seen
more than a normal soldier's career-span of peacekeeping in some of the most troublesome spots in
the world. Now, he was the number one man in
Bosnia, a job that, on most days, he wished he
would have turned down. In his own mind, not
his "official" one, it was bad enough that he was
under-equipped and his sparse team of
peacekeepers overworked, but it was the egos and
outright lying of the Bosnian field commanders,
on both sides, that made his blood boil—that and
seeing the effects of the wanton killing of non-com-
batants.

Each unit, whether it be a Serb or Muslim
armed camp, seemed to be its own little autoc-
racy, working almost independently of what its
provisional leaders were spilling out at the peace
talks in Geneva. Meanwhile, mortars dropped in
schoolyards and snipers shot those too slow to
escape their eye; and bastards, such as these, hijacked food earmarked for starving babies. It
seemed that was business-as-usual in Bosnia. In
another time, in another place, he would have regarded the short, stocky Serbian man as one would
a horsefly, bothersome and sometimes a pain in
the ass, but not lethal. But in Bosnia, men like
this were a large part of the problem, and that
made him dangerous.

"Colonel Patric, I am the commander here.
Please let *me* get to the bottom of this." Carruthers
almost yawned as he spoke.

Sulking, the Serb drew away and took a cigarette from Ilic. Then the two resumed their heated discussion, trying to keep the volume down and away from any prying ears.

A French lieutenant sauntered over and handed Carruthers and Dorey each a cup of coffee, the steam rising into the twilight of the frigid afternoon. "*Mérci, Georges*," nodded Carruthers. Greedily taking a sip, the general began to chuckle, his normal personality surfacing. "Look at those two, Tom. Whatever it was they had planned, you seemed to have put it in the shitter."

He drained his cup and the lieutenant, standing by with a plaid thermos, poured him more. "Do you think they wanted to use the APC to hijack the convoy?"

Captain Dorey took a swig from his cup, drawing the hot steam into his nostrils. "I think they wanted a UN vehicle to penetrate the TDF positions." Tom walked over to one of the large, green duffel bags that the attackers had with them and kicked at it. The rope holding it closed unraveled, spilling out half the contents into the snow.

"Yup. Blue UN flak jackets, patches and blue hats. With a little luck, and a white APC, one small group of shit disturbers like these yahoos could give the whole Serb militia an end-run behind the Muslim positions. Then wouldn't we have looked stupid!"

Carruther's long whistle said it all. "Jeeze, it would've caused a lot of bad vibes between the Muslims and us. They would, in turn, claim we helped the Serbs, grabbing the moral high ground and getting our asses kicked straight out of Sarejevo in favor of Muslim reinforcements from Afghanistan and even maybe Iran. Then, Serbia would jump in and help their Bosnian-Serb cousins and then the world would *really* see a bloodbath."

Dorey smiled grimly as he scanned the huddle of disheveled militiamen. "So, what happens to them?"

"Oh, the usual," spat Carruthers. "They'll go back for questioning and some UN bureaucrat writes it all up...and then they get a lecture on the advantages of a lasting peace, and then they go free."

"Par," deadpanned Dorey.

The big general laughed like an undertaker, causing Dorey to grin. Jay was Jay again. "Y'know Tomboy, I get these dreams every now and then about a Dutch boy with his finger in a little hole in some big dam, just like the fairy tale, except this dike-runner is wearin' a blue beret and there's UN patches on his shoulders. Funny, huh?"

Dorey chuckled. "So when do we get the wooden shoes?"

Carruthers slapped the captain on his Kevlar jacket. "Well, you won't have to worry about that. You and your lucky regiment are getting out of this frozen place for a well-deserved vacation in the tropics." The general's voice had the ring of a game-show host giving away a prize.

Dorey's eyebrows raised and a smile curled his thin lips. "You wouldn't be jiving an old buddy, would ya, Jay?"

"Nope, you're goin' to the southern Sudan to set up a feeding station. It'll be a milk run after this place. Just think of the suntans."

"The boys will be doing handsprings over this one. Who do I thank?"

"New York. Seems they have this hankering for Canadians over most other nationalities and, since our armed forces' *Buyout Plan* has culled a swack of our *regs*—career soldiers—we have only the reserves. And most of them are either in training or stretched to the limit in other duties."

Dorey clucked. Up to now he believed his parachute regiment would be disbanded and his men spread out over the remaining units. "So, the Paras get to stay together?"

"For the meantime, Tom. God knows every staff officer in Ottawa has been fighting this idiotic downsizing, but the government thinks there's no need for a regular army anymore."

"So, what're you gonna do?"

Carruther's beamed, the patented twinkle in his eyes telegraphing either a joke in progress or a funny tale. Dorey knew him better than he knew any family member. "Well, our Minister of Defense thinks I need more punch over here so they've given me another maple leaf for my board. I'm now a major-general."

Letting out a whoop, Dorey shot his hand out and gripped the general's. "Congratulations, Jay. And to think you almost blew it with that little boat ride in Cyprus. You know, you, me, a couple of local girls and a pissed-off father who complained that they were only seventeen—"

"Eighteen! That's my story and I'm sticking by it!" laughed Carruthers. As the chuckles tapered off, the general's eyes panned the cliffs above the road, as if searching for a way up the steep face. "Tom, we sure had some good times in this goddamn army, didn't we?"

"Hell yes," replied Dorey, "but I think it's time to hang them up."

Carruther's face dropped and his eyes drilled into the junior officer. "What do you mean, Tom?" His voice sounded incredulous. "You're gonna take the buyout?"

"Might as well," quipped Dorey, not sure by the sound of his voice if it was irritability returning to Carruthers or he was genuinely dismayed.

"Ah, come on, Jay," Dorey shrugged, "guys my age who haven't made the fast-track to flag rank, like you did, are dinosaurs destined to ride a desk. Well, shit, you know I'd last ten minutes at a desk and I'm getting too old to jump out of airplanes. So where does that leave me?"

A sad smile widened on Carruthers' face. He was right. Dorey wasn't the type that could ride out the reorganization of the forces. The paperwork would suffocate him.

"Well," the general replied, suddenly feeling the damp, mountain cold, "would you do this last one for me? After that I can get you bumped up to where you *should* be, a full colonel, and then you can get a better retirement deal."

Dorey laughed. Good old Jay, always dangling a deal in front of someone's nose. In Egypt, in the early seventies, Carruthers was famous for outsmarting the hucksters in the bazaars. And besides, it was hard to turn down a guy that kept him out of the brig on more than a couple of occasions. "Alright, General. A little jaunt in the sun and I'm for the lobster season in Lunenburg County."

"Hmm. Lobster. Maybe *I'll* take that buyout with you!"

CHAPTER 1

1.

August 27, 1995;
Dartmouth, Nova Scotia

"They look kinda geekish!"

"Hey, watchit! You're witnessing history, Larry ol' pal, the beginning of rock & roll as we know it." Dennis Barnes poked a button on the remote control, raising the decibel level of screaming on the large-screen television. As he eyed the inquisitive nine year old, Barnes noted that he, himself, would have been just a couple of years older than Larry when he first saw the Beatles. *Lessee*, he reminisced, stroking his brown beard, *Ed Sullivan Show, February 1964...I was bang on eleven.*

"I thought Elvis started rock & roll?" plied the youngster.

"No, he didn't...well, yes, I guess he was one of the first, alright, but these guys did it up right." Dennis' patience passed the limits of fatherly attentiveness. "Jeeze, Lar, could we watch this first, then talk?"

"Who's *Elbus*?" Sean, Larry's brother, had his face scrunched up as he stared inquisitively at his older sibling. The bowl-cut, blonde hair gave him an elfish look.

Ignoring him, Larry slunk his face between his hands and ran his eyes over the black and white images of John, Paul, George and Ringo as they bobbed on the screen. It was a credit to Larry's age group that he held back as long as he could, but, inevitably, his pre-adolescent mind finally won out.

Larry's face twisted, the way it did when he watched a commercial for girl's dolls and things. "Y'know, with those haircuts, uh, if they had the pointed ears and padded shoulders...they'd look like Romulans." Unleashed, his mind raced on. "Dad, did you know that them and the Vulcans came from the same civilization way back when—"

"Shush! For chrissake, Lar, I wanna see this!" His father's hands waved in a frantic protest. Larry shrunk down at the rebuke, scowling at a beaming Sean, who always enjoyed it when Larry was scolded. It made up for the concealed punches and cuffs across the head that were Sean's lot in life as a younger, and much smaller, brother.

Naomi just caught the last part as she came into the room. Shaking her head she knelt down in the deep-pile carpeting and massaged the shoulders of her pouting son. Paul McCartney had just shook his mopped head for the umpteenth time when she jibed, "Come on, Dennis, you're taping it. Why can't you let the kids give a running commentary now and then you wallow in your 'Beatlemania' after they've gone to bed?"

Drawing her shoulder-length brown hair behind her ears she kissed the sulking boy on his forehead. "Dad's just reliving his childhood, Larry," she said softly. "Back then, they all looked like Romulans without the ears, especially an annoying band called *Creedence Clearwater Revival*."

Dennis shot her a glance of feigned anger. "Nobody says that about CCR and gets away with it."

"What's a *Revivo*?" tried Sean, his bowled head cocked.

"Creedence Clearwater Revival, sweetie," answered Naomi, a twinkle in her hazel eyes. "They're another bunch of Romulans your father liked."

"Oh," responded Sean, satisfied.

Naomi's quip ended Larry's silence. In the next instant he bounced back to form. "Did Dad look like that too?" he giggled.

"No," she continued in the same soft voice, "I'm afraid your Grampa Henry would have scalped him with his old hand clippers if Daddy had come home looking like that." The boys snickered.

Dennis drank up the last "yah, yah, yah's" as the blend of words in the final chord was suffocated by the screaming audience. And then that was drowned out by an even louder commercial. He hit the mute button and spun around in his large, padded chair. "I still get shivers every time I see that. I'm sure glad that someone had the sense to replay the old Ed Sullivan shows."

Satisfied with his shot of history, he leafed through the *TV Companion* while revolving back until he faced the screen again. "Ah sh...damn!" he caught himself. "Next Sunday, they've got the Stones and Richard Pryor! My bloody luck that I have to leave this Saturday!" Then another thought struck him. "Oh well, I'll just set the timer on the old Betamax and watch it when I get back. Last time I set the VHS I came home to watch five episodes of *My Pet Monster*, huh, Larry." His oldest son just sunk his head behind his mother's shoulder.

When the commercial ended, Dennis hit the sound button just in time to hear jazzy circus music. On the screen was a scantily-clad girl, sporting a blonde bouffant, and balancing on a tightrope which extended from the teeth of two men in tuxedos. They flipped the rope in the air, whereby she did a somersault and landed deftly on the wire.

"Wow! See that, gang," Dennis preached, "they never show stuff like that on TV anymore. That's history!"

His wife laughed, her teeth flashing in the dimly lit room as she struggled to control her mirth. Naomi's parents had been blessed with a child that had needed no braces; her teeth were perfect tabs right out of a fashion magazine.

Their mother's jibes making them braver, the children joined in producing a muffled giggle under Naomi's sweater. It was fun to gang up on Dad.

Finally, the outnumbered Dennis snapped his head around. "Come on, you guys, let me have some fun." He shifted around in his large, brown-leather chair to get all three of them in his scope. "I mean, look at that." The black-and-white scene had now changed, showing Ed Sullivan talking to a big-eared, mouse puppet. A grin spread across Dennis' face. "Hey now, guys. Isn't that Topo Gigio a funny little guy?"

Larry, "The Bold", answered for everyone. "Sorry, Dad," he sniggered, "mice just don't cut it with us any more."

Sean cracked up, beating his fists in convulsive laughter.

"Even Fievel's passé," Larry added in an all-knowing voice, dismissing his once-favorite cartoon.

Dennis sighed, pleading with his eyes to Sean for support, but the resigned look on his younger son's red face told him that the lad would have to go along with his older brother on this one.

"That's alright, Dad," offered Naomi, patronizingly, "I'll sit and watch the little Italian rodent with you.... Kizz me goo-oodnight, Eddie!" That did it. Both boys broke up.

Thirty agonizing minutes finally ended for the youngsters with Sullivan's frigid expression, a mime copied by every comedian in some form or another for the last thirty years. A contented Dennis surrendered the remote to an eager Larry who, snapping off a well-executed signal, transformed Sullivan into a large opaque square. But only for an instant. Then the screen filled up the face of a human-shaped alien creature who was just about to shoot a paralyzing ray into a group of teenagers in colorful bodysuits.

"The Fabulous Five!" Larry beamed. "Now that's more like it!" But the joy was sabotaged from an unexpected source. An authoritative Naomi snatched the remote from the boy's hand and cleared the screen in one motion. "No Larry, not tonight...it's homework, and then the bath tub for the both of you."

The unified response was expected. "Ah, Mom! We just had one!"

"Right, about four days ago. Now Sean, pick up your Lego before someone wrecks their feet on it and, Larry, pile all your dirty clothes in the hall. Then get into your rooms and do your work. I'll call you in about fifteen minutes for the tub."

"I go before the Turd-Monster!" demanded Larry, pushing ahead of his seven-year-old brother.

"No!" countered Sean. "It's my turn, Buffalo Breath!"

Larry retaliated, socking the seven year old on the shoulder. Sean flinched, looking to his mother to even the score.

"Stop it!" she ordered. "Now, your father's got the pellet stove going so there'll be plenty of hot water for the both of you. Sean goes first. Larry, you go do your arithmetic homework, then you get wet."

Larry groaned. "You better clean it out good so I don't get fleas or nothin' like that," he replied.

"I don't got no fleas, but you do, Butt Brain!"

"Sean! Knock it off!" scolded an exasperated Naomi. "Where do you pick up such talk?"

"YTV," quipped Larry matter-of-factly, shuffling past them on his way to the bathroom. As he passed by, he poked Sean in the ribs and the younger brother kicked out at him.

Once they were settled in their respective rooms, Naomi let out a sigh and made her way through the now-quiet den into the kitchen. Looking out on the raised, wooden deck she found Dennis leaning on the railing, his longish, graying, brown hair buffeting in the warm, late-June breeze, staring out at the lights of Halifax on the other side of the harbor. This peaceful view was the inspiration for buying the ninety-year-old house and doing the costly renovations needed for its restoration.

Hearing Naomi's footfalls snapped him out of his daze. Smiling wistfully, he plopped himself onto the oak deck chair and reached into the cooler for a can of beer. Snapping the tab, he gingerly poured it past his facial hair into his open mouth.

Naomi filled a cup with hot water from the dispenser and mixed in some instant coffee, then joined him on the deck in the adjacent chair. "You alright?" she asked, feeling his mood change like a steep drop in the barometer.

"Need a trim," he said, wiping the hair around his lips. Other than that, I'll be fine." He licked the foam off the top of the can like it was a time-honored ritual. A few years ago he would have also stroked his handlebar mustache. In that instant he thought of shaving his face to just his lip hair again.

"Don't let it get you down, it's just politics."

Dennis nodded, almost absentmindedly. "Sure."

Naomi tried again, her low voice a smooth stroke to his ailing ego. "Dennis, you're still young and there will be other ships."

He tipped up the beer can again, draining the container before putting it down. For an instant he wondered why he couldn't drink bottled beer that fast.

"Forty-three isn't young and this is no ordinary ship."

Naomi recognized the tone, but played along. Ten years ago she would have chided him for being childish and then left to go shopping or visit her mother. But over the years, as she and Dennis began to feel comfortable with each other's mood cycles, her approach to his down periods changed. She realized that her husband's occupation was as complicated as some of his sullen moods and that he sometimes needed these spells to "chill out".

"Do you think Alice got it because she's a woman?" Part of her wanted to shy away from confrontation but the other, larger portion knew that Dennis' pent-up feelings had to be exorcised or he might wallow in it for days. Then everyone suffered.

"Of course!" he snapped, as if a raw nerve suddenly was exposed to the elements. "Don't be stupid, Naomi! The only other person who could have beaten her for the job would have been a crippled Inuit woman, if the goddamn Transport Minister could have found one that could drive that fucking boat! Christ, I should get a sex change, I'd do better in the 'New Coast Guard'."

Naomi just lowered her head. She knew it was difficult for such a dedicated officer as Dennis to accept the fact he was being deliberately passed over for the post of a lifetime. Still, his ego could mend and they had to get through this as a family without damaging the boys. That was more important to her than captain's stripes. He didn't mean to be cruel to them, and he never struck them, but there were some things worse than being physically abusive to children. Silence could be a devastating whip.

"Dennis," she said, her voice softening to almost a whisper. Her jaw was set and her brow crinkled in the same manner that brought instant attention from Sean and Larry. "I want you to look me in the eyes and answer this one question for me, then I'll never bring it up again."

Barnes' eyes raised up to focus on his wife's face. God she was still a knockout, he thought. Her features were still as fresh as they were in the dated picture he kept up on the bridge, the one he took on all those long, Arctic trips.

"Is Alice *only* a political appointment or can she do the job?" Naomi's pupils quivered inside her chocolate irises as she pensively waited for him to answer. He studied her face again. Not a line in sight after ten years, he thought. Ageless. She was thirty-eight going on twenty-two. But that was just window dressing. Because even if she looked years older, Naomi would be just as beautiful to him.

"She's good, honey, damned good." Dennis stuck out his lower lip and poured a stream of beer inside, a skill that had evolved with the beard. "That's what pisses me off the most. If she were even a bit green or unsure of herself then I could launch a grievance without bringing down the wrath of the Human Rights Commission. And I'd win."

"You wouldn't do that. You may get mad and kick over a few chairs but running to the bureaucrats isn't your style."

"Ah shit, Naomi, I know I'm a damn-sight better and, besides, I have more years in. That qualifies me in everyone's eyes except Frances Pilotte, *Mizz Right Honorable Minister of Fucking Transport*. Not only does that *dyke* elevate a woman to captain over the heads of some pretty good chief mates, she gives her the fucking world: the biggest ship to ever hit the ice! Babe, it's this 'political correctness' bullshit that really burns me."

Although quite unintentionally, Dennis moved his hands comically during his tirade and Naomi couldn't keep herself from cracking a smile. But she was also humored by the irony. And although deeply empathizing with her husband's situation, the images of her past struggles to get noticed within the banking hierarchy conflicted with Dennis' views entirely; although she dare not admit it right now. Maybe when he'd cooled down.

Because, in her eyes, Alice MacIsaac's promotion to a Coast Guard captain was cause enough to cheer, especially given the slow advances of women within male-dominated fields. And the fact that MacIsaac was lifted up to the bridge of the newest ship in the fleet was an absolute miracle. In her eyes, if it took a woman politician to equalize the playing field, then so be it. Naomi only wished there had been someone like that ten years before in the banking field.

A month after her twentieth birthday, armed with a junior college diploma in business, Naomi got a job as a bank teller in Halifax. Contrary to her expectations, promotion had been difficult. In fact, after five years the best she could achieve was a head teller position while a dozen young men with much less experience, and less schooling, had breezed past her and into specialized areas such as loans and mortgages. What burned her the most was that she had trained most of them.

But rather than protest the unfairness she decided to stack her deck with a Commerce degree from Dalhousie University, which she worked on by taking night and weekend courses. Of course, in the midst of that enterprise came Dennis and the kids, so it wasn't until she reached thirty that she finished her bachelor's degree.

"Uh, excuse me, *Mr. Fairness-In-The-Workplace*. Aren't you forgetting those wonderful guys down at the bank? Remember, the ones that thought that only *they* had the right to have kids and who weren't overly enthusiastic about our desire to raise a family.... And then there was the fight I had with the manager to get leave and maternity benefits when Larry arrived? Remember?" The memories of her detractors caused a pounding in her forehead.

"Yeah, alright, I know but—"

"Then, when news of an 'intended' second child reached the regional office, the atmosphere suddenly became icy. 'God help the bank. She's breeding again!' Can you remember what happened over that? Well, I'll refresh your memory. You see, they realized how much extra work that their 'management team' had to do when I was out with Larry; work they should have been doing all along but used to shuffle off to the 'token cu—' Sorry, I hate that word."

Barnes shifted uncomfortably in his chair. His mood had tempered with her words and he began to feel silly. He was suddenly tired of the subject and wanted to change it but knew that Naomi would bark at him if he did. It was her turn to get steamed and cutting out would build up enough pressure within her to drive the turbines at the power station.

"So, not only was I not guaranteed my position when I was ready to return, the 'suits' at regional office felt that an uppity bitch like me should seek employment elsewhere. Dennis, it was *you* who talked me out of enlisting a human-rights lawyer...."

Barnes slid deeper into the lounge chair, expecting another fusillade of his past wrongs to come shooting out of her mouth—past iniquities that he thought were forgiven. His wife was a wonderful person but had the annoying habit of resurrecting incidents when angered.

"And, I'm glad you did...." Naomi sighed, her anger dissipating. Barnes peered up at his wife in disbelief and found her smiling warmly at him.

"It was almost a blessing, not having to go through all those hassles. Especially with a young family and you out on icebreakers, buoy tenders and Search and Rescue ships, away for up to three months at a time. Besides, I got to raise my boys."

When she looked back on it all, except for the macho bullshit from the blue-suit set, she had to thank them; they had actually done her a favor. Not only was Naomi a stay-at-home-mom, a somewhat dying breed these days, she now had a lucrative, home-based consulting business.

"But sometimes I feel that I chickened out," she added, her spunk returning, "and that a whole lot of women would be better off right now if I had listened to my heart and castrated the bastards in the only way that they recognize: bad press and unwanted attention, plus a few hundred grand in lawsuits."

But Dennis was only half-listening to her. The

beer and the roller-coaster ride of emotions over his situation had tired him. His eyes were set straight ahead and drank up the city lights of Halifax, mesmerized by the tranquil harbor setting, glimpsing bits of memories aroused by his wife's soliloquy.

Naomi suddenly felt foolish, like she always did when she lost her composure; which wasn't often. She rubbed her eyes, a sign that she was going to retire.

Barnes quaffed down the last of his beer and stifled a belch. As Naomi got up he leaned over and put his arm around his wife, pulling her down onto the beer chest. "Y'know, Nome," his pet-name for her, "I just bet there are dozens of girls who are now loans officers, and a few who are probably heading up banks, that might still be tellers if you hadn't come along and starched a few jockey shorts."

Naomi shook her head, feeling the cool breeze on the back of her neck. "I shouldn't go off on a tangent like that. The only thing I want is for you to be happy. And being happy has everything to do with you being truthful to yourself."

Naomi knew him all too well. It was very uncharacteristic of Dennis Barnes to hold a grudge, even under these circumstances. "So, what's it going to be; Chief Mate Barnes on the *Canadian*? Or Captain Barnes on the *Mackenzie King*? The *Mackenzie King* offer still holds, doesn't it?"

Barnes eyes widened theatrically, like the coyote after one of his Roadrunner-catching ideas has just backfired and creamed him. "Naomi, I told you, the *Mackenzie King* is jinxed! Mega-jinxed! I'd rather swim along behind than drive it."

"So then you—"

"Yah, I'll be her chief mate. But if I hear one

crack from anyone, something like 'Prince Dennis,' 'Mr. Thatcher' or 'Pussy Whip,' I won't guarantee what my reaction might be."

Naomi drew closer to him, her eyelids lowered in a sultry manner. Running her hand up his bare thigh and under his shorts, she purred, "You can whip me anytime, dahlink."

2.

The birds never woke her, although their incessant bantering caused her to plow her head between the two oversized, salmon-colored pillows. Rather, it was the sound of people talking in the next room which, now that she was conscious, caused her mind to automatically backtrack to the previous night's events. A mane of auburn hair tumbled over her coppery-blue eyes as she finally bowed to the inevitability of an evil-sounding digital alarm clock, which was set to go off at six, and pushed herself up to bang on the buttons; the display read 5:58 a.m.

"Alice...what a pretty name," he had remarked in a velvet manner that he usually used on boppers in their early twenties. But then he was so handsome and smooth in his delivery that it should have worked with her; and then maybe she wanted it too. The man was mid-thirtyish, a little younger than she, slim and dark-haired with those murky, blue eyes that always turned her on. Mr. Perfect; a pleasing change from the beef-cakes and cute armed-forces types that frequented the loud Argyle Street bars.

Nope. I'm too cynical for that, she had quipped after pondering his advances for a few seconds, which amounts to almost an eternity in a night club. Besides, she had eyes for her new working companion—an interest that was double-edged.

Anxiously, she glanced at the other side of the queen-sized bed but instinctively knew before her eyes moved that he had not come home with her. Even if the feel of her nightshirt had not confirmed the fact, for she rarely slept nude, there were certain parts of her life that had changed considerably since the news of her new appointment—including these attempts of comforting herself and feeling the need to ease the odd bout of loneliness.

Her last, and only, words to him had been, "You're pretty, and probably what I could use for my ego right now, but tonight you'd be better off with one of the university chicks at the bar...they'd go bonkers over someone like you."

Then she tossed back the cocktail, causing her long, reddish-brown hair to flip back and her breasts to raise to their fullest as she drained the glass down to the ice cubes. Following that was the teasing smile before she smoothly slid off the stool and sauntered to the door. She knew that his eyes were following her ass, which moved with the perfection of a model, her high-heeled boots exaggerated the motion. *Isn't it great*, she remembered thinking at the time, *how a pair of expensive jeans can take fifteen years off your figure—if you can get them on?*

To Alice MacIsaac, life was a cycle in the most strict use of the word. Her every decision, in all matters from buying groceries to men, was worked around a schedule which required her to be away for up to three months at a time. Now, a couple of years shy of forty, she found it increasingly harder to break out of this pattern. But instinctively she knew that, in the not-too-distant future, her age would make the decision for her. And she might still be alone.

Dressing quickly, she strode to the waterfront,

just managing to catch her "ride". As the ferry picked up speed across the harbor, the breeze began to massage her face with feathery fingers, making her feel seventeen again. She loved this part of her journey to work because it gave her time to reflect on the day's challenges, but most of all it reminded her of being out on a ship again. This short trip across to Dartmouth could be a quick fix during the months of maintenance when she was shore-bound.

Mornings on the ferry were also a relaxation because the throngs of people, passing by barely a hundred yards away, were going in the opposite direction, to work in Halifax. She drank in the cool, morning sea air. Coming from the mouth of the harbor it always smelt clean and fresh despite the melding effluents from the refineries and the sulfur dioxide-emitting power plant, plus dozens of diesel engines which poured out smoke continually. The air, like the water in the port, seemed to be constantly flushing itself, dispersing the pollutants out to sea. As Alice stared at the deep, green water out past the ferry's wake she still found it hard to believe that the water below was one large toilet for the metropolitan area.

3.

"The bastards don't have the fucking guts to arrest anybody but their own people. And that's only because they know we got families here and have to come home sometime. Easy targets. Christ knows if I had no strings on me I'd tell this whole country and its chicken-shit government to go fuck themselves and I'd become a citizen of Spain...or, France, or even Panama. Then I could fish all I want because the Canadian politicians would be too scared shitless to arrest me for anything!"

The television cameraman winced at the flurry of unusable words but kept the camcorder rolling as Captain Alfred Grimshaw paused to suck on his pipe stem. Hovering beside the video technician, nodding with partial empathy, a diminutive reporter regarded the cursing as a legitimate part of the interview, a passage where the offensive words could be replaced with "beeps". However, even with the audio edits it did not take a rocket scientist to figure out that the captain's fury could be deciphered by all but the most novice of lip-readers. For in the news business, when it looks like it, smells like it and tastes like it, perform a few alterations and scoop the ratings.

"Look, you bastards from Ottawa and the like," he yelled, this time waving a colored piece of paper in the direction of a small group of tired-looking Fisheries Canada officials, "I was fishing in Bermudan waters with a fucking Bermuda fishing license!"

It was all Jane Blondel could do to withhold her brimming excitement. She had scooped the "bigs" for the interview with the renegade skipper. At first he wanted to stay quiet, lawyer's orders and all that. But then his ire got the best of him and he waved her NSTV news team over to the end of the dock.

"I'll talk to the little lady here, but none of you fucks from Toronto...and especially you assholes from the Canadian Welfare Broadcorping Castration!" he had spat at the numerous reporters gathered on the pier. To Grimshaw, any station that was even an affiliate might as well be from Toronto.

"Why don't you go out and get a *real job!*" Then with the gentleness of a mother hen he wrapped a meaty arm around little Blondel and led her away, her nervous cameraman scurrying in tow.

"Joan, I hear yer a Caper. From what part?"

Snuggled under his arm, Blondel smiled at her good fortune. This is what she wanted: a common ground with this seaman who was fast becoming a folk hero in Atlantic Canada. This was the Cape Bretoner's third arrest for fishing for tuna and swordfish off Bermuda, a practice that was legal by Bermudan standards. Bluefin tuna, however, were subject to international quotas, and by arresting Grimshaw, Fisheries Canada was trying prove to the world that it could handle its own people who defied world-wide constrictions. It was widely felt by government advisors that policing Canadian fishermen, even in international waters, might lead to an agreement with the European Union over fishing quotas on the region of the Grand Banks outside Canada's boundaries.

"Dominion, just outside Glace Bay." That produced an unexpected smile from the austere fisherman. He removed the black baseball cap that held down his longish, gray hair and wiped the chaffed skin on his tanned forehead, a definite line separating the white skin above that the hat protected from the Caribbean sun. On his cap was the name of his ship, *Harriet MacGillivary*, a ninety-five-foot longliner named for his maternal grandmother.

"I know it well. Many of my relatives live around New Waterford. My dad moved us all out to the Big Bras D'Or area when I was ten but I still have lots of relatives in your backyard. All those Grimshaws and MacGillivary's—a real crazy lot!"

And crazy they are, thought Blondel, picturing a few of his younger relatives in her mind. But with time running out before the news deadline, her professionalism prevented her from continuing on with a study of their Cape Breton families. "Captain Grimshaw, could I just get a bit more on your fishing so that Pat, here, will be able to get it on the six-o'clock news?"

The big man shrugged as he cupped the bowl of his pipe. Two streams of smoke funneled out of his Karl Malden nose, his large nostrils flaring like a horse's as he inhaled fresh air again.

"Then," she added, "I would be honored if you joined me for dinner, to talk about our home."

Grimshaw beamed. "The honor, lass, would be mine!"

To Jane Blondel, this spelled "contract renegotiation" with NSTV—maybe even an anchor spot. Because, right at this very instance, cameras from every Canadian network were filming her in animated conversation with the newest Canadian media star.

4.

Halifax; September 9th, 1995

"Who's that one sitting up over the dance floor?"

The bartender, a stocky man in his late twenties with the name "Ben" on his pin-striped golf shirt, looked up from pouring the last of eight Tequila shooters and rested his impassive, brown eyes on the inquisitor. He knew exactly which woman the well-dressed patron was asking about; it seemed everybody did.

These hotshots "from away," he snorted to himself; they buy two drinks from you and think that you will be their spotter for the evening. Ah, what the hell. "That's Alice," he answered.

Twenty feet away, a tall woman with long,

sandy-red hair was smiling as the disk jockey
changed from a cowboy hat, that he had donned
for a country song, to a sombrero as the large
speakers sounded the beginning riff of "Tequila".
Just below her a waitress placed the eight shooters on the table of a group of merrymakers who
tossed them down without touching the salt shak-
ers or the wedges of lime.

"What's her game?" From his perch on the high
bar stool the man tipped the long neck of the beer
bottle to the side of his mouth, watching the girl's
very move as if she was an Olympic skater. His
flowery, silk tie resembled a hangman's noose
where it had swung across his right shoulder when
he slipped off his suit jacket.

Out of his line of sight the barman's eyes rolled
around and his dark mustache raised in a mock
smile. It was the international sign for, "What a
fucking geek." Chuckling to himself, Ben decided
to humor him. After all, the goof tipped him well.

"Uh, she's sort of a regular customer. Works
for the Coast Guard, on those big red ships across
the harbor." That was enough for one conversation. Besides, the big party at the Metro Center
had just finished and the bar was beginning to get
crowded with thirsty conventioneers. No more time
for "Young Fuckheads In Love". Ben smiled at a
new group of patrons that had swaggered up to
the bar. "You guys look thirsty! What'll it be?"

* * * *

"Dad said you were a punctual sailor," remarked Alice.

"Gotta put on a good face for a *new captain*,"
the big man answered, his sentence ending in a
bored sigh.

Johansen eased his generous belly through the
narrow confines between the table and the wall

and then slid onto the wire-framed stool. The remainder of his 280 pounds settled slowly onto the padded, vinyl seat as if testing it for a breaking point. It never came and his body soon relaxed, dwarfing the stool.

"Want a drink, or is that part of the 'face' too?"

Alice flinched. It was a thought unconsciously transformed to words, effortlessly spilling from her mouth before she could stop it.

"Captain," the big man calmly replied, peering at her under his thick, graying eyebrows, "did you find my AA attendance record at the same place you got your new watch?"

"I'm sorry I didn't—"

"Know that I drank, uh, guzzled too much?" Johansen's rich voice penetrated the wall of sound from a nearby speaker. Alice suddenly wished they could start over with no memories of the first few sentences. Lately, it was a thought that came all too frequently. The counselor she had been seeing called it "Regretful Regression." But then what cute buzz-words would that highly-paid, government shrink say to Johansen right now that he wouldn't stuff back down her bureaucratic throat. *No, Alice, take it on the chin and hope you land on your feet...or at least your knees.*

"Well, to tell you the truth, Captain, I find that hard to believe. More than a few people all over this little world of ours has seen me at my finest. It goes, or went, with life on the ships."

Alice studied the man. He was maybe one or two years shy of retirement, but would have been in his second decade of "forced retirement" from the Coast Guard if not for the intervention of Delbert MacIsaac. Of course she knew, but she just had to— "And on *my* ship, Chief?" Jesus! My mouth again, she shivered.

"Dry, Captain," Johansen snapped. "As dry as I've been these past six years. But if we're here to discuss old screw-ups then maybe I should leave...then you can have the floor all to yourself."

As the chief engineer tensed his large torso, the first motion in the task of exiting the small confines, Alice put her hand over his. Johansen kept sliding out, the vinyl seat cover squeaking in protest.

"Eric, I'm sorry. I deserved that. You're right, I'd need a room at least this size to spread out all my messy laundry." The old sailor hesitated for a moment then shifted his weight back to the seat.

Her voice softened. "I guess I've been with so many technicians and engineers this past month that I'm stuck in 'analyzer mode.... Let's start again, please?"

"Okay, Captain. When do I get to work?"

5.

June 7th, 1996

By car, Halifax is actually closer to Boston than it is to Ottawa or Montreal, the closest large Canadian cities. Before the American Revolution, both the Nova Scotia capital and the Massachusetts center were sister cities of the British Empire, joined by a common culture and common enemies: the French and hostile natives. Many families had branches in each place. War separated them, but briefly, both the Revolutionary War and the War of 1812 where they became fierce adversaries who manned and outfitted ships against each other.

In 1917, Boston was among the first to send manpower, medical supplies and currency to aid Halifax when a nuclear-sized explosion—caused by the collision of two ships, one carrying tons of high explosives—devastated half the town.

When the Americans entered the Second World War in late 1941, Halifax was already a well-oiled war machine, a port which had almost single-handedly kept the lifelines open to a beleaguered Britain. Under the tutelage of Canadian sailors and merchant marine, American *Liberty* ships were amassed into convoys in Halifax harbor to sail across the Atlantic, for it was the Corvettes and patrol aircraft from Nova Scotia which stemmed the onslaught of German submarines.

In the 1990's, although shipping routes and commercial targets had changed drastically since the war, travel between the two cities was still lively enough to warrant direct air service to Halifax—both scheduled and chartered. The busiest times at the Halifax International Airport, that is, when flights from Toronto, Montreal and major American airlines connect, are 11:00 a.m. and 8:00 p.m. each day. The rest of the time the traffic is usually confined to small commuters from the Atlantic provinces and various charter flights. It was during these two frantic periods of the day that Staff Sergeant Dave Alexander of the Royal Canadian Mounted Police usually deployed constables with Canada Customs officers to keep an eye out for anything out of the ordinary.

Besides adding their vigilance, the khaki-shirted Mounties standing next to the Customs people—who whisked the thousands of air travelers through the port of entry—made good scarecrows. Their constant, and conspicuous, attendance was intended to funnel "bad guys" through the smaller, industrial airport where Alexander maintained a small force of plainclothes officers to watch over outgoing or returning businessmen—and well-tanned tourists. For his main concern was *not* illegal aliens or the odd bottle of Wild Turkey; rather, contraband shipments of drugs and, just as significant, large quantities of cigarettes and booze.

In the past, Nova Scotia, with its hundreds of miles of secluded shoreline, was a prime destination for drug-laden "mother ships" who off-loaded illegal merchandise onto smaller boats. These small crafts then fed trucks onshore, waiting in the thick forest, a scant ten minutes from a major highway leading to the large Canadian and American markets. This type of smuggling used to be very successful for the drug ships, but soon the RCMP gained a powerful ally which enabled them to concentrate their manpower more effectively on land: the Canadian Armed Forces.

Released from their intended use as intensive, anti-submarine warriors, the large, new CPV's—Canadian Patrol Vessels—and modern Aurora aircraft, along with the smaller minesweepers, had shifted their hi-tech surveillance systems to protecting the Canadian coast from drug traffickers and pirates; both fish and otherwise.

At first these reinforcements were catastrophic to the drug trade because the offending ships and aircraft were identified long before they ever entered the two-hundred-mile limit into Canadian waters. This was largely due to coordinated efforts with American authorities, the FDEA—Federal Drug Enforcement Agency—FBI and US Coast Guard, who advised the Canadians beforehand. But in recent months, the drug barons were trying a new approach with great success: "piggybacking" on legitimate commuter flights between Canada and the US.

* * * *

Alexander's new driver steered the white RCMP cruiser onto the gravel parking lot outside the Nova Scotia Air Freight hanger, whipping up clouds of dust on the hot, late-June day. The stocky sergeant bounced in his seat when the car hit a pothole. He muttered a curse against the bureaucrat that chose the new police cruisers. *Damn kiddy cars!* he fumed.

A small, red block flashed in the left corner of the bright computer monitor attached to the dashboard and he tilted the screen toward him. The updated information was unchanged: the freight was *human,* arriving on a twin engine, Cessna 412 *Golden Eagle* from Bangor, Maine. The plane had been thoroughly checked for drugs and arms at its point of origin by the American authorities and the occupants and pilot questioned for two hours

But what the travelers didn't know was that the search was a ruse. In actuality, their *kite* had been vigorously searched beforehand by specialists from the FDEA and ATF—Alcohol, Tobacco and Firearms—not to mention the two FBI men who watched over the process like expectant fathers. This had been done the night before, in the hanger, and the plane was found to be clean. *Not* to have searched them openly might have caused suspicion. Everything had to appear normal.

"Excuse me, Sergeant, is *here* fine?" asked the driver, a pimple-faced Mountie fresh from Regina.

"Close enough for horseshoes, Jonesy," answered the big sergeant, somewhat pleased with the way the day was going. Normally he was not that informal with new men but today was different; he had a sure collar on a dog he knew very well.

Alexander, in his exuberance, stepped out before the car stopped and had to run a few steps to prevent himself from falling on his face. "Woah, Jonesy! I don't want to break a leg before I lasso this varmint," he exclaimed in a contrived Western accent as he reached back into the cruiser for his yellow-banded cap.

The constable, Everett Jones, shut off the engine in the police cruiser and then ran after his superior, who was halfway to the large, gray Quonset-style hanger. Taking longer strides, he made sure he would arrive there before the sergeant. Then, at the door, the youngster undid the strap on his holster and gripped the handle of his automatic pistol.

Alexander chuckled, stroking his trim, graying mustache. "Constable Jones, how long have you been out of Regina, again?"

"Two months, sir," Jones responded, his attempt at a mustache twitching nervously.

"Well, I commend your diligence," he added, offhandedly. Alexander then peered through the dirty glass window as he grabbed the door handle. "But I really don't think anyone would dare shoot a dumb ass like me, especially since I got two spooks inside with Uzis."

The thin-faced constable swallowed hard, trying to remain nonchalant at the unexpected news. "Uh, I...I guess not, sir."

"That's alright, Jones. Anytime you think I'm going to head into a situation with just my dick in my hand, you have my permission to tell me." Constable Jones smiled weakly and jumped into the fluorescent confines after his sergeant.

Inside the low, corrugated building, a white, twin-engine Piper Comanche stood gleaming under the dozens of tubular lights. Below the nose of the airplane, two mechanics in coveralls were bent over a disemboweled airplane engine lying on the clean, cemented floor. They never saw the Mounties until shadows invaded their working area.

"What the—" started the bigger of the two.

"Fuck? Is that what you want to say?" Alexander smiled frostily, his hands propped on his hips and legs spread apart in drill-sergeant fashion. The lanky mechanic, seeing the yellow stripe on the speaker's dark pants, nervously looked up to see a Mountie's khaki form filling up his field of vision. Unconsciously wiping his hands on a rag, he raised up slowly, noticing the enameled chevrons on Alexander's epaulettes when he became upright.

"Uh, hi Sergeant. Something I can do for you?"

"Sure," Dave answered, checking the dirty name tag on the man's coveralls. "John, is it?"

The mechanic nodded. "Yeah, John Grenville. I, uh, run the shop here for Nova Scotia Air Freight."

"Well, John," Alexander replied, letting his Cape Breton accent get away on him, "yeh can take a break and go outside wit' Constable Jones, 'ere. He's a good buddy who has a few questions to ask yuh. So you two go have a coffee and I promise I won't let a single wrench go missin'."

John nodded numbly as Jones led him to the door. The other mechanic showed no emotion as Alexander focused his blue eyes on him. When the door shut, the sergeant smiled at the man—another RCMP officer.

"How's trick's, Dave?" the overalled man said, a sly chuckle following.

"Not bad, Lewis, not bad. Do you actually fix these things or will they fall from the sky after the case is finished?"

"Fifteen years of twisting wrenches for 'K' Division in Edmonton and three home-built, World War One Sopwith's to my credit," Lewis smirked, in a good-natured way. "I guess you could say I know a wing from a nut."

"Transport Canada will be tickled, I'm sure," kibitzed Alexander. "What's the final ETA?"

"They're on final approach now," Constable Lewis Kamisky answered, the sleeves of his coveralls straining as they tried to contain his huge arms. Kamisky rubbed his hands with solvent and then unlocked the bottom section of his tool chest. He eased open a drawer and gingerly took out an Uzi machine pistol.

"Nice drill," remarked Dave. "Any uninvited guests so far?"

"Yeah, two in the pilot's lounge. Larry's watching them."

Alexander grinned, his blue eyes twinkling and neat mustache spreading like a shoe brush over his generous upper lip. "How 'bout Johnny there?"

"He's clean, like his whole operation. A real sharp wrench-twister too."

The roar of engines halfway down the runway caught their attention, signaling that the target aircraft had just landed and was reversing the propeller pitch to brake its forward momentum. The burly sergeant pointed to the shack at the mouth of the hanger. "Well, let's help Larry with those two and then we'll greet the Royal Family.

Three men were standing out on the tarmac in front of the hanger when the large, white Cessna rolled to a stop, its twin engines whining and propellers fanning as the other employee, a teenaged boy, braved the turbulent prop-wash and slid the chocks under its wheels. When the blades stopped, the door opened and a man with shoulder-length, blonde hair appeared at the door and initiated the folding staircase.

The welcoming committee, all in casual, summer attire, never moved as five well-tanned men negotiated the small ladder and walked across the hot tarmac to meet them. The travelers were also dressed in shorts and short-sleeved shirts, carrying large shoulder bags. Sun glinted off the sunglasses of three of them as they scanned their new surroundings.

"Marcus!" the blonde one called out in an English grammar-school accent. "You really are a sight!"

The dark-haired man called Marcus threw up his hands and groaned in disgust. But before he could say anything else, a smiling Alexander stepped out from behind a parked aircraft with his 9mm pistol drawn.

"Well, well. Look at what the seagull shit. Jonathan Fergus in the flesh." Then in a Cape Breton accent he added, "How's she gettin' on, buddy?"

A surprised Fergus lifted his sunglasses and propped them on his sandy crop. Like the other four, he saw the mechanic's submachine gun and sighed as he turned back to the Mountie.

"Sergeant Alexander," he laughed, almost convincingly, "you came yourself. What an honor. You shouldn't have. Especially with all your corporals busy handing out tickets to speeding Newfie's."

Alexander's grin widened. "It's never a bother on my part to welcome the great Jonathan 'Asshole' Fergus, wherever he may try to enter, and on whatever manure truck he rides in on."

Fergus turned back to his companions, who were still in shock at their unexpected reception by Canadian Mounties; the same kind of 'good-guy-bad-asses' from their boyhood movie experiences in the US. The ones that always got their man.

Alexander chuckled. This moment was more pleasing than he had anticipated. "You and your 'band of angels' just lower your bags and step forward with your hands on your heads and we'll go over the drill with you. Then, Jonathan, you can tell me all about your world travels as we drive to your 'new operations center' at HQ. It'll be just like old times, me son."

6.

"Hey, you guys, can't you just say that I really did it and we'll call it a day? See, I'm really busy with the ship and there's really no need for me to go down again. I know it now."

Dressed in a black T-shirt and shorts, Bob Gross grinned as he shook his head. A feeling of foreboding shot through her.

"Come on, Alice, just one more flip and we're done. Then you can go home.... Hey, the water's a treat on a warm day like this!"

Jim and George, the two divers, helped the reluctant MacIsaac back into her orange "Mustang" survival suit and led her over to the simulator. Seven others standing alongside the huge tank of water, some with soaked hair plastered down on their cheeks, cheered her as she grabbed onto the steel rails and prepared to get into the steel and plastic box.

"Why?" she pleaded. "I know how to do it. Right now I'm missing a very important demonstration of one of our ship's systems.

"Come on, Alice," Bob sighed, "you know you have to do this crash without the mask. That's the regulations. Now there's three more that are waiting to run through this and the list says that you're next. Be a good sport. Jim and George are going to be down there with you so nothing's going to happen. I swear!" Bob held up his hand in a religious oath.

In the large, nondescript building in

Dartmouth's Woodside area, Emergency Products produced a variety of their water survival gear including the large, tube-shaped life rafts that were now standard on most large Canadian vessels; survival apparel such as the "Mustang" floating suits; and the heavier survival suits that cocooned the wearer against the huge swells and cold temperatures of the North Atlantic. The test facility also provided a "dunker course"—instruction in getting out of a helicopter that had to "ditch," or crash-land, on the ocean.

In his seven years of running people through the day-long exercise, Gross, a former military helicopter pilot, had seen many different types of personnel go through. It was now standard procedure that *all* Canadian Coast Guard crewpersons had to participate, as well as Fisheries officers and other government agencies. The military had also conceded that Bob's course was more cost efficient, and much more thorough, than they could provide. And private enterprises were also large subscribers, especially off-shore oil companies.

The majority of "students" went through the course with apprehension, awaiting what they thought was an uncomfortable experience but finding that it was a memorable challenge. For their efforts they received a certificate with a picture of the simulator on it and a good story to tell to their friends. Then there were those that breezed through it, like it was a carnival ride and then pleaded to go again.

But Alice was in the "other" group: those who had failed to complete it on a previous try and were attempting again. It wasn't as though she wasn't tough enough, thought Gross. Jim and the previous diver were manhandled by the frantic MacIsaac when she surfaced from her first try, three years ago. For some reason the experienced sea captain found it difficult to get out and had panicked.

One of the main purposes of Emergency Products' day-long school was intended to prepare persons who had to fly in a helicopter to their job sites over large areas of water for the possibility of a malfunction in their aircraft. The training was also was the last line of hope for Canadian Forces Sea King pilots who hovered forty feet above the cold waves listening for enemy submarines. There wasn't much time for figuring out an escape plan from that meager height. Reflexes would have to be honed to react in a medium when reasoning and logic were suddenly swept away in a frigid, disorienting rush of sea water.

The student is strapped into the simulator much in the way that he or she would be seated in a military helicopter. Raised over the dunk tank by a crane, the apparatus is then dropped into the water and then slowly settles until the water is over the person's head. Suddenly, the "helicopter" rolls upside down, mimicking the way that the heavy engine of the aircraft would flip over in the water, causing it to sink inverted. It is this reality that confuses the occupants and makes it hard to get out.

On the day's first "dunking," six students are strapped in and the cage is lowered to chest height so they can get the feel of it. The second one—which Alice also passed, barely—the student is allowed to wear a diving mask which prevents water from going up their nose and enables them to see what is going on more clearly than with the naked eye. It was tough enough to remember all the details learned in the morning classroom work and dry-land exercises without the added discomfort. Alice undid her straps, kicked out the side window and surfaced to everyone's applause, and relief of Bob Gross.

Now it was time to go bare-faced.

"Okay! okay!" she said, holding her hands up in a mock surrender. Almost shaking, she steadied herself and sat down, feeling her weight rock the tube-steel cage. Taking several deep breaths she strapped herself in and then looked up at Gross, nodding.

"Come on, Alice. Duck soup. Easy!" remarked one of the ones who wanted to go again. MacIsaac managed a weak smile as Gross gave the signal. In a heartbeat the simulator hit the water and Alice tensed, trying to remember the procedure. She wasn't to do anything until completely submerged because, in real life, the blades were still turning and might strike anyone who got out at that point.

When the water level passed her neck she felt the familiar grip of fear immobilize her lungs. A torrent of bubbles enveloped her face as she felt herself being pulled down lower. Then the simulator flipped upside down.

Working frantically, she tugged at her seat belt, feeling her body float free of the seat. The cold water in her nose stung the tender mucus membrane, distracting her for an instant. Instinctively, she kicked out the side window and tried to turn her self around to get out. *Where? Where's the way out? Which way is up...?*

The water was a thick, muddy soup. She could feel Danny grabbing onto her arm but she was slowly slipping away from the raft. Then her grip was gone. Flashes of red stung her eyes as she slipped deeper and deeper, feeling the current drag her away.

But then she could feel Danny's hands on hers, clamping them onto the old rope that dragged be-

hind the raft. Alice pulled for all her might on the
rope, finally surfacing behind the floating raft. Her
throat ached. Ached from the gritty water that had
clogged her breathing passages. Ached from vomit-
ing. Ached from calling out for her brother; again
and again and....

Alice coughed violently when the divers brought
her to the surface and was quickly propelled to
the side. Once on deck she rolled over onto her
stomach and raised herself up onto her knees,
breathing in little bursts to keep from throwing
up again.

7.

First it is faces. Those gaunt, black masks with
enormous white eyes. and large, ivory-colored teeth
that remind him of cartoonists' caricatures of bea-
vers back home.

Then it is the skin. Like the black, satin tuck
'n' roll Naugahyde that covered the customized
bucket seats in many a "muscle car" he rode
around in as a youth. And there is a shine to it,
not like the healthy radiance of tanned bodies you
see in Florida or the ebony gleam of the natives in
National Geographic, but a sickly glow as if the
figures are molded in plastic with their skeletons
purposely protruding, like...that's it, like an African version of the medical book at the local library.
Where the human body is constructed by layers of
celluloid plates, and pulling a page would expose
more innards until only the skeleton remained.

Finally, providing only the barest of protection
from the merciless sun, are the wisps of cloth that
hang from their shoulders and tiny waists which,
shrunken far beyond the bloating of malnutrition,
appear like a second neck above the large protrud-

ing, pelvic bones.

Waves of heat then begin to distort the images. Then, after a few minutes of intense studying, he is certain that something is happening to the figures, like a metamorphosis. The skin seems to expand, covering the teeth and filling gaunt eye sockets until the figures take on an almost healthy look. It's as if they are characters in Michael Jackson's *Thriller* video, their bodies gaining muscle and growing away from the tight packing of bones. They now stand straighter and begin walking toward him in a confident, almost arrogant, stride. Even their clothes join the transmutation, changing from natty shrouds to colorful robes.

Sensing no other opposition, the advancing figures begin to laugh and point at him, like he is more an object of light-hearted ridicule rather than their intended target. No problem, he thinks, fondling his automatic rifle. They're just playing games, as some of them do now that they're being fed regularly. Not the majority, just a few young ones who want to see how far they can go. Kids' games. Soon they will throw stones.

Suddenly, to a man, their smiles disappear and their flowing garb begins to change once more: from traditional raiment to black...black pajamas. The ebony faces, still smirking and uttering threats, become rounder and lighter colored, almost Oriental; now, yes, they *are* Oriental! *Vietnamese!*

Fear tries to disassemble his years of training, tries to make him freeze or force him into making an impulsive decision. He tenses as they get closer, feeling the sweltering heat suddenly shift to a cooling trepidation as he glances around for his platoon commander. But the lieutenant has somehow vanished, along with the sergeant and all of 1st Platoon.

His reflexes almost scream out in dismay at his lack of reaction to the impending danger. He's a pro. Pros don't fuck up like this...never. But he did. How?

Then the baggy, black sleeves suddenly raise with the familiar Kalashnikov AK-47 assault rifles.... Christ! No, not here! The weapons begin to fire, their familiar *pop-pop-pop* sound sending shivers through him.

His legs still refuse to move, feeling somehow encased in a tub of cement as the attackers' bursts find their mark. Then he feels the searing pain as bullets rip into his body, another familiar sensation. Like a sprung trap, his C-7 somehow bolts to a horizontal position, firing in full, automatic mode. The five black-suited figures dance crazily like they are being jerked by a puppeteer's strings, as his accurate fire stitches their "judo suits". Then, almost in unison, they flop onto the dusty road.

I see my wounds. I see the blood forming in a pool at my feet. Then why don't I feel anything? He ignores the blood streaming down his legs and limps up to inspect his assailants who are all face down. Kicking one over, his heart stops. They are not the Viet Cong changelings...they are the familiar living skeletons, Sudanese refugees who are now expanding their torn, bony chests for one last gasp, their eyes a mixture of wonderment and accusation: "The Canadian is a murderer!"

Then as their heads flop down and their corneas mist over, he hears the echo of his name mingling with the dry eddies of desert wind that gently cover their bodies in a fine silt.

"Tom...Tom...."

* * * *

"Tom!" It's his father's voice.

I am right down here, Dad. On the ground with

a shroud over my face. Yes, if you must know, I am quite dead and lying in the morgue at Command HQ.

"Tom!"

But if I'm dead why the hot breath under the white sheet?

"Are you alright in there?"

Sure, for a dead man I'm feeling fine, I suppose. Graveyard humor. He feels the vibrations of his chuckle.

Then the door to the morgue opens and there are footfalls. *A wooden door and flooring in a tent?* His comfortable resting state is shattered as a naked light replaces the muted white; like replacing a GE Softlight bulb with a spotlight.

For a dead man, I sure have one hell of a headache.

"Jesus Christ, boy, you're sweating like a Yorkshire pig in August! You're not back on the booze again, are yuh?"

Harry Dorey, his weathered hands, the size of pie plates, effortlessly ripped off the wet bed sheet and flicked it into the corner by a faded-blue wicker clothes hamper. The prone, sweaty figure blinked his eyes and screwed up a stubbled face as if he had been sucking on a lemon wedge. Then he sat up very slowly, but with surprising little effort as taut abdominal muscles, bulging under his sweaty army-green singlet, raised his torso like the door of a Medieval drawbridge. Still groggy and fluttering his eyes to get used to the morning light, the younger man studied his inquisitor. Hovering over him the large, chubby male's chest pumped like bellows as he tried to catch his breath.

"Nope." There was just enough of a lilt in the awakening man's answer to show respect for the bigger man, whose wheezing slowed as if the news had somehow been coupled with a barbiturate.

"Thank the Lord for small mercies," Harry countered between the rising and falling of his huge belly under the straining buttons of his white undershirt. Instinctively, he reached for his belt with both hands and shimmied his shiny, gray pants up to the creased lines on his shirt, where they had originally been anchored before he rushed into the bedroom. Both from the heat in the small room and genuine concern, sweat droplets on Harry's face joined together and slinked down the deep crevices to add more wet spots on his shirt.

"Come on, boy, there's cereal and muffins on the table and a jar of Solomon Gundy—pickled herring—in the fridge." Harry turned and, favoring his right knee, limped out of the room.

Tom Dorey sniffed and wiped his hands over the coarse, grayish sandpaper that covered his face. Stretching his arms out in front of him he braced himself for the shooting pains that would shoot through his shoulder and left arm, so familiar that he called them "Mutt and Jeff". Loosening up his limbs, he grimaced through the practice that most people take for granted as they started each new day; getting out of bed.

When he had worked himself completely up-right, Tom began the flexing and extension exercises that started his morning routine, a warming-up of sorts to lubricate the scarred muscles and arthritis brought on by his injuries. This took eight minutes. Then it was ten more soothing minutes of Tai Chi before he hopped into the shower and languished in the hot spray.

The kitchen of the large, two-story house was down and to the right of a steep staircase, which Tom gingerly negotiated, gripping the two oak railings and shifting his weight around the corner.

Just below the ceiling of the soft-yellow room were borders of wallpaper with images of multi-colored tulip gardens. Coffee perked in an old, see-through, Pyrex coffee pot perched on a lavish, chrome-trimmed, wood stove that Harry had converted to use oil as well. Tom smiled as the dark liquid spurted over the coffee grounds, the same way it did when he was a child. He could vividly remember the way he used to watch in fascination as the water thickened with coffee and finally hid the streams of bubbles oozing up the glass stem.

Harry was comfortably seated at the chrome and fake gray-marble kitchen suite, flipping through the Halifax newspaper.

"Get me a coffee, will yuh, Tom?" he asked, scarcely looking up through his bifocals. Harry then pushed a plate of buttered muffins across the table and stuck a butter knife in the jam jar.

"Sorry about not havin' bacon and eggs, pal, but I never got out to the store yesterday."

"No problem," Tom answered, carefully holding the glass top of the percolator as he refilled the big man's cup. Harry closed the paper and threw it aside with grunt before folding his glasses and tucking them back into his shirt pocket.

"You should get a case for those," Tom remarked, now seated.

"Christ, I got four or five kickin' around, but do you think I can find even one?"

"Maybe you should hook one to the chain from a trucker's wallet and slide the loop around your belt," Tom teased.

"With this gut," the big man said, laughingly, "I still couldn't find the pocket they were in!"

Regarding his son, his hilarity slowed and his tone became serious. "You know, your mother always kept me fit. She would get me on greens at the first sign of a spare tire...bran muffins for breakfast, that kinda thing."

"So, what happened?" asked Tom, genuinely interested in the reason that his father had gained over forty pounds in the year and a half since he last saw him.

"She fuckin' died, that's what happened!" Harry's dusty-blue eyes bulged menacingly in the direction of his inquisitive son. Maintaining full eye contact, Tom just chewed impassively. It was bound to happen some time, he mused. Well, this time they got along for six days. That had to be a record. *Old vices*, he thought. *The old man'll never change.*

The elder man's flare-up died down just as fast as it had risen. "Sorry, Thomas...well, I guess I stopped givin' a shit, you know, after she'd gone. I started eatin' at the restaurant 'cause they always made a fuss over me and gave me such wonderful food." His son nodded. There was no need to explain.

Harry looked down at his coffee mug, contemplating the name and logo: *Harry Dorey's Building Supply, Lunenburg, NS.* He spun the cup around so that the name faced Tom. "You know, that could still read, 'and Son.'"

Tom swallowed some coffee, looking away for the first time since his father's outburst. Then, just as quickly, his gaze drifted back to the heavy bags under Harry's eyes and the massed webbing of tiny purple veins on his nose and cheeks. *Food wasn't the only thing that caused the big man to grow rolls of fat*, he thought.

"Oh, uh, Angus phoned to say he's comin' over to see you at eleven," Harry added, changing the subject. Tom brightened at the sound of his uncle's name, which caused his father's eyes to drift beyond the window to the green patches of the golf course across the harbor.

"Yah, well," he added, somewhat impatiently, "I gotta get down to the warehouse 'cause there's a shipment o' cedar comin' in. Some o' those western shipments have been comin' up short lately so I want to count every Jesus board myself."

Harry made an attempt to chuckle and shifted his weight to stand up. As he moved around the small kitchen to the door he stopped and looked back in Tom's direction, just out of direct eye contact. "Tom, uh...I'm really glad you're home safe and I just wanted you to know that I wouldn't mind it a bit if you came to stay this time."

Without waiting for an answer, Harry reached for his coat and pushed open the screen door. It flipped back on its spring with a loud *slap* as his large frame slipped from view.

8.

When the gray, paint-blistered door swung open, the large white birds were huddled together at the far end of the coop. Dozens of stunned eyes followed a quivering, wire crook on the end of a long, dirty broom handle as it reached toward them. Instinctively, the bigger ones shuffled to the rear, keeping two or three of their smaller cellmates between them and the intruder. Patiently, the business end of the pole searched, pushing aside those it felt unworthy. Soon the hook found its target, first grappling the long neck, then sliding up to secure itself at the base of the small head.

"That's the one!" The man's voice sounded flat in the small confines of the shed.

In a vain gesture, the turkey protested, beating its wings as it was pulled almost effortlessly through a skiff of wood shavings on the slippery cement floor. Its feet were then clamped together by a strong gloved hand and its world seemed to turn over. Then a strange calm came over the bird as it moved through the door, upside down. And the large wings were silent.

In the next room, another old, wooden shed that had been fitted shoved up against the first, the inverted turkey was carried toward a large galvanized funnel that hung from the water-stained, pressboard ceiling by a couple of small chains. The fowl was dropped, headfirst, into the funnel, its head protruding out the narrow end, looking quite comical as it hung at a steep angle with its wings confined by the narrow apparatus.

A rusty bucket was positioned on the ground under the inquisitive head, which rotated as its blinking eyes searched for some logic to the situation. Then the gloved hand wrapped around its head, ending the sightseeing, and a sharp knife lanced into its neck. Strangely, as the dark-red, lifeblood from the wound drummed into the pail, the doomed fowl never moved.

The butcher then turned to a larger pail, from which water continually poured out from a running hose, and rinsed his gloves. He then wiped spattered blood from his rubberized gauntlets, large cuffs extending from the tops of the gloves to his elbow, where they were held by an elastic support to prevent water and gore from sliding down into the hands.

Nearly bloodless, the turkey seemed to wake up. It kicked in spasms as its nervous system tried to keep the body operational. Then, as if finally realizing its fight was futile, it relaxed, the contractions of the exposed anal sphincter giving the last hint that the turkey had once been a living bird. The carcass was lifted by the feet and plunged headfirst into a stainless-steel vat of steaming water.

Alice took small breaths with her mouth, trying unsuccessfully to get used to the repugnant smell of the slaughter residues and poultry droppings in the small confines. It was her first visit to the shed in a couple of years, and the very first time in the summer. Usually, during her previous fall and spring visits, there was barely a smell at all. In the other two seasons, winter and summer, she was usually aboard the ship.

Her father flipped an electric switch on the warped ceiling and a laterally-positioned drum, with dozens of rubber spikes bristling on its surface, began to spin on a steel platform just in front of her. "Better move back a bit, Alice. This new machine really flings the feathers."

She had just stepped back when he slid the large, damp fowl lengthwise over the revolving "fingers," in the manner of a carpenter cutting a long board with a table saw. Instantly, its wet mat of feathers began stripping away, shooting out the other side of the machine to add to the heaps left by dozens of other butchered birds. The turkey was then rotated and moved back and forth over the mechanical device until it was left naked, save for a few pinfeathers which the old man dug out with his knife.

"There!" he exclaimed proudly. "After I take the guts out it'll be the thirty-fifth one today...uh, not including the two dozen chickens and three ducks. Not bad for an old man, eh, Sweet Pea?"

Delbert MacIsaac deftly finished the butchering and then dropped the now-dismembered bird into another stainless-steel vat filled with cold water. There, the carcasses of brothers, sisters and cousins of the dressed fowl already floated in amongst the chickens, which looked like sparrows next to their larger neighbors. Afterward, MacIsaac pulled the hose from the bucket and began spraying down the slaughter tables and cement floor.

"You run up to the house and I'll join you as soon as I get cleaned up, alright?"

His daughter nodded and went out the door to the front of the shed past an old scale which sat on a discarded supermarket checkout. It was here that her dad tallied up the poundage and then wrapped the fowl for the freezer. In the ensuing days and weeks, his customers would then drop by and pick up their frozen "bricks". Then it was time to butcher again.

It was not that MacIsaac needed to keep working at seventy-three years of age. As a former naval and coast guard captain, he enjoyed a handsome pension that almost equaled what many first mates were making presently on active duty. Delbert's father had been a farmer and, as a youngster during the Depression, young MacIsaac had assisted him in the slaughtering process. Since then, Delbert had always kept chickens because, as his father used to say, "When the world goes to hell you can always pick your own eggs and slaughter your own birds; as well as those that others bring to you 'cause not everyone's suited to the business." But for Delbert, raising birds was a hobby. Butchering was business.

Alice could only remember bits and pieces of her early childhood on this acreage on the Shubenacadie River, a half-hour northeast of Halifax. The scattered memories wafted up like the misty pollen from the wild flowers on the lower fields: picnicking with her mother, her brother, Danny, and her father on this hill overlooking the red waters of the canal. These recollections featured the warmth of family.

But it had ended so violently. With scant warning her mother came down with cancer and died a few months later. A despondent Delbert rented out the farm, moving Alice and Danny in with his sister in Dartmouth while he went out for those many months at a time on a destroyer.

Alice's eyes misted when she saw the rusted remains of the swing set where she and Danny would spend every waking hour on a day like today. Danny.

Why Danny? Why couldn't you have grabbed my leg? We didn't have it that bad. Why did you hate him so much? He never killed her. He always brought us out here when he came home. For fuck sakes, why didn't you grab on, Danny? He and I needed you!

The memories sapped her strength, causing her usually-tireless legs to feel like jackhammers as she climbed the thirty-seven old, wooden stairs to the small pale-blue bungalow. On the verandah, Alice plopped down on a vinyl-seated chrome chair, another vestige from their family days, and stared out over the rust-colored waterway a half-mile below the farm. As a child she often wondered why the muddy riverbed ran out of water every day, becoming a channel of red paste, only to have the water come roaring back in the other direction later in the day.

It wasn't until she was twelve that she finally believed Danny, who had told her many times that the "river" was really a long, winding extension of the Bay of Fundy that raised and lowered with the tide, thus creating the effect of it running backward. Then, that summer, Danny's river had taken him from her, like it loved him more than she did.

"So, the day after tomorrow's the big day?" She hadn't heard Delbert walk up the stairs, still focused on the red rushing of sea water that was filling the mucky channel. The elder MacIsaac dragged a paint-blistered, wooden chair across the verandah and plunked himself down beside his daughter. At first his wet, wispy hair floated in chunks on the breeze, quickly drying and freeing the individual strands of white which then went on their own, dancing atop his balding head. Delbert had built a shower beside the slaughter-house so, as he put it, "I can leave it all down there."

"Yes, it sure is." Alice tipped back her chair, feeling the vinyl siding dent as she put her weight on the house. Without looking at him she lifted her father's hand and rubbed the wet, wrinkled skin with her thumb. "Thanks for Johansen."

MacIsaac shook his head, the bleached strands waving wildly as warm wind funneled through the porch. "Everyone has the God-given right to choose, Alice, even him."

Puzzled, Delbert's daughter leaned forward, dropping the front chair legs to the gray flooring. "But he called me up for a meeting. Didn't you—?"

"Yes, I *did* talk to Eric." The old man rubbed the light frosting of white stubble on his face and yawned. "Excuse me!" he interrupted, the words distorted in his sleepy voice.

"He doesn't like the idea much, does he?"

MacIsaac stared into his daughter's eyes. He never wanted this for his Alice. He wanted her to be married to a guy with ties to the land and have children, grandchildren for him. But, instead, probably as retribution to him for making her and Danny stay with his sister, she got married at eighteen. And to a Naval officer to boot. That ended quickly; but then there was always a steady stream of boyfriends in and, just as quickly, out of her life. And then he remembered the shock when Alice announced that she was going to the Coast Guard College in Sydney.

"Johansen said he oversaw the installation of the engines and the electrics. So I think, whether or not he likes you, or feels he owes me, he's already bonded with the ship. Call it fate, or whatever you want, but you got yourself a chief mate."

Alice nodded, almost reassured by the news. So it wasn't her Dad's influence after all, she thought. *The Chief really wanted the ship.*

CHAPTER 2

1.

Halifax Harbor; July 1, 1996

Harvey Crowley pressed his sweaty face to the glass, sucking in his ample belly in an effort to get a better view of the throngs of people on the long wharf, more than a hundred feet below his office. This was the first summer, he noted glumly, that he had not lost his customary "winter lard", in what his doctor warned was a "yo-yo diet". He would laugh at "Bones", his golf partner, and reply, "Well, *yo* to you, I lost it anyway!" For years he alone had enjoyed that little joke but the physician rarely saw the humor in it. Well, this year the yo-yo string had broken and, according to the little hi-tech gizmo that he clamped onto his arm every day or so, his blood pressure often ran the blinking LED digits into the danger zone.

But the mind can be trained to be selective about certain information and Harv would react to the data by vowing to "walk up the stairs tomorrow." Health was just part of growing old, he often said to himself in the shaving mirror. But, hell, he wasn't old, he'd chuckle. Lots of tight-bunned movie stars were sixty-something.

Unfortunately, sixty-one was a tough age in the newspaper world. He sighed. You were too old to follow the meaty stories because your best contacts were filling up cemeteries all over the country, and you were too young to be called "that venerable statesman and journalist" by other media people.

Peeling his features off the window, his gray-tinged, blue eyes raised once again to the flashes of hundreds of white and colored sails scooting atop the calm harbor. In the center of the commotion was the Canadian Coast Guard icebreaker, his old friend, the *CCGS MacKenzie King*, escorted by an umbrella of four aged, *Sea King* helicopters. His eyes then followed the darting, white moths and settled on the guest of honor: a giant ship in the center of three light-gray Canadian warships. But it was the size of the new icebreaker that took him aback; it was as big as George's Island, the old British battery which guarded the mouth of Halifax harbor.

Harv brought a fresh scotch-on-the-rocks up to his chapped lips, feeling the dry liquid clear his throat. From this viewpoint the scene reminded him of those ugly place mats that his brother, Larry, used to collect from all over the world and give him as gifts; the ones his wife used to hide as soon as Larry and his wife, Sharon, were out of sight, mercifully taking their mountains of slides with them. The laminated images always seemed too colorful, too staged, too bright to be a scene from the real world. They were surrealistic images trapped in artificial sleeves. Like Larry and Sharon. And this Russian boat.

With its football-field shape, the icebreaker was more like a long platform than a ship except the bow was raised up above the normal lines. It seemed to be pushing the water ahead of it rather than cutting a wake through the surface like the "King". And instead of the traditional cruise-ship style of most Canadian icebreakers, this behemoth sported three, sparkling-white superstructures which, against the red hull, contrasted the dark-blue water and the soft greens of the Dartmouth hills. Above it all was a robin's-egg sky, devoid of a single cloud wisp.

The forward superstructure, which was placed on the front-third of the ship, measured fourteen stories upward, almost stretching the width of the vessel before curving aft on both sides, giving it the appearance, from the top, of a short horse-shoe. This area contained a futuristic bridge and communications decks and housed the icebreak-er's crew.

Two white, rectangular boxes, one on each side directly behind it, stretched back to two-thirds the length of the ship, fulfilling the "U" shape that the forward block started. The information package had revealed that the starboard aft-structure was connected to the frontal block by twenty-foot-long skywalks every four floors. This area housed extra personnel for special projects and also research staff, from whatever area of private industry or government that desired hands-on data. The one on the port side, almost identical and also sport-ing the walkways, could accommodate almost two hundred passengers in comfort.

"Essentially," Harry had penned in his edito-rial column late last year "this is the world's first 'Scientific-Icebreaking-Cruise-Liner'. In other words, folks, our government intends to do NASA one better by not only renting space for scientific endeavors but providing sightseeing trips as well. And that's not the end. Our Russian hybrid will also have the oil-storage capacity to service remote, northern communities. So add 'oil tanker' to its moniker. Let's see the space shuttle do that!"

Directly behind the bridge superstructure, and straddled by the other two structures, was a bare deck area which ran right back to the stern. On-deck storage containers would take up most of this space while retractable helicopter hangars—up to four choppers could be maintained aboard—once fully extended, were designed to cover most of the rear one-third of this area. On the outside deck, surrounding the structures, was an assortment of cranes, pipes and deck gear.

For the occasion of this year's Canada Day celebrations, and the icebreaker's christening, tiny Russian sailors in blue uniforms and white-and-black Coast Guard crew members formed perfect lines on the bow while thousands of colorful flags, strung on long lines from the bridge superstructure, fluttered overhead like a rainbow of confetti.

Both large icebreakers had the familiar diagonal white stripe running back from the bow to the waterline—the signature of the Canadian Coast Guard. To Harvey, the familiar logo had always seemed like the government was advertising a type of jogging shoes and the ships were just bigger-than-life advertising models.

"Well, I've seen lots of pictures of this boat, Harv, but they just didn't do the big piece o' junk justice."

The voice was familiar but, for the moment, Crowley couldn't place it. After a moment's pause, he turned around to the speaker, his box-like head pulling his torso with him as if fused to it. A sly smile spread over his red, perspiring face as a slimly-built man filled his field of vision and Crowley's hand shot out toward him like a sweaty bear's paw.

"Jimmer Fucking Davis," he exclaimed softly, trying not to let the others in the large reception area outside the office hear the middle name. "Great to see you!"

"Happy Canada Day. I'm glad to see they still let geriatrics run the presses," Davis remarked coolly, grabbing the puffy hand.

"Keeps 'em from clogging up the old-age homes," Crowley replied just as nonchalantly, partly for the benefit of the interested audience, his firm grip telegraphing his pleasure at seeing an old friend.

Crowley's thick, gray eyebrows pulled his suspicious eyes together. "But I thought you big-shot journalist types stayed clear of government shows?"

Jim Davis rubbed his bald pate, briefly pausing to enjoy the pleasantly surprised stares of eavesdroppers. In Toronto, only news anchors received that kind of attention, so he rather liked being the "celebrity of the moment"—even if this was just an office rented as a viewing platform for the local media. Notoriety was where you found it.

"I'm slummin' it."

Crowley's mock attempt at an icy stare relaxed and he winked at the growing crowd of onlookers, many from his own news department. "Okay, all you freeloaders, this is Jim Davis, the famed columnist for the *Toronto Tribune* and weekly bullshit sorter for the 'Welfare Broadcasting Corporation'." The entourage broke into laughter and clapping, sounding almost metallic in the glassed-in foyer area. "As if you didn't know. Now you all can get back to partying on your company's time!"

After a reasonable amount of time, Crowley gestured with his hands for silence. "Hey, hey, we all know he's not *that* good, really!" Harv added, their level of laughter raising again.

It was ten minutes before Davis finished shaking hands and kibitzing with the others in the media before, one by one, the guests turned back to the spectacle outside the window, some glancing back every now and then to keep tabs on the scribe.

"So, how've you been, Harv?" Jim resumed.

"Not bad, not bad...for a guy whose publisher is trying to retire him."

"Yeah, right, when the navy gets new helicopters or the Pope starts giving out condoms."

Harv moved his head from side to side in a deliberate fashion and Davis suddenly felt a chill in the warm room. That couldn't be possible. Crowley was "Mr. Newsman", the biggest public name in journalism east of Montreal—and well-respected by newspeople all over Canada. In fact, twenty-five years back, he invented the one-on-one scenario with high-profile leaders in this country and it was a hit, despite the fact that his "take no prisoners" attitude had got him in hot water on many occasions. But he sold newspapers and kept many a politician and senior civil servant wishing for a tail gunner. Harv was a relentless foe when he caught a whiff of wrongdoing.

Crowley chuckled and deftly changed the subject. "The Russians could always bring out the people, couldn't they, Jim? For whatever reason, a hockey game or a war, our country gets really interested in them. And every time I see them it never fails to bring back memories of the Summit Series in '72....Y'know, after that, I hoped I'd never see that miserable Moscow again, but I did, and not just for a hockey series either. And I enjoyed the place."

Jim nodded slowly, still dealing with the

thought of Crowley being put out to pasture. Was it a buyout of the *Halifax Journal*? Or maybe some "bigs" finally got one up on the old pro, something that his influential friends couldn't easily deflect.

"If I remember correctly, there was a similar response the last time the Russians came," Davis said, an offhanded remark, more to show he had been listening, instead of daydreaming. "Those big warships, remember Harv?"

Crowley nodded. "Yah, that was July '93. I've still got a treasure trove of souvenirs from that one...uniforms, hats, banners, all with the hammer-and-sickle on them. Poor bastards hardly had enough to eat, let alone money to have a beer, even the officers. I got enough of their big, white hats to paper a room."

Davis rubbed his crystal-blue eyes which hung underneath straight, light-brown eyebrows. The brows, joined together by wisps of hair and balanced on top of a long hawk-like nose, made Davis' face looked 'T'-shaped. "Kind of hard to imagine those boys as 'Cold Warriors,' wasn't it?" Davis replied.

"Maybe," remarked Crowley, taking a sip of his scotch, "but that forest of missile tubes on their decks sure gave me shudder. And those 'boys' were trained to fire them."

After a lifetime of living here, give or take some brief assignments in various parts of Canada and the world, Crowley had seen many ships under many different flags sail into Halifax harbor. From his barest recollection of the World War II convoys filling up Bedford Basin, and the small Corvettes that protected them, to US nuclear submarines and friendly Japanese tall ships, he'd seen almost everything that could chart a course.

During his thirty-six years with the *Halifax Journal*, he had used his special status as a newsman to board and interview their crews. Whether they be aircraft, ship or ocean drilling rig, the newsman snooped and coerced stories from all ranks, sometimes placing himself in tense situations, but always coming out with a angle. And the fact that he was editor-in-chief didn't slow him down or diminish his appetite for "stirring the pot" when he felt something was newsworthy.

Davis recognized the pensive expression on his former boss' face and smiled. "Come on, Harv, lighten up. Enjoy the party and stop looking for another twist to this Russian boat. Let the young pups from King's College write this one up for tomorrow's paper and let's you and me relax at the premier's party."

He loosened his tie as a gesture for Crowley to follow, but the older man never flinched. Davis feigned exasperation.

"I can remember you as one of those King's College whiz-kids." Crowley deadpanned, lost again in thought.

"Look, Harv, what's the big deal? Really? I mean it's just a big, red tugboat that bangs into ice. In the last four years, every morsel of suspected government patronage and money mismanagement on it has been wrung out by every goddamn news bureau in the country. Face it, this boat is so squeaky clean it's like a *Brady Bunch* re-run. So let's skip out to the Media Club and we'll talk over some old times."

Crowley chuckled. "And so it seems, Davis, and so it bloody well seems. All I know is that, for a quarter-of-a-billion dollars, it better chip ice better than a big tug."

When the floating entourage reached the MacDonald Bridge, one of two spans that joined the city of Halifax to its harbor neighbor to the north, Dartmouth, the Sea Kings broke off, hovered slightly and then headed east toward Canadian Forces Base Shearwater.

"Didn't the *Mackenzie King* cost almost that much to re-fit?" The question just slipped out and a giddy Davis braced for the response. But the expected tirade was little more than a gravelly laugh from Crowley, one that transformed into a lengthy "smoker's cough." The elder man brought his drink up to his lips and downed the rest of the amber liquid, crunching the cold ice cubes with his teeth in the process and quenching the cough.

"You're probing for a quote, aren't you, you sly bastard? I should know, I was your professor." Harv laughed again, his body still shaking from Davis' feigned query. Then his head jerked from side to side in an exaggerated motion, parodying a comedic super sleuth. "Take it from me, Jim, there are people in this room who would go ballistic at the word 're-fit' right now. It still conjures up ill-memories of 'government incompetence', 'empire-building' and other such compound buzz-words...but you wouldn't be baiting me, would you now, Jim?"

Davis smiled like a kid caught with a fist-full of cookies. He knew all about the *Mackenzie King* fiasco. But it would have sounded better flowing from the mouth of the man who first brought the story into the open. The pertinent facts raced through Davis' head as he exercised his journalists' mental database:

It is the mid-1980's and foreign infringements in the Canadian Arctic are on the rise. All the perpetrators claim that the lack of a Canadian land-and-water-based presence nullifies the country's autonomy over the northern Arctic islands. In response, the federal government plans for increasing activity in the north, but needs better icebreakers to facilitate the navigation of large-scale shipping. As Canada's fleet of Atlantic icebreakers is approaching old age, with one of the largest ones slated for de-commissioning, they look toward building a new Canadian-designed ship at a venerable Vancouver shipyard. Fine idea, and patriotically correct.

But come election time there is a change in government and the Canadian-built icebreaker idea is put on hold while a cheaper method is looked into: the overhauling of existing ships. This new idea is spearheaded by Adam Ross, member of Parliament for Metro Halifax and long-time Confederal Party boss for the Atlantic provinces. Ross, grinned Davis as he slurped his drink, "The-Man-Who-Would-Be-Backwoods-Preacher-But-Turned-Politician."

As luck would have it, God, and the Prime Minister, listened to him. It seems that the citizenry of Canada's large, western port, Vancouver, had forgotten to vote for the new government so the new icebreaker idea is dumped as fast as moldy jam, and Adams sees his brainchild moved to the government front-burner. Where? Where else: Halifax.

Besides being a political pork chop to repay Ross for his delivery of the region to the Confederal Party—via the voting booths—the project also gives the local shipyard, Nova Scotia Marine Works, a badly needed shot of revenue to rehire laid-off ship workers, which makes it look good in most Canadian newspapers;—outside Vancouver.

It all works out very nicely: Ross receives political mileage in Nova Scotia for the patronage plum, the workers get guaranteed jobs for two and a half years, and the economic spin-offs in Ross' federal riding of Metro-Halifax beget more employment there. Everyone's a winner, right? Well, except Vancouver.

The first for refit is a twenty-year-old ship, the CCGS *John Diefenbaker*, which is re-done for a price of $50 million, only $5 million over budget; acceptable in any political circles. However, it is used for only five years before stresses in the hull, unforeseen during its tenure in the dry dock, render it to be unfit for further service. It is stripped of useful electronics and small hardware and sold for $900,000; as scrap. The loss to taxpayers: $48 million.

In the meantime, the CCGS *Mackenzie King*, a twelve-year-old icebreaker, goes in for a "mid-life refit". This makeover is supposed to add another fifteen years to its life, for a cost to the taxpayers of $75 million. At the time, this is not a bad deal for a fairly-new ship—half the cost of building the new one.

But then the circus begins. Hundreds of bureaucrats from Ottawa descend on Halifax—somewhat like the flying monkeys in the *Wizard of Oz*—in the form of inspectors, quality control personnel and "Deputy Ministers of Everything". This horde melds with a gaggle of highly priced marine architects and engineers, and "bean counters" from more than a dozen firms. The result is a small city of leased, mobile trailers which transforms the parking lot of Nova Scotia Marine Works into something out of a *Ringling Brothers* production. What a show it must have been! *Too bad I was in Nicaragua*, Davis thought, taking another sip from his drink.

So, before the first cutting torch is ignited by the *actual* workers, there are literally hundreds of highly-paid "consultants" and government employees on site who introduce to gleeful Halifax businesses a miniature version of Calgary's 1970's oil boom. The two-year project is highly touted by both

Halifax and Ottawa, which both look on with pride as the water drains from the dry dock and their "King" begins the rejuvenation process.

Enter Harv Crowley's nose.

Harvey-boy watches the overburden of government staff with great interest, however, like everyone else in the media, is initially caught up in Ross' spell. He knows "The Atom"—a word play on "Adam"—quite well, and has his suspicions. But being that patronage is as much a way of life in Nova Scotia as breathing is in other areas of the country, he just sits on his observations.

Finally, on one of his daily drives to work past NSMW, his news-nose starts twitching. He finally realizes that all is not roses in "Lobsterville". However, rather than let the cat out of the bag, and risk cutting off some important sources that he may have to coerce when the time is right, Crowley sends out a few young reporters to eavesdrop in the hotel lounges and waterfront pubs, the great watering holes of the Ottawa-led multitudes. Their information is carefully added to his own intelligence, garnered from his numerous hotel and travel-agency contacts.

He doesn't sit long; not that crafty bastard, chuckled Davis. A little less than a year after the *Mackenzie King* goes into dry-dock, Harv's newspaper blows the whistle. At first it is regarded as a spoof, like a joke that editors sometimes write for April Fool's Day. Then, after he releases the facts and figures, the meaning catches on and it isn't funny anymore. No siree!

Let's see now, the tall journalist pondered, his mind far from the anecdote that Crowley was now laughing about, what did he do first? Oh, right. First he reports that, in his estimation, the taxpayers had already shelled out more than $50 million and the ship is not even back in the water yet. In fact he hints that it is just an empty shell with four new motors. It would take at least two more years and another $50 million to just get it seaworthy.

Of course, indignant shipyard officials shoot back that Crowley is daft. They admit that they are "a bit over-budget" due to the unforeseen fact that the inner-hull corrosion is far greater than first estimated. New sections, they claimed, had to be cut out and fabricated. An honest mistake. So, why is this man saying these nasty things about us?

Seeing the scurrying of crawly things when the light is turned up, Crowley persists in his attacks. He gives detailed accounts of dozens of suites at luxury apartment buildings and hotels that have been rented "for the duration of the project" and are now well into a third year of occupancy—when occupied. Strange for a two-year project. Then he presents estimates that the living and travel expenses of the bureaucrats are almost one-quarter the original estimate of the project: a whopping $18 million! That does it. The public outcry across the country is deafening.

Clamoring for damage-control, all three levels of government let loose their public relations people to join those of the industrialists who are now turning their guns at the stalwart editor—a commercial form of "circling the wagons". Harv is chastised by every bureaucrat and politician east of Ottawa, as well as the rival newspaper, being called everything from a liar to "a forgotten, old sensationalist looking for a last, big story before he retires." The *Journal*'s owner even tries pressuring him to back off, but it is a half-hearted attempt. Especially since Crowley's story broke circulation and advertising revenues have increased dramatically.

Then, as Harv predicted, the national news magazines sink their fangs into it and their reports hammer like heavy artillery. Now facing new and powerful adversaries, spokespersons from different areas of the project, the same ones who had previously tried to defame Crowley as a "flake", begin to blame each other. To make matters worse, there is a story in *Popular Mechanics* that the Norwegians had built an icebreaker following the original Canadian design that was to be built in Vancouver by the previous government. They finished a ship in three years, at a cost of $120 million, and had just sailed it around Greenland. That one finally blew the lid off it. With the price tag on the *King* now approaching that figure, almost $115 million—and still not yet completed—debate in the House of Commons becomes one, long shouting contest.

As a peace offering, Adams resigns as Minister of Transport. But that crumb doesn't help his government. Other factors of greater concern to the country have already piled up. It is called, of course, "Mackenzie-gate"—these idiot news services continue to add "gate" to any alleged government cover-ups—but it is just the icing on the teetering cake of the government. In a "well-thought-out" move, the Prime Minister decides to retire and the Confederal Party joyously announces a new leader, and prime minister.

But the ruse fails to fool the public. Even after changing leaders, they are decimated in the following election, the proud Confederal party being reduced to just ten seats, two less seats than required to become an official party in the House. As per the rules, the party loses its research and operating money.

"It's next caucus meeting," writes Crowley the day after the voting, "could be held in a truck stop outside Melfort, Saskatchewan." Even Nixon didn't go down that hard; or that fast. Meanwhile, the former Prime Minister and Adams go on to become senators; "Elder Statesmen." Go figure.

Davis chuckled to himself. It was one of the most incredible events in Canadian history, and Crowley, though not among the big trumpets which blew down the Confederal government's wall, nonetheless, started the walls shaking.

"What are you snickering about?" inquired Crowley, suddenly irritated at the smoke-free status of his newspaper office. He was dying for a cigar but even *he* wouldn't risk the wrath of the keen non-smokers which now populated the newspaper. There were some things that even God never messed with, he mused—but knowing there were. Something divine had saved his bacon on more than one occasion.

"I may be an old-timer but I'm still not dumb enough to spill something in front of a shark like you." Crowley joined Davis' chuckling adding a lower harmony. "So, Jimmer, really, what are you doing here besides trying to lead me astray?"

Davis just shrugged, following the monstrous ship now passing in front of them, its bow in the shadow of the MacDonald Bridge.

"Christ, you could get a hundred different stories about it off the wire service, Davis. And I know your boss' too cheap to send you down here for just for this spectacle. Come clean, you Bay Street boot-licker, or you can drink alone at the Media Club. And you know what that's like." Crowley cough-laughed again, starting his double chin quaking up to his ears.

Davis joined in with his higher-pitched guffawing. To a passerby it would have seemed like a father and son were reminiscing, enjoying count-less bouts of laughter after being apart for many years. "Alright, Harv," Davis sighed, "I'm here for the 'Grand Sail'. I'm joining the gaggle of almost-knowns who will be gracing the ship on her maiden run in Canadian colors."

Crowley's pudgy face beamed. He slapped Davis' skinny shoulders. "I know, Al, so am I. And I'm glad that it's just out past Sable Island and back, 'cause I get seasick."

2.

Kingsburg Beach, just a fifteen-minute jaunt from his father's house in Lunenburg, had been Dorey's favorite place in the world ever since he first splashed in these waters as an infant, over forty years before.

A lot had happened in that time. The encroach-ment of humanity was evident on the surround-ing knolls, hills which once supported sheep and dairy cattle. Building contractors had poured foun-dations amongst the grassy sand dunes and it was only a matter of time before large houses grew up from them. But to Tom, regardless of the intru-sions, Kingsburg Beach was still as clean and windy as ever.

"When's the court martial?"

"They haven't told me anything yet, Unc."

The two men slowed their walk down the long beach to watch as a light-gray, Aurora antisubmarine aircraft passed over the distant is-lands, its four turbo-prop engines emitting just a ghostly whisper which followed far behind its stinger-like rear antenna.

"That's the army," said the older man, his voice softening as he studied his companion. "Well, take heart, Tommy. Nowadays, it's not so easy for them to take a man down."

Angus MacPherson put his train of thought on hold for an instant as he bent over and picked up a piece of rock-polished driftwood. After a quick evaluation with his bluish-gray eyes he placed it back on the beach exactly where it had lain before. Then the pensive look returned.

"You know, in the old days, all a brass hat had to do was *think* you talked funny and you were shipped out to the "Glass House" in Edmonton for a month or two of living hell.

"Now, the worm has turned. Hell, a *grunt*—foot soldier—just has to make *one* phone call and all these high-priced lawyers and pesky newspaper guys crawl out of the woodwork. They begin tying up the *wallahs*—officials—in their own red tape so tight that the accusing sons-of-bitches watch their case melt into a tar baby. Then, when they realize that their future promotions could go down the drain, they almost beg for a dismissal of charges."

Angus chuckled at the thought of sweating career officers. He always had, from that autumn day in 1941 when he first enlisted in the Nova Scotia Loyal Highlanders until he retired in 1979 as the regimental sergeant-major of the Royal Canadian Fusiliers; its highest ranking NCO—non-commissioned officer—and one of the highest in the country.

During this time he earned every conceivable award that a NCO could win in the British Commonwealth, including the coveted Victoria Cross for bravery under fire during the Normandy fighting in 1944. After the war he was bounced from pillar to post until finding a permanent home with the Fusiliers in time for the Korean War.

As RSM of the large Canadian Forces Base Laurier in Brandon, Manitoba, he was "God" to every serviceman and officer below the rank of colonel, as well as the civilian personnel. MacPherson, as RSM's have done throughout history in many armies of the world, literally ran the regiment. And each colonel that served as the Fusiliers commanding officer during MacPherson's long tenure knew the man's value and treated the Nova Scotian with respect as well as with a bit of awe for the bronze VC that dazzled his chest on formal occasions. They also knew that an RSM in any Canadian or British regiment, because of the years of service and knowing every inch of the base as if it were a living being, held the ultimate power—the unconditional loyalty from the eighteen-hundred-odd men who lived and trained there.

Tom Dorey always felt that power in his uncle's presence, as he did now watching the seventy-one year old glide across the beach, hardly disturbing the sand as he walked. Despite his age, MacPherson looked closer to a man twenty years younger, only in better shape. And although age had shrunken him somewhat, his broad shoulders looked almost artificial, as if they were football shoulder pads propped on the barrel that was his chest.

But it was the size of his arms that really impressed his nephew. Tom marveled that they still ballooned under the rolled-up sleeves of his shirt into large forearms and wide wrists. He looked sort of like Popeye with biceps.

And then there were his hands. Every time Dorey saw those large paws he knew that they had been responsible for ending more than a few lives in the line of duty. For Angus MacPherson had been trained as an expert killer and, in his time, had not shied away from expediting his craft.

"Soon, the government begins to feel the heat and that's when bureaucrats at National Defense get involved. Boy, then talk about shit rolling down-hill!

"Right about *that* time a few bastards actually get their own back with missed promotions, or transfers to dead-end posts to rot as 'Light-Colo-nels'—Lieutenant-Colonels. That's when you get the royal treatment. The higher-ups shuffle you around for a few years, delayin' trials and such, so's they can get rid of your ass without you embarrassin' them by showin' up on *W5, 60 Minutes*...or some other TV show that would ex-pose 'em as the no-nothin's they really are."

Tom threw a flat rock at a small, curling wave, showing a glimmer of a smile as it neatly sliced through the brownish-green breaker and skipped twice across the rolling surface behind. *The sea is so perfect here*, he thought, watching a small wave fold over on itself and then draw away, bringing along a gray soup of sand and small rocks. Hun-dreds of water fingers then slid up the slight in-cline of the beach and stalled as the inertia ebbed, foaming briefly before sinking into the sand. Sun-light sparkled off the shimmering surface, but just for an instant, for then the sheet dashed back to-ward the tides like a retreating shadow, leaving a dull, wet veneer. Then the next wave came and the cycle repeated—again and again.

"So, Tommy, believe me or not, the system can work for you. One minute, you're front page news and everyone's after your blood and then the next there's an election, or a change in command and, suddenly, you're something they'd rather sweep under a rug. Unfortunately, it takes time and pa-tience."

As he spoke, Dorey continued to pan the sandy strip of beach, seeming to barely acknowledge MacPherson's presence. But he was glad his uncle had come. Angus' presence, from the time Tom was an infant, meant a respite from any problems that may have arisen in his life during the space between the last time they met. This time he needed his uncle's proximity more than ever. For his feeling of guilt was far more complex than just a single incident in Africa. Not only had the threat of dishonorable discharge and prison haunted him, but also the fact that he felt he had besmirched his uncle's name and may have trivialized the contributions that the MacPherson family had made to the defense of Canada since 1757.

Angus' words, although gruff, were comforting to him; like hugs from his mother used to be a long time ago. Only his uncle, his mother's brother, as well as a soldier, would have understood what he was feeling right now. And to have him here, on this beach, in this time of turmoil, was soothing medicine.

MacPherson could not get used to the gray in his nephew's hair; which was also thinning. *Even when children grow up*, he thought sadly, *they tend to look the same for such a long time that you get used to them being one age.* But it also reminded the retired soldier that he, himself, was getting even older.

"Did you ever get around to buying that piece of property over there behind the old dairy? You know, the strip of land on the La Havre River where the old, Acadian ruins are?" asked Angus, suddenly grimacing as he remembered Tom's penchant for procrastination. This was not a time to add more insecurities.

"Yes, I did," Dorey replied with a smirk, surprising his uncle. "I got it when they subdivided the dairy farm a few years back, just before the Germans and Americans grabbed it all. That's who owns those fine digs up on the ridge...pretty smart operators."

Angus just grunted. In his years with the Forces he felt he knew both groups as well as any man and his opinions were well known to Tom.

"Ah, Unc," Dorey chided playfully, "They're al-right—"

"In their own way, Tommy," MacPherson interrupted, "but I don't trust either of 'em, and I think that the new government is actin' like kids beggin' for a lollipop, cow-towin' to the Europeans and Yanks for their almighty dollars!"

Dorey nodded and ran eyes over the horizon, squinting as the dancing diamonds flashed off the waves.

"Sorry, Tommy, I know you've got enough problems of your own without me poppin' off at you, but sometimes I feel that all the work that you and I, and a million other Canadians, have done all over the world in the name of peace gets tossed away by politicians looking to get re-elected. And Christ, I mean there's four MacPherson graves in the same countries that keep fuckin' us over in the fisheries and stabbin' us in trade talks. And the politicians—lawyers who couldn't make it in the real world—they smile and pat each other on the back every time France or Spain shits us a morsel and tells us it's a fucking 'positive sign'!

"And they still won't go after the fucking pirates from Honduras, Belize and all those other shit-assed countries that rape the oceans! Bastards! Why have we got those frigates and new minesweepers if they're tied up in Halifax, tell me that?"

Tom smiled and put his hand on his uncle's broad shoulders.

"No fuel for sustained patrols, Unc, so they tell me."

MacPherson's dusty eyes narrowed, his fists tightening into rocks. "But they can run 'em up to Montreal and Toronto in the summer so's the Bay Street bastards with money can have parties on their decks. And down here people are cryin' for work!"

"That's alright, Unc," Dorey laughed, "but we can still go out and bring in a bucket o' lobster for supper, or trade it for a tank of gas, so I guess we're doin' fine."

MacPherson snorted, the beginnings of a belly laugh as he caught onto Tom's wavelength. He grabbed his nephew around the neck and feigned an action that, fifty years before, had snapped a man's neck. When he straightened up, Angus had a pensive look on his craggy face. Hundreds of guys on the South Shore, New Brunswick and New-foundland were getting rich on contraband ciga-rettes, booze and electronic equipment while Rev-enue Canada officials were hauling in his unem-ployed friends for bartering and avoiding the Goods and Services Tax.

But, despite all his years and built-up preju-dices, Angus could still enjoy his nephew's dry sense of humor: "Morgue humor", Tom called it.

3.

Captain Alice MacIsaac paused briefly to catch her breath before skipping up the last few steps up to the bridge. Normally, the ninety-three steps from the deck to the helm would have been an effortless jaunt, but after several long days of run-ning through the ship she was noticeably winded.

But it wasn't through lack of conditioning. Alice

was a part-time aerobics instructor whose dedication to keeping herself fit was short of fanatical. The excess demand on her energy came from three days of government protocol or, in layman's terms, "glad-handing every politician and bureaucrat from the prime minister to the president of the Womens' Advancement Society."

Alice knew it was the afternoon wine and cheese party in the passengers' block that finally drained her. Not the wine—she wouldn't drink on duty—but just accommodating the waves of people who milked her for idle chit-chat when she was itching to be up on the bridge. To a professional like MacIsaac, it was pure torture. Maybe tomorrow she could relax, when this "floating office party" reverted back to the standard operating mode of an icebreaker.

But deep down, MacIsaac knew that would never be the case. For this was no ordinary Coast Guard ship where the important duties revolved around the task at hand, while maintaining both the ship and crew. While its main purpose was to clear the Arctic channels for the summer navigation of freighters and cruise lines, the CCGS *Canadian* was, in essence, a "working cruise-liner". So, in effect, after the scientific teams were aboard, she was running three ships at once.

That was the reason, much to her chagrin, that her new chief stewart did not come up the ranks but was an outsider hired from Caribbean & Coastal Cruiselines. However, Alice did get her way when she insisted that a veteran Coast Guard stewart be designated as the man's second-in-command—in other words, to service the crew. After all, the *Canadian*'s *raison d être* was to break ice, not to cowtow to "eco-tourists". Running a ship of this magnitude was hard enough on the crew's concentration and discipline without the distractions of *table d'hôte* in the mess and their pillows being fluffed every night.

But handling the personnel was the easy part of this watch, she sighed, at least easier than the task of having to switch from hostess to captain and back at the wave of a VIP's hand. Only one more day, she sighed, gritting her teeth, *one more day*. Self-consciously, she checked her compact mirror, patting away some beads of perspiration on her forehead, before pulling on the tubular, stainless-steel railing and vaulting up the last three steps. Those were the easiest steps—because this part of the ship was her Shangri-La.

The bridge of the *Canadian*, Alice grinned as she glided through the automatically sliding doors, was like stepping out onto the control deck of a starship. Even if you could forget the fact that it was almost half a city block wide, as well as put aside all the high-tech gadgetry that twinkled on the countless displays, the windows alone made the *Canadian* special: the large, glassed surfaces that, on the front and sides, rose from the deck the full height of the compartment and then swept back overhead, accounting for ten feet of the deckhead—ceiling. It was as if a giant greenhouse had been placed on top of a floating building to give a panoramic view of the sea and sky without leaving the compartment.

The wide bridge, although one compartment, was broken up into three areas from where the ship could be operated: the main bridge; the area dead center; and the extreme port and starboard sides, where miniature helms could operate the icebreaker when dealing with close-in tasks such as docking and taking on fuel. In between these three stations were two observation lounges where entourages of VIP's and invited guests could witness the magnificent vista.

No doubt the Canadian engineers, the ones who designed the "guts" of the ship, watched a lot of "space movies" because the layout of the main helm area was right off a Hollywood set. Rather than having the captain's chair front and center and the other specialized areas mounted around and behind him, as in other icebreakers, there was a "command area" to the rear of the bridge which was raised up three and a half feet—á la Jean Luc Picard. The captain's chair was dead center with the chief mate seated on the right and the ice observer to the left. It was the ice observer's job to evaluate incoming meteorological data and information on the ice pack and advise the captain on the course of attack.

Directly in front of them, and below, was the *piéce de resistance*; a five-by-four-foot opaque screen which, by remote control, tilted from a flat, table-like attitude all the way to ninety-degrees. Seafarers since before Columbus always relied on a primitive version of this innovation called the "chart table". The designers called this new navigational heart: COUNT—Continuously Operational and Upgrading Navigation Televiewer—a paperless nautical aid which used computer graphics instead of the old, rolled-up charts. With the screen within easy viewing the bridge crew could both monitor and change the ship's course without leaving their posts. For the COUNT system was constantly being fed information from the ship's many navigational computers, as well as satellite-born sources and data-links situated around the world—a Canadian innovation which had no peers in marine technology.

Another of the COUNT screen's uses was a

multi-tasking video monitor which enabled the command center to oversee multiple operations at once at different areas of the ship. During the pre-sailing trials, the night crew watched as many as twelve sports events at once: four of Stanley Cup hockey, three baseball, two basketball, two soccer and one Australian football. This also included the monitoring of two movies. MacIsaac wrote this up in the journal as "sustained monitor-screen check-out."

To the left of the "chart table" sat the communications officer, who was responsible for keeping COUNT up to date, coordinating all in/out and shipboard transmissions systems. He, or she, also maintained the ship's music and TV monitor system in which up to twenty different channels of music and video entertainment could be assigned to any cabin or working locale.

To the right was the helmsman, called a quartermaster, who not only drove the ship but monitored every aspect of the propulsion system: a scaled-down copy of the chief engineer's panel down in the Engineering section which allowed the bridge to have instant access to the information without having to call the engine room. During the long stays at the wharf, the quartermaster was also responsible for reconciling the ship's stores.

Captain MacIsaac and her "Back Three", as they were affectionately called, were positioned so they had a complete line-of-sight view with the ocean even if either the helmsmen or communications officer had the height of a basketball player—a panoramic view that was the envy of every skipper who had the pleasure of visiting the command area.

Dennis Barnes, looking very "Navy" in his "whites", was performing instrument checks at the main helm display when Alice popped up through the hatch behind the command area and then surreptitiously snuck down to the helm. There was no need to let the VIP's, who were presently pestering John Reckie, the ice observer, know she was there just yet.

"Well, Mr. Worf, is Data ready to get us out of the Neutral Zone, yet?"

Barnes snickered, his lips now visible through a freshly-trimmed beard. "Affirmative, Captain. Mr. Data is in fine form." He tapped the MOD, short for Modular Operational Display, a colorful, back-lit block diagram. Every piece of electronic equipment on the bridge was monitored by the MOD.

"I'm really relieved, Dennis. How's the glitch in Engineering?"

"Not bad, but not great." Barnes glanced at her but his face was deadpan. "Johansen's got both techs working on it and they say about two hours, or 23:30. There should be enough light left, but in case it's still too dark in the cargo area, we can always say we want the VIP's to watch the beauty of the ship at night."

Alice chuckled. "I've already thought of that, but our bosses want their show and so we'd better have power to those auxiliary deck lights before midnight."

"I think it's in the bag. Why don't you just relax and join the party for a while? I'm fine here." Barnes sounded sincere.

"Thanks Dennis, but I'm finally partied out. I just want this bunch to finish their speeches and then I'm crashing."

"Gotcha. I'll page you when the unit's up."

"Thanks."

Barnes stroked his gray-flecked whiskers and resumed his tinkering with the enthusiasm of a small boy in an arcade. Alice watched him for moment, marveling at the man's professionalism. This man of vast experience had once raised vehement objections to her assignment. And rightly so. He had five years experience on her. But now he seemed to have put it all aside, working tirelessly to put the ship in order. Or did he have another agenda, she thought, a skeptical bug buzzing in her brain?

Alice blew the thought from her mind as quickly as it came. She scanned the long chamber and was pleased to see that her crew was keeping the dozen or so VIP's occupied in the port-side lounge area. After the last three days of public inspection she was relieved to see them in "relax mode"—especially since "public inspection" meant shepherding the prying fingers of children, and few adults, away from the delicate equipment.

They had also been in their dress black-and-whites for nearly three days. On certain icebreakers they were expected to change out of their standard uniforms—light-blue shirts, navy pants and, on some ships with a *formal* captain: a neck-tie—and wear their navy-like uniforms—white shirt with black tie and pants—one day a week, usually Sunday. This was, in part, to give the crew some semblance of *time* on long tours of duty. But more than one day was impractical due to the lack of pristine water for washing. But now that was not a problem; not with the *Canadian*'s state-of-the-art freshwater system.

Then her greenish eyes locked on the large form of Dimitri Vasiliev, so dignified in his blue Russian uniform. The color and cut, not to mention the gently concaved saucer-like crown of his cap, set him apart from the sea of black dinner jackets and the black-and-white of the Coast Guard bridge crew. But he could sure lose that big hat, she chuckled. The top was the size of a dinner plate and it made his head look small, but not enough to detract from his fair features and wide, sharp jaw. It sure wasn't your average "Slav look," she pondered; that anemic quality that came from too many winters and not enough sun. The handsome Vasiliev could have posed for *GQ*, and then some.

Cap? Oh no! she thought, the perspiration on her spine turning to icicles as she fondled the auburn bun that was her hair. *Where in this floating hotel did I take off my cap!*

A tap on the shoulder made her spin around into the furry face of Dennis Barnes. "You left this on the helm's helicopter-video monitor. If you don't need it can I leave it there. It comes in handy when we grow tired of watching media choppers land...which would be about right *now*." Barnes feigned an examination of his watch.

"Thanks a bunch, Dennis!" Alice whispered, placing the hat over her rolled-up hair and giving Barnes one of those I-owe-you-one looks as she scooted over to the port-side lounge.

When Alice approached Vasiliev, he was half-listening to the Fisheries Minister, Jimmy McDougall, whose eyes scanned the water as he spoke. The Russian's gaze caught hers and then, without any facial expression, he conducted a lewd cross-examination of her shapely uniform. Bordering on embarrassment, Alice almost tripped over her own shoes when the Russian stuck out his tongue and wiggled it at her with an extremely bawdy intent. Instantly, the comical face became an expressionless mask when the politician turned back to him, asking him for an opinion about whatever it was he was talking about. Alice slipped between them with an austere look on her face, lest she give any indication that she was aroused by Vasiliev's advancement. But she was.

"Ah, Captain MacIsaac! I'm Jimmy McDougall." The Newfoundlander grabbed Alice's hand and shook it heartily, instantly evaporating any feelings of lust that may have lingered in her body. He was not tall, about five-foot-five, a wiry man, whose sharp nose and flickering, dark eyes gave him the look of an upright badger. There was an almost plastic tone to his weathered, bronzed skin, a texture which could only have been garnered from many years on the sea. Even if Alice had not been told that the man had been brought up with a fishing tradition she would have recognized it in a flash.

"I was jus' tellin' me Russian friend here that his country doesn't have to take a back seat to no one when it comes to boat buildin'!" After an afternoon of rums, McDougall's Newfoundland accent was slowly creeping back into his speech.

"Well, if you'd 'scuse me. I gotta slip back to da cabin and gets some sleep! Lord t'underin', byes, last night's shindig at da Premiere's place was a long one!" McDougall danced a jig over to the elevator, waving and throwing comments to his colleagues, his ginger eyes twinkling as the door closed.

"He's a remarkable man," noted Vasiliev, returning his gaze to the captain. "Just like a Russian—a tough clown."

"I'll second that...but before I do anything else, where did you go off to yesterday morning? I sure never pegged you for a guy who would walk out on a woman's hospitality."

The Russian's smile was devious. "The sun was up and I went for a long walk. Since you had your alarm set for eight, and knowing how little sleep you've had the last few days...." Vasiliev chuckled, raising his eyebrows inquisitively. "I didn't want to wake you. But, you *did* get the note?"

MacIsaac nodded, feigning a mother on the brink of scolding a naughty child. "Alright, I'll let you off this time, but in this country, cutting out of a girl's bedroom while she's sleeping is a hanging offense!"

Dimitri rubbed his muscular neck in mock horror. "Please! It will never happen again! I promise!"

"Forgiven." Then, noticing the stares from others in the VIP party, Alice slipped by him for another bout of "Twenty Questions" with the entourage. She did, however, manage to rub against Vasiliev's thigh as she passed.

4.

Shear Point; Fortune Bay; southern coast of Newfoundland

There was an arc of gray light melting into the patches of faint stars that still struggled for recognition in the new, summer sky. For the past few weeks, during the height of the summer solstice, the night had held a pale edge and would not return to its normal dark hue until sometime in August. This was the dangerous season for them and, if they were not back here in twenty minutes, their sleek shapes and pronounced wakes would be highly visible as they streaked across the lazy swells toward this sheltered cove—especially the police and Coast Guard.

But then Sean McConnell didn't bring his binoculars any more because a carefully-structured routine had evolved, one that did not require an actual sighting of the operatives themselves. For, after months watching from on the ridge overlooking the cove, Sean's ears could pick up the faint sound of their powerful engines long before they came into his line of sight. Then, almost unconsciously, he would flip open the pack containing the receiver and punch in the codes that would alert a half-dozen men; a few of whom would be, no doubt, fast asleep behind the wheels of their trucks, scattered about within a ten-mile radius of the sheltered inlet.

Within twenty minutes, six or seven nondescript transport vehicles, from old pickups to small moving vans, would be snaking down the narrow road toward a small, dilapidated wharf at the bottom to rendezvous with their seaborne counterparts. Less than twenty-five minutes later, the cove would see the last of the trucks and boats and all would be quiet. Then, Sean would go home and have breakfast.

Tonight, however, was different. Pawing his silvery stubble with the palm of his hand, Sean shuddered, realizing how soft his hands were becoming since he last worked the longliners. In all his forty-odd years of pulling in fish, Sean could never have foreseen that he could work so little and make so much money as he had in the last ten months. Hell, Linda had only been off "The Rock"—Newfoundland—once or twice in her life before the "good fortune", and that was only to Halifax. Last month she spent three weeks at her sister's in Toronto, buying up the town.

A few seabirds hovered on the cool updrafts that swept the cliffs, the only movement on the otherwise peaceful setting. Yup, he mused, money had sure changed things around for them and most of the community of Caribou Landing.

The first noticeable things that happened were communal. The town paid off its debt of ninety-thousand dollars and then fixed the streetlights and patched the roads. Less than a year later, three new teachers were hired so that all the kids could continue their learning without commuting to bigger schools down the road. Before, only those with relatives in a larger center could carry on past grade nine.

McConnell extracted a flask from his coat and unscrewed the metal top. The liquid spread warmth through his body like a hot bath as he surveyed the millions of sparkles on the dark sheet of ocean beyond the mouth of the cove. Life doesn't get any better than this, he chuckled. Then the medium-built Newfoundlander shook his head in frustration. *So why were these guys tempting fate?* The Frenchies be damned, but leave 'em alone.

Caribou Landing had existed for four-hundred years, it sheltered coves used as a stop-over for early fishermen to clean and salt their catches before heading back to Europe. Over many decades it saw the native residents, the Beothuks, hunted like the many moose and caribou that roamed its stunted forests and pushed to extinction. Then came the immigration of French, English, Portuguese, Spanish and Irish, their blood mixing as each new resident either moved in or married one of the locals. Its population had risen to a high of three hundred in the 1920's to just over two hundred; the present census.

The next decision by the town council was to hire its very first town administrator to handle, and *divert*, its newest revenues. McConnell's brother-in-law, Seamus Duffy, had stated that it would be best to do this without much fanfare, so they hired up what the mainlanders call a "headhunting" firm to do the looking. The result was Andrew Foreman: an unemployed city administrator from a town in southeastern Ontario whose tax base had eroded so badly from the loss of its manufacturing sector that it did not need, nor could it afford, such a position.

Foreman's arrival was preceded by a carefully-planned scenario which could be slowly brought out to explain his residence in the small Newfoundland town. Officially, he was hired for seventeen thousand dollars, plus given a small house, rent-free.

Sean felt his right leg begin to ache and pulled out the little rum container again. That was the one thing he did not miss about fishing; that and the constant throbbing in his lower back.

Foreman's biggest asset was his intimate knowledge of the huge underground industry that had sprouted up along the St. Lawrence River between Ontario and the US. The heavy "sin taxes" placed on cigarettes and alcohol during the 1980's spawned a movement that began with a few Mohawk natives in motorboats, mushrooming into a well-structured trade, garnering profits approaching the realms of Alphonso Capone's days during the American Prohibition days.

The "come from away," as Foreman was first called, incorporated numbered foreign companies which then "eagerly" invested in the town's population, creating hi-tech industries such as ship's navigational software engineering. These new ventures were earmarked for all the town's expenses and also paid the locals "dividends". So frequent were the checks it was almost as though a fairy godmother had touched her wand on Caribou Landing.

But old passions take a long time to quell, thought McConnell, tossing another spent cigarette away. He remembered his grandfather telling him about Ike Jones and his schooner, *The*

Marion, and how Ike had beaten up a French skipper in a saloon in St. Pierre back in 1915. It's said the French had caught up with the Fortune Bay ship when she was at anchor and her crew asleep, and scuttled her, not saving one man.

Some relatives of the crew still held hate in their hearts over that incident. But for the younger ones, the ones who cared to still fish for a living, it was a feud over scallops, and who had the right to drag for the shellfish. Others just wanted the thrills and to draw pogey in-between booze and cigarette runs.

Idle hands, indeed! These young bastards'll surely bring down the Feds on us for their "pay back," as they call it. Leave the fuckin' French to their piddly little islands and let's start to enjoy life. Christ knows us old folks deserve some peace at our age. We just wanna live and let live, not go around tossin' gasoline bottles at Jesus foreign boats!

5.

"It's Sydney on the 'secured', Sergeant, and they say it's urgent!"

Dave Anderson's bored face was a mask of perspiration. The policeman mopped the swath of sweat under his grayish-brown hair with a piece of paper towel, silently vowing to come up with a cool, summer cap for the RCMP. He loved the Nova Scotia summers with a passion, but not on the inside of a police cruiser with no air-conditioning. And he couldn't roll down a window for fear of scattering hundreds of loose papers all over the town of Bedford and the windy Basin to his left.

"Alexander here." The fact that the call was made through a scrambled satellite channel didn't seem to raise any special interest for him. Anderson knew that the "new RCMP" liked to play with their hi-tech toys. But when the sergeant's eyes twitched, his driver felt the temperature lower in the cruiser, as if a cool wind had invaded them through a large vent.

"Jesus Murphy! When?"

Constable Jones watched his boss out of the corner of his eye, which normally was a difficult thing to do while dodging the rush-hour traffic on the Bedford Highway leading into Halifax. But as much as he tried to keep his total attention on the road, the skinny Mountie could not help but tune in to Alexander's voice. "I don't fuckin' believe it!" Dave shouted. "I'll have their balls for bait!"

With each new oath from his sergeant, Jones' hands dug into the steering wheel, as if tensing from the tortuous buzz of a dentist's drill. "Ah, rat shit!" Alexander switched off the phone and tossed it into the back of cruiser.

Jones unclenched, happy that the tirade had started. Even though he had only been with the sergeant barely a week, he was well versed in the pattern of most of Alexander's outbursts. The longer the older Mountie held off, the more fiery the volcano would be when it did blow. For Alexander, tipping the scales at two hundred and forty pounds, did not take disappointment lightly and could make quite a mess when he stated throwing things around.

"Put the lights on and get us to HQ fast! Those stupid bastards! They fuckin' lost him!"

Constable Jones nailed the pedal and the big, white Capris Classic lurched forward, smoothly negotiating the dips and potholes like only a brand-new car can. When Jones glanced to his right again, Alexander had both hands on his face, pulling down as if he were trying to help nature accelerate the jowling of his cheeks. In-between his hands were pouting lips which kept speaking as the palms rubbed around them again, and again.

"Jonesy, all I asked them was *this*: Stay with the man. If he goes into a store, stake out the back and watch the front. If he goes into an apartment building, cover all exits...simple, isn't it, Everett? So simple that even a dumb Cape Bretoner like myself can follow it. *But not these jokers!*"

Its strobing, red-and-blue "teardrop" lights cutting through the summer day, the cruiser sped toward Oxford Street in south Halifax, the home of "H" Division of the Royal Canadian Mounted Police. Absentmindedly, Alexander rolled down the window and immediately regretted the action as a shotgun blast of air sent paper scurrying through the vehicle, plastering some sheets against the back window. He violently cranked back the handle and the interior of the cruiser became still.

"Sorry, Jonesy, I guess I'm about as sharp as those 'experts' up in Sydney."

"Uh, excuse me, sir," Jones ventured, carefully, as he flipped the siren to get through a busy inter-section. "What exactly happened?"

Alexander shook his head. "You'll never believe me, Everett, me son. This was the dumbest of all tricks to fall for. It seems Jonathan Fergus went AWOL on us. He was dressed in a black-leather jacket and dark sunglasses and made a few stops: a burger joint, a grocery store, even a movie. No problem. He even came back out the front door."

The cruiser pulled in front of the brick com-plex at 3139 Oxford and lurched to a stop. Picking up his yellow-ringed, navy cap, the sergeant took a deep breath, letting the air out of his lungs in a slow, controlled volley. He then turned to Consta-ble Jones, who was switching off the electronics.

"He went into a nightclub, had a couple of

drinks, then went to the can. No problem again. It's dark, but all exits were covered. Except that some joker with a blonde pony tail, leather jacket and sunglasses comes out and leaves by the side exit. Our dicks jump on the trail and follow him for a couple of hours...only he's *not* Fergus. The real Fergus puts on a short, dark wig and a sweat shirt and waltzes out the front door to who knows fucking where?"

As he shut off the engine, Jones nervously searched for something to say but held his silence. Both Mounties emerged from the paper-strewn cruiser into a cool, summer breeze and walked toward the building. There was no need to gather and sort out the documents: the plan was blown.

6.

"Captain MacIsaac, meet Jim Davis, the award-winning columnist for the *Toronto Tribune*."

Davis winced at the "award-winning" part. Although it was well-deserved, as the scribe had accomplished much in his profession, he always felt uncomfortable with public laurels. And that was precisely why Harv Crowley always did it.

"This is a marvelous ship, Captain. Congratulations" MacIsaac received the tall man's hand in a firm handshake. When Alice saw his eyes wandering down her blouse, she silently cursed the tailor again for making this uniform smaller than the one she wore yesterday.

"Thank you, Mr. Davis." She smiled graciously at Davis and then to the scaled-down party remaining on the bridge. "And I trust you all are having a good trip?"

"Great!" Five voices almost sounded in unison. The remark seemed to throw a switch in the heavens. For the ebbing of the glorious sunset, which previously had drenched the bridge in orange and lit up the sea with the colors of a prairie fire, had now immersed the chamber in a purple glow.

For the event, Alice had taken off the LDS— light deflection shields—so that the passengers on the bridge could behold the beauty without the darkening "sunglasses" effect. Because the bridge was, in effect, a large greenhouse, the designers installed the new LDS technology to protect the crew from both sunstroke and the hothouse effect of the glass enclosure, which was also counter- productive to the air-conditioning system.

It worked on a principle similar to the LCD's— liquid crystal diodes—in watches and other house- hold displays, where electric current is channeled through a bath of chemicals to form patterns of electronic circuitry which make up letters, num- bers, etc. The ship's windows were actually a con- glomerate of three parts: an outer pane of trans- parent, composite compound which channeled off water without the need for wipers; an inner panel of non-glare safety glass; and, sandwiched be- tween, a sealed compartment of LDS which was either controlled automatically by the climate-con- trol system or a manual rheostat override. When activated, the charged particles inside the glass polarized and could be moved *en mass*, somewhat like a Venetian blind, to block out the rays. The glassed deckheads on observation decks—on top of the guest and scientific structures—were also outfitted with this technology.

There were just five civilians left on the bridge to enjoy the scene: Harv Crowley, Jim Davis, William Berchstein, the US ambassador, Judy MacDonald, the Nova Scotia Minister of Tourism, and Frances Pilotte, the federal Minister of Transport, as well as Dimitri Vasiliev, the liaison officer from the Russian Navy.

"Captain, I must say that I've been to some bang-up celebrations in my time but I've never had three, one after the other before!" retorted Ambassador Berchstein. "And to top it all off, an ocean sunset! Well, it's like watching it from the top of the world!"

"Thank you, Mr. Ambassador, but I think the credit would have to go to Ms. Pilotte and Ms. MacDonald. They are the brains behind these events. I just run the ship." MacIsaac deferred to the two ladies standing with Harv Crowley, her emerald-green eyes locking for a brief instant on the sapphire blues of Judy MacDonald.

MacDonald was about the same age as Alice, and the same height, but it was the differences between the two women that intrigued the sharp eyes of Jim Davis. MacDonald seemed to have been born in a business suit, balancing on high heels. Her *coiffure* copied the latest style that the prime minister's wife was wearing which, in turn, was copied from the First Lady's White House style: a bob just below the ears, colored sandy-blonde. It was a "girlish" look that was turning up on the cover of every fashion magazine. Although it went well with her baby face and warm, light-brown eyes, the hairdo was a little too "cute" to top off her nine-to-five posture and wardrobe.

MacIsaac, on the other hand, looked completely comfortable in a uniform. In fact, although MacDonald won the beauty contest, the captain seemed more desirable to him. It wasn't so much her tall, slender figure, lovely rust-colored hair or even her spectacular green eyes that could be childlike or piercing depending upon the occasion—it was her movement. She glided effortlessly across the bridge like a dancer, no doubt largely due to the white gym shoes that she wore. Every step seemed choreographed; nothing was wasted. But despite Alice's feminine air, Davis, with the instincts of the investigator that he was, saw in her the hard edge of a commander. There was no question who was in charge of this ship.

But he also picked up the instinctive qualities that only a woman could pull off gracefully: the ability to carry on *normally* while in the presence of a detractor. He had zeroed in on a circumstance which would have eluded all but the most observant listener: a hint of terseness in her speech when speaking with MacDonald. "The Captain is being too modest," replied the tourism minister, enunciating it "cap-tain" as if it were two words.

After yesterday's soirée with Harv, who was now just one drink short of bedtime, he learned that it was no secret that "Judy Mac" had pulled strings with some powerful friends in the federal government to stretch the inaugural cruise of the *Canadian* into a "Worldwide Showcase for Nova Scotia."

The Minister of Transport Frances Pilotte, also a tad cool with Ms. MacDonald, Davis noted, had tried to block the move, citing the concerns of Coast Guard officials: that a tourism and media event so soon after launch "would cause unnecessary strain on a crew which has yet to fully master the new ship."

Although a loyal party member since the mid-1960's, Frances was overruled by the party caucus. Her debate, sprinkled with references to the RMS *Titanic*, and other disaster-prone scenarios, was politely dismissed by party tacticians as "naïve and uninformed."

Pilotte was especially chastised by Nova Scotia members of Parliament, both in and out of the party, who claimed that their province needed a well-deserved economic boost. This argument was bolstered by statistics: thousands of persons in the province had recently been thrown out of work due the closure of two armed-forces bases and the cancellation of a mega-project to build new helicopters. And their unemployment was just another page in the province's economic woes. Pilotte had no allies but the Coast Guard on this one, except the Prime Minister, and his hands were tied. His veto would have started a flood of accusations in the media from detractors within his own caucus. And, at just over a year in the job, it was still too early in his tenure to start purging these dissidents. Especially with an election looming.

The final word from the Prime Minister was a compromise, cutting back from the three-day gala MacDonald had planned: "The CCGS *Canadian* will make a short voyage from Halifax harbor around Sable Island and back, an overnight trip which will include a select group of tourists and members of the scientific community."

The cruise was to go ahead, but Pilotte, her boss and the Coast Guard got a much scaled-down version. Before MacDonald had floated out of the Ottawa meeting, Frances Pilotte, gracious in defeat, offered the Nova Scotia minister all her support. It was the way she had always played the game, and the way that kept party politics working: fight it out in the caucus like wolverines, but then face the public in solidarity. Besides, thought the petite transport minister, she had already beaten the "old boys," big-time: with Captain MacIsaac.

Frances deftly cut in. "I'm sure everyone would agree that Captain MacIsaac and her crew have performed a minor miracle in preparing this beautiful ship for today." A round of "here, here!" went up from the small group. Blushing, Alice thanked them, then excused herself to do her rounds and disappeared down the main hatchway. Almost immediately, Vasiliev waved and left.

"Well, I should be sauntering back to my room, now, if I can find it!" Harv Crowley drained his last drop of scotch.

"I'll help you, if you help me." Laughing snidely, Davis grabbed the old newspaperman by the arm and escorted him to the elevator to a chorus of "Goodnights!"

7.

"Why wasn't he held longer?"

"Because, sir, the minute we slapped the cuffs on him a high-priced lawyer from Bates, Fuller and Evans pulled up in his Lexus and tied us up with the usual bullshit."

The Crown prosecutor shook his head, almost absentmindedly.

"That fast?"

"Yes sir, that fast."

"So, it seems we've been fucked over." The lawman peered over the top of his brown, horned-rimmed glasses at the dejected form of Dave Alexander. He knew the sergeant was one of the best and had followed procedure to the letter. So where was the leak?

"Uh, Dave, read me again that rundown on the Planet Guardians' activities last year. Maybe we can shake something out of that."

Gerald Delaney knew all about "high-priced lawyers." The balding fifty year old had been one of them, before he switched sides. That was before two incidents changed his lifestyle: his wife died suddenly and the two children married soon after and moved west. Left with an empty house and a heart condition, all that competitive bullshit didn't really make sense anymore. The only thing he could envision for the future was his epitaph: *Look beside you, Betty. I died young, but I was a wealthy partner.* He felt it was time to give back after twenty years of taking.

"Well," Alexander started after shuffling through some papers, "you know that Fergus and his pirates were apprehended by Malaysian authorities three years ago for ramming supposedly 'legal' fishing boats, Chinese-style junks, really, with their New Zealand-registered trawler. The Guardians were also reeling in drift nets and destroying them." Rubbing his gray beard, Delaney nodded, beckoning him to go on.

"Okay, well, after the trial, each member of the crew was given six months in jail, despite pleas from some powerful politicians in the States, I might add. They were then deported, but Fergus was given six lashes with the *cane* and thrown in jail for an extra thirteen months."

"Really? With all the money the Planet Guardians have, he stayed in that long?"

"Mr. Delaney, I've dealt with police from some of those South Seas places, like Singapore and Indonesia. They live by their laws and they don't cotton much to outsiders' pleas. If anything, it makes things tougher on the prisoners in question."

Delaney envisioned the punishment and whistled. "Dave, what *we* could do with that kind of power. But that cane, it strips away some of the skin, doesn't it?"

"And them some. There would definitely be some unhappy folks if we tried it here."

"And some clean streets."

"Amen to that, sir."

Delaney stood up, stretching as his knees popped. "So what do you think they're planning now that Fergus is at large?"

The big Mountie, once so hot in the cruiser, buttoned the top of his khaki shirt against the cold blasts from the building's air-conditioning system.

"Well, sir, we have to look at it this way: Jonathan Fergus, a known felon, flies as bold as brass into a place where he knows he's up on numerous charges such as trespassing, assault and willful damage, to name a few. At the exact same time he's arrested, out pops the best law firm in Eastern Canada. Then he spends absolutely *no* time in jail, and his bail is set at only $50,000, which he forfeits by jumping with a well-planned maneuver."

Delaney whistled again.

"And you can do that twice for me, sir."

CHAPTER 3

1.

Finally, the buzzing woke her.

"Oh shit! I missed my *watch*!"

Four thirty-two a.m. The fuzzy LED numbers on the plastic face of Alice MacIsaac's clock-radio taunted her for refusing the services of the wake-up system, the same type of electronic paging used to rouse guests in hotels. It was her typical reason: rebellion; and stubbornness. "This is still a Coast Guard vessel," she had said—at least it was in the forward superstructure.

"Damn, damn, damn!" She bolted to the bathroom mirror, gathering up the copper, Spanish moss that was her hair into a pony tail as she ran. Her reflection taunting her, Alice then rolled and pinned the slender sheaf into a standard Navy bun and covered it with her black and white cap, silently thanking herself for at least one attribute: her laziness. The captain had slept in the lounge chaise with her uniform on saving her the time needed to change.

"Christ! They'll never let me live this down!"

The artificial fragrance in the corridor enveloped her as she shuffled toward the open elevator, a sort of pleasing industrial perfume. When she had first boarded the ship Alice had likened the aroma to that of a new automobile.

Once inside the stainless-steel lined car she fit the pass-card, hanging from the elastic band on her wrist, into the knurled control panel and the "Bridge Lock-Out" light switched off. As the doors slid shut and the motors whirred, a soft voice whispered, "Thank you Captain MacIsaac. The lift is now operational and is proceeding to the bridge."

On previous rides, despite hating the annoying sound-byte, she had felt giddy, like being the member of an exclusive club; like having the key to her own penthouse. But not today.

As her knees felt the soft pressure of the rising car, Alice couldn't help thinking that, in time of war, a captain could lose command of a ship for such an indiscretion as "sleeping in." However, brief flashes of her father's exploits passed through her mind. *There* was an irreverent sea captain if ever there was one and yet Delbert held on to command of his ship to be decorated for sinking a German submarine. Still, Alice knew what her officers would be thinking: "Miss Iron Britches is late!"

The elevator motor whined down and the car eased to a stop. Alice tensed, any watered-down thoughts of saving face washed away in a coolness that signaled unwelcome perspiration. Taking a deep breath she mopped her moist forehead and, instinctively, dabbed the sleep from her eyes.

When the doors parted the dawn's gray light, unfiltered and intensified by the calm North Atlantic Ocean, caught her pupils unaware, causing her to flinch and cover her eyes. Instantly MacIsaac realized that she must have forgotten to engage the LDS shading system in the greenhouse-like bridge before she left last night. But why hadn't one of the mates reset it, she pondered, the flash of pain receding before a parade of large, dark rectangles that marched before her eyes, negative images of the large windows that lingered on her retinas.

"Well, Captain MacIsaac! We were just going to give you a wake-up call!"

The voice was wrong and it stopped Alice cold. Confused, the captain forgot her initial embarrassment, straining her memory to place the speaker. Using her hand as a visor she squinted, peering through the glare to isolate the origin of the speech. Then she saw a dark shape outlined in the captain's chair. *Her chair.*

Slowly, Alice's eyes began to focus on the murky figure.

"You don't sound like a member of the crew. Who are you?" she asked impatiently, her irises growing into thick, olive rings, compensating for the brightness. As she spoke the perplexed captain circled to the left, around the Ice Observer's station, her curiosity overcoming an instinctive urge to trigger an alarm. Then, as the features of his face began to fill in, she beheld a man with shoulder-length, dark-blond hair and wire-rimmed glasses sitting at her command console squeezing, what appeared to be, a lime-green tennis ball in his right hand. So nonchalant, so irreverently grinning; sitting in *her chair.*

Rage welled up within her, but was kept in check, just below her calm veneer. It was her instinctive reaction to confrontation, an attribute absorbed during the twelve years she spent studying karate. Among the many things Alice admired about the Japanese was their ability to store temper, passion and fear into compartments in their mind for future reference. As if re-routed by a pro-grammed switch within a sub-microprocessor in her brain, her emotions were carefully funneled into a sort of holding area. Imitating the Japanese practice, each item would then be dealt with later, one at a time, when it could be given special at-tention and thought.

"Well, sir," she said, congenially, "it seems you have mistaken this part of the ship for the pas-senger section. I'll have a member of the crew es-cort you—"

"That won't be necessary, Captain. I feel quite comfortable here." His attention then drifted straight ahead to the colored images on the COUNT screen, as if dismissing her presence.

The analyzer in Alice burst into overdrive, an-other well-embedded attribute learned during the long climb to command—collecting and process-ing information quickly. The prankster appeared to be a taller version of Paul Williams, the song-writer: the same babyish face under straight bangs that seemed supported by his glasses. She also tuned into his cultured English accent and the cane hanging on the crook of his left arm.

The man then shifted left to face her, the black nylon jacket squeaking with the motion as he flung his leg over the arm of the chair; her *chair*. He kneaded the tennis ball as if it were clay then tossed it in the air. Nonchalantly, without glanc-ing at it, he smiled when it plopped directly in his palm.

"I see. Well, maybe Mr. Barnes—" It was then that her peripheral vision caught Chief Mate Dennis Barnes and Quartermaster Annette Potvin, the helmsman-on-duty, standing behind the port mini-bridge with two other men. Flicking her eyes in the opposite direction she picked up two other figures on the starboard side with their arms crossed, smiling.

Her attention went back to the chief mate, who resembled a beat-up puppy. "Oh, Jesus, Dennis! What happened?" Her voice wavered on the last two words.

"They came up behind—"

"And we took over your ship, Captain MacIsaac!" the intruder in her chair exclaimed happily. "Now *I* am captain and these are my crew!"

Alice glanced at the large, charted image on the COUNT screen. It showed the *Canadian* well past the northern tip of Sable Island, heading in a northeasterly direction. *No!*

In a strange collage of retro-events, ones which are sometimes liberated from the subconscious at the most inopportune times, MacIsaac remembered her aunt slapping her for grinding her teeth. Nellie Sandford had warned the ten-year-old Alice that, besides irritating everyone within earshot, in due time her teeth would be just a white paste and she would have to eat porridge for the rest of her life. Under such duress, MacIsaac had conquered the habit years ago. But now, here, in front of this intruder, this tin-pot pirate that was attempting to usurp her command, her molars slid together with such force that her vision vibrated. And the dormant temper, so carefully held at bay by oriental techniques, burst through her disciplined pretense.

"And who the hell are you, dickhead! And what are you and this scum doing with my ship!" The seated man might well have expected the rage of the slighted sea captain, especially since his research turned up her martial arts training—but he had not expected Alice MacIsaac's swift reflexes.

As she had anticipated, her sudden movement

caused him to partially rise out of his seat; but that was as far as he got. Her right hand clamped onto his arm, just above the elbow, and the combination of her leverage and his own forward energy propelled him upright. Alice let the motion continue, wrenching his arm straight and twisting it while swiping her right foot against the back of his ankles. Like a felled tree trunk, Fergus' back hit the rubberized deck, his face twisted in pain as she readied to rip his thumb back with her other hand. The whole process had taken less than three seconds.

"Knock it off, bitch!"

In the course of her training, Alice had more than adequately rehearsed the scenario of more attackers joining a fight in progress. In club sparring sessions the worthy, second-degree black belt had successfully fought off three trained opponents. But she also recognized the significance of the metallic clicking sound that accompanied the command. She turned her head around to see a large pistol pointed at her forehead. The next sound she heard was the tennis ball as it plopped on the deck and bounced a few times before rolling down the steps and under the COUNT screen.

"Give it a rest or I'll blow you away! Now, easy, let his arm down." MacIsaac had already appraised the gunman: a dark, slim man with a short beard and hair slicked back into a pony tail that flipped sides every time he moved his head. Middle Eastern. But it wasn't so much the pistol, even though, she thought later, it should have scared the hell out of her. It was beyond the barrel of the lethal weapon. It was the man's eyes: *like boiling oil.* And despite all her attempts to disguise it, or store it away like a Samurai would, her fear slid through, caressing her back like sliding ice cubes.

Audibly letting her breath out from her lungs, MacIsaac shot a contemptible glance at her captive and released her hold. Another of the trespassers, a distressed young, bleach-blonde woman in a sweat shirt and cut-offs, rushed over and helped him up to his feet. Standing barely two feet away from her, the winded man adjusted his glasses and stared into Alice's face. Defiantly, she expected to be beaten like Barnes and held her chin up for the expected blows, feeling a pang of regret below her heart; as anyone who has brought fists and feet to a gunfight would.

"Wow! You're good! I underestimated you, Captain," the winded hijacker managed, a bit disoriented as he regained his balance. "But don't worry, no one's going to harm you. That's not the type of business we are in."

MacIsaac sniffed as she regarded the swollen face of Dennis Barnes. "Oh, him?" remarked the blonde man, snapping his head back as if to get a kink out of his neck muscle. "Well, your chief mate, like you, surprised us. Only he wouldn't give us the bridge without one hell of a fight. If it makes you feel any better, as we speak, Tom, one of my crew, is getting bandaged up down in the dispensary."

Alice breathed deeply, feeling the tranquilizing effect of the oxygen somewhat soothe her simmering anger, replacing it with a building despair. "Alright, you have the guns. Now are you going to tell me what's the hell's going on?"

"Surely, Mademoiselle Captain," smiled the intruder, flashing a television smile. "My name is Jonathan Fergus, and this ship is now under the control of the Planet Guardians."

* * * *

"What's going on out here, lass?"

Jimmy McDougall caught the arm of a nervous young crew member as she scurried down the hallway, the emergency lighting strobing red flashes across the girl's face and the bulkheads behind her. She swallowed hard, anxiety gripping her heart as solidly as the vise-like hand of the lithe, old man on her biceps.

"It's a lifeboat drill, sir. We have them twice a day. Just routine. Now, if you could quickly get dressed and follow the green line on the floor to lifeboat station three—"

"Lifeboat drill? At six in the goddamn morning?"

"Uh, that's what was ordered by Mr. Fennell, sir! Really!"

"Fennell?" replied a puzzled McDougall. "But he's the first mate. Where's the chief mate? Isn't he responsible for drills? At the practice yesterday we were given a public information bulletin—" McDougall suddenly realized that he was frightening the crew member and released her.

"Sorry, Miss, I'm still not awake yet and this is confusing to me. Could you wait here a minute?" The dazed, orange-clad girl nodded, her brown, curly hair springing and light-brown eyes flitting everywhere but into Jimmy's piercing stare.

McDougall reached back into his room and picked up a piece of paper from the little desk by the door. He could sense that the young woman, barely twenty, was more than scared—she was petrified. He also saw that, unlike the drill they had yesterday in the safe confines of the harbor, this crew member was now wearing an orange Mustang suit.

Being a fisherman before his change of employment, the old Newfoundlander knew that, normally, such gear was used only for outside work in bad weather, or in Arctic conditions. The only other reason would be that the ship was in danger. *But what gives? The sea is relatively calm.*

"Excuse me, Miss. What's your name?"

"Susan Lowery. I work under the chief stewart," she replied, shuffling to the side as a handful of passengers, wincing at the barking alarm bell and flashing red lights, gathered around.

McDougall put on his reading glasses and squinted at the white sheet. "Well, Susan, it says here that the chief mate runs the drills and all other mates man the lifeboat stations. You're sure that Fennell gave you the message?"

"Yes, sir, I am. He said that Chief Mate Barnes was indisposed."

Indisposed? If it were true, the man would have to be suffering a grave illness. In his many years aboard merchant ships he'd seen seamen take their posts with broken bones and various illnesses. A couple even died. One fell overboard in a squall while the other succumbed to pneumonia. Dennis Barnes struck him as such a dedicated sailor.

"Thank you, Susan, and relax. I'm sure you're right. It's nothing but a drill. You go about your business and I'll be along to the station shortly."

For some reason beyond his logical thinking, McDougall suddenly thanked his mother-in-law's kidney condition for his wife not being aboard. Then, as the rest of the crowd began moving in behind Seaman Lowery, Jimmy ducked back into his room. He flipped open his briefcase and reached for his cellular phone, immediately dropping it in disgust when his mind registered: the nearest communication link was Sydney, over a hundred miles away and well out of cell range. All he would get out here would be static. Snapping his case shut again, he dressed quickly into jeans, sneakers and a *Tourism Newfoundland* sweat shirt.

By the time the politician closed the cabin door there were dozens of confused guests, some still dressed in their evening wear, sauntering along the green line, unsure of what was going on. The Newfoundlander eased his way to the front of the pack and held up his arms.

"Excuse me! Could I have your attention please!" The crowd hushed, exposing just the snarl of the alarm and the intermittent red lights. "Now, I'm not sure what's going on either but it's probably just another annoying drill to see who's in *whose* cabin. And I see by a few familiar faces that just came out of the wrong rooms with the wrong partner that there will be a lot of deep explaining to do!" A nervous titter went up among the passengers.

"So let's follow this line just to show we're not all color-blind, okay?" The guests complied and followed Jimmy down the corridor.

The orderly group reached the stern bulkhead and picked their way down the stairwell to the next level where they were joined by others who were also proceeding calmly, even jovially, down to the deck. Four flights later, the bulk of the guests were standing beside orange-clad crewpersons at their respective stations.

McDougall ran around to the *blue station*, then the *yellow* and the *purple*, dodging crew and passengers as he went. It took him five minutes before the Fisheries Minister reached the last of the lifeboats, having scanned the people getting ready to board at each terminal. Catching his breath, questions began to dog him; ones that he could not pass off to glitches in a new command structure. *Where was the captain and her senior officers? And where was the US ambassador and the rest of the VIP's?*

* * * *

Harv Crowley's head still hurt as he made his way across the deck. *I'm definitely too old to stay late at a party,* he cringed, as the honking alarm sent splinters of pain through his skull. However, this unorganized parade was just strange enough to keep his investigative mind active above the discomfort of a headache.

Just before they reached the lifeboat station he reached out and grabbed Davis' arm. His friend came to a halt barely a step later. "Do you suddenly feel like a sheep?" Crowley asked, his chest heaving.

"A very puzzled sheep waiting for the shepherd with the rubber boots," replied Davis.

"Yeah, tell me about it. And heading for some orange shearing barns. Jeeze, these new lifeboats look like floating dildos! Anyway, answer me this, hotshot. Do you notice this party is a little bottom heavy?"

Crowley's heavily wrinkled forehead seemed to force the thick, gray brows together. "Where's the brass? I can't pinpoint the captain or any of the big officers in this parade."

The old newspaperman coughed in the cool, sea air. As a burst of wind swept across the deck he was glad he brought his fisherman's knit sweater and light-brown corduroy pants as a change of clothes. But he knew that the chill really came from his recollections of sea disasters, ones that suddenly flashed through his mind.

Jim Davis panned the small crowds milling at their stations, his eyes stopping at the closed doors of the hangar bays. "If there was something wrong, Harv, wouldn't they launch a helicopter?"

"The only one aboard left yesterday night to help on a SAR—search and rescue—mission."

Crowley shrugged. "Hell, you could be right. Unless someone didn't want the bird to spread the news about something that was cooking on the bridge."

"Always the skeptic, huh, Harv." Davis had also felt the tug on his journalistic instincts—but for a different reason. This was a new ship, and new things tended to have "bugs" and operating systems which needed ironing out. Inconsistencies in procedures, such as lifeboat drill, could not be ranked amongst the most uncommon occurrences. To him, it was a rough example of what can happen when a ship is launched too prematurely, before training has been completed and each member of the crew knows the operation down to a science. But that was the work of politicians, not the captain.

On the brighter side it made great copy and he knew his editor would be pleased that the "Dream Cruise" had hit some rocky water. The lanky writer was already into "snoop mode", as he called it, and was automatically committing to memory details for further reference: the scared looks on the passengers' faces; the puzzlement of the crew; and the large orange "sausages" that were, at this very moment, being checked out.

"Look, Harv. You and I obviously know that this is for real. So what do you want to do?"

"Christ, Davis, I thought I taught you better than that."

Crowley followed that remark with a look of feigned surprise. The younger man's eyes narrowed, greedily anticipating the thrill of the hunt. This was the stuff that fueled the investigative fervor of all journalists.

"Come on, old-timer. Let's go find a bunch of people who are noticeably absent from this deck party."

2.

44°N Latitude, 60°W Longitude

Hank McKenna walked past the small herd of grazing horses without so much as a snort from the brown stallion, whose mane buffeted in the cool morning breeze. After sixteen years of seeing his assortment of plaid, flannel shirts and bushy-red beard, the equine population knew him well, as well as his smell and personality. It was almost as if he were the one being studied and not *vice versa*. In fact, his co-workers at Wildlife Canada would often say that the rust-haired, forty-two year old from Toronto was as much, or more, of a horse fancier than any trainer in Kentucky. But McKenna's world was far removed from the verdant bluegrass further south. For this horseman's domain was a thirty-mile-long, crescent-shaped sliver of sand and grass three hundred miles northeast of Boston called Sable Island.

Sable Island became the home to hundreds of horses for the same reason that generations of sailors and sea captains had called the narrow stretch of isolated land "the graveyard of ships". Because of the strong westerly winds, many a ship was already heading into Sable Island's shallow approaches before the island was sighted. Futile attempts were made to wheel these vessels around, but by that time their keels were stuck fast on the sandy bottom. Any surviving crew could only abandon ship and watch helplessly from the gale-pounded beach as their craft foundered, succumbed to the ocean pressures and then went over. And although the name conjures up visions of soft fur, *sable* is the French word for "sand".

Originally, interest in the island was directed

toward the rescue of the crews of the ill-fated ships, as well as the salvage of their cargoes: for profit. Horses were usually among the cargo of these voyages, especially during the 18th and 19th centuries. Liberated from their wooden confines, the ones which didn't drown swam ashore and added their lineage to the growing population. These horses, along with ones introduced from the mainland, intermingled to form the hardy breed that now inhabits Sable Island.

In the 20th Century the Canadian government began to take a special interest in the horse population and made the slim island into a national research station. Added to the beacons, survival supplies, meteorological equipment and dwellings, provisions were made to study these remarkable survivors. Soon wildlife specialists joined the marine personnel stationed on Sable.

At first he thought the objects bobbing way out on the water were buoys whose cables had snapped. One maybe, but definitely not three, or four. Then he pondered the idea that some bumpers had detached themselves from a fishing trawler. But at that range, two miles or so out, they would have had to come from a ship the size of this island. Curiosity finally got the best of him and he unbuttoned the leather case, raising the Bushnell 10 X 50-power binoculars to his eyes, a pair of protruding, blue orbs set above his thin, weathered cheeks.

Then, as if someone had cranked his pacemaker wide open, that is if he were so infirmed that he had to wear a pacemaker, Hank's heart began to pound under the sweat-stained T-shirt and flannel outerwear. For the first time since his high-school PhysEd classes, the biologist ran as fast as his feet could move. The observation station was only two hundred yards away but the rangy McKenna, ungainly leather boots and all, made it in a time worthy of a medium-distance runner. Out of breath, he burst through the paint-blistered door, grabbed the SatCom phone and began jabbing at the keys like they were red-hot coals, hitting the wrong call numbers in his panic. Calming himself, he tried again and heard the appropriate clicks.

"Mary! Listen! This is Hank. I suspect a ship down west of here. Alpha.... Niner.... Romeo. Four, maybe five, lifeboats coming in. Repeat. There is a ship down. Do you copy?"

The startled voice on the other end asked McKenna to repeat the message once more. He anxiously complied, ending with, "My God, Mary, hurry! Those boats'll be here in ten minutes!"

3.

"Look, I'm no Fisheries minister! I told you I'm Jerry James. Y'know, 'Big Jer' from COCO FM in Halifax."

The dark-featured man in the black ponytail leafed through James' wallet and grunted in disgust as he eyed up the chubby disk jockey again. Like a surreal sunset, the lifeboat alarm lights reflected like red volcanoes against the huge glass panes, now darkened to avoid outside inspection, casting crimson shadows and lighting up his face like that of an unearthly being.

The terrified James figured his interrogator was from some Arab country. All terrorists were, he anguished.

The gunman tossed the billfold back at him. "Then what were you doing in McDougall's room? Tell me!"

The radio man, at five-foot-nine and tipping

the scales at 260 pounds, sweated profusely, thankful at least that the gun was not pointed at him. That was due to the intervention of the "Englishman," who seemed to be in charge of the hijackers. Nevertheless, James, like an overwhelming proportion of Canadians, had never before seen a real pistol used in a threatening manner before. And he didn't really want to find out the consequences. Subconsciously, he ran his right hand over his bald head, pressing down the wet strings of thin, brown hair that he kept long to sweep over the patch of bare skin that adorned the crown of his head.

"Please, I told you the truth. My room was facing the inner court and I wanted one where I could watch the fireworks. Jimmy McDougall had an outer cabin. Well, he had a lot to drink and just wanted to sleep, so we traded rooms."

James' inquisitor reached into the pocket of his black sports coat and pulled out a package of *Export "A"s*. Lighting the cigarette, he smiled cynically at the "No Smoking" sign above his head. There was nothing threatening about his size. Like James, he was not a tall man, about five-foot-eight, but with a slender build underweighing the disk jockey by a hundred pounds. Rather it was his dark eyes, like bottomless holes, that rattled James.

"Are you finished, Fergus, or do you plan to go around scaring everyone on the ship with your popguns?" Alice MacIsaac stood defiantly with her arms crossed, staring at the hijacker without a shred of expression on her face, like a mannequin. Another feminine voice joined hers.

"Yes, Mr. Fergus, surely even a celebrity like you can see the disadvantages of bad press." It was Frances Pilotte dressed in a sweat suit with matching headband. Alice marveled how petit she looked without her heels and business attire.

"Stealing a ship is a bit out of your league, isn't it, Mr. Fergus? Or is your traveling group of *enviro-terrorists* just taking the cook's tour of our new ship?"

Jonathan Fergus' perpetual smile widened. He flipped the bottom of his brass-handled cane in the transport minister's direction. "Why, Ms. Pilotte. I was hoping that I would get the opportunity to speak with you. You know, you, like the captain here, are much prettier in person. Really. The press gallery should really think twice before they show footage of you in the disgusting manner they do. I mean, on television, when you rise to debate in the House of Commons, you look like a chamber maid who has inadvertently walked in the wrong room...and, by the way, my group frowns on the buzz-word, *enviro-terrorist*, please! That's why we're called *Planet Guardians*, because that is the best interpretation of what we do."

Pilotte chuckled, rubbing her eyes as she bent her head around to read the bold writing on the back of his coat. "Well, Mr. Fergus, I see you have to have the name sewn on the back of your satin jacket to remind you of who you are and what you're doing. Any uninformed observer, and there are probably twenty million or so in this country, would think that you and your bunch are sporting the name of a rock band, or a stock car."

Fergus' smile twisted into a grim mask at the attempted belittlement. "Right. Nevertheless, Ms. Minister, you and everyone on the bridge know who we are, and that's all that matters for now. I assure you that the other twenty million, and more, will know before the end of our cruise. Then—"

"So, Mr. Fergus, or Jonathan. We should be

on a first-name basis and now that we are, how can I say this, so well acquainted? Why don't you tell these people why they are being held hostage?"

The blonde-haired girlfriend slipped out from under his arm like a gopher popping up from its hole. "Jonathan is not a terrorist like you misinformed people think. And neither am I!" She flicked her head so that the corn-silk strands slid off the shoulders of the black nylon jacket and down her back, almost to her waist.

"While you live your shallow lives there is environmental genocide taking place right out there. I've been with Jonathan and his friends in the South Seas and helped pull up dozens of drift nets, some over ten miles long. One was twenty miles! All filled with beautiful creatures left to die for no purpose."

She pointed eastward, her long hair now shifting over her right shoulder. "And now, out there, the largest *bio-mass* on the planet, the northern cod population, is being vacuumed out of existence, and none of you politicians seem to care! Well, we do!"

Fergus smiled, his perpetually wet eyes twinkling in his impish face. "Isn't Carla wonderful? She's the product of 60's parents whose ideals permeated their genes and created this lovely young woman. This bright girl quit the University of California with only one year left in her veterinary degree, all because she cares about the living creatures on this planet."

He whipped around on the end of his cane to face the frightened group of two women and a middle-aged man standing by the locked elevator doors. "So, Mr. Ambassador, what do you think? She's an American, just like you. And she's a dedicated scholar."

The American, his head bandaged, gathered his courage and stepped forward, stopping between Judy MacDonald and Frances Pilotte. He was quite young looking, despite his fifty-eight years; his physical shape and brown hair dye showing a medium-sized man in his late forties.

"I do not wish to discuss the young lady's *attributes*," he began softly, raising his voice with every word. "What I would like, sir, is to, first, see my wife and then, second, be told what this is all about!"

Fergus glanced at the digital clock on the COUNT screen. It was now ten-twenty, Atlantic Time. "At this moment, your wife and the rest of the guests should be washing up on the sandy beaches of Sable Island, quit—"

"What!" Berchstein's voice trembled. A series of gasps joined his surprise, filling the main bridge area. A stifled cry came from MacDonald, who raised her hand to her mouth. Tears began running down her face again.

"Easy, Ambassador...." Like an Oklahoma preacher, Fergus raised the cane and his right hand for silence. "Thank you. Now please try to control yourselves. No one is going to get hurt, I assure you. The COUNT navigational screen, here, verified that all lifeboats reached Sable Island, safe and sound. I trust within a few hours that your wife, the other passengers and crew, will be comfortably back in Halifax, answering a gaggle of non-sensible questions from a bevy of incompetent officials.

"Actually," he added, chuckling, "I'm counting on a few days grace while those idiotic politicians and their incompetent judicial system decide whose jurisdiction this event comes under! It may take weeks! But then, that's what I love about Nova Scotia law."

Somewhat relieved, Berchstein regained his composure, the diplomat reaching out. "So Mr. Fergus. Despite what this girl has been ranting about, I trust there is some American policy that has offended you. So, let's get to the point, shall we? What, sir, do want from the United States? A Ransom. I want you to—"

"Oh, Mr. Berchstein, you flatter yourself too much!" cut in an amused Fergus. "Actually, almost every American policy offends me, but that's much too long of a subject for right now. You see, we really couldn't care less if you are aboard this vessel or at the bottom of the sea, Mr. Ambassador. However, the fact that you are here may make a few people in Washington squirm. But not many."

Berchstein frowned and Fergus smiled sympathetically. "I am sure you realize that your post is not really that important in the 'Big Picture' down south. I mean, think about it, sir. *You* are the ambassador to Canada which, in your country's order of importance, falls somewhere between Kenya and Liechtenstein."

Then, quite dramatically, Fergus' face erased its animated candor. His voice lowered and the smile seemed to freeze under his gold-rimmed glasses. "And remember, Berchstein...one more episode of *Gung Ho Ex-Marine* and Farouk, my Egyptian friend here, will show you how he really feels about the Jewish, American or otherwise. And I assure you it will be much more than just a whack on the noggin. *Understand*?"

There was a long silence after the hijacker's threat. It was MacIsaac that finally spoke. "So, Fergus, let me guess, judging by your checkered past...you, the *bimbette*, and these other *Bozos for Planet Enlightenment*—" Alice saw the fury in Carla's face and for the first time since the takeover, she felt a twinge of enjoyment; this was a nerve worth exploring. "—Uh, you want to drive this ship over to the Grand Banks and play bumper cars with Portuguese and Cuban trawlers. Just like you did three years ago, when you got arrested off Newfoundland and thrown in jail for two months."

The merry glint returned to the hijacker's eyes; eyes which lowered and followed her shapely uniform like a computer scanner.

"Well, Captain, I am flattered that you have followed my career with such interest. It's too bad that circumstances preclude any additional involvement—"

"That and the fact that I find it extremely difficult to get aroused in the presence of a coward." Everyone flinched at the same time, even the members of Fergus' gang, when the brass end of his cane shattered the pristine glass veneer of the Ice Observer's display, making it an intricate web of cracks. Everyone, except MacIsaac.

"I am *not* a coward, Captain!" Fergus' exclaimed, more a loud proclamation than an angry response.

"Then prove it and get off my ship!" Alice matched him, both in volume and intensity.

"We are here on a mission that is larger in scope than any one of you could ever imagine! It is, Captain, a crusade for the very survival of this planet and its non-human occupants!"

Fergus turned away from her and limped down the two steps to the lower bridge, his cane assisting the stiff left leg as he sauntered to the window. No one moved as he gazed at the glint of the mid-morning sun off the swells, the flashes reduced by the LDS system. Then he slowly turned on his cane to face Alice, his game leg dragging gingerly behind.

"Alice," he said, in a sincere tone of voice. "I once stood on the bridge of an icebreaker as second mate, so I know what a sailor's watch means. In my ten years with the Coast Guard I experienced a lot of what you have and, though I do not pretend that you will sympathize with my purpose, I will assure you that this does *not* reflect upon you or your capabilities as a captain. In other words, you were not singled for this enterprise, your ship was. So, please, cooperate and we'll get through this. Maybe we can even sit down and have a few laughs over a beer sometime."

Fergus' congenial smile was interrupted by the slow and deliberate clapping of Captain MacIsaac. He shrugged his shoulders and screwed up his face as if starring in a humorous pantomime—as if searching through the hardened crystal of her bluish-green eyes for a speck of understanding.

Alice dropped her hands and turned to the rest of the detained guests. "What Mr. Fergus wants us to do is applaud his hard work and sacrifice in saving seals, whales, fish, rats, bats, cats, gnus, aardvarks, and whatever. Then he wants us to overlook the fact that we are his prisoners...."

Her head turned and she fixed her attention on the silent Fergus again, his outline framed against the open ocean by the huge glass panes. "And, finally, Mr. Jonathan Fergus wants us all to watch through these very windows as he commits *murder* on the Grande Banks." A gasp went up from the hostages. Judy MacDonald sank to her knees, sobbing.

Alice's voice was barely audible as she finished. "This ship, my friends, is going to be used as an 'ocean-going steamroller' against the foreign ships on the—"

"Illegally fishing," countered Fergus in an exasperated voice, throwing his tennis ball into the air and deftly retrieving it while his eyes remained locked on the captain's. "I mean, if you are going to get melodramatic about it, Captain, get the story right, will you please?

"Under the West Atlantic International Fishing Agreement, which the European Community conveniently ignores, those fishing boats are not supposed to be there. Since our new Prime Minister is too chicken-shit to use gunships to pursuade them to leave, it has been up to a few brave Newfoundlanders in jet-boats and airplanes, who periodically harass the 'fish pirates' with stink bombs, paint-filled balloons and other non-lethal objects."

The limping man walked back up the steps, refusing help from a concerned Carla. His voice was still subdued as he addressed the hostages. "Now, since those French trawlers caught fire— the result of a thrown flare—and were shown on French television sinking off St. Pierre, the new, ultra-nationalist president of France, Monsieur Gérard Ledoux, has ordered a French frigate to patrol off the Miquelons, using St. Pierre as a base."

Berchstein cut in, hoping to use his years as a conciliatory voice in the Republican Party to attempt a compromise. "Mr. Fergus, I know that these events are frustrating. Believe me, we're on the same side with all of this. Those Europeans have little or no loyalty when it comes to commerce, but we really have made a few breakthroughs lately. The rest surely will come.

"Now, that French ship is just a veiled threat. There's no way that Monsieur Ledoux, as much a pain in the butt as he is, would—"

"No way, Ambassador?" Jonathan's voice had an amused ring to it as he jumped in. He turned to Second Mate Bill Barrett, whom he had allowed back on the bridge to man the NavCom station to the left of COUNT. "Mr. Barrett, extend COUNT's boundaries to include the western Atlantic."

The black officer glanced back at Alice, who slowly nodded. Reluctantly, Barrett tapped on his console and the large, rectangular screen refreshed itself, showing an area including Greenland on the east, the Canadian Atlantic provinces on the west, and as far south as Boston.

"Good, Mr. Barrett. And, by the way, I don't think we need to get approval from Miss MacIsaac anymore, do we? I mean, I really think it's a foregone conclusion that *I'm* in charge, so let's skip the semantics, shall we?" Barrett nodded slowly.

"Good! Now, please, magnify to isolate the area around the *nose* and *tail* of the Grand Banks. Let's say, within three hundred nautical miles."

This time there was no hesitation. A few keystrokes and the screen showcased the areas just outside Canada's two-hundred-mile limit, the last of the once-verdant fishing grounds.

"Good, good! Very impressive, Mr. Barrett! Now display all ships operating in the area."

To everyone's surprise, the COUNT system dotted the screen with hundreds of computer-generated indicators, each representing a ship or small boat.

"Well, even with as much preparation as I have gone through to familiarize myself with COUNT, I never could have imagined it was this impressive!" Fergus scanned the dots and threw up his tennis ball again, catching it behind his back.

"Alright, Mr. Barrett, let's take out everything smaller than, say, a small freighter." Bill Barrett skillfully eliminated the groups of little ships from the screen until there were five large ones left.

"Unbelievable!" remarked the hijacker. Digging

his cane into the short-pile carpeting he pulled himself to the center and plunked himself in MacIsaac's chair. He leveled his cane at the large display. "Right! Those three are in the shipping lanes, so delete them."

Three more ships disappeared.

"Good. Now magnify those last two and bring them together on the same screen." The shimmering panel shifted its picture again and the large outline of two ships emerged on a light-blue background.

"Excellent!" Jonathan jumped from his chair, his eyes locked on the screen. Then he spun around, like a child showing his parents a new skill. "There, Ambassador! As you can plainly see by the outline, the one on the left is a Fisheries Canada patrol vessel, and the one on the right is...well what do you know? A French frigate! And the amazing COUNT has even identified it: *The Montclair*."

Carla added a "Wow!" and Fergus' eyes went to Berchstein. "Well, what do you think of your French allies now?"

* * * *

The young man's attempt at a beard was helped by the new fashion of goatees, although he had made no attempt to sculpt it in that way. Reddish strands protruded from the bare, freckled skin thickening up around the chin and upper lip, where a reasonable facsimile of a mustache covered the skin. Nervously, he followed the bulky figure of Eric Johansen around the channels of heavy wire and conduit as the chief engineer checked the voltage levels on a series of massive generators, whose smooth-sounding whine could barely be heard above the muffled roar of the huge Mak diesel engines.

On the street he would have appeared harmless, a "nature nerd" strolling around awkwardly in his hiking boots, old jeans and checkered lumber shirt. But this "Junior Forest Ranger" had a 9mm Beretta tucked in the front of his pants, a formidable pistol in anyone's eyes, and Johansen had no illusions that this kid might be too scared to use it.

Still, the bunch that had taken control of "his ship" needed him and he was not about to submit to anyone who tried bossing him around. Just like he had done with everyone after becoming chief engineer, or as he liked to preach to everyone who entered his sub-deck world, he advised the young man, "I am *God* below the decks!"

"I wish you assholes would have let me keep my crew," he grumbled loudly over the low rumble of machinery, the sweat soaking his shirt so much that any dry spots appeared as islands. "Then I wouldn't have to run a marathon every time I have to make my rounds. Or doesn't your dipshit boss know how big this fuckin' ship is?"

George Brill just stared up at the rows of conduit suspended from the deckhead and shrugged. After spending the last six hours with the griping sailor, these outbursts were now becoming commonplace, even tolerable in a numb sort of way. Fergus told him to expect a fair bit of animosity. After all, it was only natural to have ill-will after stealing something from someone, whether it be a car or a ship. But he had expected a sulking kind of hostility—not this continual bitching about everything. For Johansen never stopped bitching, whether it was about Brill and Jonathan's group or the workings of the ship. He was a constant thesaurus of profanity and insinuating terms that the twenty-one-year-old Californian had never heard before this trip.

The chubby engineer took out his tortoise-shell reading glasses and walked over to the bulkhead. Placing them gingerly on the bridge of his bulbous nose, he scrutinized a series of back-lit, color diagrams that made up the Modular Operational Display, or MOD. The MOD in Engineering was intended as a master maintenance and trouble-shooting monitor so that on-sight inspections of each operating system would not be needed in the mammoth-sized engine area. Each module was an outline of the icebreaker and contained block diagrams which traced the path of the particular operation throughout the entire ship. It was even designed so that the flow of an isolated artery, whether fluid or electrical, could be re-routed if there were a malfunction—or programmed to perform that duty automatically.

An old-timer, Johansen liked the hands-on approach, so he ignored the self-operating feature. Slowly walking the length of the thirty-foot panel, he scanned the series of LED meters within each block, satisfied that all were within the prescribed parameters. Then he cleaned the lenses of his spectacles with a plaid handkerchief, tucking them back into his shirt pocket.

Brill stared at a section of the MOD, preoccupied with the futuristic-looking engineering maps and impressed by the similarity between it and the ones in the space movies. Despite his distaste for the rotund sailor, on his brief time aboard ship the young man had accumulated a healthy respect for Johansen's mastery of the huge power plant and its hundreds of integrated operations. Coming from San Diego, where people the engineer's age were stacked to the heavens in retirement condominiums, he was amazed that this cantankerous old seadog was still at the switch—and handling it all alone.

Johansen rested his bulk on one of the observation stools and lit up the remains of a Cuban cigar, the greenish-blue smoke curling above the cloudy puffs. There were three of these high chairs placed so that the engineer on duty could see the entire board at a glance. Eric had an override programmed into the area's smoke-alarm detectors that he could activate when he wanted a puff. He called it, "Executive Privilege".

Because his crew had been roused early in the morning for lifeboat drill, they were all gone. God knows where. *Maybe they were being held in the passenger or research blocks?* he thought. *Surely these tin-pot pirates never dumped them overboard. That bastard, Fergus,* he fumed, *was a lot of things, but he'd never kill in cold blood. Or would he?*

It was at that moment he saw something out of the corner of his left eye: a hand. It was stuck out from between two pipes, feebly waving at him. Immediately, he glanced back to see if Brill had seen it, but the young hijacker was still engrossed in the workings of the display.

"Uh, hey, Brillo?" the engineer called, his tone antagonistic tone suddenly changed. The hand disappeared.

"Brill!" retorted the indignant young man, flipping the shoulder-length, reddish-brown hair out of his eyes as he spun around at Johansen.

"Whatever. Look I'm going to take a leak, is that alright? There's a can over behind that mess of pipes so—"

"I better check it out first."

The engineer chuckled. "Look pal, you guys have already disabled outgoing communications and you know we don't have any weapons aboard, so what are you afraid of?"

"I dunno, you might try something."

"Right, Dumbo. I'm going to hit you over the head with a pipe and then what? Jump into a non-existent lifeboat? They're all gone. A helicopter? It left last night. Get serious before the bugs eat up the rest of your brain."

Suddenly enraged, the young hijacker wrenched out the Beretta and pointed it at Johansen's head. Then, just as quickly, he raised the barrel up and away from the chief engineer, holding it menacingly in the air, staring at the meaty face of Johansen shrouded in a haze of cigar smoke.

But rather than being afraid as Brill had hoped, the big man shifted off the stool and walked over to him, stopping four feet away from the sulking gunman. "Look, Brill, this is the deal. I'm going to the can whether you like it or not."

"I'm coming along," the young man said, his voice wavering.

"To what, shake off my dick? Are you that way, Brill?"

"Look, Fatso," Brill spat, lowering the gun, "I'm the one with the gun, got it!"

Johansen's lips slowly turned up into a smile as he puffed again on the cigar, blowing smoke toward his captor. He was in familiar territory now and he felt the intoxicating shift of power rise within him just as Brill was going to feel the anxiety of it leaving.

"You gonna shoot me, Brill? Huh? Are you? Because if you're stupid enough to shoot me then there's nobody left to run this ship. And if that happens, then even a 'nice guy' like Fergus'll toss you into the cold drink for being a stupid fuck. So, let's get something straight, alright? You put that little popgun away and if you ever pull it out of your pants again, I'll kick your sorry ass over that generator."

Brill said nothing, and his face remained calm, but the gun came forward slowly and he slid it into the front of his pants again. "That's better, pal," said the engineer, a lighter tone in his voice. "Now we understand each other." He walked past Brill and lumbered around the corner.

The corridor ran past his office, the engineering crew's mess and the crew laundry room. Johansen opened the door to the washroom and, locking it behind him, he scanned the bottoms of stalls. "It's Chief Mate Eric Johansen and I'm alone," he stated, softly.

A pair of jogging shoes dropped down in the end cubicle and the door opened slowly to reveal a ferret-like face. "You must be Jimmy McDougall!" The chief engineer's exuberance was drawn out in a breathy whisper. "They were looking all over for you but now they think you've gone with the others, wherever they are."

McDougall sighed, looking like a terrier in a running suit.

"Everyone's gone on the lifeboats."

"Really? Are they alright?"

"Fine the last time I saw them. Those rafts are pretty reliable.... What's happening, Chief? I saw guys in black jackets running around with guns, and since my mother didn't raise a fool, I hid out. I figured it out that we'd been hit by pirates. But why? And who's looking for me?"

"Jonathan Fergus and the Planet Guardians."

McDougall's eyes widened. "That menace? The same one who was involved in the seal-hunt protests and ramming fishing boats?"

"The same. And from what the little twerp who follows me around said, these assholes are going to the Grand Banks to create a little international incident by sinking a few ships, and they want to film you on the bridge taking the credit for it."

The Minister of Fisheries sat up on the counter, visualizing the destructive scene. "Ramming boats with an icebreaker? Why, that's murder! And no one is going to believe that the Canadian government would be in on something like this."

"Really? What about the French?"

McDougall whistled. "Yeah, that would be a bad scene. Relations with them since their election has been strained, and that Ledoux could use the attack to coerce the United Nations into accepting a 'French Security Zone' around the Miquelon's. Then France could claim the fishing grounds all to themselves.

"But why would Jonathan Fergus want the French to make a play for the territory?" he pondered. "It would be like the fox guarding the chicken coup. They would rather vacuum up every fish and scallop than practice restraint, like we're doing."

Johansen cut in. "Look, we don't have much time before Brillo comes looking for me. Do you have any ideas?"

"Well, I was trying to get to the bridge."

"Why do you want to go where the hijackers are?"

"Not on the bridge itself, just to the Com Room—Communications Room—on the deck below."

Johansen nodded thoughtfully, picturing the banks of computer processors that made up the nerve center for COUNT, a veritable brain trust overseeing the transmission and receiving of information. And mounted on the port bulkhead was the same type of easily-readable panel as above his console.

"Look, if you tried any form of communications

it would light up the communications MOD on the bridge...except...."

"Except what?" McDougall's anxious eyes darted around the bathroom, as if expecting a platoon of terrorists to jump out.

"The VHF and HF. They're tied into COUNT, but I think I can re-route it without it lighting up the bridge display. I watched the guys from AlphaTechniq install the engineering MOD's and they isolated some functions to test a module without bothering the bridge. One of the guys said that there had to be some form of communication in case the worst happened and COUNT and its backup systems failed. So, theoretically, the basic "wireless" should be free of the Star Wars stuff."

"But how would I know what to do? I'm just a fisherman."

"What do you mean, 'just?' You guys are like farmers. You gotta know how to fix everything, from nets to Volvo diesels. When you're inside, you'll find a way." The big man's jowls raised as he gave McDougall a sly grin.

"Leave it to me, Eric. I'll get to Com Room somehow and leave you instruct—"

The banging almost made McDougall slide off the counter.

"Come on Johansen, Fergus wants you on the bridge, now!" Brill's loud voice sounded bored.

"Alright, I'm just cleaning the sweat off me." The big engineer began wiping his face with paper toweling as he walked to the door. He nodded to McDougall, who nimbly climbed back up on the toilet seat and quietly closed the door to the stall.

Taking a shallow breath, Johansen flipped the latch and the smirking face of Brill appeared, looking for all the world like a novice make-up artist had glued on his beard in orange blotches. Without another word he scooted past the engineer, his sneakers squeaking on the rubberized flooring as he panned the floor beneath the five stalls. He then went back to the first stall and kicked the door open; then the second.

"Whatsa matter, Brillo?" remarked the engineer, in a disgusted tone. "Get your kicks from licking the skid marks on the bowl?"

Brill's face twisted into a scowl and he stepped back out into the corridor.

4.

46°N Latitude, 53°W Longitude; "Nose" of the Grand Banks

Paolo Joachiz sat motionless in the creaking wheelhouse, the static of the marine-band frequency a perfect soundtrack for the eerie, misty evening. Although the breeze through the open window was cooler than comfortable in the small, wooden room, it was imperative for the skipper of the Portuguese fishing boat to be able to hear outside as well.

For Paolo's radar was useless, as if someone had covered the screen with glowing, green confetti, and so the others in the small, five-man crew were precariously perched on the extremities of the small trawler, as well as up the mast, straining their senses to pinpoint the course of the huge intruder.

It had been this way since just before the fog rolled in and shrouded the ship in a charcoal velvet, with no vision past twenty feet of the vessel. Then a huge blip had appeared on the radar, heading on a collision course with the Portuguese fishing fleet. The large ship was more than ten nautical miles away, plenty of time and distance for it to avoid running through the bobbing flotilla. But it had remained on the same course, ghostly silent amidst a volley of warning calls.

It was then that the radar malfunctioned. Not only the screen aboard the *Maria Ponte*, but judging from the panic-stricken shouts cutting in and out on the old speaker, everyone was having instrument problems. Instinct had warned Paolo against turning on all his navigational lights, as if the behemoth was actually hunting down the small fishing boats. Besides, all the lights would inhibit his sight, like shining a car's high beams into fog.

Cupping his hands he lit another cigarette, closing his eyes tightly to avoid the glare and the momentary loss of his night vision. It was then he heard the rumble again. This time it grew louder, like a freight train in the distance picking up speed. His men yelling and himself almost petrified, Paolo started the engines as the mist to the port side of the hundred-foot-long *Maria Ponte* darkened. Then, just as he throttled up, the water boiled, lifting the boat upwards on a bubbling torrent.

In a moment of macabre fascination, Paolo felt he could reach out and touch the blood-red wall that was rapidly dispersing the mist and pushing his ship over toward the starboard side. That was his last conscious thought—along with the screaming of his men in the background.

* * * *

Just after midnight the cloud bank slid away, exposing the large, glowing crescent, illuminating the ocean and the gently bobbing fishing boats in a wash of silver. Like small Christmas ornaments, the little ships rode a dark, gentle swell highlighted by both the moon's frosting and their own red mast and anchor lighting. Some boats were fully lit, as if making a last-ditch effort to stave off impending disaster, but the relentless *Canadian* ignored the beacons, stalking and then swallowing the minute vessels under a gigantic prow of thousands of tons of iron. After each initial collision, the horrified spectators on the icebreaker's bridge felt a gentle shudder, and the horizon lifted a bit, but not enough to communicate the devastating force which was reducing seventy-foot trawlers into smashed flotsam.

Out of the sides of the icebreaker, below the waterline, a string of portals maintained a steady flow of compressed air, which created a turbulent wake along the sides. This "bubbler" system was designed to assist icebreakers to steer the shattered ice pieces to the sides after the ship had broken into the ice pack. Besides helping to prevent the slurry from moving back too quickly and trapping the escorted freighters following behind, the cushion of air acted like a Teflon coating on the hull, allowing the vessel easier access through the tons of floating ice fragments.

As the *Canadian* continued on its destructive path, the hundreds of pneumatic jets combined to form an oceanic snowplow on each side of the ship, propelling the grisly debris beyond the sides of the ship and into plain view of the side and stern windows of the bridge. To enhance this morbid vista, Fergus had the port cameras activated and the picture shown on the smaller monitors throughout the ship—as well as in full view on the COUNT screen.

The LDS system had automatically "cleared" the observation windows for night navigation, and the various MOD's, monitors and the COUNT screen, gave off a soft light, low enough to allow for night observation. The incandescent glow highlighted the tears that ran down Alice MacIsaac's dimly lit cheeks. They appeared as jewels which slid down the dark base of her neck, exposed now that she had discarded the necktie.

Alice had been strapped to the Ice Observer's chair before the attacks began, when she had attempted to sabotage the navigational system, and her taped hands prevented the captain from wiping her overflowing eyes. There had been no struggle this time, just a well-placed shot by Farouk into one of the planters. After that incident she was warned that one more act of subversion would result in unpleasantries to her guests. Then, in retribution for her initial attack on Fergus, and as a final insult, an emboldened Carla slapped her a couple of times.

With the exception of MacIsaac, Barnes, Barrett, Annette Potvin, Frances Pilotte and Ambassador Berchstein, Fergus had the VIP's and other crew members confined to the Officers' Mess. There, two decks below, they too watched the monitors in silent horror. As for the hijackers, Farouk still fondled the deadly Walther PPK in readiness and Carla sat in one of the VIP chaises, also shaking with every bout of wanton destruction, while Jonathan sat motionless in the captain's chair, directing the carnage. Four more Planet Guardians were still searching the ship for any stragglers who had not disembarked onto the lifeboats off Sable Island.

Then, as if a welcome respite from the scene, all eyes jerked toward the elevator when the doors opened. They saw the bulky shadow of Johansen appear around the divider, followed by the slim form of Brill, who nodded at Farouk. The Arab ignored him.

"Ah, Eric!" exclaimed an excited Fergus.

"What the fuck you banging my ship into, Fungus!" The portly engineer was breathing hard, both from the exhaustion of walking so much all day and also from the dread of knowing *exactly* what the icebreaker was hitting.

"Calm down, Eric," cooed the hijacker, shifting his weight uncomfortably in his seat at being reminded of his "pet name." "Your ship won't hit anything that will cause any damage to her, I assure you."

"Cut the phony English accent. It may work for that bimbo over there, and your bum-boys, but to me you're still the same smart-assed second-mate that we had to wet-nurse on the *Laura Secord*." Farouk hissed at the insinuation by the engineer.

"Listen, Eric, I may have been a Coast Guard officer once, and used to that abuse, but I am not that man now—"

"You're not any sort of a man as I can see," snarled Johansen.

Fuming, Fergus leveraged himself upright with the cane. "Look, Eric, that's quite enough! I *was* a mate on a buoy tender, but that was before I began this crusade to rid the oceans of the filth who are quite prepared to destroy it. Now, if they won't negotiate, and they won't listen to the pleas of environmentalists who *know* that their overfishing is crucifying the planet, then I will make it my business to stop them."

"Even if it means killing them." The chief's voice was somber.

"This is *war*, Chief, and in war there are casualties. I detest this act, and I will surely hang for it, but it is the first shot to save the oceans. And I do not mind giving my life for its revival."

The chief mate just stared, seemingly unconvinced. "Now, I really don't give a rat's ass," continued Fergus, "if I'm remembered in the same light as Jack the Ripper or Ted Bundy. But people will remember me, and realize that I fought for the planet against those who would destroy it."

Jonathan sniffed as he finished the speech in which his accent had transformed from that of an English grammar-school teacher to a Coast Guard second-mate and back again. But Johansen was not buying it.

"Well, *Planet Man*," Johansen countered in a low, threatening tone, "I suggest you go back into your phone booth and change out of your costume or this ship's as good as dead in the water. Because, let's face it, if I don't play ball, the ship don't go, 'cause none of your dweebs could float a toy boat. Especially without the codes. Now, stop this ship! Now!"

Johansen's face was expressionless, the dim light hardly exposed his moving lips as he spoke. It almost appeared to the captives as if he had discovered ventriloquy.

"Touché, old man!" The younger man nodded his head, approvingly. Then he spun around to the helm.

"Miss Potvin, let's humor the Chief. All stop!"

The underlying rumble of the six, large Mak diesels wound down to a bare whisper and the ship slowed, coasting on the slightly rolling surface. A sigh of relief was mixed with sobbing as the iron-willed Frances Pilotte finally broke down. She was joined by the faint hiccuping of a terrified Carla.

Without a word, Johansen walked over to Alice MacIsaac and, extracting his utility knife, cut the duct tape that held her. Peeling off the sticky tape, she rubbed her arms, wincing at the hundreds of needles running through her veins as the feeling returned.

Just then, the elevator door opened again and

six more figures appeared around the divider. "Tom, Harold! What do you have for us," Fergus exclaimed, the joviality returning. The two men who brought up the rear held guns ready in their hands, but their sense of security was satisfied when they saw the armed Farouk. Lowering their pistols, they stepped around their captives.

Tom Packard's hair was right out of an Archie comic. He appeared as though he was ready to go back to classes in a few minutes; or maybe meet with Mr. Weatherbee in the principal's office. Above his right eye was a bandage where Dennis Barnes had ripped open his brow with a punch.

Harold Becker was almost a darker-haired twin of Tom, exhibiting the same chiseled features of the young man. Alice figured they couldn't be over twenty, at the most. He flicked a thumb at his captives, a disoriented bunch whose eyes were nervously darting around the bridge. "Those two, the short, fat one and the skinny guy, are reporters. Says their names are—"

"Harv Crowley and Jim Davis! What a pleasant surprise!" Using his cane deftly, Fergus propelled himself up the stairs to stand face to face with the reporters.

"I wish the feeling was mutual, Fergus. After what we've seen on the monitor I feel like I'm meeting Adolf or Attila." Harv Crowley's face was a crescent of silver stubble bordered by a mask of sweat.

"I'm sure that you and I will have a heated debate about this incident, and the world at large, Harv," Fergus smirked, "but right now I'm a bit disposed. Let's do lunch tomorrow in the Officers' Mess, say, eleven-hundred hours?" Crowley just scowled.

The third man stood barely five feet tall. He had his head down, displaying a bald circle. Fergus bent his knees and tilted his head to get a better look at the frightened little man under the twilight glow of the night lights.

"It's either Friar Tuck, or Celso Bellini, the Italian engineer from VabCom. Well, Tuck's been dead for eight hundred years, so it must be the latter."

Packard piped up. "We snagged him just before he left his room."

"Good, good. Everything is falling into place nicely." The Italian electronics engineer never moved, or looked up.

The head interloper then focused his eyes on the fourth man, a tall, robust passenger who towered over his two captors. "And who is this gentleman?"

At his close proximity to the man, Harold had to cock his head to see the hostage's head. "He claims to be Captain Dimitri Vasiliev of the Russian Navy."

Alice's heart stopped when she heard his name. She had just finished ripping the last of the duct tape off her ankles when Harold shoved the big man forward to stand in the dim incandescence. *No, Dimitri, I thought you'd got away!*

Fergus scrutinized the athletic Vasiliev, dressed in a blue, cotton turtle-neck shirt and jeans and whistled. "You are a very powerful-looking man, my friend. Arnold Schwarzenegger's brother in the flesh." Vasiliev stared straight ahead, saying nothing.

"Now, what would you be doing on the ship after everyone else has gone, big guy?" Vasiliev still ignored him, glancing at the pistol in Farouk's hand. It was pointed at his chest.

"I know why." It was the diminutive Carla. "He's balling the Captain!" The remark was like a gunshot through the large chamber, especially coming from the small, timid hijacker. But now something had transformed her. She had somehow composed herself after the incident with the fishing boats and now stood beside Jonathan, her face beaming, looking as idiotically attentive as a Barbie doll.

"In Halifax, Jonathan had me follow a certain person around and this guy kept showing up in the picture. With his hands all over her."

Alice MacIsaac, her face tear-stained, slowly stood up as another eyeful rolled down her face. It didn't matter if the whole world knew, she thought, a weight suddenly lifting from her shoulders. She unabashedly loved the Russian. And she felt no shame—just fear for his life.

The elevator door whispered again and all eyes looked past the new hostages to two large shapes: the last two hijackers. Larry Cummings was an ex-US Marine corporal and Bart Jesso gained his military experience in the Australian army; now both were mercenaries for hire. The two men wore skimpy shirts, exposing their large, carved muscles, and baggy military fatigues. They weren't as tall as Vasiliev but they were just as well-muscled.

Cumming's recently-shaved head gleamed as he turned it under the soft glow of the bridge lights. He smiled warmly at his boss. "The stuff was right where they said it would be. And it's *hot*!"

"Ditto," added Jesso, whose long, black hair was braided like a Cheyenne brave. He and Cummings exchanged "hi-fives," adding some extra slaps and body movements in the manner of victorious basketball players.

"Wonderful!" replied Fergus. "Now why don't you two get prepared for the real show!"

"We're on it!" Cummings and Jesso scooted around the divider and back into the elevator. The doors hissed shut and the LED numbers showed the lift was descending.

Fergus eyed Captain MacIsaac, and then Vasiliev, his mouth twisting into a sordid smile. "Take the Russian down with the others in the Officers' Mess. No need to tempt the Captain's hormones. Same with the reporters. Mr. Bellini will stay and assist me on the bridge."

Vasiliev shrugged off Becker's hand as the hijacker tried to steer him to the door. "Naughty children playing with fire end up with burnt bodies," he said, sensing a wave of fear race through the young man. Then he gave Alice a wink before turning to go with the others.

When the door had closed, Quartermaster Potvin slowly raised her hand, as if expecting someone to chop it off if it got too high in the air. "Ex...cuse me, sir?" It sounded almost a whisper as she peered out from behind a swath of neck-length brown hair.

Fergus wheeled on the cane, his eyebrows raised. "Yes, Miss Potvin, what is it?"

"It may be nothing, sir, but there's a warning light coming from engineering."

Johansen walked to the chief mate's station and joined Dennis Barnes, who was already bringing up the Engineering Module on his MOD. The processor flipped through several screens, microscoping images as it isolated the source of the signal. Finally, it stopped at a page which depicted a series of modules joined together by dozens of neat lines. Johansen worked the tracking ball on the console, scrolling down the screen and enlarging it even further.

"It's the oiling system for generators. Seems there's a malfunction in the Viscosity Leveler."

"Speak English, Eric," chided Jonathan.

"Alright, on this ship we can adjust the thickness of the lubricating oil at each station by adding agents to a base-grade oil. Each system has its own specific weight additives stored in tanks at the station where it is required. The base oil is centrally located and feeds these satellites. On-site computers at each station decide how much to add, taking into consideration things such as temperature, existing level, cleanliness, etc."

"So?"

"So, if I don't find the problem, a generator may not get the required additives and burn out. Then we may have to light candles on the bridge. And then, when the auxiliary batteries go dead, you can whip out a sexton and you and the stars can guide the ship...if you can get some whales to pull it."

Fergus pursed his lips, exhaling like a parent tiring of a nagging child. "Very well, get on with it. George, take Eric back down to Engineering."

But before the bored-looking, goateed man moved a muscle, Eric cocked his head, as if he were pondering the Theory of Relativity. "Hold it. It might just be a glitch in the indicator software. If that's the case then I could probably fix it down below, in the Com Room. It would save this ball of energy here a long walk." Johansen flipped his thumb at Brill.

The Planet Guardian leader suddenly looked tired. "So you can just call out—"

"Right, Fungus, and your puppy here is going to eat a sandwich and play video games while I radio the Navy to tell them what they've heard already, no doubt picked up from dozens of distress calls from fishing boats. Not to mention the testimonies from a hundred or so ex-passengers who are just now awaiting the dawn so they can suntan on the sandy beaches of Sable Island. Give me a fucking break, Fungus! I just want to solve the problem. That is my job, isn't it?"

Jonathan flinched every time his old nickname played on his ears. Without looking at the engineer he raised his cane in the chubby man's direction. "Just get the damn thing done!"

Eric's bulky form plowed past Brill and punched the elevator button. The bored young man just sighed and followed him.

CHAPTER 4

1.

CCGS Canadian: July 3rd, 3:30 a.m.
Newfoundland Time

At first, the cacophony of whispers unnerved Jimmy McDougall as he scanned the endless banks of communications processors, the sound of dozens of cooling fans intermingling to create the haunting atmosphere in the large, fluorescent room. The Newfoundlander sighed as the rows of technological signage flashed by him, "buzzwords" of the space-aged marvels that had transformed marine radio into a system that relied on an intricate network of satellites. Confused and frustrated, McDougall nevertheless pressed on, scanning rack after rack, searching for a familiar series of letters.

Despite the bewilderment he now faced, the old fisherman found it easier getting into the Com Room than he thought. Johansen did a good job of paving the way for him, releasing the automatic lock on the doors with his keycard. He must have duped the terrorists into thinking he was just opening them instead of overriding the "Lock" command

put into place at the launching, McDougall surmised.

Next, the crafty engineer left a note written on
a chewing gum wrapper he wedged in the door-
jamb, unseen to any but someone looking for a
sign. Lucky for him, no one else did see it,
McDougall thought, rubbing his eyes underneath
his slim reading glasses. He had been up now over
twenty-four hours.

Peering around the corner, his eyes wandering down the first row of tall racks for any signs of
danger, he resumed his quest. Up one aisle and
down the other, his narrow head bobbing like a
chicken as he searched for the right piece of equipment. Feeling safe for the moment in this hum-
ming room, McDougall's thoughts began to rewind
to the carnage that he had witnessed a scant few
hours before. For, despite his single-mindedness,
he had to fight to suppress the scenes of destruction lest his eyes mist up again and fog his glasses.

Then.... *There!* HF—High Frequency—two of
the most comforting letters in the ex-fisherman's
vocabulary, just like Johansen's short note said:

*Find HF panel. Pull off plate. Touch red and
green wire. Repeat.*

Checking over his shoulder again, Jimmy took
a deep breath and began resurrecting an old language.

* * * *

Over the Grand Banks

Major Mark Corbett, eavesdropping on the
Marine Emergency Channel, listened again to the
series of strange percussive noises, trying to make
out the barely discernible clicks over the rumble
of the four turboprop engines. The HF scanners
had zeroed in on numerous Emergency Indication

Position Radio Beacons—EIPRB—in the area of the *nose* of the Grand Banks but, unlike the EIPRB's two-tone continuous wave, these broadcasts were erratic. But that was the NavCom's job—Corbett's was flying.

As a youngster, back in landlocked Coleman, Alberta, the small-framed officer would have never dreamed in a million years that he would be commanding an antisubmarine aircraft over the open ocean. At eighteen, he left the coal-mining town for the University of British Columbia to study Political Science, figuring to apply for Law School afterward. His high-school counselor had brought up the idea of applying to the Canadian Armed Forces' officers' program as a convenient way to put himself through. "Strictly *weekend-warrior* stuff," he was told. And that advice seemed quite sound in small-town Alberta where the once-lucrative oil-rigging jobs were clearing out faster than a virgin at a frat party. Corbett, not really a fan of anything military, laughed at the idea. Even the economic motivation was not enough for him to actually think of an armed forces career.

That began in second-year over a dare from a tall, pretty co-ed. Janet was a Leading Seaman in the naval reserves and Corbett thought it novel that he was seeing someone who not only towered over his five-foot-five frame, but could fire automatic weapons as well as she could iron or cook. It was also good fun to bring up his liaison with the "leftist" element of his study groups. To a PoliSci graduate student, the rationale of gun-toting females was a far more interesting debate than whether or not Raissa Gorbachev and Nancy Reagan *really* ran their respective countries; between stops at a Niemann Marcus, that is.

On a rainy, Vancouver morning in November

1982, Corbett finally decided to see *her world*. He slicked back his longish, dark-brown hair and went to the recruiting office. The next thing he knew he was in the air reserves, hoping that none of his classmates would ever see him parade in his ungainly, green uniform; the *one* and only—and boring—color of Canada's military. In war movies, airmen dressed in roguishly handsome blue uniforms.

However, Mark's spirits—along with those of the rest of the Canadian Forces—lifted when, after an almost twenty-year hiatus, the government restored two branches of the service to their original and individual uniforms and the navy got a new black-and-white look—the air force got their blues back, and the army, khaki.

Mark graduated with Honors and a ticket to any of five leading, Canadian law schools. However, somehow, during one of the "contractual summers" of training at Comox near Victoria on Vancouver Island, Corbett learned that he really enjoyed flying. So, after graduation from UBC, he ignored his Bay Street calling and went into the "regs"—regular forces. Now, ten years and twelve moves later, he was a crew commander on the Lockheed Aurora P3C turboprop, one of the most advanced antisubmarine-warfare aircraft in the world. And the last he heard, Janet, the attractive reservist, was now a marketing analyst in San Diego.

"Woodsy, it sounds like someone can't transmit vocally and is 'keying' their mike." Seated beside him, at a console in the darkened midsection of the aircraft some twenty feet behind the cockpit, the NavCom—navigations and communications officer—Lieutenant Frank Wood nodded in agreement.

Only a scant two years before, the role of Corbett's Aurora was as a formidable fighting platform, capable of locating the best submarines *any* nation tried to sneak onto the continental shelf off Canada's eastern coastline. The aircraft's long tailpiece, called a MAD—Magnetic Anomaly Detector— could pick up any suspicious movements below the surface, giving the approximate depth and location of the unknown intruder. Then ultra-sensitive pre-programmed, sonabuoy listening devices could be dropped through tubes on the underside of the Aurora to get an accurate fix—they also carried ones they could program manually. Settling at their respective depths, a long cord reached up to an antennae on the surface. The signal from the sonabuoy was then picked up by knife-blade-like "paddles" on the underside of the fuselage and read on the acoustic sounding equipment, giving the depth, bearing, type and, if the ASO was experienced enough, the identification of the boat that was prowling into Canadian waters. At that point it was a matter of communicating with the underwater craft to leave the area or be destroyed—the latter threat made very real with the launching of up to two devastating torpedoes.

Lately, however, with the threat of the Soviet empire all but gone, the Auroras had settled into such mundane tasks as locating foreign fishing boats illegally in Canadian waters, as well as spotting the odd drug ship. Even though these flights were no more boring than the defense patrols of a few years back, there was always the knowledge on an antisubmarine run that they were carrying "live" ammunition against a cunning foe. Today, the crew's blood was up for the first time since the days of underwater, Soviet incursions—it was the anticipation of finding and rescuing the survivors of a major accident out on the Grand Banks.

"How's your Morse, Woodsy?" he asked, admiring the youth's newly coifed hair—short.

"Rusty, but bearable," replied the amiable blonde crew cut, sucking on the straw of a juice pack. As he scrutinized the youthful officer's coiffeur, Corbett chuckled, remembering a time when his superior had to drag him to the barber shop. Now the younger ones, like Wood, *wanted* to look like Doby Gillis; or an extra from an early 60's beach movie.

The clicks began again and Wood raised his hand, a serious tone blanketing his face. Like a court stenographer, he methodically jotted down a series of letters on his clipboard. To his right, along the port side of the aircraft, two ASO's—Acoustic Sonar Officers—peered out of the portals on the plane's fuselage into the dark gray of the early morning. Up in the cockpit the two pilots, Captain Edward Johnson and Captain George Andrachuck, as well as the Flight Engineer, Master Warrant Officer Paul Riva, were also scanning the North Atlantic swells for any sign of the distress calls.

Corbett's day had begun normally with the waning of another hot afternoon at Canadian Forces Base Greenwood, in Nova Scotia's Annapolis Valley. Flying night patrol was fine with him because he usually got to bed around 7:00 a.m., when it was cool enough to sleep, and woke up at 1:00 p.m., when his small apartment was just getting unbearably hot.

Since this was his first watch since taking a few days off, he never heard the news of lifeboats coming ashore on Sable Island carrying the passengers and crew of "that new icebreaker" until just before his plane took off. Last night's crew had picked up the automatic emergency signal from the boats at about the same time as the red-dish-orange, capsule-shaped escape pods washed up on the small island. Something was up; or sunk, he surmised. And the *CCGS Canadian* was a hell of a big boat!

Up in the cockpit, Captain Johnson checked his fuel gauges again, dramatically tapping them like he was flying a B-17 in the classic movie of World War II bombers, *Twelve O'clock High.* "Al, what's the ETA again?"

A deep voice caressed his headphones as his copilot answered. "We'll be in the vicinity of the EIPRBs in approximately eleven minutes."

"Check. Hey Marky, we're starting to get dry but we can hang in a little longer if we refuel in Gander. Besides, I could go for some Newfie beer on George Street after a night like this."

"Sounds good to me, Teddy," answered Corbett. "Woodsy, make the call."

"Check."

Corbett reached into a pocket on the lower right leg of his flight suit and pulled out a chocolate bar. "Yo Pauly!" he quipped.

"The bird's a pip, Captain," returned the flight engineer, Paul Riva, now used to the handle from the *Rocky* movies. He usually sat between the pilots in the "mother-in-law" seat, a chair pushed back enough to allow for the cockpit console. At the moment, he was seated on the left side of the aircraft behind the cockpit bulkhead, his head pressed against a round observation portal.

"Uh, Pauly, what exactly is a *pip*, anyway? A singer, like Gladys Knight and the Pips?"

"No Cap, Riva's been watching those Archie Bunker re-runs on TBS. Edith's a pip," offered Andrachuck, the low crooner. "And, in case anyone is interested, that Yank Ice Patrol Herc—C-130 *Hercules* transport—should be around here any time now. Maybe he's seen something? Anyway, he can take over until the SAR—Search and Rescue—guys get here.... At least they've got eyes." That teasing remark prompted a pseudo-vicious look from one of the ASO lieutenants, his face getting a respite from peering out of a portal on the opposite side of the fuselage from Riva.

"Two Labs—*Labrador* SAR helicopters—are presently in a search pattern just north of us, Major," Wood reported, "And the ships carrying the big SAR gear and the FRC's—Fast Rescue Craft—are fifty nautical miles behind."

When the survivors were spotted, a torpedo-like package would be jettisoned from the Aurora when it arrived over them. On the way down these rescue packages would sprout two, inflatable life rafts, connected to each other by a rope, which would straddle the waterborne people. Food and water were aboard to keep them going until the rescue craft arrived. A built-in ELT—Emergency Locator Transmitter—would lead the surface craft and rescue helicopters to them.

"Check," answered Corbett. "Whoever's in the galley, could you bring me up a juice pack when you're finished?" The commander was answered with noncommittal grunt over the intercom.

"Major! Okay, This is what I got." The excited Wood lifted the clipboard to read it again, as if it would speed up his comprehension.

"This is unbelievable! It's from a guy called McDougall, who's a minister of some sort, maybe a preacher. Anyway, he claims he's on that ice-breaker with, get this: eight armed terrorists! He says it's those *Planet Guardians* guys. No shit! He says they rammed a bunch of fishing boats! Sunk 'em! No wonder we got EIPRBs going off all over the place."

"*Planet Guardians?*" A note of recognition sounded in Corbett's head. "I thought they just sprayed seal pups with paint, or pounded steel spikes into trees. I mean, they're a bit nuts, and they've got balls, but sinking fishing trawlers with an icebreaker? That's murder!"

"That's right, Captain, and their leader is the geek who posed with Brigitte Bardot."

"How come we don't get to pose with Brigitte Bardot?" deadpanned Andrachuck.

"Nah, too old. But maybe Cindy Crawford or that *Baywatch* babe."

Corbett smiled. "Maybe at the next smoker. Okay, get it in Woodsy and—"

"Debris! Port side, ten o'clock, maybe three NM's—nautical miles!" It was one of the ASO's.

"Mother of God!" replied Corbett when he peered out one of the portals. Then he was struck by a funny thought. *What a dumb thing to say.*

2.

Northwestern Atlantic; 44°30 N Latitude, 49°W Longitude

"*Oui, mon Commander. Il y a seulement un peu de transmissions, maintenant.*"

Commander Gilbert Roche rubbed his tired eyes and stroked out his short, brown beard. Although he found the sheer number of emergency beacons puzzling, if not unnerving, he could easily guess the reason for the weak and dying signals. All night he and his bridge crew watched helplessly as many disappeared off the monitoring screens, slowly fading until the radio operator lost their location altogether.

Each time that one of the dozens of calls for

help faded, the facts became clearer: the trans-
mitters on the majority of fishing trawlers were
not in keeping with the international codes. Besides that, European Community fisheries inspectors were very lenient and, it is rumored, easy to
bribe. So besides being cursed by the outdated
equipment they carried, the doomed fishing boat
skippers had probably ignored simple things like
the recharging of fire extinguishers and, more
deadly in this case, the replenishment of the batteries for the distress beacons.

Roche gratefully accepted a cup of expresso
from a young seaman in a cook's apron. Sipping
the steaming, dark liquid he glanced at the chart
table and then cast his eyes out past the bow of
the *Montclair*, contemplating the uncertainty behind the western horizon. The stars were now fading into the light-gray carpeting, exposing the de-
finitive edges of the black swells. And even though
the French frigate had been running at its top
cruising speed of twenty-seven knots, if they didn't
arrive on the Grand Banks soon, the dark swells
would be their only welcoming committee, as well
as some debris and, most likely, Canadian rescue
ships.

But why so many distress calls, pondered the
thirty-nine-year-old Frenchman. A freak storm,
maybe? One that snuck in under the screen of
billions of dollars' worth of satellites and aerial
meteorological aircraft? *Non. C'est non possible.*
Only a *tsunami* could have come up that quickly
and cause so much apparent devastation. But that
type of oceanic disturbance, which whipped up
forty-foot waves and sucking whirlpools, was
mainly a phenomenon that occurred in the Pacific
where violent seismic activity is common. Besides,
the scientific community would certainly have
broadcasted the news by now.

The French commander, no stranger to unsettling situations, sipped his *café* and dug deep into his past—a career which had its share of dangerous moments—for clues to this puzzle. In 1987, as XO—executive officer—aboard this very ship, he was wounded in the forearm while directing fire on two Iranian gunboats in the Persian Gulf. At the time, the *Montclair* was shepherding freighters in and out of Kuwait. Both gunboats were destroyed and Roche received his first of five decorations.

Then, in 1991, a missile from the Montclair combined with one from a Canadian CF-18 *Hornet* to destroy two Iraqi *MiG 23* fighters that had slipped through a screen of American and British defenders. For that, his ship received another commendation. After these battles, it was performing blockade duty in the waters off Yugoslavia and Haiti, tame events for the Montclair compared to the other altercations. Nevertheless, the crew served well and received the gratitude of both their country and the United Nations.

But now, after so many well-defined tours as a preserver of peace, the French frigate's mission was not as clear. His orders were to protect the French fishing fleet, even if it meant patrolling inside Canadian waters. This bothered him. After all, the two countries were friends, bound together by the sacrifices Canada made to free his country during two world wars. He had visited the huge country almost a dozen times, both on courtesy calls and holidays. But even if he hadn't joined the navy and saw Canada firsthand, the sight of thousands of Canadian headstones in military cemeteries like Bény-sur-mer in Normandy, outside Vimy Ridge and others that dotted northern France, would have been enough to endear him to the country. Now, the world seemed to be changing at a breathtaking pace. Old friends were suspect while old enemies embraced.

And the election of Gérard Ledoux as president didn't help, Roche sighed. His ultra-nationalistic party seemed to be paralleling the follies of nineteenth-century France; only this time, the neighboring countries were in complete agreement with him. Germany had reluctantly allowed the neo-Nazis to run for office in the Bundestadt under the name of the *Germany for Germans Party*. They presently held power, building a coalition of other conservative elements.

Even the governments of Belgium and Holland were being subjected to this nationalistic fervor. The same with Poland, Russia and the Ukraine. Seven European countries had cut off immigration indefinitely, a few even deporting thousands of landed immigrants—some of whom were bonafide citizens who had been born elsewhere.

But it was the building up of the military that bothered him the most. At a time when most career officers were ecstatic with the new military hardware, and the increased rate of promotion that came with expansion, Roche, a student of history, lamented the philosophical change. It didn't seem right that France should continually snub and offend her former allies while placating fair-weather friends. M. Ledoux was a dangerous man, a pit bull terrier held on a short leash by aging moderates. However, even the old guard wanted the attacks stopped on French fishing boats off the Canadian coast. That was why Roche's ship was sent.

In the beginning, the incursions were harmless: disgruntled Canadian fishermen who lobbed cans of paint and bottles of foul smelling ointment at the European trawlers from speedboats that zoomed around them like stingless wasps. *But why?* thought the Frenchman. They were outside Canadian jurisdiction. Nevertheless, it was a diplomatic affair. And besides, some fishermen he had known probably smelled worse than anything those misguided Canadians could throw, Roche chuckled to himself.

However, two months ago, several boatloads of Newfoundlanders attacked boats right in St. Pierre harbor, on the French-owned Miquelon islands off southern Newfoundland. They overpowered police and threw Molotov cocktails, setting fishing trawlers ablaze before sailing back into the safety of their waters. They were yelling, "Remember the *Marion!*" the news reporters said. One French skipper suffered a heart attack and died, and seventy-two people were injured.

The Canadian authorities, to their credit, acted swiftly, bringing the ringleaders and eighteen of the perpetrators to justice; but to Canadian courts. But that was not good enough for M. Ledoux. The deeply offended president demanded them extradited to France and threatened action if his request were not met.

Then, last week, the situation darkened. Despite a Canadian Fisheries boat patrolling off St. Pierre, they struck again. Two French scallop draggers were attacked with Molotov cocktails in French waters, twenty kilometers off the Miquelons. Five fishermen died when their boats burned and sank, and four more were sent to hospital with severe burns. The next day, Ledoux ordered the *Montclair* to St. Pierre to protect French interests and another frigate, the *Lafayette*, was to follow in a week. However, unknown to Canada, the *Mitterand*, France's new Triomphe-class attack submarine, was timed to leave the same day. And,

Roche kept asking himself, *who or what was the 'Marion'?*

And the waning distress calls...what of *them?* he thought, gingerly raising the thick, dark liquid to his lips.

"*Mon Captaine!*" The young ensign trembled as he switched the radio to the bridge speakers. "*Écoutez!*"

When the message ended, the cup in Roche's right hand clattered as it slammed down on the saucer in his left, breaking the delicate bottom and slopping scalding exprésso on his hand and trousers.

"*Mon Dieu!*" he cried, not noticing the steamy, light-brown stain forming on his white cuff.

3.

Alice MacIsaac checked the large screen again. Although the small shape on COUNT's small peripheral screens had not entered the shallow waters that made up the *nose* of the Grand Banks, the updated information showed that the French frigate was moving at a constant twenty-seven knots on an intercept course with the *Canadian.* The digital display also showed the coordinates, wind speed, temperature and the estimated time until the icebreaker's new low-level radar system would pick it up. But that was just a toy, thought the captain. Who needed low-level radar with the reams of satellite gadgetry aboard?

Unfortunately, COUNT gave the hijackers almost all the information they would ever need. Part of the data previously loaded into the system was the specifications and histories of every registered ship that operated *anywhere* in the world. This information, like the navigation input, was also being constantly upgraded through linkups with the Internet, Lloyds of London and various marine bureaus. This also included military information, which was either obtained freely or garnered from the data banks of world libraries. So when COUNT identified the *Montclair*, it also provided a detailed assessment.

Celso Bellini sat in Bill Barrett's chair with the black-tinted Navigation MOD panel opened on its hinged lid. Quietly he worked, testing various components with a hand-held device; a sad figure from a Bergman movie. His longish, wild hair encircled a shiny, bald patch of skin like a nest protecting a large egg.

"Mr. Bellini, how's your project coming along?"

Jonathan Fergus peered into the darkened main bridge from the port lounge area, which had remained clear so that he could relish the morning while eating. The LDS had been activated on the starboard side only, thus saving the Italian from the glare of sunlight off the light swells.

"It should-a be soon a-now, signore."

"That's-a nice-a," mocked Jonathan, producing titters from Carla, who was just bringing him in a plate of eggs benedict from the galley.

There were two more on the bridge as well. The ever-present Farouk, who slept only in thirty-minute intervals every three hours, calling up either Packard or Becker down in the Officers' Mess with the other hostages when he wanted a break. And Annette Potvin, the amiable quartermaster who had remained almost chipper throughout the ordeal.

"Hey Ferg!" It was the ex-Marine, Cummings, on the intercom.

"Yes Larry. Are you ready yet?"

"Fuckin' A. When's 'H' hour?"

"COUNT says two hours and sixty-three minutes."

"Uh, there's a lot of planes buzzing us. Could I get some exercise?"

"Negative, Larry. Just keep out of sight until I give you the word."

"Roger and Out!"

Alice MacIsaac's stare went from the hijacker to another Aurora that passed by the starboard bow at a hundred feet off the waves. It circled once then, slowly picking up altitude, disappeared into the noon sun. The shape of another *Hornet* skimmed over the rolling ocean about half-a-mile off the stern.

All morning she witnessed the satisfied smile on Fergus' face as the communications channels clogged up with pleas and threats from every quarter of the Canadian military and marine authority, as well as inquiries from the *Montclair*, via the SatCom. The pirate's response was a video of himself declaring that his war against the defilers of the earth had only just begun. This video, shot a month before in California, showed him in a beach setting, casually dressed in a golf shirt; your pleasant "boy next door". It was replayed over and over, always ending with the statement that if anyone tried anything before 6:30 p.m. Newfoundland Time that evening, all hostages would be tossed into the water. Newfoundland Time was half-an-hour earlier than Atlantic Time.

Then every half-hour he patched into CNN and CBC's *Newsworld* to see over how the coverage was unfolding. Jonathan smiled nervously as the solemn face of the news anchor would announce the latest toll from the attacks on the fishing boats: so far, two trawlers, nineteen medium-sized draggers and ten smaller boats; all sunk. Two-hundred-and-one lives lost; only thirty saved. A file photo of Fergus was prominently displayed in the left corner of the screen. The leader of the *Planet Guardians* was constantly referred to as "…an over-zealous murderer with no hope of winning over the public."

"Amen to that," quipped MacIsaac, noticing the lack of genuine joy in the hijacker now. She even saw the sheen of perspiration forming on his forehead and wrists. So, she thought, the man has his limits.

Fergus ignored her, concentrating all his attention on the newscaster. "Well, we'll see about that, buddy," he laughed at the screen, a slight tremor in his lilt. "It was their own bloody fault for being there in the first place; against the law, I might add."

Jonathan flipped back to CNN where Wolf Blitzer stood in the Rose Garden commenting on how the American president was playing down the incident. The commander-in-chief stated he was sure that Ambassador Berchstein would be released unharmed. Then the entertainment news came on.

"See, Ms. MacIsaac, even when Canadians get serious, the Americans yawn. Well, I bet the French and Spanish are hostile, only CNN's foreign correspondents haven't figured that out yet. But hell, it's only 12:28. In another hour there'll be screaming Spaniards and Frenchmen up the yingyang!"

Just then the miniature ship marker on the COUNT screen began to flash red and everyone on the bridge flinched.

"Are you almost ready, Mr. Bellini?"

"It is-a ready to go." The computer engineer snapped down the MOD cover down and ran a hand across his wet face.

"Good!" Fergus pushed a button on the Ice Observer's console. "Larry, take it away!"

Her senses tuned to "overload", Alice stormed over to the console and stared down into Fergus' robin's-egg eyes. "This is it, Fergus! You either tell me what you plan to do with my ship and crew, and the guests, or 'Prince Jihad' there might as well shoot me. Because I'll have those rotten eyes of yours out of your skull and on the ends of my thumbnails before he pulls the trigger, got it?"

For a moment, Jonathan ignored her presence. Concentrating on his breakfast, he scooped up a piece of egg with his fork and let it slide down his throat, savoring the taste of the hollandaise sauce. "Alright," he relented, still chewing the egg-topped pastry. "I think it's time you knew the rest."

He stood, wiping the yellowy sauce from his lips. As he rested his eyes on the captain, an ir-reverent smile returned to his face. "It's like this. At 4:00 p.m., *we are surrendering.*"

"What?" gasped an exasperated Alice, tilting her head toward him as if it would help the com-prehension of his words. "Yeah, right, you are just going to stop this ship and wave in the *Sea Kings*—helicopters—and give yourself up after murdering over two hundred people?"

Dramatically, Fergus sighed. "You still don't understand, do you, Captain? After today, the whole world will be tuned into our *cause*. The rami-fications will be long-lasting and beneficial—"

"Beneficial to whom, Fergus? You? So you can sell your memoirs for a million bucks and do the book-and-talk-show-circuit when you get out in five years for good behavior?"

"Maybe if I were a shallow person, Captain MacIsaac. And, who knows? Maybe I am. The ques-tion is: Will the 'Lady Captain of the CCGS *Cana-dian*' also demonstrate *her* shallow side when the people from Hollywood come knocking at her door for the movie rights?"

Alice clucked, shooting a distasteful glance at Carla, who was finishing up her breakfast. "By the way, just where do you find these weird and wonderful recruits for your organization, Fergus, in reform school?"

Jonathan's relaxed face shifted into a serious tone. "Captain, these 'weird and wonderful people,' as you call them, have seen more and done more on the open seas than you and your crew will ever hope to. They've been with me through typhoons in the South China Sea, fighting illegal fishing in places where drift nets sweep the ocean of every living creature. And they've been with me off the Great Barrier Reef fighting against the destruction of giant clams. Those huge, shelled creatures are three and four hundred years old—marvels of nature—only to be destroyed by greedy fishermen who kill them for the scallop muscle at the back of their shells."

Fergus lifted up a coffee cup to his mouth but stopped it just before it reached his lips. "And Captain, they were with me in a crowded jail in Singapore, awaiting sentencing for ramming a scow of a driftnetter well outside their territorial waters."

"Maybe they should have kept you longer," added a cynical MacIsaac, "because, God knows, the world could have used a break. Do you actually believe *anyone* out there sympathizes with you?"

"Yes."

"Who, tell me who?" Alice crossed her arms in anticipation.

"Ask the Newfoundlanders."

"The Newfs?" Alice's mouth dropped open in amused surprise. "Now I know you're crazy, Fergus, or you have a very short memory. Wasn't it you and that French bimbette, Brigitte Bardot, who totally annihilated a way of life by ending the seal hunt?"

"Please, please, don't give all the credit to Brigitte and myself although, heaven knows I would have appreciated more of the glory. The point is, and was, it was immoral to club baby seals. Even you know that, for God sakes!"

"Alright, I'll give you that. But it wasn't immoral to eradicate the livelihood of dozens of small fishing communities who had relied on the hunt for their very existence for centuries? What about them, Fergus? Did you and the Planet Guardians use even a portion of the money you received from your movie star friends to help these people that you threw to the wolves?

"You see, that's the problem with you and your 'animal rights activists,' and those other tree-hugging, fur-spraying hypocrites. You're so busy with trees and animals you've lost compassion for humanity. Instead of using you money and influence to help those *people* your dispossess, you go right after them like *they* are the criminals!"

Jonathan glanced nervously at the digital clock, then back to Alice's accusing stare. If the circumstances were different, he thought, an attractive, gutsy sea captain like MacIsaac would have made a great partner. "Captain, that may or may not have been handled with the greatest of tact but we had to stop it—"

"You *had* to stop it? Sure, now people can pet a zillion baby seals while you blame foreign fishermen for exterminating the cod. Did you ever stop to figure out that maybe you *enviro-idiots* threw a fuck into a delicately balanced ecological system?"

MacIsaac grinned like an executioner. "That's a good one, isn't it, 'Mr. Guardian of the Planets?' Now that the seals have no natural predators they eat, and eat, and eat cod, while tourists pet and take their pictures. So, in essence, you've just butchered almost two hundred human beings for something that you share a responsibility for."

Instead of hotly contesting the issue, Fergus grinned. "Come on now, Alice, please stop with that tired analogy. Anyone with as much experience as you on the sea knows that the seals aren't responsible for the decline of the cod. You can't be so naïve as to believe a few thousand seals are on their way to wiping out the biggest group of organized life on the earth?"

"I didn't say that. But then that's what you people do, isn't it? You twist things and come up with clever *sound bites* to promote your cause. Then spice it up with has-been celebrities.

"No, I agree, the seals aren't the only ones wiping out the cod. However, they are part of the problem and you know it. But it would be a public relations nightmare for your self-righteous bunch to admit it. Besides, it would take a few guts!"

"That's enough, Captain! I have better things to do than spar with you over things you know very little about!"

"Oh, is that so. Well give me a few more minutes and I'll be out of your hair. Because there's the matter of fur trapping. You also helped kill the fur market. Now, the natives in northern Canada sit idle all winter because your misinformation has convinced people in the fashion houses of New York and Paris that trapping is cruel. And if that's not bad enough, your gang bullies people who go into fur shops."

"Furs are an archaic fashion, a throwback to living in caves. Or doesn't your house have central heating yet?"

Alice, bent on releasing her anger, ignored him. "Did you ever use any of your money to come up with a more humane trap? No, you never. You just went to your cocktail parties and fund-raisers while a culture wilted and suffered devastating social problems for lack of markets for a *renewable resource*: furs. Bored and frustrated native children die from sniffing gasoline when they would normally be out on the trap lines with their fathers and uncles."

"Alice, killing and skinning small animals for fashion—"

"Is as bad as killing anything, is that what you wanted to say? I see you are wearing leather running shoes. Isn't that fashion? Have you ever been to a slaughterhouse?"

Alice shook her head in mock hilarity, her red pony tail whipping across the back of her white shirt. "So what's worse, Fergus, raising animals just to kill them, or culling a number of wild ones, ones which replenish themselves within the year?

"And if you think I'm full of shit, keep watching the tube. Pretty soon they'll show the grieving families of these fishermen you just killed. And you complain about being in jail a few days."

"A few days!" An enraged Carla jumped up from her seat and rushed over to Jonathan, brushing her fine, yellow hair away from her venomous blue eyes. It reminded Alice of the feigned charge of a Chihuahua. "Turn around, Jonathan!"

Puzzled and distracted by Carla's order, Fergus just stared at her. "Jonathan, I want you to turn around!" she barked again. Before he could protest she deftly spun him sideways and yanked the bottom of his T-shirt up to his neck, exposing long, pinkish scars on his back. "Take a look at this, bitch!"

Alice covered her mouth in horror at the sight of the mutilated back. Similar responses came from

Annette Potvin, as well as Barnes, who had re-joined the bridge to allow MacIsaac a few hours sleep. It was as if the activist had been strapped to a table and someone had used knife blades on his back.

Fergus gently pulled the shirt back down and turned around again. "It's called *caning*," he offered, displaying a humble posture for the first time since boarding the vessel. Silently, he walked over to the men's washroom on the starboard side of the elevator and disappeared.

Before anyone could react, a tear-strewn Carla calmly explained. "We were boarded off Malaysia and taken into jail. Jonathan was sentenced to six months in prison and six lashes of the cane. They beat him raw despite pleas from people like the governor of California."

For the first time, Alice felt a slight compassion for the girl. Despite the horrific consequences of Fergus' actions, the captain felt the terror and pain that this young woman had endured in her crusade to save animals.

"A cane is a three-foot bamboo rod that has slits in the middle. When the cane hits the prisoner's back, the splits expand from the force of the impact. Then, when it is pulled off, the cracks close around the skin and...pull...it away! And they gave him *eight!* Four on the butt and four that 'slipped', hitting his back and upper leg. It damaged a nerve. The bastards!"

The little blonde's sobbing face fell into her hands. Even Farouk, now sitting closer to the starboard observation area, had been dumbfounded by the worm-like lacerations across Jonathan's back.

"After his term ended," she began again, "we went to the jail to pick him up and he wasn't the same Jonathan. His eyes seemed hollow, listless, and he limped. He was so defeated-looking. It took two months to get to the point where he would even go out and meet people again."

As much as she fought it, Alice couldn't help empathizing with the small woman. She still seemed a child in her simplistic view of the world and needed someone like Jonathan to survive. Carla's whole universe revolved around Fergus, as well as her implacable sense of right or wrong. In some ways, the rest were like him also; all except Farouk, Packard, Jesso and Cummings. They were right out of a post-apocalyptic video game. They didn't fit.

The bell on the elevator chimed and MacIsaac saw the tops of the big doors open behind the dividers. Like a conquering hero, the large frame of Vasiliev rounded the wall, filling up Alice's field of vision. Her heart pounding, she forgot Carla.

"Oh, Dimitri, you're alright!" It might have been the strain of the ordeal, or maybe the short bouts of interrupted sleep, but the cool pose of the captain melted away as she ran to the Russian and wrapped her arms around him. His big chest, though hard and unyielding, sent a warm flush of security through her body as if the whole voyage were a movie and this was the last scene before the credits were displayed and underneath, someone like Bryan Adams was going to moan a fitting love song. His paddle-like hands gently patted the back of her head before sliding down her back and clasping at the base of her spine. She rested her chin on his sternum and awaited his next word.

But then, a strange foreboding came over her. Something puzzling that the captain could not put a finger on: an unsettling numbness that wouldn't normally interrupt the pure feelings of any woman in love. However, this felt odd and it wouldn't go away. It might have been just the way he held her; sort of limply. Or maybe his facial expression.

Her mind now disoriented, MacIsaac pushed away, slowly, her inquisitive green eyes searching the crystal orbs of Vasiliev. "Dimitri, why are you alone? I mean, aren't you being guarded?"

"No, my little captain. Fergus and his men told me that they are not at war with the Russians, even though they claim our fishing boats are illegally here. Strange, isn't it? Nevertheless, I am under a sort of 'house arrest' after promising I would not interfere."

Alice's brow's dipped. "*Interfere?* You mean you promised them that you would stand by and let them have their way with *my* ship?"

"Please, calm down Alice. There's no need for all this. It's over. They are surrendering at 4:30. There's nothing left to do but wait until then."

MacIsaac shook her head, sirens going off inside. "Do you really think that they are going to let us go?"

"Yes, I do."

"And how do you know that? Better yet," she stammered, stepping back from the Russian, "how did you know that they were surrendering at 4:30. Fergus just told me ten minutes ago." MacIsaac began shivering as if the air conditioning had crept up too high.

"Well, that punk, Tom, told me."

"Oh," she said, almost satisfied, but still mildly confused. Usually Tom and Harry were the type that never offered any more information than was asked by Fergus or Farouk; and especially not to the hostages. Oh, well, she thought, maybe Tom was feeling flushed with success.

"Annette, my dear! Progress report!" A refreshed-looking Fergus skipped down the three steps to the helm console, almost slipping as he grabbed the rail for support.

"The French ship is almost within parameters, Jonathan," quipped Potvin. "ETA to 'Welcome Wagon' is fifteen minutes."

Jonathan? "Welcome Wagon?" Alice's eyebrows raised, and she forgot about Vasiliev for the moment.

"Fantastic! I wish I had something appropriate from Shakespeare right now. *Henry the V.*" Fergus put his hand under his chin, a pacing "Thinker," but shook his beaming face.

Then, reaching into the left pocket of his jacket, he flipped a neon-green tennis ball into the air, deftly catching it in his right hand. "How about, 'Cry havoc, and let slip the dogs of war,'" offered Farouk, smiling uncharacteristically, as he monitored the communication channels.

"It's been almost done to death but I'll accept it!"

The beaten figure of Bellini crossed himself, uttering a prayer in Latin when Fergus limped over to the display. Like a father he patted the Italian on the back. To MacIsaac, whose busy mind was also sorting out the odd behavior of Vasiliev and Potvin's seemingly-mutinous actions, it was more a sarcastic display than consolation. *What's the connection? Think Alice! Think!*

Her confusion was cut short by the loud, metallic voice of Cummings, along with the exterior noises of the ship, the ocean and the wind, all thundering over the intercom. "We got a fix, Fergy. We're ready. Tell the 'Wop-talian guy,' his *patch* is first rate!"

Bellini never moved as Jonathan's hand slipped away.

"Jonathan, those CF-*18*'s have been ordered away," remarked a surprised Farouk. "Same with the *Auroras* and the SAR helicopters. Strange, isn't it?"

"Not really. It's a French warship, with an attitude, approaching in international waters. The fighter jocks don't want to give it any reason for filling the sky with SAM's—surface to air missiles. So, Larry, you're on auto pilot from here on in."

"Roger. This will be my pleasure!"

Auto pilot? thought Alice, searching Vasiliev's face for any clues. But his eyes were empty, like the discarded shells of robin's eggs. *Maybe he's scared too? But of what? What are those two doing out on the deck? And Annette? Too many questions.*

"Alright, inform the *Montclair* that we are surrendering." Fergus hobbled over to the windows and put his arm around Carla's tense figure. "This is it!"

"Wait!" Alice's cracking voice attracted everyones' eyes. "I thought you were surrendering to the Canadian authorities?"

"As I said, we are, at sixteen-thirty hours."

"Then why are you telling—"

"Patience, Captain, will reward your curiosity."

The bridge suddenly became ghostly silent as everyone watched the digital counter dip below one minute.

* * * *

"*Capitaine Roche! Nous ont capitalé!*" The young radio operator's face was a mixture of puzzlement and relief after the frustration of hours of trying to contact them.

"*Mérci, Georges*," returned Roche, his eyes blinking from a lack of sleep. He should have been relieved but there were too many questions revolving around his brain. And another one just entered his head: *Now what do we do?* There would have to be strict security measures adhered to because the Canadian ship had been hijacked by a group of fringe terrorists. *Well,* he surmised, *"fringe" or not, they still would have to be armed to some extent to push aside a captain and crew.*

Even though the *Montclair* was not large enough to carry a contingent of French Marines, it was outfitted with boarding weapons and, along with the armed sailors, a few more of his crew would be standing by with two .50 caliber machine guns. Also, just to be on the safe side, he would have his tactical team ready to deploy the front turret. Its twin 60mm cannon could fire explosive shells at a rate of four hundred rounds a minute.

There was no need to keep the SAM system's or Exocet's—ship-to-ship missiles—"at ready". Something must be done to return a show of "good faith" to the Canadians. After all, their patrol fighters and ASW planes had backed off the minute that the *Montclair* had come within missile range. And Roche's tactical team had discovered that the Canadians had *not* activated any targeting radar. Another friendly gesture. But M. Ledoux's friends in the admiralty might not think so.

When he saw the sleek object skimming over the waves toward him, Roche knew what it was, but his logical mind wouldn't accept the visual information. The *Montclair's* radar systems were functioning perfectly so why was this thing speeding toward him? He flashed a last look at his bridge crew, wishing he could have the last ten minutes all over again. *After all, I'm a competent commander, aren't I? Of course,* he thought, as the object grew larger. *And I am a good father to Michel and Collette. And a good husband and lover for sweet Monique. Why, all the guys at the institute were green with envy when I had gone up to her and asked for the first dance, long before she even entered the—*

* * * *

"You fucking bastards!"

Barnes' first kick threw Farouk away from the NavCom MOD. Then his momentum carried his body into a graceful pirouette, imbedding his clenched fist into the man's solar plexus. And before anyone realized what was going on, Farouk slammed to the deck and retracted into a fetal position, gasping for air.

Startled for a second, Fergus recovered quickly, reaching down to retrieve the pistol from the prone body of his friend. It was then that Alice's reflexes reacted like a cobra. She grabbed Jonathan's outstretched arm, a spring poised for a series of kicks that would send the hijacker into eternity. In her mind, the struggle was already over and she was looking past the encounter to coordinating the freeing of the hostages. That took all of a half-a-second.

But that was before a steel clamp immobilized her grip on Fergus and wrenched her off balance. Countering her new foe, Alice spun away from the attack and regained her balance, a split-second from striking. Then she saw Vasiliev.

"Dimitri?"

The Russian smiled coldly, rubbing his smarting thumb which Alice had twisted in her escape. "I underestimated your strength, Little Captain."

Dennis took one step toward Vasiliev but froze when he saw the Beretta. "Mr. Barnes, I admire you too much to see you become a corpse. Sit down!" Shaking with adrenaline, Dennis grudgingly plunked himself down in the ice observer's chair.

Alice felt a deep chill in her chest, as if the sea itself was encasing her heart. All the alarm bells that had sounded with this man, her lover, were now silent like the chapel tolls after a funeral. "You, you're with them, Dimitri?"

"Well, yes and no." There was a mocking tone in his voice.

"What then is your little game?" Fergus, breathing hard, had his arm around a frightened Carla. He had lost the charming veneer, and most of his English accent.

Annette Potvin was comforting the prone figure of Farouk, who was unconscious but breathing normally.

MacIsaac's listless stare shifted to the quartermaster. *"Et tu, Brute?"*

"I'm sorry Alice. I believed in—"

"Murder and mutiny. That's what you'll be charged with, Annette. You worked all those years to get on the bridge and it's all gone...along with our friendship."

As if he was a sack of flour, Potvin let the Egyptian roll onto the floor, and then broke into a staccato of sobbing.

"Well!" MacIsaac blurted, a smile breaking apart her grim face. "This certainly is a moment for reflection, isn't it? Anyone else *not* who they appear to be? Step right up and take a kick at the Captain! The floor's yours!"

But Fergus wasn't listening. His attention was focused on Vasiliev. "Alright, Russian, what's your game?"

CHAPTER 5

1.

As the *Sea King* flew low over MacNab's Island, in the mouth of Halifax Harbor, Tom Dorey pondered the mission with all the confidence of someone who has been given information on a "need-to-know" basis could muster. But what amazed him the most was that he was actually going back into the service.

Tom couldn't help but see the humor in the situation. After all, yesterday he was one of the most reviled men in Canada, at least according to the military "spin doctors". They were the ones who placated the public with his hide to protect the forces' other projects from the government's ax.

But Dorey didn't mind that, and actually applauded it. It was bad enough that anti-military lobbyists—ones who would rather see much of the defense budget slashed and the cuttings spent on special interests within their own constituencies—had used his incident to all but deliver the death warrant on the Canadian Parachute Regiment. So to prevent more disfiguring of the forces the public relations staff needed a human sacrifice. Tom Dorey was that offering; and he was willing to dive into the fire if it meant stalling another amputation. That he accepted as a professional soldier. And today he was winging his way back into the same fold that had excommunicated him.

The vibration from the old helicopter was like a welcome friend to Dorey, a nostalgic feeling that he thought he would experience maybe once more in his life—on his flight to prison. Even that might have been too much to ask as a last request, because it was cheaper for the military to send him on a commercial airline with two guards. As the greenery of Dartmouth slid underneath him he almost wanted to ask the warrant officer to open the huge, side door—for old-times' sake.

Yes, he chuckled, it was hard to believe he was back in the service. Earlier in the day, when the black Ford Taurus had pulled up at his father's house, Dorey had been chopping wood in the back yard. Instinctively, he knew it was an official call because his father had been long gone to work and no one else had been around to visit in weeks. The bad press had fixed that. Tom had already been tried and convicted on all the major Canadian news channels by a bevy of "media psychologists" and "military experts".

And that had been too hot to handle for many acquaintances and neighbors. The few, good friends, like old Mrs. Oliver who walked over daily to bring him things such as clam cakes, pie and Solomon Gundy—pickled herring—were rare these days. But, in all fairness to the press, Dorey was thankful that they had respected his wish for privacy in trade for easy access to his lawyer.

He had been especially amused by the astonished look on Colonel Morris' face, and the fearful face of the driver, when they rounded the corner of the big, white house. It wasn't everyday they saw a "half-naked savage" with an ax in his hand. At least that's what Morris compared him to during their greeting.

Dorey hadn't seen Al Morris since his arraignment, when the colonel had given a verbal character reference on his captain's behalf to keep him out of jail. Colonel Alan Morris was just the sort that one would expect of a man who has made a career out of jumping out of airplanes, training in the Arctic and performing other arduous adventures; a man like his uncle. His khaki uniform was cut extra-wide on the shoulders and chest to make room for a muscular body—not built in the relaxed atmosphere of a California-style gym, but molded through years of repetitious training in some of the harshest conditions found on the globe.

In Dorey's eyes, the right phrase to describe Colonel Morris' demeanor was "quiet strength," for the commander rarely raised his voice beyond what it took to make himself heard on the parade ground or area of training. And his leadership was never more proven than as United Nations' peacekeeper in Cyprus in the 60's. A young Lieutenant Morris' jeep was caught in a crossfire between Greek and Turkish Cypriots on a side street in Nicosia. With his driver hurt badly, and himself shot in the leg, Morris bandaged himself and proceeded to broker a cease-fire to allow his driver and three other wounded combatants to be removed to hospital. Out of respect for the Canadian's courage, the rivals withdrew.

"So what brings a landlubber to 'Bluenoseville?'" Dorey called out irreverently, his face betrayed the joy he felt in seeing his former commanding officer. His eyes wandered toward the harbor below.

Morris surveyed the huge yard and its view of

the famed Lunenburg harbor. Down on the wharf, miniature tourists were lining up to ride one of the tall, white-sailed ships. They were in for a treat today because joining the *Theresa E. Connor* at the wharf was the famous *Bluenose II*. Dorey had been a boy growing up in Lunenburg when they still built wooden sailing vessels, even though the art was dying out in favor of the modern fishing boats. So to see that sleek vessel under full sail always left him with a lump in his throat. This fact was not lost on Morris.

"Y'know, Dorey, you come from the nicest part of the country I've seen outside my own Georgian Bay. So, with such peace and tranquillity around you, what makes you such a shit-disturber?"

Tom shifted his stance and thumped the ax into the thick, maple stump. He wiped his hands on his torn and faded denim shorts then, with stride of a middle-weight boxer, he walked towards the officer with his right hand extended and his smile leaking out in the warm, morning sun.

"Good to see you outside a courtroom, Tom. You look very fit. This hard work seems to agree with you. He wanted to add: "And maybe it's the lack of booze." But this was not the time to discuss old hauntings. Dorey had been through enough.

"Captain Tom Dorey, I would like you to meet Lieutenant Colin Smith, a new platoon commander in 'D' Company." Smith, a slim twenty-five year old, was the epitome of the new officers who had been selected: not through the ranks, but from the honor rolls of Canada's universities. The stern-faced young man gave Dorey a hearty handshake. The older man, blonde-gray stubble on his face, rested his brown eyes on Smith's flawless features for an instant before looking past him to the rusty irises of Morris.

"It's a pleasure meeting you again, sir," Smith ventured, businesslike. "We met in '93 at Wainwright during Buffalo Stampede."

Dorey nodded, a smile slowly working its way as he remembered the dusty, airborne exercise with the British in northern Alberta. "Right. I remember. You were the 'second louie'—second-lieutenant—who got his chute tangled up with my sergeant's."

A flush of embarrassment gnawed through the young adjutant as if a cold auger had skewered his back from the inside. However a magnanimous, and mischievous, Dorey rescued him just before his knees went rubbery. "Nice recovery, Smith. You didn't panic like a greenhorn. Both of you eased out of your chutes like they were old sweaters and then popped your reserves. Just like the whole thing was planned." Smith swallowed hard, a glint returning to his blinking eyes.

"Don't let him get to you, Lieutenant," remarked an amused Morris. "He likes to toy with new officers."

Dorey smiled slyly at the colonel as he leaned over and picked up a ratty, black, *Grateful Dead* T-shirt and began wiping the swathes of sweat from his muscular body. Smith's heart skipped a beat when the darker dirt streaks on the ex-paratrooper's body turned out to be scars, especially the one on his face that cradled his left eye.

"Come on in for a drink." The wood chopper then added slyly, "...of root beer."

* * * *

His red beret in his hand, and seated at the kitchen table, Morris wanted to chuckle at the sight of his unruly captain in such a tastefully decorated house. The Hamilton-born officer had always pictured the Nova Scotian growing up in a one-room fisherman's shack, throwing lines into the ocean to catch the evening meal; having to fight off older boys for scraps of bread, and all that Charles Dickens stuff. But this large, white, Victorian house spanked of modest wealth and taste.

Under the whir of the ceiling fan, Tom plunked down three home-made root beers and slid onto a wooden stool beside the ceramic-tiled cooking island. After a long pull of beverage he waved the bottle in a circular motion, darting his eyes around the room.

"Nice digs for a convict, huh?"

Shaking his head, Morris thumped the brown bottle onto the padded place mat and glared at Dorey. He never knew the captain to whine or complain about anything before, and he had hoped that the strain had not beaten him into a vindictive shell of the "do-everything" soldier Morris once knew. Colin Smith just stared out of the window toward the lush, green golf course across the bay, pretending not to hear.

"My mom did all this."

Dorey tipped the stubby bottle back, relishing the cool effervescence as it washed down his throat long before he actually tasted the beverage. Morris poured his root beer into a glass and followed suit.

"She died last year."

More silence.

Finally, Dorey broke into a mischievous laugh. "Okay, Al. Let's have it! Why did you come all the way from Ontario? Have they offered me another deal to stay out of the news?"

Morris cleared his throat to speak but Dorey started in again. "Tell them to save their breath, Colonel. There will be no 'tell-all' book. I just want to be left alone, to fade away.

"Remember," he added pointing the neck of his bottle at Morris, "it was the print-mongers who created this mess, so why should I help them, for any price. Tell that scared bunch in Ottawa that it's my final present to a grateful nation."

The colonel held up his hands in a mock surrender. "Are you finished mouthing off, Captain?"

Dorey shrugged his shoulders, a lock of his longish, graying hair falling over his left eye.

"Good. Now, I never said this to you before, but you're going to listen to me." Dorey nodded, a respectful salute with his forehead that gave the floor to his former commander.

"Here's my opinion, Tom. Whether you, I, or anyone else cares. This is what I think happened. You shot a bunch of so-called 'friendlies' during a peacekeeping mission. So, right or wrong, there had to be an investigation. Especially since it was on the books that you roughed up a Bosnian-Serb major only a year before. So, if by some strange quirk, an 'insensitive-minded' defense minister hadn't have taken action, I would have ordered an internal inquiry myself. Got it?"

An embarrassed Lieutenant Smith continued to gawk out the window, catching Tom's nonchalant look out of the corner of his eye as the grizzled ex-commando took the lecture. It was a good thing that there was an interesting view, otherwise he felt his actions could have be misconstrued as impolite.

"Tom, every country in the UN wants blood for what happened, even though you'd have had to be an idiot *not* to know that the victims were Cuban-trained Sudanese rebels bent on creating just such an incident. In my book, you acted correctly, and saved your company from heavy losses. And I know they wouldn't have taken any of you prisoner if they'd overrun your position. They'd have slit your throats with machetes."

Morris cocked his head to get a better look around the side of Tom's body. "By the way, how's that arm? The bullet went through, didn't it?"

Dorey moved his shoulder in a circular motion. "One bullet went right through, chipping the rotary cuff. The other just took some skin and meat off my side."

"Thank God for that. Anyway, as it stands, our reputation as peacekeepers is just barely hanging by a thread, especially in the European Community. Those smug bastards are looking for any reason to start a trade war against us.

"Which beautifully brings me to the point of my visit. Tom, have you been watching the news, lately?"

"Who, me? Right, Al, I love to watch the same old scene of myself walking into the courtroom, hounded by the fourth estate. And, for lack of a new view of my perfect features, it repeats over and over—"

"No, not that. I mean, have you heard about the icebreaker that was hijacked? The new one."

"Yeah, sure. It was on the radio. Some animal-rights whackos demonstrating something."

"It's worse than that, Tom." Morris leaned toward Dorey, his face as expressionless as a passport photo.

"People have been killed. Hundreds. And there's hostages."

Dorey's left eyebrow twitched, like it always did when he showed concern; a souvenir from Vietnam when a fragment from a 'Bouncing Betty' tore his left cheek open, leaving his face partially paralyzed on that side. He slid off the stool and approached the table, his body odor invading Smith's nostrils.

"And three hours ago, a French frigate blew up like Mount St. Helens—compliments of a Silkworm from that icebreaker."

Tom shook his head in disbelief. A frigate, he calculated, is manned by a crew of at least two hundred. It must have been—

"Okay. I see now," Dorey, blurted out, leaning across the table to face his old commander. "You came here to recruit me. Yeah, like maybe I could help you get this ship back. That's it, isn't it?"

Without any pretenses, Morris nodded, kneading his maroon beret in his hands.

"Holy shit, this is right out of *Rambo*: The disgraced vet asked to perform one more act of viciousness, only this time for his country. What is that, Al? *Art-imitates-life-imitates-art*?"

"I have to admit, Tom, that as corny as it sounds, that's the gist of it...except I'd tone down the 'viciousness' part. They only started printing that after you shoved that reporter who compared you to Lieutenant Calley—the officer who ordered the My Lai massacre in Vietnam. Quite frankly," Morris added, "I thought you were a gentleman. I'd have broken his fuckin' nose if I had been in your situation."

Al Morris glanced at the uneasy form of Smith. "That's quite off the record, Lieutenant, as is everything that goes on here."

Smith felt a lump rise in his throat. "Yes, sir!"

The colonel poured some root beer down his throat. "Let's cut through the shit, Tom. The reason you and I are *not* staff material is that we are outspoken, cut-through-the-bullshit kind of guys. But, that approach never worked with the 'happy hour set' in the Ottawa bureaucracy. They liked to be 'schmoozed', 'boozed' and stroked a little. Well, I don't 'schmooze' well and any stroking that I might do in their presence would be with an 'Arkansas toothpick'—a large knife. As for booze, well it's gotten both of us into trouble more times than I care to remember." Dorey stirred uneasily but he could sense Morris was through with the niceties.

"To be blunt, Tom, I know I don't have the social skills to reach general...but I've reached colonel and you should have had your own regimental command five years ago. It's been your attitude and that fucking 'whisky demon' that's stopped you."

Morris swigged his root beer. His eyes drooped and there was the unmistaken look of sadness in his usually officious countenance. "Christ, as good as you are, you never lasted three months as 'light-colonel of 2nd Battalion." Dorey joined Smith's gaze and watched a tiny golf cart zoom across the verdant patch across the harbor.

"Look, here it is: with the regiment disbanded and scattered throughout the military, at least those who haven't been shoved out, we've got a shambles of a rapid-deployment force left to deal with this. What we need is someone with enough experience to pull off a retrieval of that fucking boat and to do that through official channels would take up too much time, as well as alerting the 'bad guys.'

"What I'm trying to say is this: Just for once, keep your thoughts to yourself, swim through the shit with a smile on your face and help me get this job done...at least for those poor bastards on that ship, and the many more who may die from the spin-offs if we don't stop it."

Dorey rubbed the thick silvery, stubble on his chin. "Why *me*? And even if I wanted to, the 'schmoozers' would veto it."

"They asked for you."

"But why me?"

"Because Admiral Jenkins and I insisted."

"The head honcho of Maritime Command wanted me?"

"Remember, Tom, no one wanted Patton until there was a war on...but there's someone else."

"Who?"

"Jay Carruthers."

"Holy cow. The shit certainly does roll from on high, doesn't it?"

2.

"I repeat. This is a restricted area. You will not, I repeat, *not* perform low-level reckon. Rejoin at angels fourteen—fourteen thousand feet...over."

The gray shapes of the Canadian CF-18A *Hornets* hovered over the lighter-colored American F-14 *Tomcats* like shadows imprinted on the bright, clear sky, matching the Americans' subtle course changes and other attempts to play with their authority.

"Affirmative, 'Bug' driver—an irreverent name for the Hornet. We will comply...Red Flag Two, switch to secured five-oh-three."

"Aye, aye, Ramblin' Man," came the reply from the fighter barely ten feet off the American's wing tip. The pilot and his RIO—radio/intercept operator—perched behind him like a back-seat driver, appeared to be stuck way out on a pencil-thin limb ahead of the aircraft, just in front of the large, rectangular scoops that forced air into the two massive engines.

"Okay, Billy Boy, those Canucks are blanked out. Any ideas?" asked the pilot, glancing through his canopy to the helmeted figure driving the other American jet off his starboard wing tip.

"Lead on, brother," came the reply.

"Captain, shouldn't we think about this for a

second?" cut in the RIO behind Captain Dave "Ramblin' Man" Talbot, the pilot of "Red Flag One".

"Uh, I gotta GPS—Global Positioning System—that reads that the target has been in Canadian waters for over three hours. Don't we have to respect their sovereignty, or somethin'? That *is* the law, ain't it, Cap?"

Talbot eased the aircraft into a gentle port bank and surveyed the immense red-and-white ship below them. The sunlight played on an equally-large iceberg just ahead of the vessel which reflected flashes of ultra-white light through the cockpit.

"Look, Cisco," replied Talbot, "up here no one knows *who owns what*. Greenland is over there," he said, pointing starboard, "and Canada is over there. That puts us in between. So let the Canadians and Danes bitch all they want 'cause as far as the US, government is concerned, this area is international waters."

"Danes?"

"Affirmative, Cisco. Greenland belongs to Denmark. And from what I've seen of the place, they're welcome to it."

Lieutenant Jorge Ramirez remained silent, watching the aquamarine-ringed shape of the ice mountain disappear under his aircraft. Seated behind, Talbot like the passenger on a motorcycle, his job was communications, navigation, weapons preparation, as well as making sure the fighter's operational systems were up to par. But it was the Captain's airplane.

It had been an exciting venture for the New Mexico-born Ramirez, dubbed the "Cisco Kid" by his commander, taking off from the deck of the formidable USS *Theodore Roosevelt*, down off Haiti, and flying up three thousand miles to Baffin Island. To make the trip, extra fuel tanks had been added to the fighters, giving them an additional range of five hundred miles each way. In the meantime they had been refueled by a KC-135 tanker—a Boeing 707 fitted for in-flight fueling of other aircraft—off Norfolk, Virginia and had filled up at CFB Shearwater in Dartmouth, Nova Scotia and CFB Goose Bay, in Labrador.

"Exciting" for the lieutenant also because he had never been up to Canada before or, for that matter, anywhere colder than the Sierra's. From his lofty view, the field of ice-capped mountains of southern Baffin Island and the large chunks of floating ice islands were like a PBS documentary shown on a huge IMAX screen.

"Okay, Cap, but only one pass 'cause the nearest gas station is Goose Bay. And we'll be sucking vapors *real* soon."

As the two American fighters circled at three thousand feet their CAG—commander, air group—was attending a briefing aboard the *Theodore Roosevelt*, while the carrier and its group of support ships proceeded at full speed northward. The CINCLANT—Commander-in-Chief Atlantic Fleet—had flown aboard the carrier to update the captain and his senior officers on President Thompson's response to French President Gérard Ledoux's newest threats of retribution—what the French president termed, "Canadian adventurism and expansionism."

Due to the loss of an American C-130—an aircraft flying for the International Ice Patrol, which went missing after its pilot reported a missile heading toward it—as well as the detaining of the American ambassador, the CINCLANT ordered American fighters to go long-range to keep an eye on the CCGS *Canadian*, now just one hundred-fifty miles south of the Arctic circle. Eight *Tomcats* were ordered to fly ahead to Goose Bay, an initial response, to give an immediate American presence and a "bird's-eye view," both of the marauding icebreaker and the advancing French destroyers. Pairs of fighters would continue flying reconnaissance missions out of Goose Bay until the *Roosevelt* and its support ships arrived on the Grand Banks.

Rather than a show of force, the F-14 fighters and the advancing carrier group were a subliminal reminder to the French that the US would *not* tolerate being excluded from any decisions made in its sphere of influence—mainly North America. Cuba, Grenada, Panama and Haiti were examples of this on-going policy and reassigning a carrier group was President Thompson's way of affirming this commitment.

"Roger, Cisco. Just enough for one pass, low on the deck around that 'berg and then straight for home. Copy, Billy Boy?"

"Roger, Ramblin' Man. But we may have a couple of mad *Hornet*'s buzzing around."

"What're the Bugs gonna do, shoot us down? That cloud bank ahead should do the trick. We'll just skim overtop and then bust loose."

"You're the boss, Ramblin' Man...Billy Boy out."

"Okay. Jump time. Port, on five, four, three, two, one—"

The F-14's were the newest model of the swept-wing fighter that continued to dominate the ocean skies even after twenty-five years of carrier service. Classified as a "variable-geometry-fighter," their wings could be retracted sixty degrees aft to meet the stabilizer fins, giving them the appearance of a large, flying arrowhead. Besides carrying the latest in avionics, as well as the newest weapons-systems updates, they were lighter and more powerful than their predecessors; their two huge Pratt and Whitney turbofans were capable of delivering

Mach 2.5, or 1,800 miles an hour. And that was fifty-percent more power than the *Hornets*.

To the pilots of the two Canadian fighters, it looked as though the *Tomcats* just vanished.

* * * *

The two ropes of Bart Jesso's braided hair flapped in the breeze as he waited for the two gray-white specks to disappear behind one of the three sail-like silhouettes of the icebergs, rising some two hundred feet out of the frigid water. This was going to be almost as easy as splashing the white Herc, he grinned, cruelly. That big bird's wing just broke apart and the aircraft lazily cartwheeled into the ocean swells.

Before he activated the SAM's, he rechecked the display and his eyes drifted to the launch platform twenty feet aft. Then, after four almost-simultaneous blasts, the sleek, six-foot, white projectiles slid out of their cradles toward the rolling, blue sea, their vaporous exhaust hanging in the cool air. Jesse danced and whooped as they planed out at a scant ten feet above the surface and homed in on the large, white chunk of ice that, for a moment, hid the advancing fighters.

* * * *

"SAM's! Christ, Pull out—"

The piercing warning in Talbot's headset cut out the RIO's scream. Instinctively, he jammed the throttle full forward, pinning himself and Ramirez to their seatbacks while, at the same millisecond, kicking the rudder controls. Six G's—a measure of gravitational pull on the body equaling six times the body weight—pressed the blood out of their heads like an invisible juice press, presenting their eyes with a darkened view of the bright day. Modern aviation, however, had a handle on such maneuvers with the invention of the *G-suit*, which stopped the downward squeeze of blood by automatically constricting their legs and lower torsos.

"Chaff! Flares away!" yelled Ramirez as the *Tomcat*'s ALE defensive systems went into high gear, dispersing strips of aluminum "Christmas" tinsel and white-hot magnesium flares to draw away the projectile.

Four slender pencils, visible against the dark ocean, shot toward them. The first missile went for the decoy, missing the F-14 by barely a hundred feet when the swept-winged jet rolled on its side. The explosion of the SAM, five hundred feet away, rocked the F-14 but did no damage.

And the empty detonation was an extra bonus for Talbot's fighter. Besides missing, it drew the second missile to the heat source. Instead of tracking them, like a confused bird, the projectile continued on along the sea, its sensors searching for a target. Then, less than a minute later, it plunged into the North Atlantic swells, exploding harmlessly underwater.

The third SAM went for Red Flag Two's decoys, destroying itself, but the *Tomcat* couldn't shake the last missile, which caught the second interceptor's starboard engine. Captain William "Billy Boy" Hargreaves' aircraft wrenched violently as one-third of his *Tomcat* blew away. Warning beacons lit up the console and harsh buzzing sounds invaded their headsets as the sophisticated fighter stalled. Smoke was starting to pour into the cockpit when the RIO, Lieutenant "Con Man" Considine, pulled hard on the yellow-striped "escape cables" above his head just seconds before the stricken aircraft, its aerodynamic design now a jumble of composite pieces, ripped itself apart and scattered its remains over the calm sea.

The first explosion jettisoned the canopy, which

flew back with the air current. A millisecond later, the charges beneath his seat detonated. Considine felt the bottom of his spine want to "telescope" into his skull. His face suddenly felt the blast of a cold wind whip his body behind the stricken wreck like a broken kite. Then, conversely, his shocked body was yanked in the other direction when his parachute canopy caught the air. The last view that the lieutenant remembered was pieces of his aircraft splashing into the dark, green water which raced up to greet him in its cold embrace.

"Billy!" screamed Talbot into dead air, weaving his swept-wing fighter side to side in his search for the other *Tomcat*. A minute later, out their port side, the airmen saw fragments of Red Flag Two floating on the ocean three miles away.

"Two chutes, but they were awful goddamn low," stammered Ramirez, almost matter-of-factly. "They're gone, Cap."

Before he could say another word, the RIO felt almost four G's melt his body into his seat as the *Tomcat* went into a steep bank. The fear catching up with him, Ramirez swallowed hard.

"No, Cap! We can't do *nothing*, our rails are empty. Let's—"

"There! There's someone crawling up onto the berg!" shouted Talbot, ignoring his back-seat. The F-14 cruised low over the iceberg and Ramirez strained to see who the survivor was while keeping one eye on the green, tactical-information display in front of him. They might try again, he shuddered.

"Okay, Cisco," fumed the captain, disgusted with himself for not treating the icebreaker as a hostile ship and, thus, not ordering the defensive system activated. "This time we turn on the goddamn toys! We're going in! Master Arm on!"

"But we don't have the punch, Cap! We gave up our birds to carry the extra fuel, remember?"

"I'm going to rake the bridge!" proclaimed Talbot, activating the 20mm cannon control; a fearsome multi-barreled Gatling gun. "You just do the SAM-jamming!"

The new F-14 was more than well-equipped in the area of defense. Besides *chaff*, it carried the ALQ-135 radar jammer—which isolated the SAM's tracking radar and nullified it—and some other deflectors with a technology called *POET*. These devices, once dropped, accept tracking information from the incoming missile. Then they amplified it and redirected it back, deceiving the relentless warhead into thinking that POET was the real target.

Talbot had just pulled low over the water and around the same iceberg again when Ramirez's screen flashed and naked tones went off in the cockpit. "Jesus! Someone else's locked onto us!"

In a flash Talbot veered away from the ship and put the fighter into a series of defensive maneuvers. But at subsonic speed and at low altitude, the situation remained the same.

"Cisco! What the fuck's going on?"

"Cap, it's not the ship!"

"Then who, dammit?"

"It's a *Hornet* IFF signature...the Canucks!"

"The who?" Talbot, his helmeted head resembling a large bug, twisted around to see the outline of a dark-gray *Hornet* off his starboard fin. "Those bastards!"

"What the fuck do you think you're doing?" Talbot bawled over the airwaves.

"You will break off now and climb to Angels Twelve—twelve thousand feet. Then you will proceed to CFB Goose Bay under our supervision or we have orders to shoot you down." The reply was very calm.

"By whose orders?"

"Admiral Clinton Maris, US Navy...Washington."

Talbot shook his helmeted head in wonderment. So much had happened in the last five minutes that he fought to place everything in order.

"Maris is with the Pentagon. Two stars," he said calmly. "Why would he be ordering us—"

"Please comply immediately, Captain, or you will be shot down. End of transmission."

But it wasn't the end of the transmission. This time the voice was conciliatory. "Come on guys. We're on your side. Let's go home."

3.

The response had been almost instantaneous. Within minutes, Dennis Barnes had the throttle of the FRC wide open and was heading over the dark, gentle swells toward the long, flat iceberg. Although the chief mate had practiced this drill many times before, it had been in the safe confines of Halifax harbor. Open-water drills had been scheduled for the first operational voyage; that meant now, he shuddered.

Still, the rescue system had worked smoothly for Barnes, just like the run-through in the harbor. The FRC popped out of its "nest," a notch near the stern on the port side, ten feet above the water line where it fit in the space in somewhat the same manner as toy in a display package. Dennis emerged from a special door behind the "nest," stepped into the boat, and then hydraulic arms lowered the fifteen-foot craft to the water. All he had to do from there was start the engine and lower the FRC the last three feet into the water.

The sea at the base of the mountain of ice was

a brilliant turquoise, owing to the thousands of tons of frozen, fresh water just below the salty surface reflecting the bright sunlight up through the frigid, 3° Celsius water. Barnes spotted the downed airman, a seal-like shape on the "shore" of the iceberg, and cut the engine, letting the vessel slide onto the pitted, icy surface. Then he checked his watch. It had been over ten minutes since the man's chute was spotted; Barnes was frantically racing against the threat of hypothermia. If the airman had been in the water all that time then he would have been past the point of no return. Barnes was praying that the hot sun had added some warmth to the man's dark, wet flying suit.

Kneeling over the American, the chief mate pulled out his Swiss army knife and cut through the straps of the parachute, the canopy of which still floated in the water, and then gently turned the still-helmeted man over. He popped off the dark visor and cut the helmet straps, lifting the large bowl off his head.

Barnes thanked all the Saints in order when he saw the blinking, green eyes. Bolting back to the FRC, he returned with a portable stretcher board and an armload of blankets and medical paraphernalia. Gently, fearing internal injuries, Barnes slid the board under the man's body, a task made easier because of the soft ice. He then ripped open a large, flat bag producing two plastic blankets. The first he wrapped around the flyer's head and neck, the second he tucked around the man's chest. Each sheet had a cord protruding from it which Barnes had yanked out. By pulling the cords, a chemical was released into the liquid sandwiched between the sheets of the plastic blankets. This produced a soothing heat which would delay the onset of hypothermia.

After strapping him in and bundling the air-man in blankets, he dragged the stretcher onto the boat and was soon piloting the FRC back to the icebreaker. It was when the little boat was half-way back to the *Canadian* that he noticed the American's boot-holster. But it was empty.

* * * *

"As you can see, we are not barbarians. The humanitarian effort to save the downed pilot was successful. He is, at this very moment, in the in-firmary under the care of Bill Barrett, a trained paramedic."

"Can we airlift him to a hospital?"

"I'm not stupid enough to let anyone land on this ship."

"Affirmative. Are his wounds serious?"

"I am told he has a sore back."

"Has Barrett checked for hypothermia?"

"Mr. Barrett feels the sun, of all things, saved his life."

"The sun?"

"Never mind. Just fly away and leave us. *Out*!"

An impatient Dimitri Vasiliev drew a finger across his throat and a nervous Annette Potvin cut the communication between the circling *Aurora* and the icebreaker.

"When are you going to tell me why you're do-ing this?" Jonathan Fergus' face was a blank cast-ing, far removed from the confident ship master of only twenty-four hours before. His disability was even more pronounced now and he hobbled around as if the wounds were slowly eating away at his leg.

"You know, Mr. Fergus, it was almost fun watching you and your gang of *puppies* move about this grand ship as if you were *really* in charge of it. But, to be fair, you surprised me with the efficiency in which the ship was taken over and relieved of its 'excess baggage.' Most efficient, and without injury to one passenger, Mr. Fergus. I applaud you."

Vasiliev's large form rose from the captain's chair and lorded over the bridge, somehow making the vast chamber a little smaller to the bridge crew and the *new* captives: Jonathan Fergus' Planet Guardians; but not all of them. Like a Greek god, the cable-like muscles of his torso strained against the Russian's singlet, as if they were living entities of their own in a constant state of growth and needing more room.

"And the way you got the French and the Americans worked up.... Well, Jonathan, with a few missiles you managed to provide a greater diversion than we could have ever hoped for; and I plan to make it worth your while."

Fergus' brow wrinkled under the wet locks that were pasted to his forehead, as well as stuck along the light stubble on his right jaw. His cane dug into the carpet, wobbling under his unsteady balance as he limped toward Vasiliev. When he got closer, the veins in his eyes could be seen as minute, red lightning bolts permeating the pink, bloodshot orbs around his impish, blue irises.

"What do you mean by 'hoped for'?" Fergus voice wavered on the last two words as he struggled to hold his temper.

The Russian's perfect smile was an advertisement for the dental clinics of the privileged in the old Soviet system, its outward sincerity betrayed only by a curled lip on the right side of his "beach boy" face.

"You try to confuse me with your naïveté, Jonathan. But I really think you know who I am."

"Yes," replied Fergus, nodding his head slowly and calming somewhat. "*You're with* Rasputin. You used our cause to get aboard."

"Give that man a cigar, please!" teased Vasiliev, basking in his discovery as would a person who has been named "Citizen of the Year" would. "Oh, by the way. Thanks for paying *my* men."

* * * *

The wiry figure managed to work the screws off a large, false plate on one of the communications racks with his pen knife and then, after pulling the sheet metal away, had crawled into the empty space to test it. It was a tight fit, but would do in case someone came snooping around. Under the circumstances, however, everything was quiet in the room.

Jimmy McDougall had transmitted on the HF for five minutes every hour since discovering Johansen's primitive setup, taking merely three hours off to sleep in the cramped compartment. The only downside of his job so far was relieving himself.

On the first day, the Newfoundlander utilized the services of a large soft drink container, inadvertently left by one of the installers. After urinating, he immediately capped it with a wad of paper and hid it under one of the conduit plates in the false floor. He used it twice more, filling the torpedo-shaped bottle to the top.

However, later the next day, his bowels ached beyond control. Since he could not find anything appropriate, he pried another plate open at the far end of the room, intending to use the square opening as a toilet. It was then he heard muffled voices from below. Somehow stifling his natural urges, he pulled up the insulation surrounding the neatly-laid sheaves of wiring and fiber-optic cables. Unhindered by the sound dampening, the speech became more audible and then, through a slender crack in the plates below, he saw movement.

Carefully moving his head over the sliver of light, he picked out Frances Pilotte and the US ambassador seated at one of the dining-room tables in the Officer's Mess. There were parts of other bodies as well, but his view of them was very limited. Everyone's attention seemed to be glued to CNN, on the large television screen, except the guard, a crew-cut young man in jeans and a jean jacket, who paced back and forth.

Quietly, McDougall replaced the floor covering and went to another part of the room and repeated the procedure, taking up a tile and the insulation below it. This time, he had picked a spot directly over the serving counter, between the galley and the dining area, far enough away from the captives and their guard that he could play with the light, acoustic tile below him and get a better view. Quickly dipping his head down below the ceiling of the Officer's Mess, he saw that there were five captives: the two journalists, the Italian computer expert, Judy MacDonald and the radio guy he earlier changed rooms with making up the other five. Satisfied that his lookout could not be detected by the guard, he replaced the square and repacked the insulation and top plate, leaving the area as pristine as he found it.

McDougall then cracked the door to the Com Room and listened for a few minutes. If anyone had been within two feet of the door they would have heard the fisheries minister whisper, "Lord, you've driven *this* as low as it can go without shooting down my pant leg; now grant me the serenity to get relief before I explode!"

With that he hobbled down the hallway.

4.

**Dartmouth, Nova Scotia; July 3rd,
7:27 p.m. *Atlantic Time***

Tom Dorey had fond memories of Canadian Forces
Base Shearwater, just across the harbor from Halifax. As a child he remembered watching *Seafires*—
a carrier-rigged, propeller-driven Spitfire—CF-
100's, and later *Voodoos*, fly in and out of the pic-
turesque plateau, the racket rattling off the gentle
hills that protected the north and eastern perim-
eters from ocean-generated crosswinds. Along with
an assortment of training aircraft, such as
Harvards, and other military support craft,
Shearwater had been a living testimonial to aviation history.

When he returned from the US and joined the
Canadian Forces, CFB Shearwater was still an
operations area: one which would coordinate simulated missions using its compliment of fighters for
close air support. Then, as a team leader with the
Canadian Parachute Regiment, Dorey's select
group of show jumpers thrilled audiences at several Shearwater International Airshows. In all, the
airbase had been a lucky spot for him.

Lately, however, it had become just one of a
growing number of "shells," bases which had either been decommissioned in preparation for piece-
meal cannibalism by auctioneers—and the land
sold to developer-friends of politicians—or
downsized to a skeleton force. To the dismay of
Dorey, and many others in the military, Shearwater
was one of the latter, its CF-18 *Hornet* and C-130
Hercules aircraft long gone, leaving only a compliment of *Sea King* helicopters and the static displays of the base's aviation museum.

In the last forty-eight hours, however, the base

had been a hive of activity. The usually-bored tower controller was buried in requests for landing instructions from military aircraft of all classes as the partially-dismantled base entertained top officers from Canada and its NATO allies. Armies of journalists from around the globe, although not allowed to land at the base, laid siege to its gates. Satellite dishes and receiver trucks from the world's most prestigious news services had also begun littering the compound outside the main gate, waiting to beam speculations about the Canadian government's next move in the soap opera ironically titled *The Canadian Crisis*.

So, in Dorey's eyes, with all this attention Shearwater was the last place he would have expected a high-level meeting to be called to discuss the options for dealing with the runaway icebreaker. Especially when all the action was taking place almost seven hundred miles away. However, Nova Scotia was still headquarters to the main players in the problem-solving team, the MARCOMPAC staff.

Tom unzipped his blue coveralls and picked a pool cue from the wall rack. "Do they still have wild dances at the *Sea King*?"

"Not so much, anymore. No people," replied Major Bob Higgins, head of security for Shearwater. "Hell, the last one we had could have been held in a phone booth."

Tom grunted, staring around the brick-faced lounge. The only thing that made this afternoon different from a normal one in the bar was the lack of pool-playing airmen. In their place, at each exit, were pairs of military police with C-7 automatic weapons at ready.

"Funny place for a meeting. I mean, isn't it a bit irreverent to meet in a bar?"

The air force major narrowed his eyes at Dorey.

"You don't like the *Sea King Lounge*, Captain?"

"No offense, Major. I just thought that the defense minister and the brass hats would fly thousands of miles in any direction rather than risk being seen around liquor. Especially with every camera in the world just outside the fence."

"That's why they chose—"

The major jumped to his feet as the door to the kitchen burst open. Three faceless, military policemen entered past the guard, their suspicious eyes darting about the room. Dorey mimicked him a fraction of a second later, laying the cue on the green tabletop.

Soon afterward the guard came to attention, presenting arms as a line of both military and civilian personnel entered the lounge. One, noticed Dorey, was an American admiral with two-stars on his epaulettes. It was then that he spied some US Marines skulking outside in the corridor. *You're slipping, Dorey.* He silently chided himself for letting his sharpness wane during the months of inactivity.

Giving the two standing men formal nods, the dignitaries surrounded the long, bar table flopped briefcases in front of them and sat down. Dorey and the air force officer followed suit.

After a reasonable amount of throat-clearing and latch clicking, one of the civilians, a tall man bordering on middle-age, clasped his hands and surveyed the participants. Tom almost grinned. The man was very familiar to him.

Besides Dorey, the major and the American, were Colonel Wilfred Myers, commander of CFB Shearwater; Vice Admiral Robert Jenkins, commander of Maritime Command (MARCOMPAC); and Colonel Alan Morris of the Canadian Parachute Regiment; Dorey's regimental commander.

"Gentleman, my name is Marcel Gallante. I will

be chairing this emergency meeting." Gallante's Quebeçois accent was usually considered "moderate" for a Quebec politician, but today, in front of this audience, his diction, however slow, was devoid of any Francophone nuances except to a very critical ear.

"For those of you not familiar with me, I am the Canadian Minister of Defense. I'm sure you in the Canadian Forces are familiar with the man beside me, John Balcom, the deputy minister." Balcom, a senior civil servant with only two years left to retirement, nodded his thatch of silvery white hair.

Gallante drew a sheaf of papers from his wine-colored, eel-skin briefcase and nervously eyed the front door, as if some terrorist group were about to smash through the glass panels. He smoothed back his thick, dark hair, obviously dyed to compliment his youthful appearance, then panned the anticipated looks of the committee.

"At this moment the Prime Minister is trying to set up a meeting with French President Gérard Ledoux."

That solemn announcement was met with a reverent silence lasting almost ten seconds as his eyes met those of everyone at the table. He cleared his throat and continued.

"This morning he and the cabinet agreed to a proposal put forward by Lieutenant-General Alex Jameson, the chief of staff, for a commando-style assault on the CCGS *Canadian*, somewhere in the vicinity of Nanisivik, Baffin Island—the area where the icebreaker will be in two day's time...that is, if negotiations with the hijackers can't be worked out before then."

The table became a ring of nodding heads and smiles. Gallante raised his hand to indicate he was not finished and the murmuring ceased.

"Excuse me, sir, but I thought they were going to surrender after the destruction of the French ship?" interrupted Colonel Myers, a gaunt figure whose uniform looked like it had been fitted for a larger man.

"I am sorry to say that the original players are *not* in control anymore," returned Gallante. "So it is imperative that we have a plan to take the ship back if negotiations fail." The defense minister's posture was slumped, and his expensive suit wrinkled, a sign of many hours without sleep. But his eyes held a sharp edge.

"Would it be within bounds to tell us who is in charge?" Myers' concerned posture was joined by the others as the rustling of papers and half-whispers permeated the room.

"We are not sure, Colonel, and that's what makes this operation so dangerous. I should mention at this time that reports by the media that two American planes have been shot down are, unfortunately, correct. So, gentlemen, it's a new ball game and, I should add, a more desperate one.

"At this time I would like to introduce Vice Admiral Clinton Maris from the Pentagon who will be the American liaison during the operation and advisor to General Davidson, President Thompson's Chief-of-Staff. I would also like to extend the condolences of the Prime Minister and the people of Canada to the families of the American airmen murdered by these cold-hearted pirates."

The American nodded, his expressionless, brown eyes giving away nothing to show either his approval or disapproval with the minister. His uniform was right out of a Hollywood movie: starched-white, short-sleeved shirt and pants with brass buttons, belt buckle and stars on his collars and epaulettes. Four rows of colorful medal ribbons adorned his left breast.

"Now, I will turn the briefing over to the commander of MARCOMPAC, Vice Admiral Jenkins."

Gallante sat down and sipped some water from the jug in front of him while the black-suited form of Jenkins, resplendid in gold cuff rings and epaulette insignia with maple leafs, stood and read from a prepared document.

"The assaulting force will consist of two groups from Colonel Morris' Canadian Parachute Regiment and will be under his direct command. Morris and 'Team Two', consisting of thirty men, will be airlifted immediately to Nanisivik, code-named 'Center Ice', approximately twenty to fifty miles from the expected position of the icebreaker. If the weather conditions are too dangerous to land a C-130, then 'Team Two' will have to be dropped in from high altitude."

"Dropped in?" asked Gallante. "By parachute? Why not helicopter?"

"Two reasons, Mr. Minister. First, the *Canadian* has sophisticated radar and satellite tracking systems and, from what we have witnessed in the last couple of days, the hijackers know how to use the gear. Helicopters could be easily tracked with the new low-level radar and the mission tipped off to them. Which brings us to the second reason: *Sea Kings* are not suited for such a long-range operation so they will be flown to 'Center Ice'."

Gallante shifted uneasily at the resurgence of the biggest thorn in his side as defense minister. As much as they had pushed Sikhorsky, the new American *Sea Hawk* helicopters they had purchased to replace twelve of the thirty-year-old Sea Kings were still one month away from delivery.

They had been bought "off the shelf," helicopters purchased as an "add-on" to an already-existing American production run. To keep the manufacturing going, especially since the scaling-down of US requests, Sikhorsky gave Canada a sweetheart deal in aircraft and maintenance contracts. But they had to be fitted with avionics and weapons systems that conformed with their armed forces counterparts in Canada. They were not the ultimate replacement craft for their needs, but would fill the gap until a more suitable aircraft was decided upon.

"But won't transport aircraft be as easily tracked?"

"Sure. All the way. But we had already established a pattern of C-130's and *Aurora*'s as 'watchdogs' during the rescue operations on the Grand Banks. It seems that the hijackers have allowed us that much and have almost ignored their flights as routine. So, the aircraft carrying 'Team Two' would follow such a pattern and then fly back to 'Center Ice' as if on a refueling stop in Nanasivik or Resolute Bay, whichever airstrip is being used as 'H-Hour' approaches. Except for a gentle slowing of the plane, nothing can give their sensors a clue that there is a parachute drop in progress. An American Air Force *Galaxy* transport, a loner from our gracious allies..." he smiled at the stoned-faced Maris "...will land at Nanisivik with two *Sea Kings* and off-load them.

"Won't the icebreaker detect the difference?" asked Gallante. "I mean, wouldn't it 'see' a larger aircraft?"

"We're hoping that by establishing a regular pattern of transports the hijackers won't notice if we slip a 'big one' in. The final details haven't been nailed down, sir, just the framework."

Gallante conceded the point by nodding.

"'Team One' will consist of four men led by Lieutenant-Colonel Dorey, here." All eyes turned to the civilian in the dirty *Eastern Passage Cleaners* coveralls. It was Tom's idea to ensure his anonymity within the compound. The presence of an officer charged with "war crimes" would have created a public-relations nightmare and have tipped off the terrorists that a rescue attempt was in the works. Some factions of the media would have paid handsomely for that information and anyone outside the room might let the information slip for a years' pay from a tabloid.

"This first team will assault the ship and neutralize the computer system. With the ship blinded, and Dorey's boys sheltering the hostages, Colonel Morris' team will be flown in by the Sea Kings to neutralize the entire ship."

"How will 'Team One' get aboard? The same way?" It was Maris. Dorey likened his voice to the low roll of a kettle drum.

Gallante and Balcom gave each other apprehensive glances. Jenkins answered his question by addressing the audience. "Gentlemen. At this time, with the international climate being the way it is, the Defense staff is not at liberty to divulge our methods concerning 'Team One.'"

Maris pursed his lips, glaring at each man at the table in turn. His crew-cut, salt and pepper hair accentuated his large head. "Excuse me again, sir, but I really think that the United States should be advised as to *all* proceedings, I mean, especially after the downing of our two aircraft. International law provides that the principles of 'Hot Pursuit' would have to apply here." The admiral stopped to pour some ice water into a glass. Everyone watched him drink as if his every motion could affect the outcome of the problem at hand. The ice cubes in the glass rattled like dice when he lowered the empty glass

"In other words," he continued, "the US should be able to chase that goddamn icebreaker to the gates of Hell without asking anyone's permission." His voice raised like the sudden crescendo of a symphony orchestra. "And if that's not good enough for your government they should at least tell us what the hell's going on!"

Jenkins, equal in rank in the Canadian navy as the American was in his, answered as if Maris had just offered a counter opinion in a lawn bowling tournament. His voice was cool, almost matter-of-fact. "Admiral, except for the presence of one of your ambassadors, this is a total Canadian operation within Canadian waters. We regret the loss of your airmen, but both aircraft were operating in our airspace, especially the fighters who ignored clear warnings to stay out of the area. Your government promised us that they were up there for reconnaissance only. It was only on that premise that I gave the fighter group *my* personal permission for a *recco*—reconnoitre."

"Yes. And for that I truly apologize, Admiral," backtracked the American, his tone much softer, feeling awkward for blowing off in front of another country's military. "It goes against my grain, too. Our boys are supposed to be a hell of a lot more disciplined than that. But, shit, you at least gotta let us help. What if the worst scenario happens? What if both teams are repulsed? You said the plan's pretty sketchy, so it could happen."

Admiral Jenkins rubbed his gray temples, his hawk-like face staring off toward the far window. "Then the ship will be incapacitated by whatever means we can deploy."

"You mean destroyed," the American offered.

"At this time that is *just* an option. We value human life more than prestige or one-upmanship. However, with French attitudes being the way they are, we may have to make sacrifices to avoid a serious altercation. I am not saying that we will bend to the will of the French but, in order to avoid a potentially costly confrontation with them, we may have to bend away from what *we* think is right."

Jenkins let the last sentence sink in as if preparing the officers for an inevitable decision. Unlike many Americans of his generation, such as Maris, in all his thirty-five years in the force he had *never* had to ponder such alternatives.

"But," he added, his voice lifting as he eyeballed Dorey, "we have a dedicated group of individuals, well-trained in Arctic maneuvers. I have every faith in their ability to end this favorably."

"And rightly so, Admiral," countered Maris, "but I still don't know why your prime minister rejected the President's offer of Navy SEALs. After all, with no disrespect to Captain Dorey here, our boys have been on dangerous assignments before—"

"In the Middle East, Somalia, Grenada and Panama," cut in Jenkins. "All warm places."

"For chrissakes, Admiral, we got the 172nd Infantry Brigade in Alaska. They've got specialized units."

"True, ones that know Alaska. But the Para's have jumped at temperatures that would freeze the brass balls off a monkey, and in just the territory we have designated at the target zone. So in this climate, just below freezing, they would have no problem setting up 'Center Ice' at record speed."

It was Jenkins' turn to carry the play to Maris. "And Admiral, when it comes to all-weather deployment and achievement of objectives, the Canadian Armed Forces doesn't have to take a back seat to anyone. And if you don't believe me, ask General Colin Powell, your president's former Chief-of-Staff.

Clint Maris offered some damage-control. "Admiral, there was no disrespect intended to your nation's forces and I apologize if I sounded out of line. I'd like to help out any way I can, so how about I give your Team Two some new helicopters with some long-range punch. We'll run 'em up to Nana...whatever, in the *Galaxies* and our chopper crews will take you in."

Maris acknowledged the thank-you's around the table and then the brows of his eyes lowered. "But just to make sure all of us knows the situation here, it's like this: There's two American birds down over this damn affair and you've got half the French navy making a beeline for the Miquelons. So if we don't have a pig in time for the barbecue it might be more than just a few asses that get roasted over this thing." The vocal reverberations were like drumfire.

* * * *

Dorey was walking with his three-man squad out of the hangar and onto the dark tarmac when the piercing sound of the landing F-14 *Tomcat* attacked his ears. Behind the line of purplish lights that sped down the runway in the twilight almost a half-a-mile away, came two more sets: CF-18 *Hornets* gently touching down, almost toy-like on their tricycle landing gear.

A steady, metallic whining grew louder as the American fighter, glowing rose-pink in the waning light of day on the western horizon, taxied toward the hangar area. Then it slowed, wheeled around and followed the flashlights of the landing officer, the thrust of its twin engines flattening the grass beside the taxiway for fifty yards.

As the awesome interceptor came to a halt Tom noticed Vice Admiral Maris, now wearing a khaki uniform and operations ball cap, and four US Marines waiting on the tarmac. With his arms clasped behind his back his barrel chest was a bold platform for the rows of campaign ribbons above his shirt pocket; among them was one representing the Distinguished Flying Cross for flying carrier-based *Intruders* during the Vietnam War. The American officer's physique could rival a man half his age.

There was a marked decrescendo in wail of the turbines and the long canopy of the F-14 raised smoothly. Two Canadian ground crewmen rushed out to the fighter and climbed up on the coarse surface of the wing root to assist the pilot and his RIO. Once unfettered by their safety gear and helmets, the two American aviators climbed down the wing and examined the murky, Nova Scotia evening.

"Over here, Captain!" boomed the admiral, whose silhouette loomed like an avenging angel against the lighted innards of the hangar.

The two surprised Americans trotted the hundred feet to Maris, joy replacing their lingering anger over the incident at sea.

"Captain Talbot, sir!" Talbot announced as he reached Maris.

"Lieutenant Ramirez!" added the RIO.

Both men snapped salutes and Maris returned them in a sullen fashion. "Sir," continued Talbot, "we have a formal complaint to make against these Canuck hotshots. They—"

"Lieutenant Billings!" bellowed Maris, stopping the perplexed pilot in mid-sentence.

The Marine behind him took two steps forward, pivoted, and saluted the admiral. "Sir!"

Maris eyed the two air crew in the manner of a high-court judge. Only his verdict was much swifter.

"Put these two men in irons and have them flown back to Norfolk on my plane."

"Aye, aye, sir!" The Marine bawled again and two of his armed comrades stepped forward and produced handcuffs. But before they could affix them, a stunned Talbot stepped up to within a foot of the admiral.

"Sir, please!" he stuttered, "Why are you doing this?"

Maris' eyes narrowed to two rusty, ball bearings as he appraised the aviator. "Captain, your actions have cost the lives of one, and maybe two, fine aviators and, subsequently, have besmirched the good name of the US Navy. Not to mention the loss of a twelve-million-dollar aircraft. So, as far as I'm concerned, and until a military court martial finds otherwise, you are under arrest and your rank, as well as all your privileges, are hereby suspended.

"Lieutenant, get these two out of my sight!"

"Aye, aye, sir!"

The handcuffs were fastened onto the two shaking airmen and the solemn Marines marched them toward the white, US Navy Lear Jet parked on the tarmac.

Vice Admiral Jenkins had discretely stayed away from the scene until the chastising was complete, then he sauntered over to the American. "Admiral Maris, I deeply regret that we didn't have more control over the situation."

"Admiral," the American replied, his voice sounding weaker after the incident, "Canada is a

NATO ally. And although, these days, NATO seems to have all the authority of a wet noodle, we all have to stick together if we want to accomplish anything.

"That F-14 driver disregarded a direct order from your aircraft while inside Canadian airspace. By all that's right, your boys could've shot him down and I would have had to write it off as an unfortunate incident.

"However," Maris continued, a streak of sadness easing into his voice, "the way it worked out was even more costly. That attack not only cost us *four* good crewmen, as well as an expensive airplane, it endangered the lives of every hostage aboard that damn ship. And now the bastards won't even talk to us so we can explain the mishap. *That*, Admiral, is what that captain's actions cost us—so far.

* * * *

"Colonel, that has to be the finest vintage aircraft I've ever seen," remarked an impressed Clint Maris, barely heard over the wail of the twin turbines as he and Colonel Myers approached the front of the shiny, blue-gray Sikhorsky *Sea King* helicopter.

"Admiral," Myers admitted sheepishly, "that's your ride."

"I know," laughed the American, "I was just yankin' your chain! Sometimes a little humor gets me over a tough call."

The helicopter was already fueled and warmed up and the crew completing their pre-flight checklist when the two "brass hats" stopped and waited for boarding clearance. Above a huge, black "409" stenciled on the front of the aircraft, the pilot noticed the two admirals through the cockpit window and waved them forward. The helmeted Maris shook Jenkins' hand and walked around to the starboard side of the *Sea King*.

A crewman in a flight suit, boots and jacket, extended his hand and helped the American up into the helicopter. "Welcome aboard, sir!" he shouted over the engine noise, carefully negotiating himself around his tether, the safety umbilical cord to prevent him from falling out when the helo was on maneuvers with the door open. "My name is Sergeant Gary Turner. I'll get you hooked up to the intercom."

Once plugged in, Maris noticed the four soldiers sitting on the canvas-draped benches of the *Sea King* and waved. The soldiers rose up in the cramped confines and saluted.

"The admiral is aboard, Major," Turner announced into his mike.

"Welcome aboard, Admiral," replied a voice in Maris' headset. Turner then led him past the ASW—antisubmarine warfare—console and up to the cockpit. The TACCO—Tactical Coordination Officer—Captain John Farnham, stood up to greet the admiral and the helmeted head of the pilot pivoted around from his pre-flight check duties, showing a grinning face.

"Welcome aboard, sir, I'm Major Alan Povich and this is the co-pilot, Captain Jim McConnachie." The crew stood up for a moment and shook hands with the American before returning to their stations. Turner then escorted Maris back, explaining a few features of the new ASW system while Povich ran through the remainder of his systems checks.

Farnham joined them in less than a minute. "Admiral," he yelled over the pitch of the engines, "we're just getting clearance for take-off so Sergeant Turner, here, can get you strapped in the back with Colonel Dorey and his unit. The weather is calm for this time of the year so we should have a smooth ride. The HMCS *Thunder Bay* is approximately 350 NM—nautical miles—northeast, in the Davis Strait and our ETA is 2.5 to 3.0 hours, depending on if strong winds move in over Newfoundland. Right now the ceiling is high."

Maris nodded. He could hear the chatter between the pilot and the tower, confirming the flight plan in his headset. They would proceed out of the base airspace at a height of 750 feet due east until they hit the perimeter, then up to 2,000 feet for the duration of the trip.

The high-pitched whine of the turbines increased erasing all fuselage noises and the huge blades began to rotate. As they went around faster ground, the crew, now only discernible as walking reflector vests, backed away under the spinning umbrella.

Turner assisted Admiral Maris to strap himself in and moved over to check on Dorey's group. Then with a quick half-step worthy of a trained dancer he deftly maneuvered around the cage which held the dipping sonar transducer and moved forward to talk to the co-pilot. Returning again he waved to the ground crew and closed the large bay door.

"Crew secure?" Povich's voice came through the headphones. One by one each crew member replied with their station and "check," with Turner answering for the soldiers and the admiral.

"Alright, final checklist before takeoff."

"Roger," replied McConnachie, who went over the various instruments and controls.

"Bring back full throttle."

"Full throttle," replied McConnachie and the *Sea King* began to vibrate under the power of the twin turbine engines.

"Prepare for lift off."

"Roger."

"Tower, request permission for lift-off."

The air traffic controller paused for a moment, then answered, "Merlin 409, you are clear for lift-off.

"Roger, tower."

With that the already-trembling helicopter began to shake like an old car with a front-end problem and all those who were not air crew gritted their teeth, waiting for it to fly apart. But the venerable old bird gingerly broke free of the ground and rose up into the pale, summer night, out toward the smooth, dark sea.

"Tower, permission to start climbing to cruising altitude. Over."

"Uh, permission granted Merlin 409. Please note that there are no weather changes at this time. Over."

"Roger, tower. Merlin 409 out."

"Roger, Merlin. Safe journey. Tower out."

* * * *

For the second time that day Tom Dorey felt the chest-deep thumping and numbing vibration that a passenger experiences while traveling on a cruising military helicopter. Except for the seasoned air crew, very few riders are truly comfortable on one, he mused. But, as the veteran of dozens of landings in numerous types of helicopters, he felt truly at ease on the *Sea King* as a soldier would with an old friend accompanying him into conflict.

Across from him, not exuding the same enthusiasm with the ride, was the somber face of Admiral Maris. "*Colonel* Dorey, isn't it?" the American shouted, his voice sounding hollow as his mid-range vocal sound waves were distorted by the wide range of frequencies invading the airframe. Other tones were lost due to the deadening effect of the acoustic material lining the interior of the helicopter; and also through "phase cancellation"—a phenomenon that occurs when two wave forms of equal frequency and opposite polarity are combined, eliminating that frequency.

"*Lieutenant-Colonel*, sir," he yelled back, his words quickly melting into the din. Then he added with a mischievous snicker. "They gave the rank back to me before I got aboard."

Dorey looked a lot more commanding to the admiral after he had exchanged his dry-cleaning duds for an airborne jumpsuit.

"Gave it back?" smirked the American. "Were you busted?"

"Big time, sir," chuckled Dorey. His voice bordered on the "cartoonish" side in the noisy confines of the helicopter.

Confused, Maris leaned over so that he could hear the soldier better. "Can I ask why?"

Dorey shrugged, a wry smile widening his face. "I went on the offensive in a couple of peacekeeping operations."

Maris scowled, trying to sort out the puzzle placed before him without sounding too nosy. The Canadian chuckled. "Sorry, Admiral, I shouldn't be so casual. I manhandled a Bosnian-Serb officer in the former-Yugoslavia and then I gunned down some Sudanese rebels in the southern Sudan. And you can probably guess the incidents didn't do much for the image of the boys in the powder-blue berets, or," he added, "our own airborne regiment. Some pissed-off politicians are for disbanding the unit."

Maris' dusky eyes widened in surprise, almost twinkling in the thick pouches above his cheeks. "I heard about that. The Pentagon called it a 'snow job'. It's a shame that all the good work you did would go down the tubes just for a couple of judgment calls from foreign journalists. Especially since neither of those places is a cut-and-dried example of peacekeeping."

"Canada is sort of a 'peacekeeping factory', Admiral. Aggression, even in self-defense, is considered, in some political circles, the result of 'faulty equipment'. And those parts are scrapped."

"I see. So, you mean to tell me that the 'part' was *you*?"

Dorey shrugged, suddenly wishing he had not quit smoking along with his self-banishment from alcohol. He was dying for a cigarette right about now. "Well, a couple of my men got a burst in before they were hit and I got away a clip or two from my C-7, what you would call an M-16."

Through the muddy light the Canadian glanced up at the dormant ASW—antisubmarine warfare—gear to his right. The TACCO was up in the cockpit conferring with the two pilots.

"You lost some guys, didn't you?"

"Three. And five wounded. One lost his arm."

"But it was self-defense, right son?"

Dorey's head nodded solemnly, pumping his fingers together to ease the urge for a cigarette. After two months he shouldn't have *nic fits* he thought. "The Sudanese had been raiding the border villages. They were gangs of kids, really, but heavily armed kids like the ones that knocked down that *Black Hawk* of yours in Mogadishu."

Maris cracked his knuckles at the remembrance of the American bodies being dragged through the streets of the Somalian capital after their helicopter was shot down. It always amazed him how such heavily filmed, gruesome scenes could sway his government's policies overnight.

Now, they, like the Canadian across from him, would never be remembered for saving millions of lives through their brave and orderly famine relief—just chastised for being overexuberant in a few cases.

"From the radio reports and *recce* patrols we knew they were getting bolder and would probably test our 'feeding station.' We had an efficient perimeter and the nightly intruders were easily scared off by flares and such. Then, one night, the incursions just stopped. For two additional nights everything was quiet. I knew something was up, so had all the men prepped for trouble.

"On the fourth day, we saw a group of refugees coming down the road past the hundreds of little refugee hovels that had sprung up outside the camp. Our interpreter, a wonderful Somali woman educated in London, went out to greet them.

"When she got close to them she stopped and looked around at me with terror in her eyes. Instinctively, I barked out an order but the 'refugees' were already slipping guns out from under their robes." Dorey snapped the knuckles on his right hand as the memory tore at him.

"She was in the line of fire so we couldn't help her. Their first burst cut her in half; her face just disappeared in a puff of red. Then they started spraying everything that moved: women, children, us. I didn't have to order our guys to shoot, we all just responded. No one dropped or took cover. They would have flanked us if we had flinched. The guys just stood tall and fired like they were at the 'Gunfight at the O.K. Corral.' That was the deciding factor. It intimidated the rebels and they began falling back.

"We were taking hits but we kept reloading and

shooting. In a short time, the surviving attackers scattered, but we were too shot up to chase them. Patching ourselves up, we waited for another attack but, thankfully, it never came. I guess we'd mauled them too badly. But it wasn't until nearly dark that a relief helicopter came in carrying Dutch troops."

Maris cleared his throat. "Jesus, what a firefight! But what was all the fuss about with the United Nations? You acted in a normal procedure, returning fire on a bunch of ambushers and thus saving your command, as well as the whole village. Them bastards would have murdered everyone."

"Admiral, by the time the Dutch got there, the attackers' weapons were gone. Disappeared. They slipped back and got them while we were regrouping further back."

"So?"

"So, what the Dutch found was a bunch of fifteen and sixteen-year-old kids dead without any sign that they had attacked us."

"Look, over there sixteen is *old.* And surely your wounds and those of the men—"

"Same caliber, 5.56mm. We knew they were stolen weapons but word was discreetly passed on to some journalists that the Canadians had been drinking heavily. And supposedly, they said, we were angry at 'being kept out in the desert with a bunch of niggers' instead of 'in the cool mountains of Canada drinking beer.' Certain elements of the foreign press ate it up. Their official story was that we got drunk and began shooting the refugees and then those of our own that wouldn't go along with it. Our own losses and wounds were as a result of drunken infighting."

The American drove his left fist into the palm

of his right hand. "Yeah, and that news hit my plate like what it was: utter bullshit! No one in my office believed—"

"No?"

"Look, son, what we heard at the Pentagon, off the record, was that you got into a firefight with these rebels and some civilians were hit by 'friendly fire.'"

Dorey reached down and pulled a leather-sheathed, KABAR knife from a long pocket on the legging of his jumpsuit. Holding it on the blade end he handed it to the admiral.

"Do SEAL's hit what they shoot at, Admiral?"

"Damn straight!" he exclaimed, taking a pair of glasses out of his shirt pocket and perching them on his nose to examine the weapon.

"And so do the Paras. And nothing more," replied Dorey.

Slowly and deliberately, the American raised his reading glasses and peered at Dorey's face, a ghostly apparition under the faint light of the interior instruments.

"*You* were a SEAL?"

"April 1971 to late '72, Admiral."

"Jesus H! I was flying A-6 Intruders off the *Coral Sea* then!"

"I was never on the *Coral Sea*, sir. Just an assortment of river boats."

"Rotated out?"

"Nope. 'Bouncing Betty.'" Dorey pointed at his deformed cheek and a healed scar across his lower neck.

Regarding the sickly-white crescent under the Canadian's eye, Maris solemnly extended his hand and firmly shook Dorey's.

"I'm real glad you're aboard, Colonel...and there's nothing 'light' about your rank!"

5.

HMCS Thunder Bay: July 4th,
1:57 a.m. Atlantic Time; 085700Z;
Davis Strait, 69° N Latitude,
64°30 W Longitude

The *Sea King* slammed onto the green deck, jarring its riders.

"Down! Down! Down!"

With that affirmation by the pilot, the probe on the belly of the helicopter locked into the "bear trap." This was a clamp-like apparatus built into the flight deck of the patrol frigate designed to secure the hovering, seven-ton aircraft after it had been winched down to the deck by cable. After the occupants had disembarked, and the blades retracted, the nitrogen-gas-powered "bear trap" crept toward the bow along a slot running down the center of the deck, towing the helicopter directly into the large hangar.

After thirty years in the navy, the American admiral never lost the thrill of a night landing, even if it were dropping on the deck in a helicopter. At first, the golf-green surface of the landing pad on the HMCS *Thunder Bay*, awash in halogen lights on the dark night, looked like a tiny gas station; an oasis to those who just spent two hours in the air over rocky land surfaces and, later, the sub-Arctic ocean. As the helicopter closed the distance, the scene changed to that of a park. And, with a little imagination, the spectacle could have been what the occupants of the Goodyear blimp saw when they approached a football stadium for a night game.

Then the flight officer's station, a turret-like dome of Plexiglas embedded on the starboard side of the deck just in front of the hangar, became distinguishable as well as the flight observation mini-bridge, above and to the port side of the hangar—where the deck lights are supervised and fire control is coordinated. The hangar itself, open in readiness, glowed red like the maw of a giant sea creature waiting to devour the firefighters, space-suited figures waiting on the edges of the deck.

As the frigate was moving at nearly its top speed of 30.8 knots, each intricate operation of the landing—usually done at much lower speeds—was painstakingly thorough, requiring the mettle of every crewman.

Finally, the *Sea King* wafted over the green mat at twenty feet and dropped the winch line, the umbilical that guided the aircraft to the security of the deck. Facing the helo crew, at point-blank range, was the formidable Phalanx Close-In Weapons System, the last chance against any missile that might get by the ship's outer defensive perimeter. The Phalanx's automatic Gatling gun—which fires at 3000 rounds a minute—appeared like a cannon sticking out of a miniature farm silo. Then the pilot crash-landed the aircraft onto the deck, which was standard procedure when landing on a frigate.

"Welcome to the *Thunder Bay*, Admiral. I'm Commander Greg Smart. I trust your ride was smooth, under the circumstances?"

"Not bad, Commander. And I had good company."

Smart, trim-bearded and just a few months over forty-five, struggled to keep his cap on in the vortex of air at the stern of his fast-moving ship. He pumped the admiral's hand and quickly led him into the cavernous hangar. Out of the wind, Dorey and his squad, the flight crew and Maris were helped out of their bulky "Mustang" survival suits by the ship's crewmen. Once they were approaching open water, the commander thought it would be a good idea if the "guests" were so attired. As much as Maris grumbled he knew it was prudent when flying in Arctic waters. With the hissing of a giant snake, the "bear trap", like an iron mole, began pulling the *Sea King* into the red cave.

"Admiral, this is my XO, Lieutenant-Commander Henri Lemaire."

"Welcome aboard, sir! We have food and coffee set up in the mess, Admiral," offered Lemaire. Lemaire was a half-foot shorter than the other two officers and sported a dark, pencil-thin mustache.

"Thanks, son. Look, if it's all the same to you, Commander, could I have a bite to eat and a coffee on the bridge? It's been a while since I've sat in on a *real* operation." Maris stretched, relieved to be out of the hot, orange suit.

"Certainly, sir," replied Smart. Lemaire saluted and disappeared through the hatch at the bow-end of the hangar. The rest followed, taking the inner corridors to the bridge.

* * * *

"This is a nicely laid-out bridge, Commander! Very clean and easy to move around without bumping into things, like dozens of extra seamen!" Maris chuckled at his last remark. "After an aircraft carrier, it's sort of like riding in a compact convertible."

"We like to equate it to a Porsche, Admiral, and if we had the time I'd show you how she turns on a dime and accelerates, somewhat like a big PT-boat."

"That's it!" remarked the American. "This is like a jumbo-sized PT-boat. Fast and, by the looks of your weapons systems, *deadly*."

Smart regarded the amused looks from his bridge crew, replacing the awkwardness that they usually showed on the arrival of such a high-ranking VIP aboard their ship; especially since their ship hadn't yet been commissioned.

"Commander!" interjected Lieutenant Biggs, bounding up from his seat. "We have a sonar reading at fifty-four degrees west, sixty-three north. It's about ten miles off the starboard bow."

"Great timing! Proceed at present course and speed for another five minutes then cut the turbines and engage the diesel. We have to conserve fuel if we want to follow that damn ship any further. Where's that tanker, anyway?"

"Presently its refueling the icebreaker CCGS *Terry Fox* off Clyde River. On diesel we'll be there tomorrow afternoon."

"Good timing again. And the *Canadian*?"

"Still running at twenty-five knots, just north of Clyde River."

"To match her we'll have to line up another fuel ship. But if she goes into Lancaster Sound we'll need.... Oh to hell with it! Anderson, get me that Fergus again on the blower."

* * * *

CCGS Canadian, 75 miles east of Clyde River, Baffin Island;
Davis Strait, 70°N Latitude, 64°W Longitude.

"It's the commander of that frigate that's following us," remarked a fatigued Bill Barrett at the NavCom MOD.

Vasiliev took a sip of his coffee, surveying the brilliance of the northern lights through the glass dome above him. "It's unbelievable to see them so clearly this high up. Any further up toward the Pole and they usually just disappear!"

The Russian put down his cup and ordered Barrett to connect him with the frigate. "Yes, Captain *Whatever*, and what gems of wisdom do you have to offer me tonight?"

Smart's voice was smooth and relaxed over the bridge's sound system. "I believe we haven't met, sir. My name is Commander Greg Smart—"

"Yes, yes. Get to the point." Vasiliev's voice was irritable.

"Well, sir, I have the responsibility of escorting you in order to make sure that no more incidents take place...like the one with the American fighters. Y'know, I'm like a shepherd."

"And so you can get close enough to pull something brave but, otherwise, stupid, I take it?"

"Negative, sir. If you check your COUNT data-based system, you'll find that we are *not* even armed."

"What?" Vasiliev pointed to Barrett and the navigations specialist worked the keypad on the console. First, an engineer's diagram of the Canadian patrol frigate design appeared on screen, detailing all the weapons systems in an "exploded" view.

"Yes, sir," continued Smart, "We were on 'engine and systems trials' when we were ordered to 'escort' you."

Barrett changed *pages* and the side views of the twelve Canadian frigates appeared. With the pointer, Barrett isolated the last one, the *Thunder Bay*. It then appeared on the refreshed screen with all its data below. Dimitri scanned the particulars and smiled.

"Well, Commander Smart, it seems they've given you an *unloaded gun!*" He laughed for a few seconds, his mirth ending in a low groan.

"Yes, sir. As I said, we carry nothing that could

be harmful to your ship."

"Fine. Now tell me, Commander, why would they send an unarmed ship after me."

About ten seconds of silence followed Vasiliev's query.

"Because we're the only ones around." The reply was sheepish.

* * * *

Smart heard another hearty laugh through speakers on his bridge. "Commander, you may tag along. In fact, I think it's a capital idea to have a reasonable voice behind us. We'll even slow down so you can catch up."

Then the voice turned cold. "But I warn you, if I even suspect you have a strike force on board, or a helicopter with missiles, I'll put a *Silkworm* down your throat. Understand?"

"Yes," returned Smart. "I assure you, as one officer to another, that no strike force will attempt to attack you from *my* ship and that we have no helicopter with missiles."

"Then come ahead, commander. Besides, I think the company of another military man will be most stimulating. Out."

No one spoke on the bridge until Maris' booming voice shattered the silence. "Christ! You mean you have no weapons?"

Smart shook his head. "None that would hurt that big boat."

"Well, where in the hell is the rest of your damned navy? I know you have ships because I saw the status report at the Pentagon!"

"Well," Greg started, sounding tired, "half the frigates are on the west coast. And of the other half in Maritime Command, two are in dry dock, one is with your navy, and our only supply ship is helping to enforce the embargo off Haiti, and the

last two are in their namesakes cities, Toronto and
Montreal, for the Canada Day celebrations. They're
open for public inspection and photo opportuni-
ties with politicians." Smart's last sentence dripped
in sarcasm. "Both are said to have wrapped up
their public relations assignments and are, at this
time, under way."

"As for the destroyers, one is in dry dock and
the other was decommissioned two months ago
and is now awaiting towing to its new assignment
at a razor blade factory in Malaysia."

Maris whistled and shook his head in disappointment. "Jesus H. Christ! They're scalping you
too, huh?"

Smart was silent, now self-conscious at spout-
ing off in front of an American admiral, as well in
the presence of his own crew.

"Commander," continued Maris, "I know what's
happening, and I truly feel for you and your forces.
We've had to tie up two whole carrier groups and
mothball a swack of great ships. And I don't know
where it's going to end either.

"Funny thing, though. The world doesn't appear to me to be getting any safer and here our
governments are destroying our capacity to defend ourselves."

Smart chuckled. "Come on, Admiral, I'll show
you the *real Thunder Bay*, the 'cook's tour'."

"Damn straight!" The admiral moved toward
the bulkhead with Smart and then stopped unexpectedly, a perplexed look on his face. "Commander, what about this sonar reading? You gonna
let me in on that?"

The Canadian skipper shook his bearded head.
"Sir, all I can tell you is that it'll all become clear at
0730 Zulu—Greenwich Mean Time—in two
hours.... Oh, by the way, Admiral, Happy 4th of

July!"

Maris smiled. For the first time since long before he was a Boy Scout, he had forgotten his country's birthday.

CHAPTER 6

1.

July 4th, 0605:00 Zulu; Yellowknife,
Northwest Territories.

The two men in pastel trousers and polo shirts, sitting up at the bar, laughed as they teased the bartender, a twenty-two-year-old college student from Saskatoon, Saskatchewan. They were having the time of their lives, leaving all their worries and deadlines below the sixtieth parallel while they fished and played golf in the "Land of the Midnight Sun." The bartender didn't mind either; they were tipping her three bucks a round.

Another two men were down on the lower part of the small lounge, the shorter one staring out across the miles of stunted trees that struggled for life on the rocky landscape. He adjusted his baseball cap and leaned back in the chair, discreetly checking the couple ten feet away on the next level. They were holding hands and far too interested in what was going to happen later than to eavesdrop on the two men below.

"Alright then, it's set. Tomorrow at 8:30 a.m. we do it while everyone's entertaining some shareholders on a fishing trip," said the taller, bearded man.

"So we leave today?"

"In one hour we'll meet at the hangar. We'll file a routine flight plan to Spence Bay. We'll improvise after that."

"The pick-up?"

"Easy. The *ice* is out for show and tell but there'll be nobody with guns, just computer disks. We just walk out with it."

"Smokin'."

2.

"ETA in five minutes, Commander."

"Right, let's do it," replied Greg Smart, stroking his beard. Then he stared at Admiral Maris, letting the American's inquisitive eyes meet his. "Okay, Admiral, come on with me. There's something back here that you may *never* have seen before...'cause I sure in the hell haven't!"

Mystified at the Canadian's clandestine manner Admiral Maris followed the commander back through the bulkheads of the frigate, exiting past the helicopter hangar onto the windy flight deck.

"We're just into Baffin Bay, seventy-two degrees north latitude, approximately fifty nautical miles north of Clyde River, Baffin Island, and five degrees and some minutes north of the Arctic Circle, which sits at sixty-six degrees, thirty minutes. We usually have an initiation, sort of a 'hazing,' for those who have never crossed the Arctic Circle but, under the circumstances, we'll have to invite you back for that one. Besides, with this new crew, we'd be hazing for two days."

The admiral, just awakened from a six-hour sleep, grunted in mock amusement. Not having spent much time in the north, he was uncomfortable with the continual presence of light.

"As you can see, the sun never went down. It just scratched the horizon at around 2300 hours and came back up at 0100. Quite a view, isn't it?"

As the ship progressed into the Davis Strait the sea was calmer, even more so than when the helicopter landed, although spotted with numerous *growlers*—small icebergs.

"Aren't those icebergs dangerous to this ship?"

"Affirmative, especially at this speed. Lieutenant McGuire and the ASW team have their hands full right now computing the size of these things below the water. That's why the ship's been doing some quick course changes."

Smart checked his watch again. Then he surveyed his black-suited crew, nervously reminding himself that many of these men had never before attempted a lateral transferal of personnel. He, himself, had only overseen the process a few times when he was XO on one of the earlier frigates. But never at this speed.

"There! Starboard side!" The cry came from a sailor with binoculars above them on the hangar. In one motion, Smart jammed the binoculars to his eyes and beheld a group of black sticks moving through the syrupy water with a white, roostertail wake furrowing behind. Then he passed the binoculars to the puzzled American who buried the glasses in his meaty hands and pressed them to his eyes.

"Jesus, that's a sub! But how did the—"

"It's not one of yours, Admiral...." Commander Smart cut in. It was time to bare his soul to the American officer. His orders had compelled him to reveal the information only when the submarine surfaced. For all intents and purposes, especially up here in the Arctic, this was close enough. "It's *ours*."

"Yours?" mouthed the admiral, watching the objects speed through the sea like a group of very skinny water skiers. "One of your old, diesel Oberons?"

"No, sir, she's almost brand new. Its an *Akula*-class—"

"Russian?" The binoculars fell from Maris' eyes like they were cement. The wide-eyed look through the puffy, jowled face said it all.

Smart swallowed hard. Now was the time for, what Admiral Jenkins briefed him as, "diplomatic damage control," a tall order for a mere commander, Smart sighed. The forces had a public relations division for that task. But then, at this moment, he was the highest ranking naval officer north of the Arctic Circle, and Maris was his "guest."

"Well, sir, it's like this," Smart said matter-of-factly as the wake of the periscope grew in size, "the Russian-Canadian icebreaker venture was modified by our prime minister to also include the last *Akula* launched from the Komsomolsk shipyard, before it was completely changed over to a civilian operation."

Fatigue now usurping his shock, the admiral exhaled slowly, his lower jaw dropping as he turned his eyes back to the masts of the approaching submarine. When he again put down the glasses Smart produced a manila envelope from under his arm and held it out to Maris.

"Admiral, if it makes you feel any better, I was just informed of this myself, via two information packages that arrived on the same *Sea King* with you. I opened the first one and my instructions were to open the seal on this second package, in your presence, at 0200."

The American slowly ripped the seal on the envelope and scanned the documents.

"There's the sail!" cried a crew member.

The remark was greeted with enthusiasm from the black-bereted sailors, who clapped and cheered as the dark rectangle of the submarine's "fairwater" slid above the gentle swells like a small, black boat.

As the surfacing submarine approached, Maris lowered the documents and sighed, a rush of air escaping loudly through his lips. "You know, Commander, there was a time when everyone knew what side they were on. It was *us* versus the *Commies*; nice and simple. Now, it says here that Canada bought this sub to protect its sovereignty in these northern channels that America, and most of the world, thinks is open water. Well sir, things just got a lot more complicated."

* * * *

The commotion over the sub's arrival had just begun when Jim Dorey and his three comrades arrived at the rear of the hangar dressed in camouflaged, Arctic gear: white fatigues with various darker shades to break up their silhouettes in snow and ice conditions. In an officious tone, he read off a list as each man silently checked his kit for items such as knives, sidearms, ammunition, explosives, navigational aids and survival gear —and a hand-held rocket launcher.

The squad—Dorey, Lieutenant Brad Flemming, Sergeant Terry James and Corporal Ed Anderson— walked ahead to the mouth of the hangar and watched the submarine grow in length under its tear-drop sail until the stern pod appeared, indicating that almost all of the 113-meter boat was on the surface. The only parts remaining submerged were the seven-bladed propeller and the extreme bow section.

"Jesus!" remarked Flemming. "It looks like the *fastback* version of the Russian navy!"

"Yeah, like a '67 Mustang," added James, twisting his red, handlebar mustache.

"*Fast* isn't the right word when you pull thirty-five knots underwater," added Dorey.

"And they want us to ride in that hot rod?" Anderson's quip rang with excitement, his head a glowing dome barely hidden by his "flat-top" haircut.

Amidst all the crew's excitement, Commander Smart walked through the hangar and approached Dorey, a wry smile filling up his bearded face. "I wish I was going with you, Colonel. In fact I'd give up my command for just a joyride. Not really, but the temptation is there!

"We can proceed with the transfer as soon as the lines are attached, oh...in about ten minutes. I'm sorry I can slow down much because, even though I know we're shielded from the icebreaker's radar by those 'growlers,' who knows what they can see with that new low-level radar. As well, I can spread some anti-radar chaff around, and that sub's acoustic coating should at least confuse it, but then anything out of the ordinary might spook that bunch."

"Thanks, Commander, especially for the great spread."

"Yeah, well, Maris and his two Marines weren't too hungry after that *Sea King* ride so I'm glad it didn't go to waste."

"Later," Smart chuckled and shook Jim's extended hand.

"Later. Colonel...look, I hear you're from the South Shore. How about driving up to Halifax for a beer at the Fleet Club, say, Labor Day?"

"Sounds like a date." I wouldn't mind a root beer with a frigate driver, he thought.

"Oh, and by the way, Colonel, congratulations on your promotion...and nobody I know believes any of that shit that went down in the Sudan."

"Thanks again, but at least there's not a hell of a lot they can do to me up here, is there?"

As Greg shook his head, the large, dark figure of Chief Petty Officer Warren Mills trotted up. "We're all set!"

* * * *

Dorey heard the *whiz* of the mountaineers' clasp as gravity hurled him down the bowed, nylon cable toward a group of sailors on the deck of the cruising Russian submarine. The drama associated with sliding down a slippery wet, thirty-meter cable between two parallel ships maintaining twenty knots ranked up there with some of his most difficult parachute jumps. As the light-green swell rose up to meet him, he gripped the neck of the pulley and straddled the dripping line, using his boots to slow him down. The small-looking crewmen on the sub began growing to full size at a rapid rate and then, *clunk;* his boots hit the rubberized surface. Then the Canadian felt hands all over him.

"*Nostrovya!*" exclaimed Dorey to his helpers, the adrenaline still pumping from his fast descent.

"Save it, Grunt, we're Canadian," came the casual reply as they steadied him on the gently rocking surface. To any soldier or airman, "Grunt" was a fighting word—Government Reject, Unfit for Naval Training. But not today.

Dorey chuckled nervously. "That's *Colonel* Grunt to you."

3.

**July 5th, 1327:00 Zulu; CCGS Canadian,
Lancaster Sound, 74°N Latitude,
75°W *Longitude.***

"The range of the chopper is now two-hundred-fifty miles."

"Let's get it on screen, Mr. Barrett."

Bill Barrett pressed the required symbols on the MOD display and a large diagram of a helicopter appeared at the top right-hand corner of the COUNT screen. Vasiliev then read the information supplied with the picture out loud, as if trying to reassure himself that his plan was going well. "*Bell Ranger*, registration Gulf, X-ray, Bravo, Charlie. Owner: Northwest Territories Air Survey, Yellowknife, NWT. Flight Plan: Pellat Lake; Bathurst Inlet; Cambridge Bay; Spence Bay…. As they say in your country, *Bingo!*"

He jumped up from the captain's chair and surveyed the small bridge crew. Annette Potvin, Bill Barrett and Dennis Barnes were all that were left. The rest were in detention in the Officer's Mess, carefully watched by Tom Parton. The Russian keyed the intercom and the husky voice of Bart Jesso boomed through the sound system. "Jesso!"

"It all checks out, Bart. But just to be on the safe side, keep a lock on it. We can't leave anything to chance. *Out.*"

The Russian then walked down to Barrett's console and, leaning over the navigations officer, he firmly squeezed the man's shoulder. "Bill, you are doing a grand job. Just a few more hours and we'll be off your ship so, please, bear with me and hold down the temptation to be heroic, okay?"

The black officer nodded but he never believed

the part about the "few more hours." Fergus had made the same promise.

"Good. Now, have you plotted the sonar readings and *Ice View*—ice density—reports?"

"I have," the officer said, emotionless, but holding back his growing anger. But despite his lack of sleep and edginess, the Haligonian held his tongue. Barrett had sailed with some pretty tough captains in his Coast Guard career, but none had the authoritative tone of Vasiliev. The Russian never threatened or coerced. He had no shepherding gunman, like Fergus did. And the only accomplices seemed to be Cummings, Jesso, the missile launcher, Harold, Farouk; who was resting after his beating, and Tom; who was guarding the prisoners. But he never called them except for information.

No, thought the Canadian officer, it was the sheer power in the man's aura, as well as his physical size, which precluded any thoughts of reprisal from the 180-pound Barrett, regardless of his pugilistic skills. Barrett had been a Canadian lightweight boxing champion and couldn't remember ever fearing a larger man. He had grown up in Halifax's north-end, fighting bigger kids and, later, men, until he began boxing. But this Dimitri was different: he had the air of a cold-blooded killer.

"None yet, except for the popping and grinding of the ice pack."

Satisfied, Vasiliev walked back to the captain's console.

* * * *

As he carefully extracted the insulation from his listening post, Jimmy McDougall's stomach growled from lack of food. To douse the loud inner protests, the Newfoundlander poured some more water down his throat, shaking off the urge to run down to the galley and surrender so he could stuff himself with pancakes.

However, despite his forced *fast*, his back felt better now that he had bravely ventured out of the Com Room and slept in the electrical supply room, just down the hall. Behind the rows of spare part racks, Jimmy had stretched out on a veritable sea of "cloud-soft" acoustic-foam rubber. And, just in case someone walked in while he was sleeping, the wiry ex-fisherman had pulled a mountain of sheets over him to dampen any snoring.

It seemed strange to him that not one of the hijackers had ventured to the Electrical Floor; there hadn't been a soul on the level during his two-day occupancy. The elevator was used fairly often, but went right down past his level to either the Officer's Mess floor, which also contained the highest breezeway to both the scientific and passenger superstructures, or past it to the main deck and engineering. It was the same when it came up.

So far, from his listening post, he was able to discern that the Planet Guardians were no longer in control of the ship. This he had keyed out on the HF, along with updates garnered from listening to the hostages and the guards in his perch above them. However, for all his bravado, he was finding that his spying was far less effective than he thought. According to television reports, from the monitor in the mess that was continually on, it seemed that the media was finding out about the hijackers as quickly as he because Fergus had been telling them his intentions. *So why am I sending these archaic messages?* he thought. *Why don't I just hide out until they leave the ship? Or surrender and get something to eat?*

But that was before the destruction of the French ship and the two American aircraft. Now his temptation to do nothing until rescue, or surrender, was usurped by a greater thought; *they might destroy the ship and kill all the hostages.*

Kneeling, he slowly slid the familiar tile off its mounting and lowered his head, letting only one eye slide below the ceiling level of the galley. At first, the glare from the sunlit room caused him to retract his head so his eyes could get used to the brightness. Then he tried again, figures appearing as his irises focused.

There was a new batch of, what appeared to be, hostages. A diminutive blonde woman was asleep on the shoulder of a sleeping blonde man in one of the booths facing the bow windows. Beside them was another sleeping figure, a big man: Jerry, the radio guy. Then came the card-playing duo of journalists, and over to the far end of the room, Captain MacIsaac, who was watching the television with Frances Pilotte and Judy MacDonald. All three looked in need of a refreshing dip in the pool in the passenger area. Asleep in one of the chairs was the Italian radar engineer that he had been introduced to at launching ceremonies.

Finally, the guard, a young brush cut, was playing solitaire in front of another television showing a Bruce Willis movie. Beyond the windows, the ocean was scattered with sheets of ice. *Ice? Christ preserve us*, he sighed, almost too loudly, *we're in the goddamn Arctic!*

As if the good Lord was trying to torture him, the smell of eggs and fresh coffee wafted up, almost causing him to lose his grip. Someone was busy cooking in the galley but it was out of his line-of-sight. *Who?* After careful consideration the Newfoundland politician raised up his head and carefully replaced the roofing materials. Then he sat, cross-legged, on the floor for a few minutes, pondering a new idea. *Why not?*

McDougall crept around three banks of processors before kneeling down again on the hard, marble-colored tiles. Reaching down on the floor between two electronics racks he lifted up one plate, repeating the methodical procedure of taking up the ceiling tile on the level below. Then, once more, he paused before lifting the acoustic panel to the galley.

However, when he pulled the square out of its grooves this time, the edge of the brittle acoustic board caught on a bundle of wire and a small piece broke off. As if he were living in slow motion, he watched helplessly as the triangular chunk fell down and bounced off the stainless-steel ventilation hood that hung over a trio of fat fryers. Then he shuddered as a hand picked up the piece and turned it over, examining it.

McDougall wanted to pull his head away, but he couldn't. If this was to be the end of his holdout, then so be it. He was too tired and hungry to live like a ship's rat anymore. *Christ protect you, Jimmy, this is it!*

His eyes first beheld a large belly entering the square field of vision below him. Then a huge face looked up.

It was Eric Johansen.

4.

HMCS Thunder Bay. Baffin Bay:
74° N Latitude, 74°30 W Longitude.

"It's the same scratchy Morse we've been hearing since the 3rd, Commander."

Greg Smart lifted the cup of herbal tea to his

furry mouth, inhaling the cinnamon vapor. The continual daylight had messed up his regular cycle of sleep and now he had insomnia. So, for the six hours since the submarine left, he had desperately tried to flush the two days' worth of caffeine from his system.

"What've you got today?"

The radio operator, Lieutenant Robert Follett, hidden behind the XO's station, scrawled out letters on a piece of paper, turning the percussive signals in his headphones into words.

"How long before we run out of gas?"

"At twenty-five knots, less than an hour, sir," replied Lieutenant-Commander Henri Lemaire. "Then we're on diesel."

Smart winced. Running the twin gas turbines at twenty-four knots had almost sucked the tanks dry. When they switched over to the single Pickstiel diesel engine, the ship could make barely nineteen knots—and that was pushing it.

"So, how long before we have visual?"

"We should have it now but there's that 'berg field up ahead. It's so thick we don't even have a radar image. But based on the GPS readings, and verified with the reports from the *Herc's*, the icebreaker is just under twelve miles away at seventy-three degrees, forty-five minutes latitude."

"They're probably turning into Lancaster Sound right now."

"Affirmative, Commander," added Follett, now finished with his deciphering and back to monitoring satellite surveillance information. "They've just passed seventy-five west longitude."

"Well, nice to see that the 'space junk' is playing ball with us, at least."

Follett chuckled. There was nothing like a trial run to watch the "bugs" come crawling out of the bulkheads and into new equipment. The screen of the Loran 'C' positioning system, so precise and clear in port, was now a jumble of computer characters bouncing around on the glowing, green screen above the chart table.

"Speed?"

"That last C-130 from Namao puts them at just under twenty knots."

"Hallelujah!" cried the commander, his hot tea spilling on his white shirt. "That fish-lovin' bastard is slowing down and letting us keep up to him!"

"Uh, Commander," interrupted Follett, a glum look on his bulldog face, "if any of this HF *drivel* is correct, that Planet Guardian bunch is not in control anymore."

"What?" The surprise caused a twitch on Smart's face. His dark eyes, purged of their luster by lack of sleep, resembled those of a deep-sea fish.

"It says here that a Russian named Vasiliev has taken control. He's the one who steered the ship north." Follett passed the paper up to Greg, who scanned it and then folded the message, slipping it in his pocket.

"Get a coded message out. They'll probably pick it up, but they won't know the contents."

* * * *

CCGS Canadian, Lancaster Sound

"What was that message you sent out in code?"

In another situation the voice would have been pleasant, maybe even friendly, but in this circumstance, Smart could feel the hardness behind it, especially over the small, mid-frequency, heavy bridge speakers. This confirmed the Morse message in his mind. The man he spoke to now was *not* a member "filling in while Fergus slept." He was running the show.

"It was a ship's status report," he lied. "Regulations state that such reports are classified and no one gave me the authorization to change the procedure during this 'exercise'. Do you want me to read it out to you?"

The chuckle was dry, but cold, like a night wind in the Arizona mountains. "I suppose you have one all written out for me, don't you?"

"Status report, July 5th—"

"Forget it, Commander. What do you know, anyway. But answer me this, and let me remind you that if I don't like this answer I won't let you follow me through the ice pack, alright?"

"Affirmative."

"Why did you suddenly slow down?"

The Canadian cleared his throat. "We have three engines: one Peilstick cruise diesel for cruising and two GE gas turbines. To keep with your speed of twenty-seven knots we were running the two turbines, usually reserved for combat or other special circumstances such as search and rescue. As we are brand-new and supposed to be on a 'shakedown cruise' we had to power down below eighteen knots for thirty minutes to check the systems...."

"And to do what else?" the voice baited.

"What else could we do? Did you pick up any helicopters?" Smart's tone bordered on sarcasm. Wincing at his unprofessionalism, he made a mental note not to repeat the slight. "Sorry, sir. I'm a bit tired."

"Apology and explanation accepted." The voice, far from conciliatory, reverberated through every speaker on every deck within the frigate. It was as hard and hollow as the bulkheads themselves. "Because if I had detected a helicopter you would be just another bobbing piece of flotsam in the sea and your ship a sinking mess."

Smart shuddered again, thankful that the ice-breaker's COUNT system had not been pro-grammed to sort through the shroud of chaff that he had ordered deployed to shroud the ship from radar waves during the transference. If the low-level radar had enough range to pick up the *Thunder Bay*, at almost one-hundred nautical miles away, he had hoped that the millions of ejected particles would have appeared as interference, a temporary spotting. God knows what kind of "cloak" that COUNT used to sneak a Silkworm in on that French frigate. The satellite report showed that the *Montclair* was there one minute; *and then it wasn't!*

"So, Commander, since everyone knows where we are, anyway, and I enjoy our brief conversa-tions, I will let you follow us into Lancaster Sound for as long as our 'protest' lasts. I'll let you ap-proach to within six miles so you can follow us into the ice pack.

"*But*," he chuckled, an odd accent hanging off the word, "there's no guarantee you will get out, is there?"

5.

"Welcome to the HMCS *Sam Steele*, Colonel. My name is Captain Petr Shishkin." The man's accent was heavy, almost like he was doing a spoof of a Communist spy from a 1960's Hollywood flick.

Tom Dorey gawked at the heavy, blue uniform of the Russian officer, his epaulettes and sleeves trimmed in gold piping and his upper, right chest adorned with campaign ribbons.

"Please, sit down. Your men will be well taken

care of in the mess. Can I get you a coffee?"

Dorey, shooting off glances in all directions within the small confines of the officers' mess, nodded mechanically. Then he remembered his manners. "Yes, sir. Thank-you, sir."

Captain Shishkin placed two hot cups on the table and slid onto the bench seat across from him. "I can well imagine that all of this must be pretty bewildering to you, Colonel." The Canadian smiled, half-heartedly, wondering if the understatement was intentional.

"Since you will be going out soon, I asked Commander Ellis if I could have the pleasure of meeting you. He will be here after he finishes the diving procedure and analyzes the sonar readings."

Dorey sipped at the scalding liquid, appraising the svelte man across from him. Shishkin was far different from his impression of a Russian sub commander. He was bald and lacked the stereotypical rough-hewn, "Russky" features that defined the officers of "the evil empire" that President Reagan continually warned the world of in the 1980's. When he first met the man, the Canadian thought the brown-eyed Shishkin could have been an accountant or a grocery clerk, but with every passing second his stingy moments and confident air gradually usurped his "civilian" features. In a scant few moments, Dorey would find himself in awe of the Russian.

"Colonel, to be very blunt, I am now the property of the Canadian navy." The Russian leaned back in his chair, letting the comment sink in before he continued.

"The *St. Petersburg*, a compliment of crewmen and myself, were traded along with the *Vladivostock*, the icebreaker we are following, for food and various sundry items that my government feels it needs. In other words, we were *bartered*."

Tom picked up an air of irony in the captain's words. Trading a modern attack submarine for "groceries" must be demeaning for a commander of Shishkin's status, he thought. In a flash of humor, Dorey also wondered if the Russians picked up "a draft choice and future considerations", jargon from professional sport trades.

"However, my opinions about the arrangement changed when I was given a tour of your country. I was greatly impressed by your people and what they thought of your place in the world. Your country is acting out of a genuine desire for the peace and security of its people. Needless to say, I found myself settling into my new role as a Canadian officer quite comfortably."

"*Canadian* officer?" Dorey was confused.

"Yes, it's quite a perk, Colonel. You see, I was originally selected to train your commanders to use this submarine but, as we submariners all know, you do not just learn to command this 'shark'. For officers to become proficient in attack boats takes an officer years of examining the characteristics of each vessel and familiarizing himself with every detail and every seaman's duty. There was also a great concern amongst your military chiefs as to exactly how much classified information I would be allowed to see while doing this training."

The Russian sipped some more of his coffee. "So I solved the problem by offering to become a Canadian citizen, while retaining my Russian heritage. I believe you call it 'dual citizenship'."

"So you are now a Canadian officer?"

"Yes, but they have allowed me to continue wearing my uniform for the sake of my twenty crewmen who volunteered to go along with me. *Esprit de Corps* and all of that. My sailors get to keep their "boat-style" caps too. After all, they are some of the best submariners in the world and should be allowed to keep the uniform in which they worked so hard to become proficient."

"I think you have the best of both worlds," remarked Dorey, impressed with both the logic of the Canadian military and the commander that sat across from him. In one fell swoop his government, that gaggle of politicians who couldn't agree on a helicopter, had a world-class submarine and one of the top commanders in the world driving it. Of course it helped that those legislators had a new leader who understood world politics extremely well.

A Canadian naval officer, bearded and looking almost too tall for submarine duty, walked into the mess and saluted Shishkin. "Captain, we are ready to make course changes to enter the Navy Board Inlet." His message delivered, he smiled and extended his hand. "Commander David Ellis, Colonel. It's a pleasure to have you aboard the HMCS *Sam Steele*."

Shishkin chuckled. "They changed the name, Colonel, but I find it rather invigorating to have my ship named after one of your nineteenth-century Mounted Police heroes. Now, lets go to the *conn* and the commander, here, will show you what we are planning to do."

Dorey followed the Canadian officer through the clean, narrow hallways of the submarine while Shuskin followed behind them. The sailors they passed were a mixture of bereted Canadians and "boat-capped" Russians who seemed to melt into the bulkheads as the officers passed. Like an acrobat, Ellis shot up a hatch and Dorey clambered after him, emerging into a world of blinking, electronic wizardry.

"Colonel, this is the control room, or *conn*. This is where it all happens." Ellis beamed as the soldier's eyes widened.

"Right now we are going through preliminary checks before we initiate a high-speed turning maneuver. As XO, or executive officer, I will advise the crew to that effect so they can brace for it just as you and your team did when we dove after you came aboard."

"Ellis picked up the microphone on a hook just below the deckhead and alerted the crew. Then he walked over to the helmsmen, a pair of seated, Russian "drivers" with steering wheels in their hands.

"Depth?"

"Thirty meters below the keel, sir!" the sailor answered in accented English.

"Depth below ice pack?"

"On screen, sir!"

Ellis glanced over at a twenty-six-inch, television-style monitor which depicted a three-dimensional view, something like an engineer's CAD computer program.

"Colonel," he remarked, the tone of his voice softening as he once again became tour guide. "This is called a Continually Operationing and Upgrading Navigational Televiewer, or COUNT system. It is an awesome piece of technology that was developed by our guys especially for this submarine."

Dorey thought he heard the Russian captain grunt with amusement but held his attention on the images on the televiewer. Although he was thoroughly briefed on COUNT, Tom had never before seen one in action.

"Unfortunately," Ellis continued, "the ice-breaker has the same system. They were carrying the engineers and computer scientists that were supposed to fine-tune the programs before we became completely operational. As it stands, we have only the ice-scanning capability, an underwater version of the old Ice View system which plotted and gave the drift information of icebergs, and the ice pack itself. The COUNT system on the icebreaker has *everything* functioning, which was why it was able to coordinate the missile attacks with a portable Silkworm and SAM launcher. This full use of COUNT, Colonel, is what makes the *Canadian* a very dangerous platform."

Dorey examined the numbers on the screen images. "Is this the depth of the ice?"

"Correct. It goes from two to a maximum of thirty-one feet, or just over nine meters. At twenty meters we're well below that, but we're going to be doing some tight turns in a very narrow channel, and at a good clip, to skirt Bylot Island. Some spots in the passage have barely twenty-five meters between the ice and floor."

"Why so fast?"

Ellis refreshed the COUNT screen with a computer-generated map of northern Canada. With the tracking ball on the side, he isolated a small area and enlarged it. "Right now the *Canadian* is in Lancaster Sound, at seventy-eight west longitude and seventy-four north latitude. And we're here, in Eclipse Sound, off the southwestern tip of Bylot Island, the most northern part of Baffin, at about...seventy-nine, and change, west longitude. To come out ahead of the ship we have to shoot down this dogleg channel called Navy Board Inlet and skirt the coast once we get to Lancaster Sound. You and your team will be let off here, behind Prince Leopold Island, bang on ninety-degrees west."

Suddenly, the realization that this was not a

training mission, but involved putting live soldiers in harm's way, dawned on the commander. It was something that a naval officer like himself had never before done. "Colonel, we're going to put you on the lee-side of Prince Leopold."

Ellis clapped Dorey on the back, an empathic gesture. "Alright, Mr. Parker...speed?"

"Twenty-two knots!"

"Initiate right-hand turn to two, seven, six degrees on my mark.... Eight, seven...."

Dorey glanced around the small, red-lit room, his eyes resting on the serious faces of the crew, all concentrating on their consoles as if the world depended on their actions. In actuality, it did. Their world was the *Sam Steele*.

"Four, three...."

His gaze rested on the pensive, but satisfied, face of Shishkin. The Russian commander hadn't taken his eyes off the markings on the plastic-laminated chart since Ellis began the procedure.

"Two, one...initiate the turn!"

The narrow chamber tilted and Dorey heard the muffled popping as the submarine's outer hull protested the maneuver. It soon straightened up and the relief of pressure spawned a chain of soft groans.

"Course?"

"Bearing two-seven-five, Commander!"

"Speed?"

"Twenty knots and climbing!"

Ellis turned to see the mischievous look in Shishkin's face.

"Captain?"

"Well done, Commander. And you did it without the benefit of a television screen," returned the Russian. "Remember, my gifted protégé, a submarine is a living, breathing organism and we are its corpuscles and cells. Like your own body, the boat relies heavily on 'brain-power' but, also like the human body, instinct and quick reflexes are crucial to survival. Whatever your COUNT screen was meant to replace, it is only an *aid* to the commander and is no substitute for good judgment."

"Aye, sir!" returned Ellis, quelling the urge to smile. It was one of the few compliments Shuskin had allowed him during their three month acquaintance.

A beaming Ellis returned to his countdown checks before making the first dogleg in the narrow straight. In less than ten minutes he would have to switch directions again, bringing him back on his original course.

"Speed?"

"Approaching twenty-seven knots!"

The Canadian sub driver grinned at Dorey. "Well, Colonel, two more fast turns and we'll have you swimming with the seals in six hours, tops."

6.

094500Z04JULY
FR: USSFARGO
TO: COMSUBLANT
TOP SECRET
1.SONAR CONTACT. SSN \VIC-TOR III CLASS AT 60N 58W \22 KNOTS HEADING NW\DAVIS STRAIT.
2.SONAR CONTACT. SSN\LE TRIOMPHE CLASS AT 45N 50W\28KNOTS HEADING W.
3.SURFACE SONAR CONTACT VERIFIED AS TWO FRENCH DE-STROYERS.

4. REQUEST PERMISSION TO
FOLLOW LE TRIOMPHE.

He had met the US president a few times before, at social functions, but Ambassador François Clemente had only been to the White House once: to present his papers when he arrived in Washington. That occasion had been shortly after the election of his employer and good friend, Gérard Ledoux, seven months ago. From then until now it had been business as usual for the French ambassador: smoothing out trade missions, attending official functions and the like. Some of it was very droll, but most times the tall, thin man had to pinch himself in reminder that he was France's premier man in the world's most powerful city.

This meeting, however, was as far away from the mundane workings of an embassy as he could get. First, he had been *ordered* by the US president to attend this meeting; and second, a green and white United States Marine Corps VIP A *Sea King* helicopter from Quantico, Virginia made sure that nothing came between him and his intended appointment. Finally, he was ushered directly from the turbulent vortex of helicopter blades—that spun at just under full power for security reasons—into the waiting room of the Oval Office.

President Gordon Thompson was staring out of the thick, polycarbonate, bullet-proof glass window when Clemente entered the legendary workstation. Although, at fifty-three, the president's light-brown hair was thinning on top, his face revealed a man ten years younger. If not for the fact that he was receiving the French ambassador, he would have worn something less formal than the conservative, charcoal suit. Also in the room, seated to his left, were Secretary of State William R. MacMillan and Gerri Lawson, the president's personal secretary.

As if waking from a dream, Thompson rose from his large chair with his hand extended, a smile of perfect teeth intending to soothe any deep anxiety Clemente might still have due to the unexpected summons. Although he was nervous, this had more to do with airsickness. François had never felt comfortable in helicopters, even in one of those official "taxis" reserved mainly for the First Couple.

The president's handshake was as firm and strong as a tennis player's. *"Bonjour Monsieur Clemente. Comment allez-vous?"* The President's French was very good, thought the ambassador, still disoriented. For a moment he tried to find something regal to reply with but finally blurted out, *"Je tres bién, et vous, Monsieur President?"*

Thompson laughed. *"Je tres bién, aussi...*uh, sorry, my French is rusty. Welcome to the White House, Monsieur Clemente. I apologize for your 'kidnapping' and hope that this sudden meeting did not cause undue alarm for you and your family. By the way, how's Madame Clemente's famous garden coming? I hear that all Washington is drooling with envy regarding her flair for growing beautiful flowers."

The President's interest in his wife was mildly relaxing for François, even if he knew the American had been coached. It proved that the president thought it important enough to inquire about the lifestyle of a mere ambassador such as himself. Not even *he*, himself, gave much thought to whether or not Marie could grow things.

"She will be thrilled that you complimented her penchant for growing things, Mr. President." Subconsciously, Clemente's left hand produced a handkerchief whereby he quickly dabbed his trim, dark mustache. It was a good thing that there was not a mirror anywhere in sight or François, meticulous about his appearance, would have noticed a "cowlick" of dark-brown hair protruding at the back of his head. This would have been devastating to him, especially now that he was slowly relaxing.

"I love gardens and admire people who have the discipline and gentle hands to nurture them." Thompson then introduced MacMillan, a balding, middle-aged man whose former occupation of an accountant was hard to disguise; and Gerri Lawson, his secretary. Lawson, his aid when he was a southern governor, had followed him to Washington after the election. A tall, fortyish lawyer with many hard-won battles behind her, Gerri smoothed out her tailored suit dress when she stood to shake the Frenchman's hand.

"Coffee, Monsieur Clemente?" Lawson asked.

"Yes, please."

After four cups of *café au lait* were steaming in front of the group, the President unfolded his gold-rimmed glasses and perched them on his long nose. "Excuse me for a second, M. Ambassador, I just want to look over this dispatch again. It came in yesterday evening from our Atlantic Fleet operations center in Norfolk, Virginia."

Thompson's attention to the message was his way of heightening the drama; lighting a fire under the Frenchman to see if his body language would reveal anything. Clemente's eyes darted around the Oval office, his misgivings over the paper numbed by the sheer honor of sitting across from the most powerful man in the world. The other two sat watching Thompson.

The President bobbed his head thoughtfully as he folded up the spectacles. When his eyes found those of François, he clasped his hands on the desk and forced a congenial smile. "M. Clemente, I'll get right to the point. Our intelligence sources have confirmed that two French destroyers are, at this very moment, one hundred miles outside Canadian territorial waters. I trust you know this?"

The Frenchman slowly nodded before he spoke. "Yes, I am fully aware of that, Mister President."

Thompson scratched above his right ear as if trying to rid himself of an annoying insect. Then he leaned across the table, his musky, blue eyes gripping Clemente in a frozen stare.

"M. Ambassador, I have to be honest with you. This bothers me. This *really* bothers me, but it doesn't bother me as much as *this*...." Thompson turned the piece of paper on his desk around so that the ambassador could read it. On first glance, Clemente knew what it was but feigned a deep concern as he read the report, his anxiety returning. *What was Gérard doing?*

"Now—" Thompson continued, leaning back in his large chair, the one belonging to John F. Kennedy. Lyndon Johnson had turfed this very piece of furniture from the White House within days of Kennedy's death—a part of Johnson's paranoid process to purge the hallowed office of Kennedy's aura. Thompson, a devoted follower of the assassinated president, from the time he joined Kennedy's brand new Peace Corps in 1963, had it and the desk on loan from the John F. Kennedy Museum. "—it seems that your newest missile submarine, *Mitterand* is also lurking around the Grand Banks, just off Newfoundland, contrary to a certain agreement concerning the North American continental shelf area. And besides," he added with a folksy concern, "it just ain't neighborly!"

Then, as if someone flipped a switch,

Thompson's face went blank and out of the corner of his eye Clemente caught the tense looks on the faces of MacMillan and Lawson.

"For some reason yet unexplained to me, Mister Ambassador, your President Ledoux has seen fit to conduct war-like maneuvers off the continental shelf of North America without discussing the matter with the United States. And what pisses me off the most, if you forgive my frank colloquialisms, is that these type of actions have become part of the *modus operandi* for M. Ledoux—as well as for his economic allies in the European Community, who seem to follow his every lead like a flock of sheep. In other words, instead of trying to solve trade and political differences between us in a civilized manner, the EC chooses to just stand back and give the US 'the finger'.

"Well shit! That puts me in a very difficult position, sir, because my constituents, the people of the United States, will surely want to know why I sit here, in this office, while France pretends this is 1805 and Napoleon Bonaparte is once again marching to fucking Austerlitz!" The president surprised even Lawson, a loyal assistant for over fifteen years, when his big fist hit Kennedy's desk.

However, the action seemed to produce a calm within the athletic-looking man. Unexpectedly, his tone changed and his voice reached out to the Frenchman, almost as though Clemente held the key to the dilemma. "Usually, Mister Ambassador, I would conduct negotiations on a personal level with your president, but his arrogant attitude in dealing with our State Department, and numerous other trade bureaus, precludes any friendly overtures or suggestions of high-level discussions from this office.

"So," he continued in the same tone, "this is

what I have done, Monsieur Clemente. I have already informed the other European ambassadors that their fishing fleets *will* retire from the entire continental shelf areas of North America or face confiscation of their boats as well as suffer stiff retribution. As we speak, the US and Canadian Coast Guards are preparing to become the world's largest towing companies.

"So, here's the deal. Your President Ledoux calls all your fishing boats and warships home *immediately*. They have forty-eight hours to be out of the prescribed area. *Fini!*" Thompson's glasses came off his nose and his musky, blue eyes stared right into the soul of the Frenchman. "Do I make myself clear, Mister Ambassador?"

Feeling hot and cold flashes at the same time, a breathless Clemente felt as though he had been mugged. The former college professor had never before experienced such a roller coaster of emotions.

"Yes, Mister President."

"Fine," Thompson replied, returning to his "awe shucks" demeanor. "Then I suggest you have a pow-wow with Monsieur Ledoux and relate what I have just explained. Thank you for coming, Monsieur Clemente, and tell your lovely wife that the First Lady would sure love some cuttings from her beautiful lilacs."

Very quickly, Thompson stood and extended his hand, his eyes back to their merry twinkling. After the handshake, the President abruptly turned away and walked to the window, staring off into the gray skies over Washington. Clemente could just barely remember shaking hands with the other two before being led out. But he remembered filling up the airsick bag during the helicopter ride back to his residence.

CHAPTER 7

1.

July 6th, 0901:26 Zulu; 5 miles
west of Prince Leopold Island
74°N. Latitude, 91°W. Latitude.

"Depth?"

"Ninety-three meters. No exceptions."

"Ice thickness at Oscar Charlie?"

"COUNT shows 1.2 to 1.8 meters, sir!"

"India Bravo?"

"India Bravo is twenty kilometers east, bearing 125."

"Bingo! On target!"

Over his shoulder, Commander Ellis studied the jagged images on the COUNT screen, appearing like stunted stalagmites on the ceiling of a large cave. In-between two of these downward-pointing bumps was a thin area, and below that was the silhouette of a submarine moving upward toward it.

A yawning Captain Shishkin walked into the comm and edged in beside Ellis. "Status report?"

"Captain, this boat is prepared to surface."

"Very well, Commander, commence vertical ascent."

"Commence vertical ascent!" The call went through the various stations: ballast, trim, electronics surveillance. Valves were opened and the tanks surrounding the boat's pressure hull were purged of water.

Jim Dorey and his team, forward in the weapons-loading compartment, felt the upward motion and the sounds associated with a surfacing submarine as the sea water's pressure diminished on the steel hull: popping and groaning.

"Twenty meters." Shiskin grabbed the handles of number-two periscope and activated the video camera. Standing back he and Ellis surveyed the underside of the ice pack on the monitor: a greenish mass with, what appeared to be, dark veins running through it.

"Ten meters." At this depth the ice pack lightened considerably, the individual chunks becoming noticeable, interspersed with thousands of bubbles. Shishkin smiled. It was what the bottom of the ice in a glass of bourbon on the rocks looked like.

"Five meters."

"Prepare for impact!"

* * * *

The lone, male polar bear recoiled from the shock as the ice burst up in front of him. Lumbering away from the cracking and groaning of the ice pack his head flipped back to see a huge, black thing poke out of the broken pieces of wet ice which glistened in the eternal, Arctic sun. When the noise ceased and the huge intruder seemed to have frozen solid in its position, the large, cream-colored bear stopped, his curiosity winning over his initial urge to flee.

* * * *

Even with sunglasses covering half his face, Captain Shiskin, resplendid in his Soviet navy greatcoat and fur hat, winced as he finished his climb up onto the mini-bridge on the fairweather. The low-lying, morning sun accentuated the glare, its rays bouncing off every irregularity on the ice pack with the exception of the six feet of protruding, black sail. The air was fresh but unusually warm and the captain soon found that his heavy, woolen coat soaked up the summer Arctic sun too well.

While Shishkin and Commander Ellis basked in the warm atmosphere, Dorey's team, just wide of the cracked surface that hid the dark behemoth below, unfurled their white, nylon-skinned equipment packages. The snowy, camouflaged figures, almost invisible except for their faces and hands, were too preoccupied with their preparations to notice their audience.

However, no one was too busy to forget thinking about their target, barely nine miles away around the other side of the small, striated vestige of Prince Leopold Island. To their right was the long shoreline of Somerset Island, another six miles of ice pack away. Off its cliffs they could hear low drum rolls, the deflected sound of the icebreaker as it pulverized the ice with a never-ending appetite.

If they were any other surfaced sub, Ellis mused, the icebreaker's keen sonar and radar capabilities, that were an important part of their fully-operational COUNT system, would have surely picked them out by now. In preparation for this, the smaller COUNT system aboard the *Sam Steele* had quickly computed the fairwater's radar image and was continually changing it as the icebreaker closed the distance between them. The "offending frequencies", ones which might bounce back and alert the hijackers of the submarine's presence, were isolated and "neutralized" by sending back simulated readings of the surrounding landscape behind the submarine—a sort of "cloaking device." Hence, the *Sam Steele*'s instruments would show a normal ice pack consistent with COUNT's data: areas of flat ice, intermingled with raised ridges of porous, frozen sea water. That is, until they were close enough for a visual analysis of the icescape. But that wouldn't happen until the *Canadian* rounded the wind-blown island and was almost on top of them.

Dorey and his men also wore the new "Cool-Soot": thin coveralls, with a hood, worn underneath their Arctic camouflage. Webbed with miles of tiny capillaries, these suits coursed with a coolant to mask the body's "heat signature" which would fool any infra-red sensors on the ice-breaker—another "cloak".

Also, thanks to satellite jamming, the *Canadian* could not receive updated information. The United States and Great Britain had agreed to the Canadian government's request to "blank" their satellites, a costly maneuver that required reprogramming the codes to place COUNT's space-dependent, data system inoperable over that area of the Arctic. That meant that close-up photos from space could not be taken or processed; photographs from above which might show a black, elliptical object stuck in the ice.

Just as Shishkin was beginning to enjoy his view of the Arctic, a sort of "invisible man's-eye view," which he conceded was made possible by COUNT, he saw Commander Ellis' eyes suddenly go wide with shock under his headset.

"ETA? Ah, shit!" When Ellis' stunned face found the doe-eyed captain and he almost bellowed the report. "Company's coming! Some helicopter in the area suddenly changed course and is on an intercept heading with India Bravo. She'll see us in less than ten minutes!"

Shishkin reacted coolly, as if the situation were a mere drill. His voice was regular and deliberate, and Ellis felt suddenly ashamed for being so excitable. But that was not the way he meant it.

"Prepare to dive."

"Aye, sir!"

The commander disappeared from the bridge, hooking his feet around the ladder railings and sliding rapidly down to the conn. Captain Shishkin waved to the group and a hooded Dorey came running over to the low-slung monolith, his white, Arctic boots crunching on the rotten ice surface. In less than ten seconds the captain explained the situation to him. Flying above them the intruder would easily make out the dark shape of the sub below the ice.

"Good luck, Colonel," he yelled as the Canadian commando trotted off to join his comrades. "I would very much like to meet you in more relaxed times!"

"Thanks for the lift, Captain," Tom replied. "And you can count on it!"

Shishkin smiled and dropped below just as the diving klaxons began blaring, sounding thin as they wafted up through the hatch. Then, with the sealing of the submarine, they disappeared altogether; abandoning the foursome in the quiet, white world.

Inside, Commander Ellis reported to the arriving Shishkin. "Captain, the boat is ready to submerge. Ninety meters under the keel. No exceptions."

"Vertical dive."

"Vertical dive!" echoed Ellis, subconsciously knowing that the command would spread faster than wildfire through the entire submarine.

First, the diving officer, Lieutenant Sokov, ordered the aft-main ballast tanks flooded. His chief hollered back an affirmation when the deed was done and the indicators on the ballast control verified that the valves had opened. Then the tanks around the pressure hull flooded and the HMCS *Sam Steele* began to sink, first heavy to the stern to clear the propellers. Then the call went out to flood the forward tanks and the mighty Akula pulled down and away from its icy grip and sunk into the frigid, green world that it knew so well.

Tom Dorey and his threesome, a hundred yards to the side, watched from their prone position as the fairweather disappeared in a menagerie of grinding sounds, the tons of ice plates, protruding at angles, trying to fit back together into the space left by the retreating submarine, like a giant jigsaw puzzle that has been lifted and then placed down again. The monstrous rift of ice that once hinted of the length of the boat lodged underneath the pack, settled in a series of crunches and pops. Then all was still in the glaring, Arctic vista.

Dorey checked to see if any excess cracking had occurred around his area. Satisfied, he and his men proceeded to unfurl their camouflage "blind"—the one they would hide behind to launch the time-detonating rocket at the communications room of the icebreaker. Unlike the years he had spent trying to keep people from killing each other, the Canadian was in his element again: leading a group of men in an operation that required every ounce of knowledge that he had garnered in over a quarter-century of wearing a uniform.

Checking the position of the icebreaker on his hand-held receiver, he smoothed the camouflage material over his team, carefully spreading pieces of ice over them before he crawled under the tarpaulin. After the passing of the "visitor" they would redeploy, making their way over the dunes of frozen white and turquoise toward the small island.

Their "blind," as well as serving as a visual camouflage, was also designed to confuse radar signals with synthesized magnetic pulses, simulating the natural conditions experienced by their proximity to the Magnetic North Pole. They were to be one-half mile south of the target before 1155:00 Zulu. At that time they would launch the wire-guided missiles, steering the armor-piercing, high-explosive projectiles from a small, hand-held console. These would be steered toward the communication deck below the main bridge of the icebreaker. With the Com Room destroyed, the huge ship's power systems would stop, rendering the icebreaker dead in the water, or in this instance, the ice.

Since entering Lancaster Sound, COUNT's integrated scanners had been greatly impaired by the loss of satellite communication. But its surveillance capabilities were still a formidable threat due to the low-level radar and the already-stored data, readily available for automatic comparisons and retrieval. If the hijackers had any hi-tech Russian SA-N-12 missiles left, it would still be extremely dangerous for the fighters to venture within fifty miles—not to mention Morris' attack force—even without the GPS and other satellite aids.

With COUNT officially "dead", the missile launchers could only rely on the radar and heat-seeking capabilities of their SAM launchers. However, once activated, the radar was a pariah to the launcher because the CF-18's maintaining a constant vigil could then lock on the signal and take out the exact position of the launcher with HARM—anti-radar—missiles.

The back-up plan—if in any way the TOW system was rendered ineffective—entailed a more dangerous mission: boarding the moving ship in much the same way. But instead of the hand-held TOW's, Maverick air-to-surface missiles would be fired from one of the many *Hornets* who had been taking turns making wide circles around the ship for more than twenty-four hours.

This was not the favored plan. COUNT would

pick up the launch immediately and, even though it had no protection against the projectiles, could allow the hijackers time to prepare to repel borders and even kill the hostages—which was the reason the ship hadn't been boarded in the first place. The *Hornets* were still required to keep a distance of thirty miles; if called upon, their missiles would still take a few minutes to impact. To quicken that time would require a closer orbit which would definitely alert COUNT and cause added danger to the captives, canceling any advantage.

In a few moments the hidden commandos heard the intermittent sputtering of a helicopter. Tom lifted the tarpaulin and poked out his long-range glasses to have a look. It was a Bell *Ranger*, five kilometers away, on course for the target. But why?

2.

Alice MacIsaac watched Vasiliev wince as the wash from the helicopter whipped up some dust on the green flight deck. But his new-found smile, viewed from high up in the officer's mess, was something that even he could not hide with his usually cold expression. Once upon a time, Alice found the expression attractive.

The whine of the engines decreased and the rotors slowed and became visible as individual blades. Then the doors opened and two men in coveralls jumped out, each carrying briefcases. A joyous Vasiliev embraced them both.

She turned back from the huge window and shifted her attention to the slouching figure of Tom Packard in front of the television. He reminded her of one of those dipping birds. His eyelids tapped together each time his head dropped, but when his chin hit his chest it woke him, momentarily; and then his crew-cut head raised to repeat the procedure. This scene had been going on for almost fifteen minutes. Beyond him, half-sleeping and half-gazing through the windows, the rest of the hostages waited. It was almost time.

Eric Johansen surveyed the room. The American airman, his hands tied behind his back, was dozing but every so often he would go into a fit of coughing and awake, if only into a stupor. MacIsaac would then lift up some hot tea or administer cough syrup. She knew he was out of danger from hypothermia, but was still weak. He had asked Vasiliev to let him lie down but the Russian wanted no suicidal acts of revenge so ordered him tied in a sitting position.

The two journalists were still playing cards, teasing each other as if they were on a cruise ship instead of a hijacked vessel. That was good, Johansen thought. It gave the impression that everyone was waiting to be released through negotiation.

At least that was what he overheard the "new hijackers" talking about: trading lives for money and a flight to North Korea. Why anyone would want to live there, even with hundreds of millions of dollars under their belt, was beyond him. *Those* people had the sense of humor of a stillborn octopus. Still, there was no way in hell that extradition could be arranged. That country was a sealed enterprise.

When the bulky engineer lifted his 280 pounds from the chair, no one really paid much attention. Every five minutes or so there was someone going to the bathroom or into the kitchen to fix themselves a sandwich. In fact it was so commonplace that, after two days as guard of the small group,

Packard was more worried about Vasiliev finding out about his lax attention than rebellion from his charges.

But the threat was there, lingering just below the surface of his calm exterior. The "college boy" already made his point, and made it well, when he put two holes in George Brill's forehead, the back of the surprised young man's reddish-haired skull exploding as his brains splattered on the wall outside the men's washroom. Five of the hostages, including Johansen, Brill's charge, had witnessed it and the look in their eyes told Packard all he needed to know: an example had been set. "Besides," he had later gloated, "what could you guys do if you ever made a run for it—turn into seals and swim?"

The big chief engineer's next move caught everyone by surprise. In a couple of seconds he had quietly moved up behind Packard's lounge chair and, as if Johansen was going to playfully wrestle with the hijacker, his huge forearms were around the man's head, covering his mouth.

Fully awake, but his face buried under the tattooed muscles of the engineer, Packard's hazel eyes flipped open as wide as any human being's could without his eyeballs popping out. His arms, like wing beats of dying chicken, flailed uselessly at Johansen. Then, with about as much effort as lifting a portable television, the engineer twisted his large body and Packard's neck made a sickening *snap*, the sound instantly conjuring up images in Alice's head of her father butchering turkeys.

The young man's body twitched and vibrated as Johansen dragged his limp form toward the galley past a gasping audience of horrified onlookers. When he had deposited Packard in the freezer he reached up and shifted a loose ceiling tile. Then he banged three times on the upper floor. Two responses followed. "My guardian angel," the engineer chuckled. "Now, let's get going before that Russian fuck gets back with his friends."

Judy MacDonald, a haggard replica of the sophisticated politician who flirted with Prince Charles at the premier's party just a week ago, was the first to stand. Her red eyes fluttered wildly. "I wish *I* could have broken his neck. I wish I could break all their necks!" she cried, her voice stuttering with sobs. Her unkempt head fell onto the shoulder of Frances Pilotte, who led her out of the room. The rest followed along like zombies, wishing more for uninterrupted sleep than escaping.

A dazed Jonathan Fergus felt Johansen's amused eyes appraise him and shuddered as he passed by, almost being led by his little blonde shadow. "Wait!" Eric dug his hand into Fergus' shoulder and the Planet Guardian leader felt his knees go weak.

"Fungus, I rather enjoyed snapping the neck of that little fuck," he explained, much in the same way that a golfer would recount a well-played game. "Now, I know that you won't hang for what you've done because our country doesn't see fit to get rid of its murdering shitheads...."

Fergus suddenly felt his head hit the bulkhead, stunning him as the engineer's huge right hand held his throat in what could have easily been a death grip. With the other hand he held a frantic Carla away with as much effort if he were fending off a puppy. Then, like a vampiric monster, he leered in Fergus' face "But I will squeeze the life from you if you cause me one bit of trouble, got it?"

Fergus' bloated face was a bright crimson when he nodded. When Johansen released his grip he slumped onto his knees, fighting for breath. But the engineer hauled him up again and shoved him after the others, flipping the sobbing Carla after him.

A smiling MacIsaac patted Eric on his large right shoulder. "You have great patience, Eric. I might have squeezed harder."

The engineer shrugged. "The day isn't over yet. Besides, I've got *you* to keep watch over him. And who do you think he's more afraid of?" Alice grinned, the sparkle returning to her emerald eyes.

"Now, just like we planned, you find Jimmy and stay put until I've done my stuff." MacIsaac gave him a "thumbs up" and then hurried down the hallway, skirting the quiet group.

Johansen motioned for Barrett. "Okay, Bill. Once more: you lead them to the guest quarters and use the pass key I gave you to get into a room on the first floor. Get them under the beds and tell them to stuff pillows around them. You sit low and watch from one of the windows. When the shit starts flying, so will a whole pile of metal, so run into the can and get in the tub."

Then, his heavy brows turning upward, Eric produced Packard's Baretta. "You ever seen one of these before?"

"No, not that model," replied Barrett, "but I've fired pistols. I can figure it out."

Johansen looked deeply into the black man's eyes. "Bill, this is for keeps. They might want to come door-to-door to polish off some witnesses, so don't be afraid to use this. No one in this universe would treat you less than a hero for wasting these bastards. So, remember, it's just like the Olympics. Hit 'em hard and take no prisoners, got that?"

Bill nodded solemnly, his thoughts flashing to

the three rounds of toe-to-toe brawling with his South Korean opponent in Seoul in '88. The judges ruled him the loser on points but the Korean boxer went down twice—and then had to accept his medal in the hospital.

He shook Johansen's large hand and ducked out to lead the tired gathering waiting on his instructions in the hallway.

3.

Dorey worked frantically to stem the flow of blood from Corporal Anderson's shredded arm, finally tightening the tourniquet around the greasy, scarlet limb. A stunned Sergeant James, the pulp on the right side of his face bandaged, poured hot water from his canteen over Flemming's trembling, white lips. The captain's numerous wounds had been tended to but Tom had grave doubts that he would last—and Flemming knew it. All James could do was give him comfort. And beside them, with tufts of creamy-white fur rippling in the gentle Arctic breeze around a dozen or so red, plastered areas, was the blood-splattered corpse of the polar bear.

Tom lifted up the corporal's head and gave him some tea, silently thanking his foresight to fill his canteen with something hot. It was supposed to be a perk, something soothing to sip while waiting for the icebreaker. Now, it comforted a comrade who had all but lost an arm and might yet slip away unless he could be evacuated.

Captain Brad Flemming had been the only one to free himself from the camouflaged tarpaulin when the polar bear jumped on the blind and began swatting the covered team with vicious claws. At first, all they could do was cover up and try to protect themselves from the blows. But the carnivore soon ripped through the meager protection and was attacking the exposed men still trapped by their equipment.

While the other three tried frantically to free themselves from under the weight of the eight-hundred-pound tornado of teeth and claws, Flemming, managing only to extract his knife, tackled the whitish demon in a brave attempt to distract it; his eight-inch knife blade plunging repeatedly into the bear's heavy fur and skin. Given a brief respite, Dorey freed himself from the mangled webbing.

Once he dragged himself out, Tom frantically ripped away the Velcro strap holding his semi-automatic Glock in place on his leg and pulled free the pistol. But he couldn't get a clear shot with Flemming in the way, and the man and beast continued their bloody dance.

Then suddenly, as if tiring of the close-in fighting, the bear swatted the captain away, the officer's limp body hitting the hard ice pack like a bloody rag doll. In the instant that he saw daylight between the animal and Flemming, Tom instinctively fired, pumping four 10mm soft-point bullets into the bear's shoulder and chest. The impacts of the lethal rounds threw it off the beleaguered captain like a battering ram had struck it. Then, Dorey blew the carnivore's head apart with three precise shots.

When the colonel finally lowered the pistol, he saw James, blood streaming down the left side of his face, crawling out from under the remains of the tarpaulin. Anderson was now sitting up, a numb, shaking mannequin, his arm streaming blood from a severed artery.

But then his eyes rested on Flemming, the commando's form resembling a tie-dyed body-suit that

Dorey had once seen on a girl in a club somewhere; only this dye was blood. His friend's body had been ripped open by the long, scythe-like claws and his right shoulder almost gnawed in two. Brad's face, however, was calm. He just stared across the bright, frozen plain, his eyes blinking.

Appraising the situation quickly, his analytical mind conjuring up a crude form of triage, the commander jumped into action. He ripped off a piece of the blind and tied Anderson's upper bicep as tightly as he could, stopping the flow of blood. After that he sat the stunned James down and placed a piece of ice in the man's hands, getting him to hold it against the bloody slash on the corporal's face.

But moving along to Flemming, his old friend, tears came to his eyes. Even if a MedEvac had been close by, the captain was too ripped up to make it; his breathing was like a rattle of small stones. As Dorey plugged up the wounds with most of the gauze from the first-aid kit, Flemming swallowed hard and grinned, his eyes fighting to stay open.

"In Sudan...we fed a pile o' people...right, Tom-boy?"

"We sure did, Flem.

"Do you...." He coughed, his body vibrating with a series of convulsions. Tom sighed as a rivulet of blood ran from the side of Flemming's mouth. "Do you think anyone'll ever know that?"

"The ones that count know. Now you—" But Flemming wasn't listening. His heart had given out.

Concentrating to keep his hands from shaking to utter uselessness, Tom reached his blood-caked hand into his long, pant-leg pocket and pulled out a sealed, plastic package. With his knife he peeled off the shrink-packed plastic liner, revealing an oblong, gray transmitter. There was an

LCD display and a keypad, in which he could dial out much like a cellular phone—but he was only interested in the red button.

4.

Had this been any other ship in the Coast Guard, Chief Engineer Johansen would have had an easier time stopping it. However, the new automation system on the *Canadian* had been programmed so that everything could be controlled from the bridge—which relied on the Com Room for its control systems. In order to get there, or anywhere without alerting the hijackers, the Intership-Video-Surveillance system would have to go down. To accomplish that, a *mole* was needed; and his mole was Jimmy McDougall.

His throat feeling as parched as dried cod, the Newfoundlander watched the digital clock on the MOD: 1059:50 Zulu; ten seconds. Five minutes before, he had tapped in the codes that Johansen had given him, gaining access to the Accessory Control Unit. Sweating profusely, he held his hand above the modular diagram that displayed caricatures of the dozens of cameras throughout the ship.

As the appropriate time flashed he jabbed the master control pad and, instantly, the miniature camera icons disappeared from the MOD as the banks of video recorders directly behind him automatically switched off. The surveillance system was dead.

Two minutes later, he heard the required three knocks and opened the door to find the welcome figure of Alice MacIsaac. Even though they barely knew each other, the two fell into each other's arms, hugging momentarily before the seriousness of their task fell upon them. "Captain, let's shut 'er down!"

Alice whirled around the racks of equipment and faced the long Com Panel. With quick, deliberate taps she entered her personal access code. A green light soon appeared above her hand, followed closely by the words, "ACCESS ALLOWED," glowing in red. Then, watching the digital clock in much the same manner as had McDougall, a scant six minutes before, she waited for one more minute.

At 1107:00 Zulu, Alice began a series of procedures that absorbed her total concentration for five more minutes as she shifted back and forth along the panel. Pressing batteries of buttons, her eyes moved up and down the board, monitoring the progress of her methodical procedure.

Jimmy watched in fascination, trying to fathom how someone's mind could operate so quickly while knowing precisely how each system operated. His amazement, however, was briefly interrupted so that he watched for intruders through a crack in the door.

* * * *

"Good girl, Alice!" shouted Johansen, as the lights extinguished on the main engineering board, releasing control of the six massive, Mak diesel engines from the bridge to him. The chief engineer had already initiated manual procedures so all he had to do was punch six buttons. And "punch" then he did.

As if the gods on Mount Olympus had thrown a switch, the great ship came to a grinding halt in the ice pack, its lights and systems shutting off in sequence. Underneath, the muffled wane of the massive engines powering down provided a dramatic soundtrack. Minutes later, in the breathtaking silence, the emergency lighting cast an eerie glow in the cavernous engineering control center, quiet for the first time in over a year.

Johansen wiped his hands together and a mischievous smile grew under his large, bulbous nose. Then he sauntered to the machine shop to get some added insurance.

* * * *

"That's impossible! The captain and the engineer have to be at their stations to do—"

Vasiliev's mouth twisted into a grotesque shape and Dennis Barnes thought for sure the muscular Russian was going to break him in half. He could only stare at the flashing LED warnings which indicated that the ship's propulsion and navigation systems were off-line. The CCGS *Canadian* was in "Dry-Dock Mode".

Just then the huge form of Jesso appeared, a new Russian AKR assault rifle slinging from his shoulder. "They're all gone and Packard's dead, hanging like a slab of meat in the cooler!" the Australian snarled, swiping a rope of his braided hair back over his muscular shoulder.

Dimitri took a deep breath and scanned the Emergency MOD. It would take too long to power up now even if he had the knowledge of the engineer's controls. And it was unlikely that Barnes knew Johansen's codes. Not because of any security reason, he fumed, *but because these lazy, fucking Canadians never got around to it!*

Vasiliev glanced at his watch again: 1117:23 Zulu. His expression softened and a grin tried to win over his face. Even if the Canadians launched an attack now from, say, Resolute Bay, it would take well over an hour. Besides, he remembered, Jesso still had plenty of SAM's left and the Canadian frigate was stuck with no firepower. And even if it did, Smart wouldn't make a move with hostages aboard.

Hostages! He had to find them and parade them on the deck to show that they were still alive—

otherwise they might be attacked. If he got them on deck a surveillance aircraft would pick them out and alert any assault team that he meant business.

He turned to the shorter, but still hulking, figure of the Australian. Although Vasiliev was rather fond of the mercenary he knew that Jesso's mind had been "bent" by steroids, and so watched him carefully. Before the operation, and under the threat of death, the Russian warned him against any further use of the drugs. "Bart, we have to find the hostages. They'll most likely be in the tourist section. Find them but don't hurt them. Hurry!"

After Jesso left he turned to the bearded Coast Guard officer, whose face still bore the purplish reminder of his beating. "Barnes, you will send this message on the Emergency Channel immediately. Then, you will transmit this other one at 1130:00, repeating it every five minutes, is that clear?"

Dennis nodded. "Good. Now, Barnes, I am going to lock you in here to make sure you fulfill your mission, but if you don't, I'll send that troll, Jesso, back here to make your death very painful and slow. Understood?"

Barnes' thoughts flashed back to his peaceful verandah overlooking Halifax harbor—his beautiful wife and great boys. Then the image was rudely interrupted by the vision of the brutish Australian snapping his fingers back in a sickly, cracking motion. "It will be done to the letter, sir!"

"Good. And Dennis," he added, his voice softening, "it may not mean much but I enjoyed working with you in Halifax. You and your family were very kind to me. I want you to know that this is strictly business and has no reflection on you or Alice. If it means anything, I did have feelings for her...good-bye Dennis."

Barnes attempted a smile when he thought of the barbecues at his place, and Dimitri's stories of Russia keeping his wife and kids enthralled. But then the memories stopped—and so did his smile. Like the Russian had said: this was business. And so was ridding the ship of Vasiliev and his thugs.

When Dimitri closed the door, Barnes heard fumbling in the hall and knew that he was rigging up a device to keep him in. When it stopped the chief mate began transmitting:

Ship disabled. Passengers safe. Hijackers still aboard.

Do not attempt rescue. I repeat.

Ship disabled. Passengers safe. Hijackers still aboard.

Do not attempt rescue.

"Come on, Dennis, let's get out of here." Alice's voice was calm as she placed her hand on Barnes' shoulder.

"Jesus!" he started as he saw his captain's face, but then remembered to release the mike key. "How?"

"We were hiding in the rack."

Barnes looked over to see the grinning face of McDougall.

"Now, let's get you out of here before all hell breaks loose."

Momentarily disoriented, Barnes mentally went through the day's events, trying to comprehend the situation. His confused look was met with a pull on his arm from his captain. "Come on, Dennis, we'll explain later."

Barnes was momentarily distracted by the tears in Alice's eyes. "You heard, huh?"

The captain nodded her head, a drop running down her cheeks and falling off to the floor. "Old news, right? Now let's go."

"Where are we going? We're locked in."

"T'rough dah floor, bye, t'rough dah floor," added McDougall, letting the Newfoundlander in him loose.

5.

HMCS Sam Steele
74° North Latitude; 87° West Longitude;
Fifty kilometers east of
Prince Leopold Island.

"Range to India Bravo?"

"Fifty-three kilometers...uh, she just stopped, sir."

"Stopped?"

"Right dead in the ice. No movement, no sonar."

"Where's the contact now?"

"Contact bearing zero-eight-zero, eleven thousand meters and closing at twenty knots."

"Right, eight-degrees rudder," returned Shishkin. "He's right in front of us."

"Is that really a Victor?" whispered Ellis, incredulous. In all his nineteen years in submarines he had never played a waiting game with such a powerful adversary. A few months ago the mere mention of the Russian boat in the same sector would have sent shivers up his spine.

Shishkin chuckled. "*Michman* Malova is one of the best sonar men I have ever worked with. He has been tracking the Victor since the Davis Strait. We broke contact when we took the short cut to both pass the icebreaker and to get far enough ahead of him to surface without being detected."

The Russian's eyes sharpened, coming alive from their usually-passive posture. "Now we have the advantage. Are you ready for combat, Commander?"

Ellis stared at Shishkin, his mouth drying at the captain's remark. "Combat, sir? With one of your subs?"

The captain shook his head, slowly. "No, not really. It is a *rogue* whose captain has succumbed to greed. He figures to gain a great amount of money after selling his command, and his soul, to the North Koreans for hard currency. That kind of man is no longer a naval officer. He is a pestilence that has to be sprayed."

"But, sir, how do you know for sure?"

"Our last bulletin from MARCOMPAC stated that a Victor was presently operating in the eastern Arctic. The Russian navy confirmed that it has no Victors on this side of the Atlantic. It also said that the Russian government had informed it and the Americans that one of their boats was missing and was reclassified as a rogue."

Shishkin placed his hands gently on the Canadian's shoulders. "Rogues are dealt with very severely by both our nations because they are 'loose cannons,' sold to the highest bidder. And that country may use the nuclear weapons in something like a *holy war.*

"Now, Malova knows the *signature*—distinctive underwater sounds made by the hull and propellers—of the rogue Victor. With the help of your COUNT officer, Lieutenant McKenna, he was able to filter out the ice noises. It is the *Skobelev*, captained by Viktor Plekhanov. He was a *zampolit*, or political officer, in the old Soviet navy. Through connections in the Gorbachev government he was able to remain in the fleet as an executive officer, and later made captain despite his deep Communist convictions. Now, he belongs to a group of similar-minded jackals called 'Rasputin,' an extremely dangerous group who are going to deliver a very dangerous weapons platform to the North Koreans."

Ellis whistled. "Alright, Captain, let's get us a rogue."

The captain spun around to the conn.

"Battle stations."

"Battle stations!" echoed Ellis.

6.

HMCS Thunder Bay;
74° North Latitude; 89°30 minutes
West Longitude;
Nineteen kilometers northeast
of Prince Leopold Island.

"Roger! India Bravo just went dead in the water, sir! Range, five kilometers."

"Confirmed, Commander," added the XO, Lieutenant Lemaire. "All its systems are showing offline, including COUNT. But we've got another HF bulletin. This time, it's vocal."

"Voice? Who?"

"Speaker doesn't ID himself."

On the quarterdeck Commander Smart lifted the binoculars to his sunglassed face and scanned the white superstructure of the icebreaker. He uttered his first wholly-martial command aboard the new ship, the first ever on an uncommissioned frigate:

"Battle stations!"

"Battle stations!" repeated the XO into the mike while Smart panned the ice pack around them.

"Get me the ice conditions on Sea Sweeper, Henri."

Henri Lemaire, the executive-office, keyed the

mike to the bridge. "Ice report? Roger. What's the wind speed and direction?"

Lemaire paused as he was told the information.

"Roger. Ice View confirms twelve knots, southwest, sir."

"Damn! In less than two hours we'll be stuck fast."

7.

**Nanisivik, Northwest Territories;
73° North Latitude, 85° West Longitude.**

The native children, broad smiles widening their cherubic faces and hiding their almond-shaped eyes, danced with excitement as the funny-clothed soldiers handed out spearmint gum and juice packages. A few youngsters crept closer to the two large, black helicopters, waving to the smiling man at the door—the one who held the large gun and the bandoleers bristling with bullets. Some older Innuit men and women, sitting further back on an overturned boat, acted as if nothing was going on. They smoked cigarettes and laughed at some of the things they saw funny in the white man's helicopters and dress. Because in their Inuktitut language, *Nanisivik* meant "the place where one finds things." And, in this instance, the meaning held.

Running flat out as he made his way across the loose, smooth rocks on the beach, Colonel Allan Morris stumbled, then caught his balance as he approached the whining Sikhorsky UH-60A *Black Hawk* helicopters. The gunner, ballooned in an oversized, gray flak jacket, caught the colonel's arm, yanking him inside where ten men in Arctic combat regalia greeted him with tense, expectant eyes.

Before he could get seated and a headset over his ears, the gunner tapped him on the shoulder and pointed out a dark silhouette skimming across the water. The American Army AH-64 *Apache* attack helicopter, complete with 2.72 inch laser-guided anti-tank missiles and a 30mm rapid-fire Chain Gun, had just finished hovering around the crest of the hill overlooking the Nanisivik mine site so its instruments could verify that the icebreaker's radar system was fully off-line.

Satisfied, the pilot of the helicopter carrying Morris' small party lifted off and followed the American bird, with another *Black Hawk* carrying Squad "B" of Team Two. A few minutes after they had leveled off, well past the airstrip, two *Galaxy* transports touched down, one after another, to off-load Squads "C" and "D", as well as two more Black Hawk helicopters; also lent with their crews by the US military.

But a civilian helicopter had beaten them all out of Nanisivik. Seconds after the Apache had signaled the go-ahead, a Hughes MedEvac stationed at the Nanisivik airport, following Morris' instructions, lifted off and was already heading for the position of Dorey's ill-fated expedition.

8.

1157:24 Zulu; 6 kilometers east of *Prince Leopold Island.*

The sun was overhead but the high, overhanging haze made the Arctic noon almost indistinguishable from any other time of day. That is, other than when the sun disappeared for its two-hour hiatus, eleven hours later. It was then that the Arctic was in its twilight, a mixture of bright pastel colors that stretched across the vista. But now, mired in this washed-out landscape, like a beached relic, was the CCGS *Canadian*. And one, lone figure, a speck on the frozen desert, trudged toward the silent, red monster—an ant bent on decapitating an elephant.

Tom Dorey's left arm hung limply by his side, a burden that periodically erupted in pain as he ambled on toward the icebreaker, now a mere kilometer away. His helmet was gone, a mottled red mark on his cheek where the polar bear had ripped the kevlar-cushioned shell off with one swat.

But it had done its job, just like the flak jacket, torn on the shoulder from one swipe of the deadly claws, the force of the blow setting his old wounds afire. It wasn't until after he had patched up his crew that the adrenaline finally wore off and the pain registered. Now the appendage was a throbbing counterweight to the satchel and rifle he carried on his right shoulder.

And the light-blue stains on his torn Arctic fatigues were all that was left of the "Cool-Soots", its coolant having drained out during the attack. The constrictive fit of the coveralls and hood had been an extra impediment in escaping from under the camouflage.

But with his team "inoperable"—a clinical, military word to describe the broken bodies he had to leave behind on the ice—and himself still more than ten kilometers from the icebreaker, Dorey had set out to attempt *Phase 2* alone.

Originally, because it would take the helicopter assault team an hour to reach the target, Dorey's group was to use grappling lines to climb to the low-slung FRC station of the now-dormant ship and blow the portal, thus gaining entry. Knowing that there were less than twelve "bad guys" they would break into two pairs. One twosome would try to find the hostages before the main rescue force came, or the hostile kidnappers killed them. The other would stay below decks to sabotage any means the hijackers had for escape. He would continue that plan—himself.

Confused, as well as in great pain, Dorey stopped in his tracks. *The ship was dead in the ice!* Crouching, he scanned the dark, lifeless windows carefully shielding his eyes against the glare from some panels. Nothing. And no engine noises. Not even a fan. Using his rifle he pushed himself up and continued walking.

Despite the severe setbacks of the bear attack the mission seemed to have gone off without his small force. Someone aboard the ice breaker seemed to have done it for them without the benefit, nor the destruction, that he and his crew planned to accomplish with the portable TOW launcher. However, it would still take Team "B" seventy minutes to reach the target: *Phase 3*.

By the time Tom reached the FRC bay he calculated that there were still forty-five minutes remaining before *Phase 3*. It was then that he realized the immenseness of the *Canadian*; like a sleeping giant in the middle of the Arctic—but, in reality, a mega-beast that had killed many times. Dorey eyed the surface rust covering the lengthy gashes along the ship's lower hull and shuddered. His mind conjured up visions of the large fishing boats that had been tortured under her long keel, horribly rolling, crushing and disgorging their human crew, before being relegated to scrap at the bottom of the sea.

As he got closer to the ten-story, blood-red hull, he stumbled over the sharp ice ridges; crushed ice pack that had been built up from the pneumatic pressure of the *bubblers*—in some places to six feet. Satisfied that he was still unnoticed, or that no one was yet in position to shoot at him, he tossed the grappling hook into the FRC, anchoring it onto a railing.

Climbing up took an excruciatingly-painful five minutes because his left arm was almost powerless. Once on board the rescue craft he crawled across the tarpaulin covering and tried the wheeled latch. *It moved!* The information from the mystery man was correct. He *had* left the door open.

Expecting a trick, Dorey eased out his Glock and pushed open the oval hatch with his boot. Nothing. Not a shot, warning, nor the shuffling of feet. Carefully he removed his C-7 rifle and shoved the stock in the opening as a decoy.

Still nothing.

Taking a deep breath, Tom leaped into the opening, dropped down and rolled in behind a cluster of pipes. When no human movements could be discerned he doffed his sunglasses and poked his head into the dim passageway, illuminated only by the emergency system. The dead ship, although devoid of human voice, was far from quiet. Pipes clattered intermittently, as if mice were running on the inside in army boots, and groans from the stresses of the ice haunted the halls.

Dorey, relieved at the absence of a welcoming committee, gently raised himself to his feet and reached into a breast pocket, pulling out a miniature, laminated map. In two minutes he was oriented and began stealthily making his way down the passageway.

* * * *

Bart Jesso yelled as he kicked in the door to the handsomely-decorated room, and quickly jumped back behind the bulkhead in case anyone inside had a weapon. He had chosen this room out of the dozen others on the floor because he had heard, what he thought was, whimpering coming from inside. The door slammed against the wall, bouncing back to a half-way position, causing a surprised scream from a woman inside. The Australian smiled. "Pay dirt!" he yelled. With great care, he eased his AKR around the door frame first, then slipped around to see the panicking form of Judy MacDonald sitting in the far corner beside the large bed.

Jesso stepped through the doorway with a nimbleness that one wouldn't have expected from such a stocky man, the barrel of his machine gun searching out would-be ambushers. Watching the bathroom entrance carefully, he leaned over the bed and whipped off the cover, revealing the soles of someone's shoes.

"Fair dinkum!" he remarked. "Alright, outta there! And be quick about it, mates!"

One by one, five bodies stirred from underneath the bed. As they did, Jesso carefully sidestepped to the bathroom entrance, reaching his hand around to flip on the light switch. Taking his eyes off the emerging captives for a split second he pointed the Russian weapon into the small room. Satisfied that it was empty he watched in great satisfaction as Bill Davis, Harv Crowley, Celso Bellini, Judy MacDonald and Frances Pilotte stood up and adjusted their clothing. With the exception of Crowley, their eyes telegraphed their fear.

"Well, well. I'd say we have here one-half of the ship's Brady Bunch." Jesso keyed the small mike on his vest. "Jesso. Got half the buggers on Deck Two."

"Coming right down," was the electronic-sounding response.

In another situation the bulky mercenary's grin

could be taken as the mirth of a big, lovable guy in a television sitcom; a cop or an ex-football player who is always outwitted by a kid. But something unearthly seemed to lurk behind his glazed eyes, and all it took was the lowering of Jesso's eyebrows to remind them of it.

"Now, you've given us a merry chase. But all will be forgiven when you tell me where the rest of your gang is. Right?" He pointed the weapon at Crowley. "Okay, Fatso, spill your guts...but don't get shit all over the place, right mate?" The boisterous laugh that followed tapered off to a maniacal snigger.

Crowley, looking like a hungover Hemingway character, just nodded. "Sure, beefcake, they went for a swim with the walruses."

There was an almost unified gasp at his remark. Nonplused, the white-stubbled Crowley sat on the bed and rubbed his toes, seemingly unperturbed by Jesso's size and gun. It was then a guttural sound emerged from deep within the mercenary, raising in volume and timbre to the wail of a banshee. He swiped at the newspaperman with his fist, knocking the chubby Crowley over onto the mattress. "You fat fuck! I'll fucking kill you!"

The old journalist sat up and wiped the two streams of blood off his upper lip, the effect making him appear as if he pasted on a red mustache. "It's all over, Jesso," he casually remarked, as if speaking to a fallen politician. "This boat's dead, and in about ten minutes it'll be crawling with guys carrying guns. *Big guns.* So, if you're smart, you'll just drop that thing and maybe they won't shoot you full of holes."

The Australian nodded thoughtfully and everyone braced for Crowley's expected thrashing or, at worst, death from the AKR slung over his shoulder. Instead, Jesso latched onto MacDonald and yanked her over to him. Out of a sheath on his waist he extract a long, wide-bladed knife and sliced off a piece of the woman's hair close to her temple. She whimpered as he held the three-inch lock out in front.

"Next time, fat boy, I'll cut off Sheila's ear!"

Crowley saw the flashing, ten-inch knife shift over to the long, golden earring on the right side of her short-coifed hair. Slowly the journalist stood up and, holding her gaze, reached out for MacDonald's hand.

"Okay, you win. Just lower that knife and I'll tell you."

"Deal! But make it fast!" The knife lowered but he still had a vise-like grip on the woman's wrist. Then he spun her away and raised the barrel of the Russian assault weapon again.

"Come with me. I'll have to show you myself."

"Right, Fatso, so this bunch can get away again?"

Harv shook his head. "Listen. With rescue a few minutes away I don't think—"

"No one's going to rescue you! You're coming with us!" The Australian's crazed, brown eyes popped out of his head as he swung the barrel of the AKR at the journalist, knocking him over the bed and onto the floor. Luckily for Crowley, the short, silvery hair on his cheeks had almost the same effect as Teflon, deflecting the steel muzzle and preventing a tear on his cheek. But the blow loosened two of his molars and the muzzle sight cut the side of his mouth.

"Get up, old man!" Jesso screamed, backing out into the hall. "Show me where they are, now! One more fucking word out of your smart face and I'll blow your fucking kneecaps to mush! Get it, you—"

When Bill Barrett reached the senior amateur ranks in boxing, most of his opponents were already skilled fighters, ones who bobbed and weaved, draining the effect of even the most devastating punches he could throw. Not only did he lose, it was frustrating. He soon perfected that style because, in a three-round fight, every hit was crucial. There was the odd, solid connection, but mostly the fighter depended on outpointing his adversary and wearing him down. Boring, but that was amateur boxing. So when Barrett's right-cross connected with the side of Bart Jesso's jaw it was like the fulfilling of every fighter's dreams.

The second mate had crept out of the next room when he heard MacDonald screaming and waited just outside the door, hoping for such an opportunity. He literally stopped breathing when the Australian backed out, amazed at the huge shoulders and biceps ballooning out of the mercenary's five-foot, ten-inch frame. Thankfully, Barrett's instincts took over. The sound of the mercenary's jaw shattering reverberated down the passageway: like a meat cleaver hitting bone.

Jesso hit the deck like a fallen tree, spewing gobs of red and pieces of teeth down his cheek. But, unbelievably, his dazed eyes didn't close. The second mate watched in horrified amazement as the Australian rolled over onto his stomach and spat out another bloody mess. Then Jesso raised the muzzle of the still-slung weapon up at Barrett and slowly pulled himself to one knee, his chin a leaking faucet of blood.

In a panic, Bill reached for the Beretta in his pant's pocket, his brain screaming with indignation over the fact that he hadn't been better prepared before he threw the fist.

"Bye, bye, nig—"

Barrett winced at the loud racket of automatic weapons' fire but, instead of feeling bullets tear him to shreds, he saw Jesso dance and the wall behind him spot with crimson holes. The stunned mercenary managed one word before he collapsed like a bloody rag doll: "Bugger!"

It was then that the second mate saw a man dressed like a dirty, white tiger trot down the hallway toward him, a wisp of smoke trailing from his rifle. He looked as dangerous as the man he just shot and Barrett tugged again for the pistol.

"I'm a good guy, pal," the running soldier said, calmly, as if reading his mind, "and, judging by that punch, you must be one, too." He never looked directly at Barrett, instead his head bobbed and his eyes darted all around the corridor. Bill had wisely decided that, even if the guy were a hijacker, he could easily kill Barrett before he got the Beretta out.

Unceremoniously, the approaching soldier rolled Jesso's corpse over with his foot, revealing a darkening mass of red glue underneath. "Scratch one bad guy," he said, impassively running a hand through his short, gray-brown hair. Barrett swallowed as the man looked up from the mess on the deck, noticing that his Arctic fatigues were brown-stained with old blood.

"I'm Lieutenant-Colonel Tom Dorey, Canadian Parachute Regiment...and you are William Lawrence Barrett, second mate," he remarked casually to Barrett.

Then he shot out a callused hand. "It's a real pleasure, Bill. I saw you fight three or four times in Halifax. Great stuff. But they really robbed you of the gold in Korea."

Dorey peeked past him into the room. When he saw the frightened stares from the rest, he smiled reassuringly. Frances Pilotte stopped dabbing the small cut on Crowley's mouth, and Judy MacDonald, clutching the lock of hair that had been cut from her head, began crying again. "Is this it?" Dorey asked

"No," replied Barrett. "There are more next door, including the American ambassador and a pilot. The captain and chief are busy shutting everything down and a guy named McDougall's in the Com Room."

Good Christ, thought Dorey. He or the F-18's could have killed the Newfoundland minister of fisheries if *Plan A* had've gone on schedule. "Okay, you're fine now. There are helicopters coming to pick you up so let's just sit tight and wait." A sigh of relief went up in the bright room.

As the commando glanced about for danger, a stunned Jim Davis watched his every move. Without looking in the journalist's direction, Tom deadpanned, "Don't worry Davis, you may have hung me to dry over the Sudan deal but I won't let the bogeymen eat you."

Then he turned around and gave the journalist a wry smile. "This is quite a picture, isn't it, Davis? Did you ever think you'd see, what you termed as, 'The perpetrator of Canada's Mei Lai Massacre,' armed and in the flesh?"

When a nervous Davis looked away, the others caught on. Their savior's identity was the man whose pictures had adorned every news magazine in the country for almost a year. This was the guy who they said gunned down those unarmed and undernourished Sudanese people.

"Alright, listen up! I'm going after the others so everybody get into one room and stay down. Barrett here will watch the door with this Russian peashooter, so just remain calm and this whole thing will be over shortly."

Dorey shed his Arctic jacket and popped a full clip into the C-7, placing the half-empty one in a pant-leg pocket. It was better to have sustained firepower than find the need to change clips in the midst of a firefight. Strapping the satchel over his shoulder he waved to Barrett and ran silently down the passageway.

CHAPTER 8

1.

All nonessential activity ceased aboard the HMCS *Sam Steele* as the Russian-built attack submarine hovered near the bottom of the frigid Arctic waterway. No one went to the toilet or cooked. In essence, no one made a sound.

Captain Shishkin snatched the headset from the sonar man and listened to a barely-audible, single propeller pass within one kilometer of his boat. Suddenly, the bronze blades stopped churning the water and the cavitation sounds died off.

"He's stopping," remarked the captain giving the headphones back. "But why? Can he possibly hear us?"

"No, Captain," replied Malov, clamping the headset to his ears again. "He is raising his periscope, and probably communications antenna, too."

"Then it is time. They're going to make a run for it after he rendezvous with the icebreaker. By that time it might be too late for the hostages."

"So that's what the sub is here for," replied Ellis.

"Yes, but to do that he must surface or—"

He turned to Commander Ellis, a perplexed look on his face, and pointed to the glowing screen to the right of the sonar panel. "Commander, can that COUNT thing over there tell us if the *Canadian* carries a DSRV? You know, a deep-sea-rescue-vehicle, the small sub used for rescuing submarine crews. Do they have one?"

"Good question," replied the XO as he moved in front of the display. He began tapping the keypad in front of him and a CAD engineering diagram of a small submersible appeared on the screen. Using the track ball he scrolled through different images until he came to a diagram showing the finished vehicle.

Captain Shishkin smiled. "That's it, Commander. That GRU bastard and his pirates are going to transfer to a mini-sub right under the noses of the commando teams."

Ellis pondered Shishkin's statement for a few seconds, his brow furrowing. "Captain, what did you mean by Vasiliev being a 'GRU bastard'?"

"Because his real name is Comrade-Captain Valeri Ilia Surikov, GRU, or Naval Intelligence in the old Soviet system. He is the leader of 'Rasputin.'"

Ellis whistled again, a habit that Petr rather liked, a sort of instant verification when he was suitably impressed. "But COUNT has Vasiliev down as a marginal communist who was largely responsible for handling the ice clearing for the Northern Fleet."

Shishkin chuckled. "Finally our Mr. COUNT finds a topic that he is very naïve about. Vasiliev has what you in the West call, 'a fabricated past.' If your government only knew what his job was in Afghanistan was they'd—"

"Captain!" It was Malov again. "The *Skobelev* is now transmitting."

"Can you tune it in?"

"Affirmative. But it's in some sort of code." Everyone was silent while they watched Malov's concentration.

"The surface contact matches the coordinates of the icebreaker, India Bravo...." Then, as if they had transformed into red-hot steel disks, the sonar man wrenched the earphones away from his head. "Captain! He is diving!"

Ellis wiped his brow as he watched the icon on the COUNT screen lower and then stop. "COUNT shows him at 204 meters," the XO confirmed. "He's almost at the same depth as us."

"Alright," said the captain, calmly. "Let's put this business to rest." Shishkin stood with his hands behind his back for a few seconds as if weighing his next words. His shiny, domed head jerked to the left in a robotic fashion and his eyes bore into a young officer in a boat-shaped cap. "Flood the forward tubes!"

The Russian fire-control officer saluted and worked a series of switches. "Flooded and clear," replied Igor Golikev, in passable English—which had been the official language of the ship since its "unofficial commissioning."

"Torpedoes?"

"One through four activated with Mark C's."

"Check range."

"Nine hundred forty-two meters. Elevation angle zero."

"Firing solution?"

"Confirmed sir."

Shishkin rubbed his bald pate, feeling the droplets of sweat mix into a swath that dripped down onto his neck. He had fired a "live" torpedo only in mock battles. And those were at dummies. This was for real; and two, maybe, three dozen Russian seamen, many of them decent sailors, despite being talked into this folly, were going to die.

"Fire both tubes."

"Firing one.... Firing two!"

Everyone in the *Sam Steele* felt the air-compression blasts as the two wire-guided torpedoes, both twenty-one inches in diameter, plowed out of their nests and surged through the dark, Arctic sea.

"They are powering up to make a run for it!" remarked Malov, his voice shaking. "Fish at forty-eight knots. Ten seconds to impact.... Heavy cavitation from target."

Petr knew he didn't need the insulated wire-guides at this range but wanted to be thorough. With this type of torpedo, five kilometers of wire is coiled in the aft section and spools out behind it after launch, acting as a communications umbilical with the submarine. The underwater missile can be accurately "steered" toward the target, much like a surface-launched TOW, until the on-board radar sensors have a positive lock on it.

The Russian hung his head, the wistful look his brown eyes broadcasting to Ellis that he almost wished for the twin tubes of death to miss. He could only imagine what those poor bastards were doing right now....

"Three seconds."

The first quarter-ton torpedo almost missed when the sub reversed engines, catching the dome of the bow during the doomed evasive maneuver. But the second hit aft of the *Skobelev*'s nuclear reactor. The pressure hulls quickly deflated in the sections nearest the impact and a tidal wave of ice-cold sea water flooded a third of the Victor submarine, drowning any surviving personnel in these areas very quickly. Captain Plekhenov and the control room crew, tossed like human dice during the forward explosion, were either unconscious or suffering from broken bones as the huge sub lurched to starboard and began sinking lower into the cruel Arctic water. There had been no chance to activate controls to "blow" to the surface—an emergency surfacing procedure in which the water in all ballast tanks is quickly forced out, enabling the stricken submarine to ascend very rapidly.

Inside the *Sam Steele*, the conn crew, shaken from the enormous blasts of the Mark C torpedoes, winced as bubbling and crumpling noises poured through the sonar speakers. Then there was one long, horrific groan....

2.

1257:00 Zulu
CCGS Canadian; Helicopter Air Crew
Lounge: Hanger #1

"Why doesn't that jackass, Jesso, answer?"

Dimitri Vasiliev dropped the walkie-talkie on the padded chair in the spacious lounge and stared out at the *Thunder Bay*, three miles behind and stuck as fast in the Arctic ice pack as the immobilized *Canadian*.

"Dunno. Bart's been acting rather strange lately. Maybe he's been really juicin' it." Larry Cumming's remark was so offhanded that he never thought anything of it. But Vasiliev turned his huge body around to him, his eyes venomously boring through the shaved, bald head of the American.

"What do you mean 'juicing?'" Cummings made the mistake of shrugging his shoulders, a natural response for the ex-Marine. But before his *faux pas* registered in his mind he felt his two hundred and ten pound frame lifted up and slammed against the wall by the Russian Goliath.

"Cummings, has Jesso been injecting himself with steroids again?" Vasiliev's calm tone belied the dangerous slint in his eyes.

Farouk grinned as he usually did when retribution was handed out. Even the beating he took from the hands of the "infidel" had not softened his addiction to watching violent acts. As long as it wasn't *he* that was on the receiving end, that is.

The American mercenary's face transformed to a large beet with bulging eyes as the Russian's huge forearm immobilized his Adam's apple and could only nod.

"Damn him!" With that his grip relaxed. The air rushed into Cummings' lungs like a pumped up accordion as Vasiliev eased him down. Like he was distracted with other thoughts, he backed away and the ex-Marine slid down the wall to his knees, gagging as if he had breathed in chlorine gas.

It was then that the big Russian turned his attention to his two accomplices with the briefcases. "I had originally planned to present the new government of Kim Jong Il with the added gift of an American ambassador, but there's no time. The Canadians will surely have a rescue squad here in less than a half-hour...and we have a bloody maniac like Jesso running around the ship complicating things!"

Like switching a television channel, Vasiliev dismissed the incident entirely and helped the coughing American to his feet. "Forget Jesso and the others. We have to get going."

Picking up the walkie-talkie he led his cohorts through the cavernous hanger to the staircase on the other side of the bulkhead. Since the lack of power had negated the service elevator they took the stairs nine flights down into the bowels of the ship to *Scientific Deck J*. It was sealed off from the rest of the ship, to prevent wayward passengers from interrupting any researchers sharing the same vessel, but all locks had been disengaged when the emergency power switched on; a safety feature.

The hatchway on *Scientific Deck J* was a standard ship's wheel-lock door which opened to expose a short passageway lined with diving paraphernalia. That entryway in turn led into another chamber where a yellow-and-white submersible sat suspended in the middle of its launching bay, sunken into the deck.

Vasiliev grinned when he saw the mini-sub. "Gentlemen, that's our ride! The submarine holds only four men so it will take two trips to get us all aboard it. Cummings, call Becker and tell him to get his ass down here or we're leaving without him. Then get the sub checked out. I'll give *Dolphin* the green light."

The Russian then opened up the control panel on the gray bulkhead and turned the power switch to "emergency". He smiled when the light flipped on and the MOD panel lit up. Reaching into his pocket he pulled out a slip of paper and began pushing the icons on the panel. The module flashed a set of numbers. Nonchalantly, he leaned toward the fixed microphone on the board and began transmitting.

As Vasiliev waited patiently for the answer, Cummings, his call to Harold Becker completed, went to work on the submersible. But his face dropped as he approached the DSRV.

"It's fucked, man! They fucked it!" The gleaming pate of his head flashed under the red lights as he darted around the small craft.

"What are you yelling for?" The Russian's vicious sneer almost stopped the mercenary's heart. Cummings just stepped back and pointed.

"What he means to say, Dimitri," added Alvin Mackie, one of the helicopter passengers holding a briefcase, "is that the submersible has been tampered with. It's *no* good."

Vasiliev lurched away from the console and glided across to the submersible, easily pushing the American aside to inspect the craft. The stabilizer fins had been hacksawed off and a sheaf of cockpit control cables hung in a rat's nest of wires and fiber-optic cables. His eyes transformed into lifeless orbs of slate blue as they bore into Cummings.

"I thought these things were built heavier than this?"

"Uh, this is not really a DSRV. I mean, it'll do the same thing, all right." Cummings, not known for his tactful speech, continued with the carefulness of a Wall Street lawyer. "This is mainly for scientists to go under the ice and look at fish and stuff. It's not built for being banged around so it's easy for some clown to fuck with it."

Vasiliev grunted, tossing a nest of wires on the deck. "Then we'll have to get *Dolphin* to surface." His eyes flashed back to the emergency MOD and he was stunned to see the message:

NO SURFACE AND/OR SUBSURFACE RESPONSES

A chill went up Vasiliev's back.

"They have to be there!"

For the first time since his odyssey he felt fear; the fear that he might be captured and extradited back to Russia. There would be no doubt as to his treatment: torture and a labor camp. Then, after a few years when people barely remembered him, he would have an *accident.*

"That bastard Plekhenov has deserted us!"

The helicopter pilot, Gordie Callahan, a small-ish man in his early forties, piped up: "Look, I think we should get out *now* before any more time is wasted."

"And where do you suggest we go, Callahan?" Dimitri's eyes scanned the little pilot, who would have easily passed for a jockey.

Unfazed by Vasiliev's threatening glance, Callahan's eyes lit up like jack o' lanterns when he spoke. "Thirty miles north of here is a Coast Guard helicopter refueling depot. It's a collection of shacks and drums with aviation fuel. We could duck in there—"

"And give ourselves some time and...." Vasiliev's mind worked rapidly and he grinned genuinely at the diminutive form in overalls. "Yes! Good! Larry, Farouk! We need *hostages*! Now! Find them and then meet us at the hangar. Gordie get your chop-per ready. Alvin, go with him." Mackie, the tall, bearded passenger nodded, feeling a deep threat in the Russian's words.

* * * *

Large, amber lights flashed from the emergency systems in Com Room, a subtle warning that there were less than twenty more hours of reserve power to keep the RAM—random access memory—in the processors alive. At the twelve-hour mark, red lights would flash intermittently with the amber. The amber would then go off at six hours. Red strobing lights would replace the flashing. Finally, for the last hour, a klaxon would join the lighting. Then there would be one long, electronic tone as all emergency power terminated; dumping all pro-grams. After that the CCGS *Canadian* would be, in actuality, what it now looked like from outside—

a mountain of red and white scrap metal embedded in the ice pack.

If that happened, a team of electronics personnel would have to be flown up from the Ship Electronics Workshop in Dartmouth. At best it would take them two weeks to replace any damaged chips—from any power surges during the emergency—and "boot-up" the processors for the icebreaker to run under its own "steam" again. In a worst-case scenario, some of the systems might require the services of commercial programmers— from the companies who designed the equipment— which would take a week or more on top of that.

To Tom Dorey, the yellow laser-like warning lights and twinkling colors emanating from the huge MOD gave the room the look of an arcade. Checking the hallway again, he carefully closed the door behind him, his pistol ready as he scanned the racks of electronics for human movement. Not that he really expected any. Vasiliev was trying to activate the submersible. *Have fun, fuckhead!* smiled the commando.

The errant thought took his mind off the search for only a millisecond, but that's when a huge arm wrapped around his head like a vise and began dragging back. The powerful attacker was simultaneously trying to tear the Glock away from him. *The man is strong, unbelievably strong!* Tom thought, quickly weighing his options as he tried to get a breath.

Then, just when spots began to form in front of his eyes, Dorey, his instincts guiding him, dropped onto his knees and twisted his whole body like a crocodile spins. The tactic worked on the amateurish heavyweight, whose grip was broken by the unexpected move. Then the ambusher felt the cold tube at his neck and braced for the bullet that would end the long battle for the icebreaker; *his icebreaker.*

"Freeze like a stump, shithead!" panted Dorey, not seeing his captive too well against the flashing yellow lights. The figure stopped as if suffering from instant paralysis. "Now give me a real good reason why I shouldn't kill you!"

As the large, chunky man swallowed, he felt the cold pistol barrel follow his Adam's apple. "Chief Engineer Johansen, he said, softly." It was then he noticed his adversary's combat fatigues. "Say, you're not one of them, are you?"

Dorey's pathetic chuckle sounded like cackling through his heavy breathing. He drew back the pistol and rested against the bulkhead, his arm aflame. "No, I'm Colonel Dorey with the Parachute Regiment."

"Glory be," sighed Johansen, beads of sweat blending to form slick creeks down the crevices of his face. "You finally come!"

"Not 'we'. Just *me*. But have no fear, the others are on their way."

His adrenaline still pumping, Tom felt, rather than saw, the movement behind him. Without so much as a warning to the big engineer, he dropped to one knee and spun around, his pistol ready to fire at the intruder.

"Jaysus!" cried Jimmy McDougall, jumping back in fright. "Please, I'm a good guy too!"

Dorey sighed and raised the gun, instantly recognizing the man. He had been a fraction of a second from firing. And wouldn't that have looked good to the newspapers: Criminal Commando Shoots Newfoundland Fisheries Minister. "For Christ's sake, I hope the rest aren't a bunch of sneaks or I'll be as nervous as a cat in a room full of rocking chairs."

"Sorry for sneaking up. I'm so tired I didn't know what I was doing. My name is—"

"I know, Jimmy McDougall. Who else is there running loose?" inquired a rattled Dorey, his arm on fire again from his tussle with the engineer.

"Just me," replied a feminine voice, almost shyly, a tousle of long, auburn hair falling off the shoulders of a uniformed Coast Guard officer as she inched around a stack of electronics.

"Captain MacIsaac." Dorey had no trouble identifying Alice.

A wave of relief swept over Alice. "We're *really* happy to see you, Colonel! Like Jimmy said, we've been without sleep for so long that we're all a bit punchy.

Dorey was instantly impressed with the captain. Sleepless or not, she looked good in his eyes.

"So, now what?" Johansen's inquiry broke the gaze between Alice and Tom.

Feeling the mutual attraction, Alice self-consciously looked away. And the emotions disappeared when she saw the MOD panel. "The starboard FRC door is opening again!" she cried.

The other three leapt around the display. "Again?" asked Dorey. "Did you know that I came in?"

"Sure, we're the ones who left it open for you. Jimmy radioed the information on the HF."

"So, that was *you* giving us all the specs!" Dorey grinned, impressed with the amateur team. "But why is it opening now?"

"Who is it, Alice?" asked Johansen.

MacIsaac followed the block diagram of the emergency systems, which included both port and starboard rescue ports. "Can't tell from this. Maybe the others are making a break for it."

"But I told them to stay put!" Dorey blurted

out, at once sorry that he sounded so domineer-
ing.

"Maybe they got spooked," MacIsaac shrugged.

Tom looked out of a small portal at the stern-
side of the room and saw the light-bluish silhouette of the *Thunder Bay*. When he popped the
round, brass and glass window he heard the un-
mistakable sound of gunfire.

"The passengers!" he cried, flying out the door
past the startled threesome.

3.

When Bill Barrett hit the release valve the Fast
Rescue Craft sank smoothly to the icy ridge below, automatically stopping when its sensors felt
the frozen, jagged slabs. One by one he helped the
passengers out onto the craggy surface, silently
thanking God that everyone had on some sort of
tennis or aerobic shoes.

Dennis Barnes and Berchstein were the last
out, half-carrying the American airman, Lieutenant Considine, who was still suffering from the
after-effects of his ditching: bruised ribs and a fe-
ver. Safely out of the FRC the ten weary ex-hos-
tages began trudging over the rough ice plates toward the smoother, bluish-green surface of the "old
ice"—hard ice pack which had formed years before and had compressed into a solid layer.

At this moment, the grim-faced Barrett was
not a man to be trifled with. His head was still
swimming with the altercation that had just taken
place back on the ship. For physically bumping
into Harold Becker had been one chance in a million and he had just such luck on this trip.

Bill had just returned to the room after dragging Jesso's body to a supply closet when the slight

figure of Becker rounded the corner. This time Barrett never hesitated. His finger squeezed the trigger on the Russian assault rifle, filling the hallway once more with a deafening roar. The AKR made a clacking sound when the clip was finished, with Becker a ripped-up carcass staring lifelessly up at the deckhead. Behind him, the bulkhead was decorated with dozens of globs of bloody tissue. An emotionless Barrett just shrugged and ordered his charges to abandon ship.

The second mate depressed the "Raise" lever, sending the small boat back up to its dock. Once reaching the top, the small crane assembly retracted the vessel into the recessed port in the side of the ship. Satisfied, Bill followed the rest.

* * * *

"Commander! Quick! I see nine, no, ten people walking away from India Bravo. One looks hurt." The leading seaman on lookout resembled a baseball catcher in his short-sleeved shirt, flak jacket, and cap turned backwards. Because of the intensity of the Arctic sun the commander had allowed the crew to exchange their black berets for baseball caps and sunglasses.

Greg Smart raised his glasses and whistled. Even if he had the authority he didn't have time to get the armed *Sea King* aloft in time. He had been given explicit orders *not* to launch the helicopter. "Henri! Get a boarding party out after 'em!"

"Commander! They're getting shot at.... Holy shit! Two, no three, down!"

"Locate bad guys!"

"The starboard FRC bay!"

"Target!"

"Aye, sir!"

"Fire on my command."

"Aye, sir!"

* * * *

When the stragglers had trudged only twenty yards from the ship, Dennis Barnes heard a sound like a snap roll on a military snare drum. He watched in fascination as small explosions ripped up small pieces of ice in front of him. Suddenly, he felt his legs burn and go out from beneath him, then he pitched to the hard, turquoise surface. Beside him, Considine grunted and also began falling, pulling Berchstein down.

"You fucks get back here!" a male voice screamed from the FRC hatch. Another ten yards ahead of Barnes and his other prone accomplices, the main group halted, terror in their eyes again. In tears, a fatigued Frances Pilotte looked off towards the *Thunder Bay*. So close, she thought, rubbing her red eyes.

It was then that she and the others noticed the steaming, dark-red mass forming under Barnes and Considine. "My God, they've been shot!" she cried. A sad-faced Harv Crowley wrapped an arm around her shoulders, shielding her from the scene. She lay her head upon his shoulder and sobbed, her shoulders heaving uncontrollably. Judy MacDonald just stood in her tracks, blue eyes darting and her frail body shaking like a rabid animal.

The chief mate slowly rolled over and checked his wounds. He had been hit twice, once in each calf. Then his eyes drifted over to Considine and the ambassador. The airman had also been hit in the leg and Berchstein, although shaken, was unharmed.

"Next time, I'll aim higher. Now get back here!" bawled Cummings. "Or I'll waste—"

The former Marine, discharged a few years back because his sergeant called him a "walking time bomb," was surprised at first when he heard the "backfire" sounds. Instinctively, his Kalashnikov tried to rise to the new threat but he found, to his dismay, that his right arm didn't work. His legs went numb and he slumped back into the hatchway, knocking a similarly surprised Farouk back with him.

The Beretta jumped a couple more times as Bill Barrett fired toward the port area, not really caring if he hit anyone else, but just as a warning to keep any others back.

"Come on! Keep moving!" Bill yelled to the rest. "I'll stay with these two. You have to go!"

Jim Davis ran back to Barnes and began ripping the chief mate's pant-legs apart to get at the wounds. He doffed his own shirt and ripped it for a tourniquet, feeling strangely warm amongst the tons of ice around him. Tightening the knot around Barnes' bloody leg he chanced to look up; his whole body froze.

Up in the FRC port was the figure of Cummings, red streaming from his right chest, raising his machine-gun in his left hand. To Davis, who had been a film critic in his earlier days with his Toronto newspaper, it was like a bit from a "B" grade movie. The bleeding hulk in combat fatigues tries one more time to stop the hero and—

Barrett's chrome pistol began jumping in his hand again, the reports echoing off the steel mammoth like someone pounding on an out-of-tune Jamaican steel drum. The spent, brass shells continued to fly over his right arm until the last cartridge exploded and the breechblock sprang forward with an audible *click*.

A stunned Cummings, hit three more times in the chest and once again in the thigh, pitched forward, bouncing off the FRC. His body then cartwheeled and struck a ridge of ice with a sickening *slap*.

The threat passed, Davis went back to bandaging up the chief mate, his shaking, blood-stained hands just barely able to tighten the knots. And Berchstein, he noticed, although rattled by the circumstances, was doing a good job patching Considine's wound. In less than five minutes the two injured men were able to be lifted.

Barnes, his calves knotted in pain, smiled at the ex-boxer. "Jesus, Barrett, I promise to go easier on you next cruise. Especially now since you're *packing*! You're going—"

"Well, the piece he's packing seems to be empty now!" The voice was familiar and evil, a one-two combination that spelled Farouk. He stood in the hatch doorway with Cummings' Russian weapon pointed at them.

In disbelief, Bill stared down at the empty pistol and then back up at the sinister face of the ponytailed hijacker—the one who loved to inflict pain.

"No more pissing around. Especially you, Barnes."

As he braced for death, Dennis glanced over his shoulders and smiled; the passengers were almost two hundred yards away and out of harm from the short-range machine-pistol.

"Oh, I don't give a shit for them. It's just you I want."

Farouk shook his head, his black ponytail sliding over his shoulder. His dark eyes spat hate. "Let's play a game, just you and me, okay? Let's see how long you can live as I take you apart, piece by—"

When they heard the big gun fire, Frances Pilotte and the rest of the passengers were approximately 205 feet from the icebreaker, striding toward their intended rescuers now barely a half-mile distant. The Minister of Transport later told a television interviewer that she spun around to see the FRC dance a few times and then explode into smaller, smoking chunks which flew upward before drifting down to the ice. Horrific metallic noises accompanied the destruction as smaller explosions dented the heavy steel around the bay. It was only when she got aboard the *Thunder Bay* that she was aware that a burst from the 57mm Bofors rapid-gun on the bow of the frigate had destroyed the small vessel in less than four seconds with sixteen rounds of explosive cannon fire.

Jim Davis wrote a personal account of the incident in his bestseller on the hijacking, stating that:

"...the little, red boat bucked, rocked and rolled in its enclosure; the tarpaulin shedding like tissue paper while the crane assembly blew away. Then the FRC seemed to tear itself to pieces. Anwar Farouk, the Egyptian-born hijacker, disappeared in the fusillade, pieces of him interspersed with the smoking fragments of the FRC which melted fast into the ice pack."

4.

"The passengers are off the ship now. A party of armed sailors are leading them back to the *Thunder Bay*," recounted Tom Dorey, as he ushered Alice MacIsaac, Eric Johansen and Jimmy McDougall down the staircase of the forward superstructure.

"What was that loud gunfire from the frigate?" Alice frowned, her emerald eyes shot Tom a puzzled look.

"Yeah," added Johansen, "was anyone hurt?"

Tom nodded grimly. "I can't say for sure because I was leaning over the port railing, trying to get a shot at the hijackers. But I saw three down on the ice; looks like they were wounded. Then the frigate opened up with her fast cannon and blew the shit outta the rescue craft area. What a noise! But it seemed to stop the hostile shooting. Five or six sailors are crouched down a couple of hundred yards off the starboard stern, just waiting."

"So, where now?" asked McDougall.

"I figure either the starboard FRC dock or one of the gangway hatches," replied Dorey.

"The safest would be the bow gangways," interjected MacIsaac, "since the hijackers will probably be trying to get off the stern. There are emergency slides there, just like airliners have." In another brief moment, Dorey's mind was sidetracked by Alice. He suddenly felt good to be here, helping these people—helping *her*. Then his professionalism kicked in.

"Good idea. Lead the way, Captain."

As they cautiously made their way down the emergency staircase, Dorey checked his watch. About ten or so minutes until the reinforcements arrived. In fact, if they had been out on the deck they could have heard the far-off rotors of the approaching helicopters. "I have to check in," he said, stopping at the main deck entrance. "You guys go ahead. By the way, what level is this escape hatch on?"

"*H Level.* When you get there make a right and follow the main passageway. We'll be waiting." Alice smiled at the rugged Dorey, a mess of grease and dried blood staining his Arctic assault fatigues. Returning the gesture, he almost lost himself again in her green eyes. Recovering, he slapped hands with Johansen and MacDougall and shouldered his C-7.

"God speed, Colonel!" the Newfoundlander called out as Dorey ducked out of the forward superstructure.

Once on deck he crouched behind a storage shed, checking the area for any hint of danger. A minute, buzzing sound emanating from the southeast. *They're here!* he thought, a grin spreading across his stubbled face. Satisfied, he stood up slowly and keyed the mike from his tiny radio transceiver.

"Sunrise, this is Sunset. Do you copy? Over."

A hollow, beating sound greeted his ear from the transceiver as he cautiously scanned the deck back to the stern, his rifle in readiness. "Ah, affirmative, Sunset. Great to hear your voice, Tomboy! We see India Bravo. ETA, eleven minutes. Are you alright?" The beating disappeared.

"Affirmative, Sunrise. Maybe five 'Bad Guys' on the stern. Two known dead. Two possibles. 'Yellow Submarine' dead. 'Big Cheese' possibly still alive. Over."

"Sundown reports nine 'White Hats' okay. No discards. Good job, Sunset. Take a shower. We'll take over. Sunrise out."

Dorey's grin returned as he stuck the Velcro-backed microphone to the transceiver on his chest. The passengers had made it to the frigate with no "hard" casualties. It's time to let Colonel Myers and the rest of the Paras get some credit, he thought, rubbing his throbbing arm. As of right now I'm retiring. Maybe I'll ask that redheaded captain if she wants to go somewhere warm to recuperate...like Bermuda.

But when Dorey turned back toward the hatch he pitched forward as a series of blows struck his back—like he had been hit with a pick, or a sledge-hammer. Before he blacked out he had a weird thought: *Wasn't Bermuda too hot in July?*

* * * *

"Your commando is dead, and you, my lovely Alice, are coming with me," ordered Dimitri Vasiliev, shoving a shocked MacIsaac ahead of him as if her one hundred and twenty-five pounds was a feather pillow. He acknowledged the other two with an unconcerned shrug. "I would kill you two but, as a former intelligence officer, I have this admiration for the both of you. Especially you, McDougall. You kept that fool Fergus hunting for you for five days while you transmitted under his nose. And you, Johansen, for shutting down the ship. That was a stroke of wizardry. Consider this my parting gift."

Then the Russian's eyes narrowed. He swung his AKR and barked at the Canadians. "Now go! Get out the escape slide before I change my mind!" McDougall and Johansen looked like a modern version of Laurel and Hardy as they skipped through the hatchway, following the flashing exit signs toward the exit hatch.

"Now, my sweet, you are going for a romantic vacation with your 'boyfriend'."

5.

"Duckling to Mallard, I see rotors turning on the civilian helicopter. Over!"

"Affirmative, Duckling. Back off a hundred and wait for the cavalry. There could be mucho sparks. Over."

The feeling was completely powerless. It was like that day when he realized that alcohol was dictating his life. Eric Johansen seethed as he watched the lieutenant holster his transceiver.

Vasiliev had won and Dorey was dead. With rubbery legs he stepped into line with the group of black-suited sailors as they began to carefully draw back from the icebreaker. At least, he sighed, he had beaten the "'whisky demon".

It was then that he heard the turbines from the Team Two echoing off the thick iron hull, just before the thumping of their helicopter's rotor blades. *Well now, this could be interesting.*

* * * *

Vasiliev heard the incoming assault team just as he was ushering Alice through the empty hangar toward the helicopter on the exterior pad. The blades moved slowly on the *Bell Ranger* and the small figure of Callahan could be made out through the bubble, quickly performing his pre-flight checks. Stopping for an instant, as if expecting someone to jump out at him, the Russian's eyes scanned the cavernous chamber whose walls were neatly lined with fire fighting and maintenance equipment.

"It's about time you got here!" yelled Alvin Mackie over the whine of the engine, the black briefcase still manacled to his right wrist. "But what about them?" he added, pointing at the black dots approaching from the south.

Vasiliev pushed MacIsaac aside, painfully twisting her wrist in the process. "We're going to need proper clothing. Put on those survival suits," he said, pointing to the "Mustang" coveralls hanging from the bulkhead.

"We've got our parkas in the chopper," replied Mackie.

"Get two for us." Dimitri thought a moment, then grinned. "Tie her. And be careful, she can be dangerous!" He tossed a roll of duct tape to Mackie, who started to bind her arms together.

"Wait!" Alice cried, ripping her hands away. "If you're going to tie me, I want the suit on first! I don't trust your pilot." Then she added, defiantly, "Or just shoot me here." Alice was tired and frustrated. And serious.

With the approaching helicopters getting closer, Dimitri threw up his arms in disgust. "Get the bitch in her suit, then tie her."

The Russian ducked into the flight officer's turret—a recessed dome of plexiglas just outside the hangar where the FO directed helicopter landings—and keyed the transmitter microphone. He grinned arrogantly as he punched in the emergency frequency. There were few functions on this ship he didn't know. After all, the Canadians had spent a year and a half training him.

"Attention incoming attack force! This is *your good friend.*" A pause followed. Then a mechanical noise blared through the overhead speaker.

"Go ahead!" was the reply, a muffled voice over the din.

"We still have hostages. Repeat. We have hostages. You will land on the ice pack *now* and turn off your machines. Then you will wait until our helicopter lifts off before coming nearer. Do you copy?"

All was quiet for ten seconds then the noise returned. "Affirmative. We will land."

Vasiliev jumped out of FO control and nodded to Mackie, his face almost featureless under his dark beard, who began trotting toward the helicopter.

* * * *

"You wanna go for a swim?" joked Tom Dorey as Jimmy McDougall helped him past the large swimming pool on the top deck of the passenger superstructure.

"You're coughing blood, Colonel, give it a rest. The assault team is just over there! Let them finish this!"

"No. They won't attack the helicopter with Alice aboard. And that Russian'll get away."

"Where? Man, for God sakes you're a mess! You—"

"Please," interjected Dorey, his lips greasy with scarlet saliva. "I gotta do this or that bastard'll kill her. The CIA called him *Rasputin*, and that's what he calls his cutthroats. Ex-GRU. In Afghanistan he used to push rebels out of helicopters for sport. Even the Soviet commanders were sickened by his brutality. He'd snuff Alice in a New York minute."

Jimmy nodded and half-carried him past the twenty-five meter pool towards the stern. He had gone back for Dorey after the huge figure of Johansen was safely at the bottom of the emergency slide; and unable to talk him out of it. Starting at the spot he last saw the soldier he found a light blood trail. Following it, he found a delirious Tom dragging himself up the stairs in the passenger's superstructure. Vasiliev's burst had pounded his kevlar assault jacket like the swings of many sledgehammers, not penetrating the body armor, but cracking his left shoulder blade and breaking two ribs; not to mention severely bruising his skin and, more seriously, sending a rib splinter into one of his lungs.

As they approached the back edge of the superstructure, Dorey sunk down and checked his C-7, thankful that his whole torso was numb from the shock. Peering over the railing, five stories above the main deck, Dorey was almost directly overtop of the fanning helicopter. A man with a briefcase was standing immediately beneath him, half in and half out of the hangar. Although the angle was steep, he knew he could get the pilot, but the curved Plexiglas and slowly rotating blades might deflect a burst from the light 5.56mm shells and harm Alice.

Putting down his automatic rifle he eased out his Glock, the pain in his back from that simple movement almost causing him to chew his tongue in half. The heavy 10mm "hot loads" from the pistol would hit flat and mushroom, hopefully shattering the plastic dome and causing instrument damage.

Breathing heavily, Dorey keyed his transmitter. "Sunrise, this is Sunset." The muffled whining of turbines poured through the two-inch speaker. Dorey had heard Vasiliev's order and was glad that Morris hadn't shut down the helos.

"Sunrise, here. Christ Dorey, what's happening? That Russian told us to back off or he'd kill the hostages. You said they were free!"

Dorey coughed, flecks of scarlet covering the black mike like a shot from a red spray bomb. "Change of plan...I was hit and the captain is with Vasiliev."

"Are you hit badly?"

"I'll be alright."

"Look, stay put! We'll—"

"Is everyone but her accounted for?"

"Counting the ones presumed dead, Mallard now reports there are still two other Planet Guardians at large."

Before Dorey could answer, Vasiliev and Alice appeared, trotting toward the helicopter. He dropped the mike, which swung on its coiled cord, and cocked his pistol. But he never fired because the man with the briefcase in front of them suddenly fell.

* * * *

Mackie pitched headlong to the rubberized, grass-colored decking, the black briefcase sprawled in front on its chrome wrist-chain. He tried to get up but slumped down, his eyes gazing off toward the ice pack. Then the bearded face relaxed and blood dripped from his lips.

"So much for your fucking plans, *Rasputin*!" grinned Jonathan Fergus, pointing an AKR at the Russian. "Alice, back away from him!" MacIsaac, her arms taped behind her, wrenched away from his grip and moved back into the hangar, her eyes darting quickly between him and the smiling, baby face of Fergus. Beside Fergus, the small figure of Carla huddled in the shadows of the firefighting equipment, her face as pale as parchment and her eyes glazed with fear.

Dimitri's head moved in small jerks as he searched for a possible escape. Callahan, the helicopter pilot, was sliding to the aircraft's door and, so far, Fergus hadn't seen him. For now he could play with this fool.

"So, Mr. Fergus. You hold all the cards. What's the game?"

Jonathan smiled and moved closer so he could be heard above the helicopter, a mere twenty feet away. His limp was more pronounced as he moved without the aid of a cane, both his hands gripping the menacing machine pistol as if it were a lifeline.

"Why, for you to join me in prison, of course!" Fergus sounded as if the experience were going to be a carnival ride. "Then, when you get extradited back to Russia, I'll sit in my nice cell in Kingston and watch CCN explain how you mysteriously disappeared from a labor camp. How's that hand? A *Royal Flush*!"

Vasiliev laughed, catching the slowly-opening

helicopter door out of the corner of his bright-blue eyes. "That will never happen, Jonathan. I'll be in the next cell because everybody knows that Canada doesn't extradite people back to countries with death penalties. Maybe we can get to know each other better."

Now it was Jonathan's turn to laugh. "Well, Dimitri, or whatever your name really is, it doesn't really matter because you and I are going to wait for those soldiers to land and handcuff us. So we might as well get comfortable.... By the way, I must commend you on planting Becker and Packard into our organization. Farouk, Jesso, Cummings...."

Gordie Callahan's pistol rested on the door hinge, trying to get a sight on Fergus, who was partially blocked by the little blonde girl. *I may be a thief*, sighed the pilot, *but I'm not a murderer*. To him, shooting Fergus was self-defense.

"They were hired for their talents, but I almost raised those other two. So you must tell me, Vasiliev. *Why?* What did—"

There! Good girl! Callahan held his breath and squeezed the trigger on the semi-automatic pistol.

* * * *

From his lofty perch, Tom's eyes we're pinned to the area right below him, where one of the hijackers lay sprawled after being shot by someone from inside the hangar. *But who?* Not Vasiliev. He wanted what was inside that briefcase, so why kill him now and have to spend extra time retrieving the contents? He could have done that anytime; but not now, with time running out.

Then, from the corner of his eye, he saw the glint of something metallic below the slowly rotating blades and adjusted his gun sights to the helicopter. It was a pistol. At that instant the muzzle flashed and the resulting gunshot echoed off the superstructures, amplified by the huge steel enclosures.

Dorey waited a few seconds, then fired the Glock.

* * * *

Fergus clutched his stomach and felt his legs give out. With reflexes honed through many years as an operative, Vasiliev dove at the slumping Planet Guardian, bowling him over. He wrenched the AKR from Fergus' hands and, for an instant, contemplated ending the life of the man writhing in pain at his feet. With a sly smile, he leaned over, his face bare inches from that of the wounded man. "Guess what, Fergus? You're gut-shot!" he said, chuckling. "By the way, your puppies' loyalties were *bought*—"

But Vasiliev's mirth was short-lived by a muffled sound from outside the hangar. When he looked up he saw Callahan's body jerk back into the helicopter, obviously hit from some unseen gunman. Dimitri pointed the gun toward Alice, motioning her to stay put. The gesture wasn't needed. The captain was now too tired to care about escape.

* * * *

"One pilot down!" remarked Dorey calmly, as he grabbed his rifle and rested it on the railing. "Now, watch this!" Jimmy poked his head over the side and recoiled at the sight of the bloody body of Mackie, sprawled in front of the helicopter. Dorey then let go a burst from the C-7. The black rectangle attached to the dead man's wrist exploded under the hail of bullets, its stuffing shredding into satin ribbons. The next thing that McDougall saw was a glittering mass spread out around the smashed briefcase.

* * * *

Vasiliev's mouth dropped as the briefcase blew apart in front of his eyes. Fergus, his midsection a large, red stain, indiscernible from his left hand, which tried to stem the flow of blood, stretched his neck and pulled himself up to lean on his left arm.

"*Diamonds,*" he remarked calmly, just as if the sparkling mass of stones was salt. "That bastard used my *cause* to pinch some fucking diamonds!"

Jonathan Fergus tried chuckling but found it hurt. *I'm tired,* he thought, *too tired. Someone else's going to have to take over for a while.* He then motioned for Carla who sat shivering in the corner. "Come on, Carla. It's time to go home. Give your Jonathan a hug."

That seemed to snap Carla out of her traumatic state. The minute blonde girl, her red eyes almost too big for her face, grinned bravely as she crawled over and cradled the smiling Fergus in her arms.

"Jonathan," she said, sniffing as she wrapped her small, nylon tour jacket around his shivering shoulders. "Could we spend some time at the beach house this summer? I'm really tired of all this travel."

Fergus nodded. "Yes, Carla, we have all the time in the world, now."

"That's good...because...." A relaxed Carla fell asleep before she finished her sentence.

When she awoke, much later, on the hangar floor, Jonathan was still lying in her arms. But there were all these strange men standing around them: sympathetic-looking soldiers in white with black and beige markings. She knew without looking at his blood-flecked face that Jonathan Fergus was dead.

* * * *

His right eye trained down the barrel of his assault rifle, like a cobra's ready to unleash venom by the minute, Tom patiently watched for any sign of Vasiliev and Alice. Jimmy McDougall was still leaning over the rail, staring in wide-eyed wonderment at the contents of the briefcase. Just then, Dorey's transmitter came on, the turbine noises of Team Two's helicopters singing in the background.

"Sunset, we got orders to finish this. Get down—"

Tom never heard the rest and certainly wouldn't have been able to reply. His instincts went into overdrive. He grabbed McDougall's shoulder and yanked his body back just as a burst from Vasiliev's AKR raked the railing of the high deck with ricocheting .225 caliber bullets. Barely out of the way, McDougall cried out and fell back, an almost-spent bullet tearing through his right ear and fragments from another hitting him in the chin and left hand.

Dorey caught a round in his left forearm, causing him to drop the C-7 over the railing. Splinters from another bullet hit him in the neck. Drunkenly, the commando stepped back and sank to him knees, clutching at his neck.

* * * *

Dimitri pushed Alice into the helicopter, completely ignoring the diamonds on the flight deck. *That was their cut*, he grinned macabrely. Callahan was still breathing, but barely. He was dying of shock, thought the Russian. The slug from the Glock, having expanded to the size of a Ping-Pong ball when it hit the left rotary cuff —arm socket— had blown away a large chunk of his shoulder.

Vasiliev calmly reached over with his AKR barrel and, turning Callahan's body as a shield, blasted the wrist-chain, releasing the briefcase from the pilot along with a piece of his hand. As Callahan shrieked in pain, Dimitri unceremoniously shoved him out onto the flight deck and slid over to the bloodied pilot's seat.

Vasiliev was going through a quick cockpit check when he caught a dark shape to his left. His heart almost stopped. The iron-nerved Vasiliev felt fear for a second time when the surreal shape of a US *Apache* attack helicopter rose from beneath the outside of the deck.

Having crept up along the deep hull, the slim *Apache* hung like a cocked trigger, barely thirty-feet away, its rocket platforms portraying a cartoon character in an old Western movie waiting to go for his gun. The sixteen 2.75-inch rockets and the 30mm rapid-fire Chain Gun were aimed right at him, as if using an elephant gun to hunt snipe. Two helmeted shapes of the crew, one behind the other, stared impassively at Vasiliev. Then the pilot grinned at him as if to say, *"Go for it!"*

Taking a deep breath to calm himself, the Russian slowly keyed the mike. "Very impressive, guys, very impressive indeed! But the media wouldn't like it if this lady got blown away, would they?" Vasiliev raised his machine gun and pointed it at Alice. "Now, call off your dogs or the lady captain is dead."

The figure in the rear of the tandem cockpit nodded. The helicopter lifted off to the right and moved back a hundred yards. Dimitri smiled at the bound figure beside him. "Now we'll see how much you're really worth."

With that he did a quick cockpit check, then jerked the helicopter into the bright haze of the Arctic sky.

6.

"Sunset says he's got orders to let 'em go."

"*Let them go?*" Admiral Maris stared in disbelief. He was angry enough with Commander Smart for letting him sleep so long: fourteen hours.

"They're off the ship and the hostages, with the exception of Captain MacIsaac, are safe. The best way to get the captain back is through negotiation, even if it just gives us time to set up for another try."

Maris grumbled but he had to agree with Smart even though this had been the most frustrating campaign of his career. It would have never entered his mind that he could be stranded on a mere frigate, stuck in the middle of the Arctic in continuous, boring daylight. "Uh, sorry, Commander, this midnight sun has got my clock all screwed up. I'm still a bit disoriented."

"Sir, helicopter taking off from the deck and it's turning this way," reported the XO, Lieutenant Lemaire. I have cameras running and—"

A tone sounded on the bridge, reverberating through the metal confines. Not so familiar a tone that just anyone on the frigate would have known the cause, but a startled Henri Lemaire's jaw dropped. In a blind panic, he spun around to the weapons-control console, but the indicators informed him he might not make it.

The *Thunder Bay* was 1.5 kilometers behind the *Canadian*, turned at a forty-degree angle to port. Because of the threat of a Silkworm missile attack, which had already destroyed one ship of her size from dozens of miles away, Commander Smart had activated the Phalanx Close-In Weapons System. In a naval engagement, if anti-ship missiles were fired at the *Thunder Bay*, the STIR fire control system would launch up to sixteen Sea Sparrow missiles to intercept. Then, any that got through that formidable shield would be faced with chaff and decoys which, when fired, try and steer the projectiles into a cloud of floating Mylar strips and flares.

The HMCS *Thunder Bay* had not yet been equipped with Sea Sparrows, and the Shield decoys and Ramses electronic countermeasures were not to be tested on this "trial run." But the Phalanx CWIS was. It was installed and operational.

The white, silo-shaped Phalanx over the helicopter hangar, nicknamed *R2D2*, had been left on automatic and now tracked the helicopter's radar. This was because Commander Smart, after opening the briefing package on Operation Sundown/ Sunset, had Lieutenant Lemaire set the IFF frequencies on the weapons control so that no "friendlies" would be identified and fired upon— which meant no friendly *military* aircraft.

The arrogance of Vasiliev—the brash and cruel *Rasputin*—demanded that he snub his detractors one last time. He decided to do a "fly-by" of the frigate before turning westward, as if to bare his butt at the impotent warship. But, unfortunately for him, the ship's robots didn't understand such displays of contempt.

By flying straight toward the ship on his takeoff roll, at a height of one hundred feet, the helicopter was instantly evaluated by the *Thunder Bay*'s weapons system's computer, which searched for favorable IFF codes, which would label it a friendly aircraft. Finding none, the six-barreled, Gatling gun below the white dome jerked to starboard in readiness as the CWIS tracked the incoming helicopter. When the "target" had reached two thousand-yards distance from the *Thunder*

Bay, the gun fired, sounding like a huge bed sheet being ripped apart.

Lemaire's quick reflexes transferred the CWIS to "Standby" a split second after the firing had started. Then he shut down the weapons control system.

* * * *

Two things were in Vasiliev's favor. First, only fifty-three 30mm shells were fired by the Phalanx before it was deactivated. Second, a sudden updraft of Arctic wind caused the aircraft to bounce up and saved it from thirty-nine of the projectiles, which passed by underneath. In a few seconds they reached their maximum range and then arched down to the ice pack miles away. But that's as far as the Russian's luck went. The remaining fourteen tore into the aircraft, shattering the Plexiglas dome and reducing the engine to a collection of smoking junk. One shell exploded Vasiliev's right knee and his left eye was gouged out by a piece of flying plastic shrapnel.

Alice was miraculously untouched by the projectiles, but the left side of her face was bleeding from splinters. The survival suit deflected the rest. She recoiled in horror at the once-handsome face of Dimitri. The Russian was babbling incoherently through the mess of gore, which was being whipped across his face by the air blasting through the cockpit of the rapidly descending helicopter.

Then, just before the aircraft hit the ice-strewn water, the slender sinews holding his right leg together gave way and the lower part of his limb fell into the mass of blood on the cockpit floor. The helicopter slammed upright into a soup of ice and water a mile north of the ice pack. It sat there for a few seconds, buoyed at first by the frozen slabs until water flooded the lower fuselage; then it began to sink slowly.

At the sight of the rising water, panic overtook Alice's shock. The icy sea streamed in through the open front, mixing with Vasiliev's blood to form a frothy, pink wave rising up to snuff out Alice's life. She gagged as the mess reached her face, trying to push her head through the roof to get more air. Unlike the simulator which settled slowly in laboratory conditions, this bird was now going down fast. Then the frigid, green liquid covered her head, biting her face. *No! I've forgotten what to do!*

With a sudden lurch the helicopter, its blades idle below the icy surface, tipped over from the weight of the overhead engine and began sinking upside-down. Holding her breath MacIsaac, who had not been strapped in, hit her head on the cabin roof and felt the frigid, dark sea water run up her nose she struggled to orient herself. Through the murky water she saw the tortured face of Dimitri clawing at her as if she were his salvation. With her hands still manacled behind her back with duct tape, she kicked at him, propelling herself against a hard, clear surface. *It was the door window!* Green bubbles streamed past the window as she booted it. The pane finally gave way and sank below, allowing bubbles to stream into the sinking cockpit.

By now Alice was numb and exhausted. She wanted terribly to exhale. Before she had been too scared to be cold but her struggling was slowing and now she felt the cool water caress her. Alice saw herself dying, just as in her nightmares. But this time she didn't mind it. Then it got darker, and darker....

It's sort of pleasant down here. She was seeing people she knew. Things that she hadn't thought of for years came to mind. Her first date. Her Dad's return from the Suez. Danny's—

Danny! She saw him floating and reached out

to his sad face. *Come and get me, Danny!* But her brother just shook his head and began floating away, a smile replacing his forlorn features.

Come back, Danny! The figure stopped and pointed up; then vanished.

Up! Alice coughed, and as the bubbles escaped she felt her lungs fight to keep in the remaining air. *Think Alice! Release, kick, swim. Release, kick, swim!* Looking up there was a flicker of light green and she felt herself rising toward it. It got lighter and she saw the ripples of the surface—

* * * *

"Got her!" Sergeant Lawrence Jaworsky, a SAR diver from Shearwater, grinned as if he had a ten-pound Arctic char instead of the orange, choking figure of Alice MacIsaac.

"I got her, and she's still alive!" The muscular figure latched onto the tether from the *Black Hawk*, as its huge blades beat the slurry thirty feet below, and slipped the loop around Alice. Then, with his diving knife, he cut the duct tape that held her arms behind her back. The captain was winched up into the American helicopter.

Once aboard, Alice was taken out of her "Mustang" suit and wrapped in blankets. The big aircraft settled down on the ice pack and Alice was rushed up the gangway to the *Thunder Bay*'s sickbay. There, while her wounds were being dressed, she was given hot soup.

Before she slipped into a long sleep she recognized one of the uniforms and whispered, "Tom?" Colonel Myers smiled and gripped her pale hand. He would be Tom if it would keep her alive.

Alice never knew that, seven hours later, she had been moved back aboard the *Black Hawk*. Then the large helicopter lifted off and flew over the CCGS *Canadian*, carrying the captain away from her first command.

CHAPTER 9

1.

24 Sussex Drive, Ottawa, Canada;
July 6th: 2:00 p.m.

"*Diamonds*?"

"That's right, Mr. Prime Minister. Seventeen million dollars worth. Plus the nuclear attack sub for North Korea: the Victor-class, *Skobelev*, that was destroyed in Lancaster Sound yesterday morning. That would've probably added another oil sheik's dowry to the Russian gang's fat kitty."

Defense Minister Marcel Gallante handed the prime minister a series of computer printouts and sat silently as he scanned the pages. His lack of sleep compounded his Quebeçois accent.

"I must have been away from this country too long, Marcel. Is there really that much interest in diamonds in this country? I mean, I thought they were a fad, something to wish for."

"No, sir. The rush for diamond claims in the Northwest Territories has outstripped even the Klondike. The gems are found in a volcanic rock called *Kimberlite* and the Pellat Lake Mining Company sits on one of the richest claims of the diamond-bearing rock in the world."

"Where the hell is Pellat Lake?"

Gallante reached into his wine-colored, eel-skin briefcase and pulled out a map of the Northwest Territories, unfolding it on the large teak desk. "It's right here, about halfway between Yellowknife and Bathurst Inlet. 'K' Division RCMP Headquarters, in Edmonton, sent us a FAX identifying the pilot: one Gordon Adam Callahan. Seems Callahan was Pellat's head pilot. He organized the heavy chopper crews that flew in the camp setup and its personnel, so he got to know the geologists really well. He also had a couple of priors for drug smuggling to the North. Nothing that got beyond the misdemeanor stage. You see Callahan's got, or *had*, Inuit blood in him and the courts are really touchy about giving northern natives jail time these days."

"Callahan's classed as a *native*?"

"It's very thin blood, but it holds up on the books. The Crown prosecutor flies right into the mining camp and exonerates him. So Mr. Callahan gets off."

"Flies in, why?"

"Because that's the way it's done with the majority of minor offenses up North. It's less costly to fly the court officials in than to haul people out and have to put them up in those expensive Yellowknife hotels for a few weeks."

"Gotcha."

"Anyway, Callahan, as a pilot, stays off the bad books so he can get bonded by the mining company. He lines up with a crooked mining official from the US, Alvin Mackie, who floated the mining company's shares on the Toronto Stock Exchange. It seems Mackie wanted to make a huge haul without waiting for the stocks to mature so he cooks up this scheme. Only he needs wings to pull it off so, I guess by criminal attraction, he picks Callahan."

The man across from Gallante shook his head in disbelief. Studying the map again, he picked out the spot where the *Canadian* stopped and asked, "So why the Russian connection?"

A sly grin came over Gallante's face, one reminding his superior of a meager attempt at doing Sherlock Holmes in a high school play. "Alvin Richard Mackie graduated *magna cum laude* from Harvard Business School in 1972. In the following decade he was considered by various Wall Street companies as a 'wonderkid', a virtual Einstein of the commodities market. In the '80's he got extremely wealthy during the 'junk bond' hype and, like Michael Miliken, went to jail for various breeches of the US Securities Act. He was let out in '89 and was considered *persona non grata* in New York, Chicago, etc. So he floated, no longer wealthy but living nicely off what the US government allowed him to keep."

"Marcel, this is a nice story, but you're going to have to wrap it up soon. I'm expecting a call from the President any minute now."

The defense minister shrugged. "Alright. The fast ending: The Berlin Wall goes down, the Cold War ends. Mackie gets a call to help the Russians with their capitalistic stock market. He does a superb job establishing some large companies on the new exchange and is handsomely rewarded by those that benefit from the system. That's when his dark side takes over and he and a consortium defraud the market of thirty million dollars US. Somehow, when a housefly couldn't, he slips out of Russia as the stocks deflate."

"I saw that! Right when I got back from Bosnia. Thousands of people lost their life savings. That was him?"

"The same," Marcel nods. "Anyway, lounging

away in his St. Kitts beach mansion in late '93, he gets a call from one of the 'old consortium': one Valeri Ilia Surikov."

"So?" shrugged the man across from him.

"Better known as Dimitri Vasiliev."

"Vasiliev! Holy shit, now it fits!"

"Right, the same. You see, as one of a dozen 'Russian Technical Advisors' to the icebreaker program, Surikov went to the north many times. He was once stalled at the Yellowknife airport during the rush for diamond claims in the early '90's. In the lounge of one of the hotels he listened to drunk geologists and miners spill their guts, naming Pellat as the biggest find."

"He bumps into Mackie and they cook up a plan."

"Exactly. Mackie takes seed money from the Russians, plus a bit of his own, and buys a respectable amount of the fledgling company. Then, as a director, he gets the property listed. The other directors—mining people, not financiers—are overjoyed at the swiftness of their dream and begin to mine the kimberlite."

"Okay, but why the submarine?"

"Surikov and the consortium thought of this plan long before the diamond idea and hooked the two together."

"*Who*, then, are the consortium?"

"We're not sure about the personages but the new Russian security force describes them as old party hacks and KGB bigshots who socked away enough money to ensure their influential status after the fall of Communism. Surikov was the 'Rasputin' operations manager. An ardent Communist, he was recruited by his superiors because of his reputation while a *Spetznaz*—or Russian commando—leader in Afghanistan."

"But I thought he was a *sailor*?" Carruthers eyes fluttered with fatigue. It was his body informing him that sleep was needed. He was too old to do these three-day stints without it anymore.

"He *was*," continued Gallante. "He officially held a rank equivalent to Lieutenant-Commander in our navy."

"Double threat?"

"Very much so. It's too bad that Colonel Dorey didn't—"

"Tom was an experienced operative, Marcel. He never took any situation lightly. It's damn amazing that he...well, let's not discuss that now."

Gallante nodded solemnly. "Anyway, sir, that's the gist of it. Surikov's pals, despite having absconded with a modern submarine, wanted to crown their achievement by pulling off the diamond heist of the century."

"And unless there was a revolution in North Korea," added the Prime Minister, "no information on them would ever get out. They could live like kings."

The tall Canadian leader leaned back in his chair and rubbed his clay-blue eyes, suddenly feeling much older than his forty-nine years. "Shit! The sub! All we need now is for the media to pick up on the fact that a nuclear sub was destroyed in our Arctic waters before *we* get the facts on it. We're going to need an environmental assessment on the nuclear fuel spillage as soon as possible—on the QT."

"Maybe they don't need to know," offered Gallante, his dark brows coming together over the loose wrinkles on his forehead, which never failed to remind his boss of a Labrador puppy's face.

"What?" The Prime Minister's hands fell from his cheeks.

"Think of it, sir. We're not hiding the fact that there's radiation in the Arctic because previous testing expeditions show traces already. If you remember, the old Soviet policy of dumping radioactive waste in the northern hemisphere goes back to Khrushchev so—"

"You want us to hide the fact that a nuclear-powered submarine was torpedoed?"

Gallante just shrugged, but could see that the Prime Minister was slightly warm to the idea. "In a matter of speaking. Remember, that was a lethal weapons platform that was saved from the hands of a belligerent country, who might have used it to catastrophic ends. Even if we did reveal the facts—"

"You mean to say, 'tell the truth', didn't you, Marcel?" The Canadian chief of state cocked his head, eyeing his defense minister. Gallante was a good man, he thought, even if he had the politicians' vice of sometimes "calling a camel a horse."

"Yes sir, I meant 'tell the truth'," Gallante corrected himself. "But if we did that the North Koreans would just deny it. So we would blow the secret of our new sub, as well as cause a panic and bring unwarranted criticism on the government, for no advantage except accurate wording."

"Come on, Marcel, it can't be much of a secret now."

"Who's seen it, sir? The frigate crew thought it was a Russian submarine helping us. So only the ship's commander, who has sworn an oath to his country, and a US admiral know the truth...and the Americans *definitely* don't want that news to get out."

"So, it's classified until—"

"Until we want the world to know. Remember the Stealth F-117 fighters? They were always *officially* deemed a 'product of someone's imagination' until the Gulf War in '91, even though thousands of people had seen them besides the ones that built them."

"So, I guess it's settled. We don't officially *own* a sub."

"Actually, sir, *legally* we don't. Not until all the agricultural assistance have been transferred...in 2006."

"Oh, you mean *The Great Tractor/Submarine Heist*, Marcel," the tall man laughed. "Now, that was a trade worthy of a Phoenician pirate. You bought up every used tractor in the west—"

"And don't forget pick-up trucks, combines, balers, steel sheds, *et cetera*. Not to mention every ounce of surplus grain unsold from last year's crop."

The Prime Minister chuckled. "Christ, you cleaned up the West, Sheriff! Is there anything left out there?"

"Cash...plus the 'multiplier effects', the business spin-offs in hundreds of farming and manufacturing communities. Hell, within a week, five farm-equipment manufacturers in Ontario went on three shifts. And the last word was they might be going at that rate for four or five years."

The Prime Minister straightened up in his chair, a grin still stuck on his sculptured face. "Do you think we got enough people happy to call an election?"

Gallante's next swallow was dry. No politician was ever ready to call an election in this country, even if there was an employment rate of one hundred percent. "Can we table that discussion for another time, sir? I mean, we do have over two years left," he chuckled.

"Not a bad idea. At this moment, I have no desire to criss-cross the country in a bus for five weeks."

Gallante grinned as he checked his watch. "Well, time to go.... Uh, by the way," he added, his voice sobering, "have you heard any updates on Colonel Dorey?"

"It's not good," the other man sighed. "As you know, he's busted up pretty badly. And the last report I heard was that pneumonia's set in."

"My prayers are with him," offered Gallante

"Yeah, well, include one from me."

* * * *

3:06 p.m.

"Good evening, Prime Minister. And how are you today?"

"Good evening to you, Mr. President. I'm doing just fine."

President Thompson paused a few seconds to lean over and untied his shoes. Kicking them off one by one he lifted his hot feet onto his desk with a soft *clunk* that was picked up by his speaker phone. The Canadian prime minister also thought he heard a pleasurable sigh emanating from the other end.

"I imagine your first months in office have been memorable ones, to say the least."

"Yes, they have, Mr. President. It's a lot different than being ambassador."

"I can well imagine, I can well imagine." Thompson loosened his tie and waved to his secretary to bring him another bowl of chocolate-covered peanuts. He had met Jay Carruthers once when the prime minister was the Canadian ambassador to the US, during the first two years of Thompson's term, and knew that the ex-United Nations' lieutenant general was like no military man the president had ever met before: a career-soldier with all the poise and patience of a skilled politician. In his books, that beat even a tenured senator in both tenacity and diplomacy.

"Look, Jay, I've got a problem here and I think you know what I'm talking about?"

"I believe I do, Mr. President. Ambassador Beaumont filled me in last night," replied the Canadian, his resonant voice taxing the audio limits of the speaker-phone on Thompson's desk.

The secret service agent's eyes raised when the president slid his feet off the desk and leaned forward, as if preparing to attack the ivory-colored apparatus. Popping a handful of the nutty confection into his mouth, he silently ground his teeth, as if contemplating his next move. But the three other staff members in the Oval Office, Secretary of Defense George Myer, General Davidson, the chairman of the joint chiefs of staff, and Presidential Secretary Gerri Lawson—knew Thompson's drill. *That Canadian*, they smiled, *had to be squirming like a salted leech.*

"Well then, maybe you can tell me something more than your Ambassador Beaumont cared to relate."

There was a pause on the other end. Finally Thompson prodded, almost irritably. "Uh, Jay? Are you still there?"

"Yes, I am Mr. President. I'm just trying to remember if I missed anything.... No, I don't believe I did." Carruthers' voice was steady, betraying no hint of sarcasm or disrespect. "Gilles Beaumont was a former commander of mine and is a stickler for details, Mr. President. I could name no man better for his position."

Thompson's patience was slowly eroding. "Carruthers, level with me, alright? What the fuck are you trying to do, go to war with France?" He ran both hands through his steely hair, almost barking at the speaker-phone.

"No," replied Prime Minister Carruthers, a slight titter in his voice. "In fact, I have attempted through countless diplomatic channels to diffuse the situation, but Monsieur Ledoux refuses to negotiate. His personal responses, when he cares to answer my calls, are intended to belittle both myself and this country."

"And now this icebreaker mess has him determined to place hostile forces, that is, hostile to Canada, within your two-hundred-mile limit."

"That seems to be—"

"Don't bullshit a bullshitter, Carruthers! I know what the fuck's goin' on! And I just chewed the ass out of the French ambassador's pants yesterday mornin'. Told him to get his warships the hell back to France. As you probably heard from your Mr. Beaumont, they ordered their new sub into your waters, too."

"Yes, I have been aware of that since they passed Newfoundland. It's still there." Carruthers let another long pause linger on the secured line connecting the two countries.

"You mean you found them with that *Russian* sub you bought. You know, the one you picked up without first conferring with us, your ally?" Thompson's voice was tinged with acid.

"No, as a matter of fact we tracked it through our system of anti-submarine listening devices, the same way we do your submarines."

"*Ours?*"

"Yes, Mr. President. By this week's count there are a total of four US subs in Canadian waters; two SSN attack boats; one SSBN 'boomer'; and one diesel trainer. We even know the identity of each boat, but that is immaterial right now."

Thompson shifted uncomfortably. *How the hell could they track them?*

"Uh, look, Jay, let's get back to your new *Russian* sub? Why weren't we consulted about that?"

"Because, President Thompson, you would have tried to 'nix' the deal. We both know that the United States does not, and never did, want a post-Cold War Canada to be more than a 'lookout' nation with a few boats and planes—and a whole lot of empty space to confuse any enemy incursions into our hemisphere. Well, now that you are chopping your forces, we feel that it's only fair that we should add a bit of punch, albeit a small showing, to ease your *burden*."

General Davidson's face seemed to shrivel up under his graying crew cut. He attempted to say something but Thompson shook his head, as if trying to find the patience to continue. "Okay, let's drop that for now. What about this icebreaker thing? Is it under control?"

"Ambassador Berchstein and your airman are fine and the belligerents have been neutralized. I would like to personally thank you for your support on that, Mr. President. Those helicopters were a *vital* part of the rescue."

"Great! Berchstein's a stand-up guy," Thompson exclaimed, resolving to put the other Canadian matter on the back burner for now. "And now I can call both their wives with the good news.

"Now Jay," he continued on another track, rubbing his tired eyes under his glasses, "come clean, and please don't hand me a bunch of flag-waving bullshit. What are you going to do about this fishing stuff? As we speak I've got every congressman with a view of an ocean tying up my phone lines."

The sound of Carruthers clearing his throat sounded similar to a dog's bark through the extension speaker. "As of 1700:00 Zulu, Greenwich

Mean Time, Mr. President, our territorial water has been extended to include the shallow areas of the Continental Shelf known as, the *nose* and *tail* of the Grand Banks. These will be enforced by two of our coastal patrol frigates, and be under constant surveillance by our anti-submarine aircraft."

"And that *damned submarine*," Thompson blurted.

"No, that will be mostly up in the northern archipelago to protect our Arctic passages."

Shaking his head in amazement, Davidson got up and waved his arms. "What the fu—"

"Jesus, Carruthers," Thompson cut in, giving the general a cutoff sign, "I can't get on common ground with you on anything! Everybody on this goddamn earth knows those are international waters!"

"As far as we were concerned, they never were. It was only when the world knew that Arctic shipping was possible that anyone bothered to question the fact that we laid claim to them many decades ago. But now it's official, sir. As of 1700:00 Zulu we also reconfirm our *original* declaration of Arctic sovereignty that dates back to the beginning of the century."

"Carruthers, a sub can't patrol all that."

"No, but that new icebreaker can. It will be our Arctic eyes and ears, as well as a formidable weapons platform. The sub will feed off its information."

"You are going to *arm* one of your Coast Guard ships?"

"Not really. It will resume being just what it was intended to be: a *scientific-icebreaking-cruiseliner*—only a 'curious' one with large eyes and ears. And, in times of conflict, it can be converted to military use in less than twenty-four hours—

the time it takes to get all non-essential personnel off the decks.

"You see, President Thompson, as a former United Nations field officer I have witnessed enough bloodshed and misery firsthand to know what happens when soft approaches are taken toward belligerent nations and terrorist organizations. But, I also know that every possible angle, short of capitulation, should be used to negotiate with them.

"With President Ledoux's *ultra-nationalism*, he is providing a bad example to the rest of the world: that it's alright to take what you want because nobody with the power to stop you wants to create a fuss. Just like a guy called Hitler did; or one named Saddam.

"Well, Mr. President, Canada is going to *fuss*. If we don't, then there's only going to be *you*, because Britain's new Labor government is slowly backing away with every bone thrown it from the EC. And the Pacific Rim countries are too busy making money. So, now do you understand?"

Thompson cleared his throat, accepting a glass of water from his secretary. "Well, when you put it that way, I can see your point.... But for now let's keep this Arctic thing low key 'cause I got a whole lotta people in the House of Representatives who would blow a gasket if it got out. Understand?"

"Will do, Mr. President."

"And Jay...*do* cut me some slack on this salmon problem in the Pacific, will you? I got an election coming up and the whole damn region is slipping over to the Republicans."

"I'll handle it personally."

"I know you will."

When the line was disconnected Thompson poured some water into his whisky and drained the yellowish liquid with relish. "I got no problem with generals turning politician. But hell, why can't they all be like Eisenhower and play golf while someone else runs the goddamn country?"

As the President's eyes panned his three subordinates, the Oval Office became silent. Then a frustrated-looking Davidson stood up and began refilling everyone's glasses.

2.

July 7th, 2008 Zulu
"Nose" of the Grand Banks,
100 miles southeast of Cape Race, Nfld.
47° N Latitude/50° W Longitude

"Contact, Captain! I think we got him cornered!"

"Jesus Murphy! Nice goin', gang, we just made the big leagues....Woodsy, advise MARCOMPAC for instructions."

Captain Mark Corbett grinned at the sonar display as he sipped from a juice pack. The operation had worked perfectly, just like it was just another exercise. No equipment breakdowns; no procedural screwups; and no communications misunderstandings with the other two partners. The frigate and the Sea King crew had been right on the money. Christ, he thought, was it supposed to be this easy?

Actually, Corbett had been briefed on the possibility of an antisubmarine maneuver three days ago, before his flight. Unbeknownst to him, it was on that morning that Prime Minister Carruthers, Minister of Defense Marcel Gallante, and the Commander of Defense Staff General Brydon Hornby, had met in Halifax with the Commander of Maritime Command, Vice-Admiral Robert Jenkins, and decided that the interloper would be introduced to Canada's state-of-the-art submarine "welcoming committee".

Going on precise data sent by MARCOMPAC, garnered by the American submarine which was shadowing the large Triomphe-class sub *Mitterand*, the frigate HMCS *Hamilton* proceeded to a certain area of the Grand Banks to conduct a search for the French boat. Newly presented to the Canadian forces from it shipbuilders, the *Hamilton* had just entered the Atlantic from ceremonial duty in its namesake city; where it had received its "christening". Now it would receive its official baptism.

Commander Alex MacKee had received the FAX from MARCOMPAC in code, a first for the *Hamilton*'s computers which efficiently typed out the instructions in readable English. It also contained a technical breakdown of the intruder and its location, as well as orders for bearing and speed to be taken to intercept. At the same time, Corbett and his PC3 *Aurora* crew were being briefed with the same information at CFB Greenwood in Nova Scotia.

At approximately one hundred nautical miles from the target vicinity, the *Hamilton*'s *Sea King* left the deck and went on ahead to join the *Aurora* in the vicinity of the intended search. As commander of the *Aurora*, Corbett was also the leader of the operation and responsible for coordinating the attack.

Within the hour the *Sea King* arrived in the area and Captain Corbett ordered its commander to execute a series of "dips" along a stated pathway—which entailed the lowering of its sonar transducer via a long cable by its winch. While the *Sea King*'s ASO crew listened for the submarine at each spot indicated, the Aurora dropped seven sonabuoys—small floating, listening devices set for different depths—from the belly of his aircraft in a twenty-mile radius of the target area. These were monitored by the *Aurora*'s ASO's.

To Corbett's delight the *Sea King* picked up a reading on the first pass, verified by one of his airplane's sonabuoys. It was then he ordered a second series of the acoustic instruments dispersed from the sonabuoy tubes to triangulate the position of the submersed vessel. That produced a positive fix.

"MARCOMPAC says to bring it up, Cap!"

"Jesus Murphy! They did? Okay then, boys, let's go get it!"

As the frigate headed toward the position of the French submarine, Corbett ordered the *Sea King* to "go active." That meant the use of "pinging," or sending sonar waves through the water. When the target was hit by this frequency it would send back a signal to the receivers, identifying the position of the sub. The other motives for this action were to let the boat know it had been located— and also to annoy it.

The submerged boat was in a quandary. Even if the French destroyers were not heading back to France, there would be no rescue for the sub now because it had to be within antenna depth to send a message. And that would be like committing suicide, as the birds of prey above would easily kill it.

In less than an hour and a half the *Hamilton* was in the section. Using its advanced CANTASS— Canadian Towed Array Sonar System—and keel-mounted sonar, it picked up the French sub and moved into position.

Corbett then gave the command to use depth charges. "Talley Ho, *Hamilton*! Good hunting!" In their overhead platform, every crew member watched in awe as a line of spots in the dark-gray water began to boil white and then shoot up in violent volcanic spurts as each charge detonated.

"Marky, I got a wake off the port stern! I am turning now to get a better look. The four-engined turboprop banked as Captain Eddie Johnson followed the tiny white streak on the surface of the gray ocean, five hundred feet below.

"Affirmative, Captain! I'll confirm!" remarked Master Warrant Officer Paul Riva. "Holy shit, it looks like the bastard's coming up!"

"Mother of God!" exclaimed Corbett. "Do you see that, *Hamilton*?"

There was a pause as Mark watched the cluster of tiny black objects rise into the foamy wake of a submarine sail. "I see it," deadpanned Alex MacKee, "but I don't believe it. She looks like she's surrendering."

* * * *

Ottawa, 3:07 p.m.

"Jay! MARCOMPAC reports the *Mitterand* just surrendered to the HMCS *Hamilton*!"

Startling the CDS, General Brydon Hornby, and Marcel Gallante, Carruthers leaped from his chair. "Was anyone hurt?" His hands gripped the large, oak desk.

"No, sir, it went off without even a callused thumb."

At that news the tall, lanky Carruthers danced a jig. "Yes! yes!" he exclaimed, grabbing the smaller Brydon Hornby by the shoulders. "We did it!"

In a few moments he had calmed down but the wide grin still adorned his face; but Marcel had never seen his eyes so lively. "First, Brydon, get out my personal congratulations to everyone involved in this operation. Then, after I calm down, I'm going to get Gérard Ledoux on the line. I think he'll talk to me now."

Clapping his hands slowly he paced the large room, chuckling almost like he had won the lottery. Realizing he was being scrutinized, he stopped and sheepishly eyed his staff. "Sorry, I was always the kind of commander who liked missions to come off without casualties. Especially after what has happened in the last week." His giddiness waned and he added pensively, "I guess, in a way, *The Marion* has been avenged."

"What was that?"

"Oh, it was a Newfoundland fishing sloop. I'll tell you about it sometime."

Gallante had to smile; but for a different reason. From the day Carruthers first threw his hat into the ring for leader of the party, the member of Parliament from Montreal had never thought it a good idea that military men run for public office. In fact he had gone up against the popular general, carving out a third-place standing in the second round at the convention before being persuaded by his campaign strategists to back Jay. It was either that or watch Burgess Williams from Toronto, a popular Bay Street blowhard, win. If that had happened the party would have had no chance of winning the next election. With Jay, a hero in the eyes of the world, they could win again.

In gratitude, Carruthers gave Marcel the Defense portfolio, plus made him deputy prime minister. But until now, their association had been strained; mostly due to Carruthers' stalling of Gallante's proposed military cutbacks. However, rather than ostracize Marcel, the prime minister tried to win him over by showing him *his* side of things, using his many years as a UN officer to impress upon him that the world was still a volatile place. The Quebecker was finally convinced. *If not for Jay Carruthers' poise, and luck*, thought

Gallante, *there would be Americans and French in our Arctic and French warships patrolling the Grand Banks.*

"So, the *Mitterand* is being escorted to St. Pierre," added Gallante. "Of course we will stay out of *French waters*, but the submarine commander has been told it must tie up and await French officials. Any submerging would bring a renewed attack."

"Now the real bargaining begins," quipped Carruthers.

"Precisely. But it would be prudent to make Ledoux understand that the sub is *not* a bargaining chip. It was only ordered there because St. Pierre is the nearest French port. In actuality we want to keep it in sight until we get an agenda from the French for territorial negotiations."

"But of course!" laughed Carruthers in a Maurice Chevalier voice.

"What was that?"

Hornby and the Montrealler joined in the merriment but suddenly stopped when they saw that Carruthers' humorous mask became washed with a pained look. The prime minister snatched a piece of paper from the ivory-colored machine on his desk and solemnly handed it to Gallante. "This just came over the FAX."

The brows of the minister and military man both furrowed up into a worried attitude. "I'm sorry, sir," said Hornby softly, "I understand that you and he went back a long way."

"Yes, Brydon, a long way and a long time."

3.

The blood-splattered robes took shape like black balloons were being pumped up within them.

Then they rose from the ground, regaining the vengeful, white eyes that burned in their sweating, ebony faces. Assault rifles materialized from under the bright, flowing garments, spitting out streams of spent, brass cartridges that flashed like bits of gold in the merciless sun. Then there was Lena, innocent little Lena, still trying to protect the two children in her care; her face a shower of flying gore.

Strings of small explosions gouged out circular chunks in the mortared walls of the Catholic church, then stitched through the bellowing cattle and their surprised herders.

"The church!" cried Dorey, waving his hand at two fellow platoon members frozen in their tracks by the sudden attack.

"No!" he screamed, as the puffs of death ran across their chests in small red spouts. They pitched headlong to the dust.

Dorey and the others, eight in all, dropped to their knees and began returning fire. The attackers were stopped in an intense barrage, their robed bodies ripping apart in bloody strips of cloth. Then....

* * * *

"Please stay," invited Harry Dorey, just entering the room as Angus MacPherson got up to leave. "I know you and I, well, we never ever saw things the same way. But don't leave just 'cause of me. *I* want you here, and so does Tom.

"Sure," replied MacPherson in a shaky voice, patting the elder Dorey on the shoulder as he glanced around the sterile room of tubes and blipping electronics. "If you don't mind, Harry, I got a piper outside. Could he play a while?"

Harry Dorey smiled, a tear running down his face. "Tom'd love that. Thank you, Angus."

* * * *

But, like before, the bloodied bodies on the road stood and their features became flush and full. They raised their assault rifles and began stalking the platoon again. Dorey looked around for someone to command but saw none of his men; nor bodies. He was all alone under the blazing African sun.

The attackers then transformed into yellowish-brown figures in black pajama-like outfits. Some wore straw, peasant hats while others wore bandannas to keep the sweat from their eyes; and they all had the same look of vengeance in their eyes. It was then that Dorey noticed his weapon had disappeared. He was not only alone and defenseless, he faced his old enemy: the Vietcong. He braced himself for the painful blows that would end his life.

But when the attackers were within ten feet they stopped and lowered their guns, as if knowing they could kill him at any time. Maybe, he thought, they wanted to torture him. Maybe they wanted to prolong his agony, as if knowing what buttons to push to keep it going.

Then one of them spoke; one with a black bandanna. "Come on, Tom," he said softly, a gentle smile turning up the corners of his mouth. "It's time to go home."

He reached out his hand and Dorey's shaking hand clutched it. When Tom looked at the others, they were also smiling, and their eyes filled with tears.

Feeling oddly relaxed, Tom looked up into the jungle canopy for a moment and listened. It was bagpipes. Bagpipes in Vietnam? Then he nodded, knowingly, and said, "Hey Unc, tell Dad to put 'and son' on that sign 'cause I'm coming home."

Then Tom Dorey walked down the road with his old friends.

* * * *

"He's gone, sir," uttered the doctor, Captain Louise Smith, her words a sympathetic whisper.

MacPherson put his arms around his brother-in-law, tears misting his eyes. "Come on, Harry, it's done. Let's go get a coffee."

Harry Dorey nodded, slowly getting up and wiping his nose with a tissue. He took one last look at his son and managed a weak smile in the doctor's direction. When they were out the door, MacPherson sadly nodded to the piper, who switched to the mournful strains of "Flowers of the Forest."

As the ballad wafted down the white hallway, Harry stopped and looked into MacPherson's red eyes, a smile forming through the mask of pain. "You heard him, Angus, didn't you?"

"I sure did, Harry," MacPherson returned. "I sure did."

CHAPTER 10

Dartmouth Coast Guard Base
October 14, 1996

A vortex of warm wind scuttled the leaves that had piled up against the podium. The dark, purple shells of the past summer's vibrant foliage scattered across the broad, green flight deck, some cartwheeling between the feet of the dozens of visitors gathered there. Dwarfing the guests, and casting long shadows on the verdant surface, was a Canadian Forces *Sea Hawk* helicopter, newly painted in the gray of its *Sea King* predecessors.

Naomi Barnes' smile suddenly became as radiant as the sunny, autumn day when Dennis' name was called out through the ship's public address system. As the last tones echoed through the massive, gleaming-white superstructures, she helped her husband up from the chair to balance on the two aluminum walking canes. Their children, Larry and Sean, squinting as the diamond-like reflections on the harbor from the low, October sun flashed in their eyes, each grabbed onto an arm.

"Chief Mate Dennis Andrew Barnes," repeated the tall man at the podium, "for extreme bravery under adverse conditions, and for placing your life in harm's way to protect your fellow citizens, I, as Prime Minister of Canada, award you the 'Star of Courage,' your country's highest award for valor."

When Jay Carruthers draped the medal around Barnes' neck, the racket from the cheers and applause from the hundreds on hand could be heard across the harbor on Privateer's Wharf. Besides the invited guests and families of the recipients, scores of spectators lined the red and gold-colored hill above the Dartmouth base to view the festivities while dozens of yachts of every description bobbed just off the Coast Guard jetty. Overhead, cramming the rails on the outside walkways of the superstructures, the event was witnessed by hundreds more onlookers: tourists on board for the maiden voyage of the icebreaker.

"Thank you, sir," replied Barnes, scratching his beard self-consciously. It was his fourth time standing for an honor.

"It has always been a great pleasure for me to hand out medals, Dennis." Carruthers put his hand on the chief mate's shoulder and glanced down at the boys. "Your dad's going to be home for hockey season, right, guys?"

"Nope," quipped Larry Barnes, "just for the first half."

"Really?"

Barnes cleared his throat, placing a fist to his bearded face. "Uh, that's right, sir. The doc at physio says that if I work hard for him he'll clear me for the winter cruise."

Jay grinned, his milky-blue eyes focusing on Naomi. "I imagine you'll have a heart-to-heart with this doctor, isn't that right, Mrs. Barnes?"

"No, Mr. Prime Minister, on the contrary, I'm going with him for a few weeks. First Class cabin. Indoor poolside."

Carruthers laughed and shook her hand. "Something tells me I'm going to like the *new* Coast Guard, Mrs. Barnes."

* * * *

"Did you ever think you'd be on this goddamn boat again? Or in Nova Scotia, for that matter?"

"Harv, I didn't want to be anywhere near the fucking water!"

Harv Crowley brought a glass of cranberry juice to his mouth, sipping the liquid until the ice cubes froze his upper lip. "I don't know, I think that, in a weird sort of way, we're a part of this tub, er ship, now. Karma, or whatever you '60's freaks call it."

"But not enough to leave the harbor, right Harv?" quipped Jim Davis, fondling a bottle of Schooner beer.

Crowley sniggered. "So, when does the book tour start?"

"In about two weeks."

"You sure cleaned up on this, didn't you?" he teased.

"What about you, Crowley? Christ, besides letting you keep your old job they offered you half the media conglomerate to stay at the *Journal*— television commentaries, national magazine."

Crowley belly laughed, refilling his glass with sparkling water. Then he brought up the tumbler in a salute. "Hey, it was a big thing you did, Jimbo, printing the retraction about Dorey. You coulda just let it lie."

"No way. I never was a weak knee when it comes to taking flak about a story after the fact, but when I got home from the Arctic I had a lot of time to think about Dorey. His actions up there didn't quite define a 'loose cannon.' So, I started reviewing my sources on the Paras. Then one of my many phone inquiries turned up a decent source; a Swiss reporter with *Paris Match*. The guy turned me on to a Belgian relief worker who confirmed that Dorey's company was set up by the 'Red Flag', an offshoot of the Sudanese Patriotic Front. The culprits were a suicide squad of kids using UN weapons. It made it look like the Canadians were on a drunken binge and got out of control."

"But why would they go to the trouble?" Crowley's inquisitive stare was almost comical to Davis. In less than four months the old-timer had lost thirty-five pounds, giving his facial features more definition. The irony in it for Davis was that, although Harv's abstinence from drinking alcohol and his new fitness regimen was a blessing to his friend's health, he missed the bouncy, semi-obese Harv.

"Because peacekeepers get in the way of warring factions' political aims. And since the Canadians are the best and most respected peacekeepers in the world, discredit them."

"And you give the heavily-armed assholes, and their foreign friends, a free reign to go in and 'straighten things out because the UN can't handle things.' Gotcha."

"Precisely...unfortunately, I never caught that angle from the start. Like a rookie I relied on Dorey's history of alcohol abuse and insubordination as the slant and the rest, in a non-professional burst, just seemed to write itself. And him being a former US Navy SEAL just added to the rumor of his unusual behavior. After Vietnam it seemed tough enough for *regular* veterans to 'turn it off' let alone the Special Forces guys."

Davis let the last words fall off in a sigh, but Harv picked him up. "Hey, Jimbo, after the beating death of that civilian, that the other battalion was charged with in '93, even *I* thought that the whole Parachute Regiment was coming unraveled. And I'm a big supporter of the military."

"It doesn't excuse the fact that I *wanted* Dorey to be guilty because I thought our country didn't need a bunch of *gung ho* bastards like him any more. It went against ever bone in my body to passively stand by when the tax payers were funding a unit whose only purpose, it seemed, was to jump from airplanes and kill people—seventy different ways.

"Unfortunately, I overlooked the fact that their high degree of training and *ésprit de corp* was what enabled them to set up those distribution centers in the Sudan in record time. They fed over half-a-million people before the other civilian agencies, or UN forces, got unloaded. Fast and efficient."

"So, how do you feel now?"

"I'm not sure, Harv," he sighed. "The only thing I am certain of is that I made a grievous error in judgment over the Pibor Post, Sudan incident. And Tom Dorey was publicly whipped as a result."

"Look, you corrected it," Crowley countered, "both in your book and in the national papers."

"But what about Dorey's excommunication? He died knowing the world thought he was a villain."

"I know, but that's the breaks in this business. We all make big mistakes. If you remember, I crucified Bob Stanfield's Wage and Price Controls issue in '74 and a lot of people believed me that it was madness. Pierre Trudeau vowed to never use it and then popped it on us a year later. After that election, Stanfield was finished as the leader of the Tories and my rantings, though not the main reason that he lost the election, had a lot to do with killing his support east of Montreal. In other words, I sabotaged a fellow Nova Scotian and the truest gentleman I ever met in politics."

"Aren't we a couple?"

"None finer, Davis, none finer. Here's to your book."

* * * *

Angus MacPherson's eyes misted as he and Harry Dorey stared at the bronze medal lying in the blue-velvet case. Governor-General Janice Howard then placed it in Harry's hands. "From a grateful Commonwealth, Mr. Dorey."

Standing a few feet away Jay Carruthers shook Alex's hand. "I always wondered when I'd ever run into the hardest RSM in the goddamn army," he whispered. "I saw you a few times when I was a lieutenant stationed in Brandon, but by the time I achieved enough rank to approach you without my knees feeling weak, you were retired."

MacPherson laughed as he wiped his eyes. "You're doing a great job with the country, General...but how did you manage this?" he asked, pointing over to the medal in Harry's hands. His brother-in-law was still conversing with Ms. Howard.

"I got a special Order-in-Council, a unanimous decision in Parliament to petition the Queen for the honor. Your nephew was a long-serving member of the forces, long before the new Canadian medal. The Governor-General gladly put the matter to Her Majesty. The Queen never even blinked an eye.

"In fact," he grinned, "she remembered when her father, King George VI, presented you with yours in '45. And she was only seventeen years old."

"I remember seeing her there, but so many guys were getting medals—"

"But only one was given the Victoria Cross.

You. And now Tom has honored Canada again with one...plus President Thompson is presenting the Paras with a Presidential Unit Citation. That hasn't happened since Truman honored the Princes Patricia's Canadian Light Infantry in the Korean War."

MacPherson shook his head. "Well, General," he said nodding at the Halifax dockyards and then the new *Sea Hawk*, crouching on the deck like a huge dragonfly, "and keep up the good work."

"If I didn't, Sergeant-Major," Carruthers remarked respectfully, "I would be making light of both yours and your nephew's achievements." And then he smartly saluted the old warrior.

* * * *

"Tom Dorey first demonstrated his mettle in Vietnam as a member of the elite US Navy SEALs. On April 10th, 1972, when his unit was discovered during a mission to free a captured US gunboat and crew, a wounded Dorey single-handedly fought a rearguard action against North Vietnamese regulars, allowing the escape of his comrades and their charges. For that action he received the US Navy's highest honor, the Navy Cross. Two weeks later he was wounded again in action, receiving a second Purple Heart, but was hospitalized for four months.

"Tom joined the Canadian Forces in January 1974, after being honorably discharged from the US Marines, and served Canada in both peacekeeping and security roles. I, for one, know that these are difficult jobs because the enemy is never clearly defined, being as diverse as terrorists and famine. In every situation, Tom Dorey proved himself above reproach.

"Colonel Dorey was the epitome of what the duties of a member of the Canadian Forces are in today's uncertain world: To endeavor to alleviate suffering and hostility. That mission is *our* standard, and that is why this country is in such demand when crises evolve.

"So, it is in this spirit that I re-christen this fine ship, the CCGS *Thomas Dorey*, with the knowledge that its combined mission of research, knowledge and security will be in keeping with the ideals of our country and the spirit of citizens like Tom."

Jay Carruthers nodded to a misty-eyed Harry Dorey, who took the champagne bottle from the hands of the young Coast Guard crewman. Giving the vial a gentle push he grinned as it swung in a wide arc on a long, colored streamer toward the large bow of the icebreaker. As the dark bottle disintegrated against the brilliant, red-colored hull a loud cheer rose up from the guests, now gathered on the pier in front of the green buildings.

* * * *

"This is the captain speaking, raise the gangways!"

A cheer went up from the throngs of well-wishers on the docks, as well as the ship's compliment, when the telescopic pathways retracted into the red hull of the huge ship.

"The bridge is yours, Mr. Barrett," announced Delbert MacIsaac, the "honorary captain" for the harbor cruise. He was dressed in his old Navy uniform, complete with his battle ribbons and campaign medals. His daughter had commented earlier that, "I doubt if too many turkey farmers cut as good a figure as you do, Dad!"

Acting-Chief Mate Bill Barrett ushered his son, Devon, over to the starboard lounge where his wife, Melanie, and daughter, Tiffany, sat smiling at their officer-Dad. "Time for Dad to go to work!" Barrett announced. Devon grinned and saluted before sitting down.

"Port thrusters, one-third!" he ordered, hearing his command echo back to him. A slight lateral movement was detected as the icebreaker pulled away from the long jetty.

Although Barrett was a fill-in for Chief Mate Dennis Barnes, he had been promoted to first mate on his return from the north. In fact, it was he who had brought the huge ship back to Dartmouth after refusing an immediate paid leave of absence. To him, it only seemed fitting that one of her officers bring her back.

Like Barnes, Alice MacIsaac, Jimmy McDougall and Eric Johansen, he had received the Canadian civilian heroism medal: the Star of Courage. The New American ambassador, David Malloy, also presented Dennis and him with President Thompson's compliments and an invitation to the White House to receive *The Medal of Freedom* from him, personally.

"So Dad, how does it feel to be 'Captain for a Day'?"

"Lousy!" the elder MacIsaac grinned, "Lousy, because it makes me realize how much I miss it."

As the icebreaker made its way out into the harbor, an honor guard of the 78th Highlanders from the Citadel, resplendent in their early-19th Century regalia, bearskin hats, kilts and muskets, knelt in precision on the wharf and fired a volley in salute on the loud command of their sergeant. Then the first of the three rows of red-jacketed infantrymen broke ranks and pulled back to reload, the second taking their place, kneeling and firing in the same manner. This was followed by the third, and last, whose smoky reports lingered on the autumn air.

Overhead, an honor guard of T-33 *Shooting Star* trainers, CF-18 *Hornets* and P3C *Auroras* flew by as three *Sea Hawks* skimmed over the blue water under them. Three frigates, the HMCS *Hamilton*, *Thunder Bay* and *Montreal* joined the destroyer, HMCS *Iroquois* in a salute of gunfire.

Far above the Halifax side of the harbor, on the parapets of the restored fortress on the Citadel, a loud cannon answered them. Lastly, a flight of gray-white F-14 *Tomcats* from the carrier USS *Theodore Roosevelt* zoomed overhead with Lieutenant Considine taking the spot as RIO in the first fighter.

"The bridge is yours again, Captain MacIsaac!" The bemedaled Barrett shook hands with the old Corvette skipper and rejoined his family in the starboard lounge.

"Permission to approach the helm?" asked Delbert's daughter.

"Permission granted...but first tell that contrary bastard, Johansen, to put on another stoker, we need to get a head of steam up quickly!"

Alice laughed. "I wish it were that simple, Dad. He owns this ship!"

"Just like he *owned* mine." Delbert put his arm around his red-haired daughter. "You know, you belong here, Alice, just as much, or more, as I did on the *Wetaskiwin*. This is a tremendous vessel and, like the prime minister said, 'You have made your mark on it. It is yours to command!'"

Alice's emerald-green eyes misted. "Does that mean that you finally approve of my career?"

"Yes, I do. I always wanted you kids to be happy," he said running a finger across his eyes, as if he had something in them. Danny, well—"

"Danny's feet were stuck, Dad. He couldn't grab the rope. I know that now. Back then I said he didn't want to live because you didn't want him...but I was a frightened little girl whose only family seemed to be an aunt who was very hard on her."

Alice put her hands on her father's face and stared deep into his tearing eyes. "You did the best you could with what you knew at the time. And that included moving us to Dartmouth where you thought we'd be well taken care of. It's not your fault that your sister wasn't cut out to be Mary Poppins."

Taking out a tissue, she dabbed her eyes, automatically straightening her cap afterwards. "Alright, Captain," she said stiffly, "let's see if we can get this floating hotel out to Sable Island and back again without taking out a dozen or so sailboats!"

"Aye to that, Captain. Aye to that!" Then Delbert honored her with a crisp, regulation salute. And Alice somehow knew that it was better than any he had ever managed during his entire career in the Navy.

EPILOGUE

Beechy Island is not really an island, but an extension of the southwestern tip of Devon Island into Lancaster Sound. It was here in 1847 that the ill-fated Franklin expedition foundered and went mad due to lead poisoning from their canned provisions. After spending many winter months holed up in their stranded, ice-bound ship, they set out on foot from their ship, carrying beds, china and other useless items across the frozen wasteland; only to perish.

Today, pieces of skull and bone, gnawed on by Arctic carnivores and scavengers, are intermingled with the round stones, polished during the great movement of ice during the last Ice Age. The cold has preserved them, preventing the passage of time from carrying out normal decomposition; a boon to scholars studying the doomed party of explorers.

As the CCGS *Tom Dorey* pulled out of its Dartmouth mooring, an object washed ashore on this bed of smooth rocks and gravel. It was a long, stringy carcass that had been picked at by Arctic char and other seaborne creatures, but ignored by seals and aquatic mammals as it bobbed for two months in the water. Then, when it came ashore, polar bears played with it and Arctic terns and gulls extracted morsels from every hollow until the resulting white segments gleamed in the pale, northern sun, now well past the equinox.

Before Beechey Island took on its frozen, winter appearance, the large pieces were broken down into smaller ones with each passing predator until the fragments of white intermingled with the ancient gray chips of Franklin's sailors. With each daily pass of the slowly-sinking Arctic sun, some of the bits sparkled. These were the carefully sculptured refinements of privilege: gold fillings that only influential members of the Party could have afforded.

About The Author

Born in the mountains of British Columbia, Kim began writing in elementary school but put it aside as a teenager when his love for music won out. Many years later, as a successful musician, he went back to writing with the expressed purpose of penning his experiences, but found that history and suspense seemed to usurp his career episodes.

Ice Break is one of four novels he has written, along with numerous magazine articles and an awared-winning short story. He is presently working on a World War I submarine thriller.

A compulsive traveller, Kim lives in Nova Scotia with his wife and four children.

The Maiden voyage of the world's largest icebreaker, billed as "a short V.I.P. cruise," turns into a long nightmare as environmental terrorists hijack the CCGS *Canadian* and use it to destroy European fishing boats on the Grand Banks. While Captain Alice MacQuarry and her crew work clandestinely to regain their ship, an international crisis brews, led by an arrogant French president. Canada's Prime Minister, a former United Nations major-general, recommissions a disgraced officer of the Canadian Parachute Regiment, Captain tom Dorey, to stop the icebreaker. But can the behemoth be stopped before French warships arrive?

Ice Break

by

Kim Kinrade